Stewart Balfour

An Elementary Treatise on Heat

Clarendon Press Series

Stewart Balfour

An Elementary Treatise on Heat
Clarendon Press Series

ISBN/EAN: 9783337149840

Printed in Europe, USA, Canada, Australia, Japan

Cover: Foto ©Andreas Hilbeck / pixelio.de

More available books at **www.hansebooks.com**

London

.

MACMILLAN AND CO.

PUBLISHERS TO THE UNIVERSITY OF

Oxford

PREFACE.

IN this work the Author has endeavoured to place before his readers in an elementary form the facts and principles of the Science of 'Heat,' and also to give some of the most prominent practical applications of our knowledge of this subject.

His object has been to begin with the study of well-ascertained facts and to proceed onwards to general principles. Accordingly, the work has been divided into three parts; the first of which embraces the study of the various effects produced by heat upon bodies.

In this part many of the most recent investigations, as well as the apparatus used in conducting them, are described at length, while numerical examples are given, which, it is hoped, may enable the student to attain to the accuracy needful in physical research.

The second division contains the laws which regulate the distribution of heat through space, and includes radiation, conduction, convection, and the measurements of specific and latent heat. Theoretical views are here for the first time introduced.

The third and last part relates to the nature of Heat, its sources, and connection with other properties of matter. In this part Heat is viewed as a species of motion, and the leading principles of the science of energy, by which Heat becomes related to other forms of motion, are discussed.

It may be well to state the basis on which the reasoning of this part has been founded. It has appeared to the Author that the foundation which involves the smallest amount of assumption is that adopted by Professor W. Thomson, namely the denial of the possibility of a perpetual motion of any kind, and it will be shewn in the sequel that the denial of one form of perpetual motion involves the principle of the 'conservation of energy,' while the denial of another form involves the principle of the 'dissipation of energy.'

In our ignorance of the ultimate constitution of matter it would thus appear that both the 'conservation of energy' and the 'degradation or dissipation of energy' should be viewed as principles having very strong claims to recognition, and as increasing these claims every day by the new facts which their employment as instruments of research is constantly bringing to light.

A few words with regard to the mode in which the subject of temperature is viewed. Some eminent philosophers are of opinion that our methods of subdividing a range of temperature are to a great extent arbitrary, so that provided we always adhere to the same method we shall not be led into error.

Be this as it may, there can be no question that some methods of doing this are much more convenient than others; nay, even that one method, that by the air thermometer, enjoys such a pre-eminence of convenience that it may with propriety be termed the proper method of sub-dividing a range of temperature.

Starting with the assumption that there is a proper method of measuring temperature, it is shewn near the beginning of this work that even if we are ignorant of this proper method there is yet an advantage in employing an air thermometer. This advantage consists in the fact that we may use any permanent gas we choose for our air ther-mometer, and yet obtain results as nearly as may be identical with one another if all our instruments are read on the same principle; while, on the other hand, the indications of two thermometers filled with different liquids, and both graduated on the same principle, are not strictly comparable with each other. If we determine to prefer an air ther-mometer we still have to decide on what principle it ought to be read, and, while this principle is indicated at the commencement of the work, the reasons in favour of its adoption are not fully discussed until the end.

The author cannot omit the opportunity of acknowledging his obligations to several scientific friends for the suggestions and advice they have kindly given him; more especially is he indebted to the organizing Secretary of this Series of Works at Oxford for much valuable assistance throughout the book.

TABLE OF CONTENTS.

INTRODUCTION.

BOOK I.

EFFECTS OF HEAT UPON BODIES.

CHAPTER I.—*Temperature, and its Measurement by Thermometers.*

CHAPTER II.—*Dilatation of Solids.*

CHAPTER III.—*Dilatation of Liquids.*

CHAPTER IV.—*Dilatation of Gases.*

CONTENTS.   xi

CHAPTER VII.—*Change of State.—Production of Vapour and its Condensation.*

CHAPTER VIII.—*Effect of Heat upon other Properties of Matter.*

BOOK II.

ON THE LAWS WHICH REGULATE THE DISTRIBUTION OF HEAT THROUGH SPACE.

CHAPTER III.—*Theory of Exchanges.*

CHAPTER IV.—*Radiation at Different Temperatures.*

CHAPTER V.—*Further Remarks on Absorption.*

Chapter IX.—*Specific Heat.*

Chapter X.—*Latent Heat.*

BOOK III.

ON THE NATURE OF HEAT, ITS SOURCES, AND CONNECTION WITH OTHER PROPERTIES OF MATTER.

CHAPTER I.—*Remarks on Energy.* (*Historical and Preliminary.*)

CHAPTER II.—*Relation between Heat and Mechanical Effect.*

CHAPTER III.—*History of Heat Engines.*

CHAPTER IV.—*Connection between Heat and other Forms of Energy.*

𝕮𝖑𝖆𝖗𝖊𝖓𝖉𝖔𝖓 𝕻𝖗𝖊𝖘𝖘 𝕾𝖊𝖗𝖎𝖊𝖘

AN

ELEMENTARY TREATISE

ON

HEAT

BY

BALFOUR STEWART, LL.D. F.R.S.

SUPERINTENDENT OF THE KEW OBSERVATORY

EXAMINER AT THE UNIVERSITIES OF EDINBURGH AND LONDON

𝕺𝖝𝖋𝖔𝖗𝖉

AT THE CLARENDON PRESS

M.DCCC.LXVI.

INTRODUCTION.

1. The word 'Heat' is used in the following treatise to denote that agent which produces a certain well-known sensation when applied to the human body.

2. But this sensation while so familiar to us that every one must immediately recognise what agent is meant when the term Heat is used, is yet not sufficiently definite or constant to afford us the means of accurately measuring the amount of heat which a body possesses. The same substance may at the same time appear warm to one individual and cold to another; nay, it may even be pronounced warm by one of our hands and cold by the other. Our judgment with regard to the amount of heat possessed by the substance in question is thus found to depend upon the state of our bodies, and as this changes from time to time we cannot therefore make use of our sensations as a means of measuring heat.

3. In the study of this subject it is thus of primary importance to become acquainted with some instrument by the aid of which the state of bodies with regard to heat may be accurately determined. The Thermometer fulfils this requirement, and a description of it will therefore form the commencement of this treatise.

4. When the Thermometer has been described the various effects produced in bodies by the presence of heat may next with advantage be studied.   Such effects are change of volume; of condition; of hardness; chemical change; with other effects which will afterwards be mentioned.

5. The laws which regulate the distribution of heat will next be considered, and under this head it will be necessary to recognise two distinct modes of conveyance of this agent from one body to another.   Every one is familiar with the fact that the contact of a cold body with a hot one, whether solid, liquid, or gaseous, will cause the latter to part with some of its heat.   But this is not the only way by which heat may reach us; for we derive a very considerable amount from the sun, although this luminary is at a great distance from the earth, while the intervening space does not contain that gross form of matter which serves to convey heat by contact.

We are thus taught that a hot body parts with its heat in two ways,—

(1) By *contact* with a cold body;

(2) By *radiation* through space.

And we believe, moreover, that radiant heat traverses space with the enormous velocity of 190,000 miles per second.

6. We have thus the means of making a very convenient and easily perceived classification of the modes in which Heat exhibits itself to us.

There is, in the first place, what we may call *absorbed heat*, which resides in a hot body, and often remains in it for a considerable time; and we have, in the next place, *radiant heat*, which is heat in the act of passing through space with a very great velocity.

7. In treating of the laws which regulate the distribution of heat this distinction may with propriety be observed, and this part of the subject will thus divide itself into two. It will be desirable to consider, in the first place, radiant heat—its nature, and the laws which regulate its distribution; and then to consider the laws which regulate the distribution of absorbed heat, while under this last heading the capacity of bodies for heat will be brought forward.

8. In treating of radiant heat theoretical views will for the first time be introduced. It is well known that there have been two distinct theories regarding the nature of Heat. In one of these it is viewed as a substance which insinuates itself between the particles of a hot body, while in the other it is regarded as a species of motion taking place amongst these particles. Such views could not well be introduced at an earlier stage of the work, since the more prominent effects of heat upon bodies form a set of phenomena that are capable of being explained tolerably well by either hypothesis. They are therefore somewhat unsuitable as tests of a theory, while, on the other hand, they are of extreme importance as facts. But the study of radiant heat enables us to pronounce with a near approach to certainty that this influence is not a substance ejected from a hot body, but rather a description of undulatory motion transmitted through a medium pervading all space.

9. It would appear to follow, as a corollary from this view, that ordinary heat into which radiant heat is transformed when absorbed must also be a species of motion, and this idea will be abundantly confirmed in the next part of the subject, where the various sources of heat will be treated of, and the nature of this agent as well as its connexion with other properties of matter fully discussed.

10. Lastly, this treatise will contain throughout notices of some of the most important practical applications of the laws of Heat, and also of certain terrestrial and cosmical adaptations in which these laws play a very important part.

It will be observed throughout that the term Caloric is avoided as much as possible, since this term has come to be associated with that theory which regards heat as a substance and not as a species of motion.

BOOK I.

CHAPTER I.

Temperature, and its measurement by Thermometers.

DEFINITION OF TEMPERATURE.

11. The temperature of a body may be defined to be its state with respect to sensible heat. When the amount of sensible heat in a body increases, its temperature is said to rise, and when this diminishes its temperature is said to fall. It is expedient to discuss at the outset certain fundamental principles which underlie all measurements of temperature.

12. If there be two substances, as for instance water and mercury, in such a condition that when brought intimately into contact with one another and shaken together neither of them changes its state with respect to heat, then these two bodies may be said to be in a state of equilibrium of temperature with each other. Suppose now that the mercury is in a similar state with respect to a third substance, oil. We have thus the water in equilibrium of temperature with the mercury and the mercury in equilibrium of temperature with the oil. Now we know, as the result of experience, that we shall also have the water in equilibrium of temperature with the oil. In fine, if a series of bodies be in equilibrium of temperature with each other in any one order they will be so in any other order; and no matter how they are brought

together or mixed up with one another, they will always retain unchanged their state with respect to heat. All such bodies are said to be of the same temperature.

But if when the water and the mercury are brought together the water parts with some of its heat to the mercury, then it is said to be of a higher temperature than the mercury; and if, on the other hand, the water receives heat from the mercury, then it is said to be of a lower temperature than the mercury.

13. It will be inferred from what we have said that if two bodies of different temperature be intimately associated with one another they will both at length attain one common temperature.

Let us now suppose that we have a large mass of liquid whose temperature we wish to measure by means of a thermometer. Strictly speaking, when the thermometer and the liquid are brought intimately together, a common temperature will be attained, but if the mass of the liquid be very much greater than that of the thermometer the former will not be appreciably changed in temperature by the immersion in it of the latter, and the result will be that the thermometer will denote with sufficient accuracy the temperature of the liquid—only it is necessary that this instrument be very small. But if the temperature of the liquid be kept constantly recruited by some natural process, as for instance that of boiling, the thermometer will in such a case, whatever be its size, at length attain the temperature of the boiling liquid in which it is immersed; but a small thermometer will attain this temperature sooner than a large one.

14. **Requirements to be fulfilled by a good Thermometer.** Having stated these facts, let us now point out the requirements which an instrument for measuring temperature may be expected to fulfil. 1st, it ought to be of small size and easily portable. 2nd, it ought always to give the same

indication for the same temperature, or to be capable of doing so by a simple correction. 3rd, it ought to do something more than merely denote that one body is hotter or colder than another. For the difference between two temperatures, such as the freezing and the boiling points of water, is one which we conceive to be capable of accurate subdivision into any number of equal parts, which form as it were successive equal steps by which we may mount from the lower to the higher temperature. This last requirement is the most difficult one, for it implies not only a knowledge of the agent Heat, but also of the changes which it produces upon bodies, since we must evidently make use of some one of these changes in the construction of our instrument for measuring temperature.

While a mercurial thermometer may probably be so made as to fulfil the first and second of these requirements, it is an air thermometer which will best satisfy the third; but the reasons which lead us to suppose that this instrument gives us the means of measuring temperature with great accuracy cannot well be discussed at the outset of this work. These will be given hereafter: in the meantime, let us take it for granted that an air thermometer does really fulfil this requirement, and refer our readers for a description of this instrument to our chapter on the dilatation of gases.

15. But while an air thermometer gives a very correct indication of temperature, it is nevertheless an instrument difficult of construction and awkward in use: it ought therefore to be employed rather as a standard of reference, by means of which the errors peculiar to some other instrument of easy construction and simple form may be determined.

MERCURIAL THERMOMETER.

16. An instrument of this kind is found in the mercurial thermometer, which is constructed upon the principle that mercury when heated expands very much more than glass.

In making a mercurial thermometer a bulb is first blown at one extremity of a tube of glass having a capillary bore, the other end of the tube being open to the atmosphere. The bulb is then heated so as to drive out some of the air which it contains, and the open end of the tube is inserted into a basin of pure mercury. As the bulb begins to cool and the pressure of the air within it diminishes, part of this mercury will be driven up the bore into the bulb. The mercury is then boiled, and the mercurial vapour drives away any air or moisture that may have adhered to the tube. While the instrument is hot and full of the vapour of mercury its extremity is once more plunged into the basin, by which means, on condensation of the vapour, the bulb and tube will be filled with mercury. When the tube is full of mercury it is hermetically sealed, and when the instrument has cooled the mercury ought to fill the bulb and part of the stem, the other part being empty. If now the bulb of this instrument be heated the glass envelope will expand, and also the mercury with which it is filled; but the mercury will expand much more than the glass envelope, and in consequence the mercurial column will rise in the capillary tube. If the bore be fine enough, a considerable rise may thus be produced even when there is only a small expansion of the mercury, and by this means a very great amount of delicacy may be given to the instrument.

17. Calibration of the tube. If the instrument is to be as accurate as possible, it is necessary to know the relative diameter of the bore at different parts of its length, since this is always variable even in the best tubes.

To accomplish this the tube is made by the glass-blower in such a way that by a simple mechanical contrivance a small column of mercury, occupying the length of about one-third of an inch in the bore, may be detached from the main body of the fluid. This column is then made to travel from the one extremity of the tube to the other, and its length is measured by a microscope at each short stage of its progress. It is obvious that this column will be long where the bore is narrow and short where it is wide, and that by this means we may obtain the relative diameter of the bore in different parts of the tube. The detached column having served its purpose is now reunited to the main body of the mercury. It will be afterwards seen (Art. 20) in what manner the information thus obtained is made use of.

18. **Determination of the fixed points. The freezing point.** Our object in constructing a thermometer presupposes the existence of at least two fixed points of temperature. The two universally adopted are the freezing and the boiling points of water. Suppose that a substance ascends from the lower to the upper of these temperatures through a certain number of equal stages or degrees, it is the office of the thermometer to indicate these. In order to determine the lower fixed point, a wooden box is perforated in the bottom with a few holes to permit drainage, and placed in a room whose temperature is above the freezing point of water. It is then filled with snow or pounded ice in a melting state, and it has been ascertained that the temperature of this melting ice is under ordinary circumstances absolutely constant. The thermometer is now placed vertically in this mixture, the ice being heaped about the stem, and is so left for a quarter of an hour, or until the mercury has become stationary. The tube is then marked with a scratch at the termination of the mercurial column, and the lowest of the two points is thus determined. Presuming that Fahrenheit's scale is to be employed, this point will denote 32°.

19. The boiling point. The next process consists in determining the boiling point of water. This, unlike the freezing point, is not strictly constant, for the temperature of steam in contact with water depends upon the pressure under which it exists.

It had been observed by Gay Lussac that water boils under the same pressure at slightly different temperatures in different vessels; but Rudberg afterwards found that the nature of the containing vessel altered only the temperature of the water and not that of the steam. It is therefore in steam, not water, that a thermometer ought to be plunged in order to have its upper point determined. Hence also if steam escape from an open vessel containing water into the air, the temperature of the steam, which depends upon the pressure under which the steam exists, will therefore depend upon the atmospheric pressure, since this must be the same as that of the steam. The temperature of the steam of water boiling in an open vessel will therefore vary with the barometer; but if we know the law of this variation we can make allowance for it in graduating our thermometer.

The Commissioners appointed by the British Government to construct standard weights and measures, and the Kew Committee of the British Association, have both agreed that the upper point of a thermometer graduated according to Fahrenheit's scale, or that adopted in this country, shall be taken to represent at London the temperature of steam, at the pressure of 29.905 inches of mercury reduced to the freezing point. This is therefore the true meaning of 212° Fahrenheit, and the temperature of steam at other pressures may be found from the following table.

Temperature of steam at different pressures.

Tempera-ture.	Pressure in inches of mercury at 32° Fahr.	Tempera-ture.	Pressure in inches of mercury at 32° Fahr.	Tempera-ture.	Pressure in inches of mercury at 32° Fahr.
211.0	29.315	211.7	29.727	212.4	30.143
211.1	29.374	211.8	29.786	212.5	30.203
211.2	29.432	211.9	29.845	212.6	30.263
211.3	29.491	212.0	29.905	212.7	30.323
211.4	29.550	212.1	29.964	212.8	30.384
211.5	29.609	212.2	30.024	212.9	30.444
211.6	29.668	212.3	30.083		

We are thus furnished with the means of determining the higher point. Let the instrument be immersed in steam arising from boiling water, mark off as before the termination of the mercurial column, reading the barometer at the same moment. If the pressure of the atmosphere be 29.905 inches, this point will denote 212°; and for any other pressure the true value of the mark may be found from the above table.

In performing this operation it will be found most convenient to employ Regnault's apparatus (see page 12). The arrangement will best be perceived from Fig. 2, which represents the interior of the instrument.

A is a thermometer having its bulb a little above *E*, the level of the boiling water. The course which the steam is forced to take is denoted by the arrow-heads. It is thus seen that the steam must pass up along the thermometer tube and down again, until finally it leaves the apparatus by the orifice *C*. The whole of the tube of the instrument is thus thoroughly surrounded by steam, and by a cylinder of the temperature of the steam. *D* is a bent glass tube, open to the atmosphere, and containing a little water, which shews by a difference of level in the two limbs if the pressure of the steam in the interior is greater than that of the atmosphere without. It has been ascertained that, if the orifice is sufficiently wide, this difference is too small to affect the temperature of the thermometer, and thus the gauge D may be dispensed with.

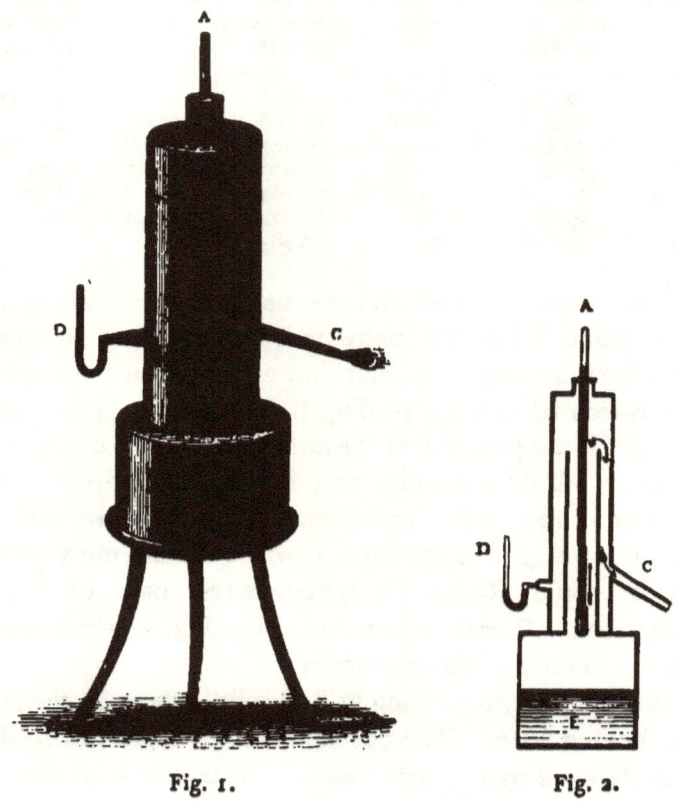

Fig. 1.   Fig. 2.

The thermometer is inserted through a closely fitting slit in a thick piece of india-rubber which rests upon the top of the apparatus, and the stem is lowered until the column of mercury just appears above the india-rubber; and thus nearly all the column as well as the bulb is exposed to the vapour of boiling water. This apparatus is generally formed of copper, and distilled water should if possible be used. It ought also to be noted that in marking off the points the lower or freezing point should always be determined first; the reason for this will be afterwards given.

20. Graduation. Fahrenheit's scale. The relative diameter of the bore at different parts of the tube having now been determined by calibration (Art. 17), and the two fixed points marked, it is easy to graduate the instrument. If the scale is to be that of Fahrenheit, the lower point is called 32° and the upper point (provided the atmospheric pressure be 29.905 inches) 212°. There are thus 180 divisions between the two points, and these are marked upon the tube in the following manner. The whole instrument is covered over with wax sufficiently thin to allow the two marks (previously blackened) to be visible, and a needle attached to a dividing engine scratches the graduations in the wax. The thermometer is then exposed to hydrofluoric acid or its vapour, which attacks the glass where the wax has been scratched off. The length of each degree is regulated by the previously determined diameter of the bore in such a manner that the internal capacity of the tube between the two marks is divided into 180 equal parts. The graduation is generally extended below the freezing point, and sometimes above the boiling point. In this thermometer a temperature 32° below the freezing point is termed *zero*, while one ten degrees lower is called *minus* 10°, or 10° below *zero*, and so on.

21. Other scales. Besides Fahrenheit's scale there are two others, those of Celsius and Reaumur. The former of these is also called Centigrade, and is used throughout France, and the latter very generally in Germany.

In the Centigrade thermometer the freezing point of water is termed 0°, or *zero*, while the boiling point is reckoned equal to 100°. A degree Centigrade is therefore greater than a degree Fahrenheit in the proportion of nine to five. The boiling point in this thermometer, or 100°, is defined to be the temperature of steam under the barometric pressure of 760 millimètres, or 29.922 inches of mercury reduced to the freezing point of water at the latitude of Paris. This is slightly different from the corresponding point, or 212°, in Fahrenheit's scale, which, as we have seen, denotes the temperature of steam under the pressure of 29.905 inches of mercury reduced to 32° at the latitude of London. It must, however, be borne in mind that the force of gravity, and therefore the absolute pressure towards the earth of the same mass of matter, is somewhat greater in London than at Paris, so that 29.922 inches of mercury in Paris are equal in absolute pressure to 29.914 inches at London (see Art. 143). This still leaves a slight difference between the absolute pressure of the steam in the two cases, and hence the upper points of these two instruments will not quite correspond in temperature; but this difference is so very small that for ordinary purposes it may be neglected.

To reduce Fahrenheit to Centigrade the following formula is made use of, $C = (F - 32)\dfrac{5}{9}$; while to reduce Centigrade to Fahrenheit we have $F = \dfrac{9\,C}{5} + 32$.

Thus, were it required to find what degree Centigrade corresponds to 77° Fahr., we should proceed in the following manner. Subtracting 32° from 77° we find that this temperature is 45° above the freezing point, or Centigrade zero, and taking $\frac{5}{9}$ of 45°, since Centigrade degrees are greater than those of Fahrenheit in this proportion, we find that 25° Cent. corresponds to 77° Fahr.

Again, were it required to find what degree Centigrade corresponds to —38°.2 Fahr., we should have, as above—

$$C = (-38.2 - 32)\frac{5}{9} \ \text{ or } \ C = -70.2 \times \frac{5}{9} = -39°.$$

In the scale of Reaumur the distance between the freezing and boiling point is divided into 80 parts, and the boiling point is defined to be the temperature of steam under the pressure of 760 millimètres of mercury, the force of gravity being that which corresponds to latitude 45°.

To reduce Fahrenheit to Reaumur we have therefore the following expression, $R = (F - 32)\frac{4}{9}$; while to reduce Reaumur to Fahrenheit we have $F = \frac{9R}{4} + 32$.

22. Correction for change of zero. It is found that thermometers are liable to an alteration of their zero points, especially when the bulb has been filled not long before graduation. This displacement is of the following nature. Immediately after graduation 32° will of course denote the temperature of melting ice, but when some time has elapsed a thermometer placed in melting ice will no longer give this reading, but one somewhat higher, perhaps 32.4 or 32.5.

When an instrument has been graduated shortly after the filling of the bulb, this displacement may in the course of years amount to nearly 2° Fahr., but it is believed that this is the extreme limit of the change. But if the bulb has been kept for some time before graduation, and has also been well annealed, the change is much less : nevertheless it may possibly amount in the course of years to six or seven tenths of a degree. Besides this progressive and permanent change there is also a temporary one, produced by heating and suddenly cooling the instrument. For instance, if a thermometer have first of all its freezing point determined by melting ice, if it then be plunged into boiling water, then suddenly withdrawn, and finally plunged again into ice, the freezing point will be found to have changed—the instrument may now read 31.8, and it will not recover its true reading until ten days or a fortnight have elapsed. This is the reason why the freezing point is always marked off first in constructing the instrument.

To correct for change of zero the thermometer ought to be plunged from time to time into melting ice, and its reading noted. The amount of alteration thus becomes known, and the requisite correction may be applied, which is of course constant throughout the scale.

23. Other sources of error. If a thermometer have its fixed points determined in a vertical position it must always be used in this position: in like manner if these points are determined in a horizontal position of the instrument, then it must always be used horizontally. The reason of this is that for the same temperature the same instrument will give a higher reading in a horizontal than in a vertical position, since in the latter the hydrostatic pressure of the column of mercury will tend not only to compress the particles of mercury into less volume, but also to enlarge the capacity of the bulb.

For a similar reason the reading of an unprotected thermometer in vacuo will be different from its reading in air.

24. Again, when the volume of mercury in the stem of a thermometer is exposed to a temperature different from that of the bulb, a correction must likewise be made on this account.

For instance, if the bulb and the column of mercury up to freezing-point mark have the temperature of boiling water, while the remainder of the column is exposed to the atmosphere, which we may imagine to be at $32°$, then the instrument will not indicate $212°$. It would have done so had the whole of the mercury been heated up to the boiling point, but this is not the case, for nearly 180 degrees, or the distance between the freezing-point mark and the extremity of the column, is exposed to the atmosphere, and may be taken to have the same temperature as it has.

In order to find the correction which we ought to apply,

let us denote by unity the whole volume of the mercury when it is all at the temperature 32°: unity will therefore also denote the internal capacity at this temperature of the glass envelope up to freezing-point mark. Now it will be afterwards shewn (Art. 52) that this mercury when raised to 212° will have the volume 1.0182 nearly, and also (Art. 40) we may perhaps suppose that the internal capacity of the glass up to freezing-point mark will have, when raised to 212°, the volume 1.0026: this however depends upon the nature of the glass. Hence a volume of mercury equal to 1.0182 — 1.0026, or .0156, will exist in the tube above the freezing-point mark provided that the *whole column* of mercury be heated up to 212°; and it will under these circumstances occupy 180 degrees of the bore. The question to be answered is, how many degrees of the bore will this portion of mercury occupy when both it and the tube containing it are at 32°. Evidently the absolute volume of this portion of mercury at 32° will be $.0156 \times \dfrac{1}{1.0182} = .01532$.

Hence if we imagine the bore of the tube to preserve a constant volume for all temperatures, the rise may easily be found. For if the volume .0156 occupy 180 divisions, the volume .01532 will occupy $180 \times \dfrac{.01532}{.0156}$ or 176.8 divisions. But the bore of the tube in which this rise takes place does not preserve a constant volume throughout, but, being only at 32°, is really of smaller capacity than it was at 212°, in the ratio of 1 to 1.0026 : the rise of 176°.8 will therefore have to be increased in this proportion, and will become 177°.2, or the mercury will indicate 209°.2 as the boiling point of water; a correction of + 2°.8 must therefore be applied.

This example will convey to the reader sufficiently well the method to be employed in finding this correction, but it ought to be borne in mind that it is much better when practicable to avoid the necessity for it, by exposing the whole column of mercury as well as the bulb to the influence of the temperature which we wish to estimate.

25. Lastly, even when a mercurial thermometer has been constructed with the greatest accuracy after the method indicated in the preceding articles, so that the freezing point is denoted by 32° and the boiling point by 212°, while each degree denotes precisely the 180th part of the capacity of the bore between these two points, it does not follow that the instrument will give an intermediate temperature with absolute exactness.

For, in the first place, it does not follow that the expansion in volume of the mercury above that of the glass envelope up to freezing-point mark for a true rise of 90° must be precisely half of its expansion for a true rise of 180°.

In the next place, it ought to be borne in mind that the rise of 90° takes place in a bore of which the temperature is only 122°, and of which therefore the capacity is smaller than when the temperature is 212°, in the proportion of 1.0013 to 1.0026.

Both of these circumstances will introduce errors, and Regnault has found that when the graduation is extended much above 212°, the difference between the mercurial and the standard air thermometer becomes very considerable at high temperatures, and also varies with the nature of the glass. But between 32° and 212°, and for a range extending not too far beyond these points, a mercurial thermometer well graduated may be considered to be a tolerably good though not a strictly accurate instrument. Since the best thermometers made in this country are all formed of the same kind of glass, it would be desirable that a few of these should be compared with an air thermometer at temperatures between 32° and 212°. The writer of this work hopes that he may ultimately be able to make this comparison.

OTHER THERMOMETERS.

26. Alcohol Thermometer. It is well known that mercury freezes at about $-38°$ Fahr., while it boils at about $660°$ Fahr. A mercurial thermometer cannot therefore be used below the former point or above the latter. But while the superior limit of its accurate employment is considerably below the higher temperature, its indications may probably be relied upon very nearly to the point at which the mercury freezes. It is, however, often desirable to register still lower temperatures, and in order to do so a thermometer filled with absolute alcohol is employed. Such an instrument is not capable of being constructed with the same amount of exactness as a mercurial thermometer; but yet if it be carefully made, and used with caution, very good results may be obtained. An alcohol thermometer ought before graduation to be marked off at $32°$, and at some higher temperature by comparison with a mercurial standard thermometer. The freezing point of mercury ought also, if possible, to be made use of as a fixed point; and it has been ascertained that this, like the freezing point of water, is of constant temperature, its true value, on Fahrenheit's scale, being $-37°.9$. An alcohol thermometer may be used for very low temperatures, since this fluid has not yet been frozen.

When a very accurate determination is desired, this thermometer should be kept in a vertical position, bulb downwards, for some time before it is read.

The reason of this is that alcohol, unlike mercury, wets the capillary glass tube which contains it, and is also very volatile: great care ought therefore to be taken that there is no liquid above the main column, whether condensed or adhering to the sides of the tube.

27. Maximum and Minimum Thermometers. Maximum. It is often of importance to know not merely the present temperature, but likewise the highest or lowest point to which an instrument has been exposed. Meteorologists, for instance, should be able to register every evening and morning the highest and lowest temperatures of the atmosphere. This, when not accomplished by a continuous photographic registration of temperature, is done by maximum and minimum thermometers.

In Rutherford's maximum thermometer the stem is placed in a horizontal position, and the bore contains a small index made of iron or graphite, which the mercury pushes before it when it expands through increase of temperature; but when it retreats this index is left behind, since there is no cohesion between it and the mercury. In Professor Phillips' maximum thermometer this index is part of the mercurial column itself, which, as in Fig. 3, is separated from the main body of the

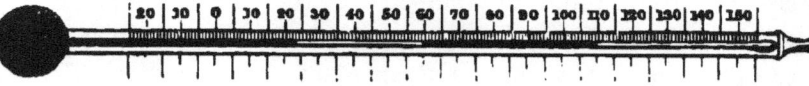

Fig. 3.

fluid by a little air. When the mercury expands, the elastic force of the air pushes the index on before it; but this is kept in its position when the mercury again contracts. By this arrangement there is no risk of the index soiling the mercury or becoming entangled with it. It has also been found that when the bore is sufficiently narrow the instrument may be used in a vertical position, bulb downwards, and it is thus of service in chemical operations. Both of these maximum thermometers when read must be reset by shaking the index down towards the mercurial column as far as it will go.

Negretti and Zambra's maximum thermometer is exhibited in Fig. 4. When used the stem of this instrument ought to be inclined downwards. The bore is nearly choked at *A* by means of a bit of enamel or glass. When the mercury expands, it does so with sufficient force to push its way past this obstruction; but when it contracts, that part of the column past the obstruction is kept there, and the contraction takes

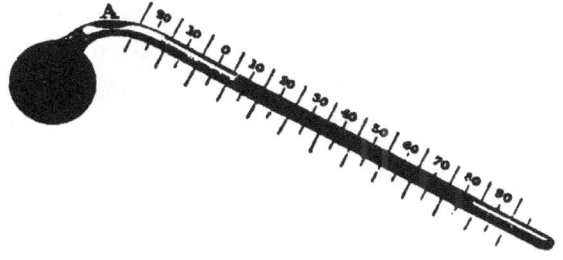

Fig. 4.

place by the mercury to the left of *A* withdrawing into the bulb. It does not matter if the column past the obstruction go down to the bottom of the tube, for when the instrument is read it is gently tilted up until this detached column flows back to the obstruction, where it is arrested, and the end of the column will then denote the maximum temperature. In resetting the instrument it is necessary to shake the detached column past the obstruction, in order to fill up the vacancy left by the contraction of the fluid after the maximum had been reached.

28. Minimum. In Rutherford's minimum thermometer alcohol is used, and a small glass index is immersed in the column of this fluid. When the instrument has been set this index is at the termination of the column which is kept in a horizontal position. Now should the temperature rise and the alcohol expand, it will flow past the index; but should the alcohol contract, it carries the index with it, for the fluid does not readily permit of its concave capillary surface being broken. The minimum temperature is thus registered.

In order to overcome the objection attached to the use of

alcohol, L. Casella has lately proposed a mercurial minimum thermometer. The principle of this instrument will be understood from Fig. 5. Its peculiarity consists in a side chamber, *AB*, the bore of which at *A* becomes smaller very abruptly, and afterwards swells into a pear-shaped termination.

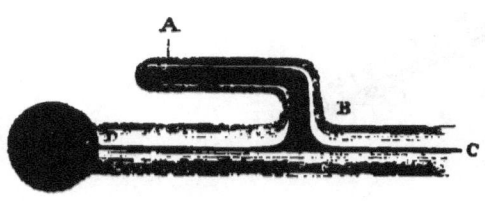

Fig. 5.

But even after it has been abruptly narrowed this bore is still much wider than that of the main tube *CD*. When the instrument is set, the mercury fills the side chamber as far as the abrupt termination *A*, but the pear-shaped vessel is left empty. Suppose now the temperature to rise—instead of the column in the main tube moving, the rise will take place by the mercury at *A* flowing into the pear-shaped vessel: the reason of this probably being that the bore is here wider than that of the main tube, and there is consequently less resistance to the movement of the fluid. Suppose, next, that the temperature falls—the fluid in the pear-shaped vessel will first contract, but when the mercury has reached *A*, or the point at which the instrument was originally set, the effect produced by the flat surface at *A* will prevent the mercury receding farther, and the contraction will now take place in the main tube. Thus any fall below the temperature of setting takes place in the main tube, while any rise takes place in the side chamber; and hence the instrument serves as a minimum thermometer. A comparison at Kew Observatory has shewn that the indication of such an instrument agrees very nearly with that of a Rutherford's minimum thermometer when the latter is carefully used.

29. Leslie's differential Thermometer. Sir John

Leslie has constructed an instrument for shewing the difference in temperature between two neighbouring substances or places, and which is hence called the differential thermometer. In this instrument two bulbs, *A* and *B*, filled with air are connected together by means of a bent tube, as in Fig. 6 : a little coloured liquid fills the lower part of this tube, and rises to the levels *C* and *D* when both bulbs are of the same temperature. But should *A* become warmer than *B*, since air expands very much for an increase of temperature, the column of liquid will be pushed down at *C* and made to rise at *D*; and this motion will be reversed when *B* becomes warmer than *A*. Such an instrument will

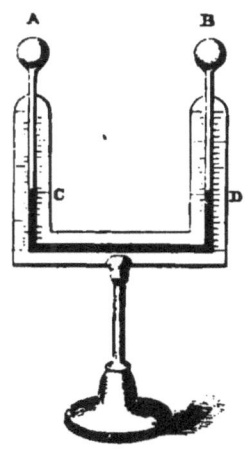

Fig. 6.

therefore indicate any difference of temperature with great delicacy. The fluid in the tube ought to be one which is not volatile—sulphuric acid is frequently used. We shall find afterwards (Art. 165) that the thermo-pile registers any difference of temperature with still greater delicacy than this instrument.

30. Fluctuation Thermometer. The author of this work has proposed an instrument for summing up fluctuations of temperature. If a bulb be blown connecting together two horizontal glass tubes of different bores, and if this instrument be nearly filled with mercury, it will be found that this fluid will expand in the tube of wide bore when the temperature rises, and contract in the other when it falls. Thus the mercury will gradually travel toward the extremity of the tube of wide bore, and its position from time to time will indicate the amount of fluctuation which the temperature undergoes. This instrument is however difficult of construction.

31. Other instruments for measuring temperature. Wedgwood's pyrometer is an instrument for measuring high temperatures, and its action depends on the contraction which takes place in baked clay when heated. An air thermometer furnishes, however, a much more accurate means of obtaining the same result, and this will be afterwards described.

Breguet's metallic thermometer is another instrument which may be used in measuring temperature, but a description of it must be deferred to a future occasion.

CHAPTER II.

Dilatation of Solids.

32. In the present chapter the relation between the temperature and the volume of a solid will be investigated.

It is a general, though not a universal law, that when such a body increases in temperature it also expands in volume, or dilates, and that when it diminishes in temperature its volume contracts, so that when restored to its original temperature it resumes its original volume.

The subjoined apparatus (Fig. 7) is used to illustrate the expansion of solids through heat. A rod A is fixed at one end by a screw B, while the other end presses against the short arm of a lever, whose long arm P forms a pointer. This pointer exhibits by its movement along a graduated scale any change of length in the rod—thus, were the rod to expand, the pointer would be pushed upwards; and were it to contract, the pointer would fall downwards. Any small change in the length of the rod is thus rendered visible.

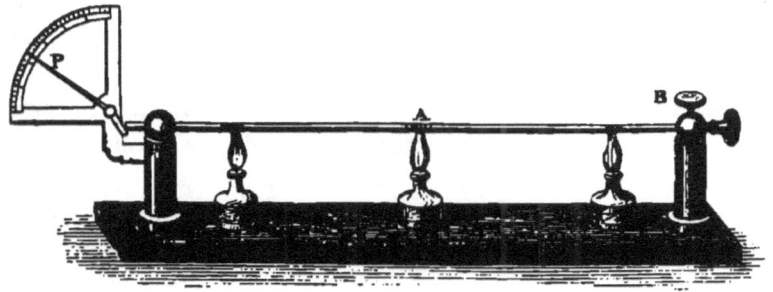

Fig. 7.

But the way in which a solid expands is different according as the substance is crystalline in its structure or amorphous, and hence the subject naturally divides itself into two parts. In the first of these the expansion of uncrystallized solids will be considered, while in the second the behaviour of crystals under change of temperature will be shortly described.

DILATATION OF UNCRYSTALLIZED SOLIDS.

33. In some cases it is the increment of the volume of a body that we wish to estimate, while in others, as for instance when we are considering a substance, such as a bar, of which the length is the important element, it is change of length and not change of volume with which we concern ourselves. The former of these is called *linear* and the latter *cubical* dilatation or expansion. We shall commence with linear expansion: but let us first proceed to define what is meant by "the coefficient of expansion," whether linear or cubical. The coefficient of expansion of a substance is the expansion for one degree of temperature of that quantity of the substance whose length or volume (as the case may be) was unity at a certain standard temperature, as for instance at the temperature of melting ice.

Thus if the length of a brass bar be unity at 32° Fahr., at 33° it will be 1.00001 : hence .00001 is the linear coefficient of expansion of brass for 1° Fahr.

34. Linear dilatation. Lavoisier's method. Several methods of finding the linear dilatation of solids have been proposed. In one of these, namely that adopted by Lavoisier and Laplace, a telescope is placed upon a horizontal axis between two pillars, as in Fig. 8. This axis carries a

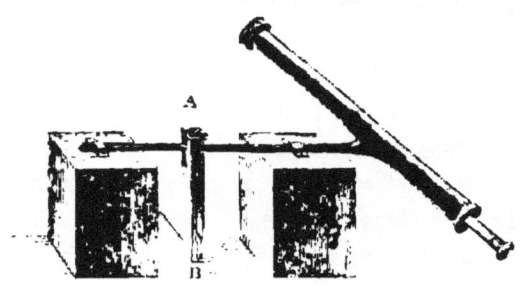

cross piece AB rigidly attached to it, and a bar (not shewn in the figure) fixed at one end is forced to expand by means of heat, and to press against

Fig. 8.

the cross piece in the direction denoted by the arrow-head. This pressure will move the cross piece and turn round the axis of the telescope to which the cross piece is rigidly attached, so that the telescope will now point to a different object. Suppose that the object to which it is pointing is a vertical scale of inches at a considerable distance. If a horizontal wire be placed in the telescope so as to appear in the centre of its field of view, this will seem to have travelled over a considerable distance on the vertical scale for a very small expansion of the bar. It will be seen that this apparatus is similar to that of Fig. 7, the telescope and vertical scale of inches performing the part of the pointer and graduated quadrant.

35. Ramsden's method. In Roy and Ramsden's appa-

ratus there are three troughs, the first and the last containing
iron bars, while the middle one contains the bar of which

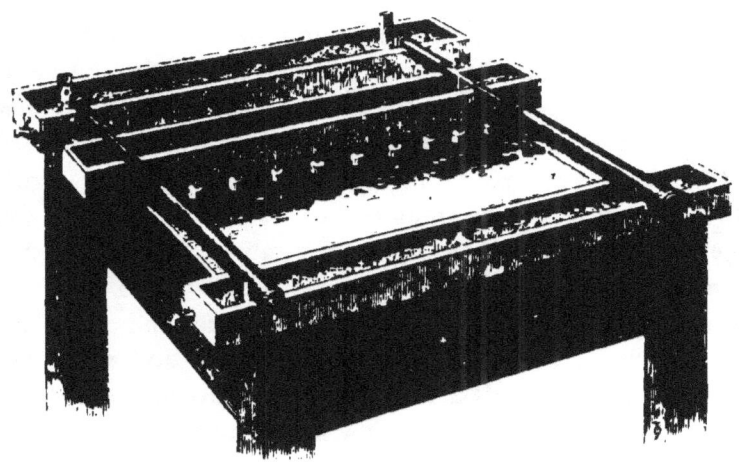

Fig. 9.

the dilatation is to be measured.   To the two extremities of
the iron bar contained in the first trough there are fixed the
eye-pieces of two microscopes, the object-glasses of which
are fixed to the corresponding extremities of the bar in the
middle trough.   These microscopes are directed towards
two marks attached to the extremities of the iron bar in
the farther trough.   The first and third troughs are kept
filled with melting ice, so that the iron bars in these are
always of the same temperature.   (These bars are per-
manently fixed at one end and moveable through a collar
at the other.)   Hence the points of attachment of the eye-
pieces of the two microscopes to the first bar may be
regarded as rigidly fixed, as well as the points of attachment of the two marks, which are fastened to the extremities
of the iron bar in the third trough, inasmuch as there is no
expansion or contraction of these two bars through change
of temperature.   On the other hand, the bar in the middle

trough is first of all placed in ice, and afterwards in water, of which the temperature is varied by means of lamps, in order that the dilatation of this bar may be measured. This middle trough rests upon rollers, and by means of a screw attached to the table (not shewn in the figure) the left-hand end of the bar is always kept in the same position, so that the object-glass of the left-hand microscope which is attached to the middle bar may be regarded as fixed. But the right-hand extremity of the middle bar, and consequently the object-glass attached to it, is moveable, and will move towards the right when an expansion takes place. At the left side therefore the eye-piece, object-glass, and mark are fixed, while at the right side the eye-piece and mark are fixed but the object-glass is moveable. Now the right-hand eye-piece has in its field of view a vertical thread, which at the beginning of the experiment, when all the three troughs are filled with melting ice, may be supposed to coincide precisely in position with the right-hand mark. But when the object-glass of this microscope has been moved owing to the expansion of the middle bar, this thread will no longer coincide with the mark: nevertheless it may be made to do so by means of a screw attached to the eye-piece and which moves the thread. It is thus apparent that the number of turns and fractional parts of a turn of this screw necessary to bring back the thread to coincidence with the mark affords the means of calculating the expansion of the middle bar, which may thus be determined with very great precision.

36. Pouillet and Daniell's methods. In the last method, as well as in that previously described, the bar of which the dilatation is to be measured is immersed in a liquid, and therefore cannot be heated to a very great extent. If we wish to measure the dilatation of a substance at a high temperature we must use some other method. Pouillet has devised an instrument by which the amount of dilatation may be measured at a distance, while Daniell has effected the same object in the following manner. The bar of which the expansion is to be measured is inserted into *A*, a black-lead tube, and pushed to the bottom; above it is placed an index *B*, which is pushed down into contact with the bar, and which is kept somewhat tight by means of a collar *CD*. When the bar expands through heat this index is pushed up, but is left in its place when the same bar again contracts. Thus by an arrangement similar to that of the maximum thermometer the expansion of the bar may be determined. It may be easily shewn that in this apparatus the index *B* (neglecting its contraction since it is small) will remain pushed out by a quantity which represents the difference between the expansion of the bar and of the tube containing it. For suppose that at the highest temperature reached the

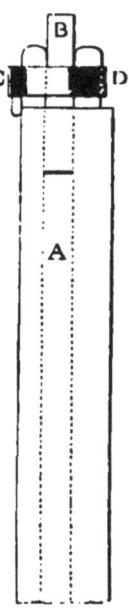

Fig. 10.

bar and the index *B* are in contact together. As the temperature falls the bar will contract, leaving a vacant space between the bar and the index; but, on the other hand, the whole tube as it contracts will tend to diminish this vacant space, and to push the bar and the index nearer together. The vacant space will thus be the difference between the expansion of the tube and that of the bar, and indeed it is evident that if the bar be composed of the same material as the tube there will be no vacant space. In using Daniell's instrument it is therefore necessary to obtain independently the expansion of the tube.

37. The following table will exhibit the results obtained by these various instruments, and it is instructive to notice sometimes the coincidence between the determinations of different observers, and sometimes the difference between those of the same observer when operating upon different specimens of the same substance.

Table of linear dilatations of solids.

Name of substance.	Length at 212° of a rod whose length at 32° = 1.000000.	Name of observer.
Glass (tube without lead)	1.000876	Lavoisier and Laplace.
„ „	1.000898	„ „
„ „	1.000918	„ „
„ (English flint) . .	1.000812	„ „
„ (French with lead)	1.000872	„ „
„ (tube)	1.000776	Roy and Ramsden.
„ (solid rod) . . .	1.000808	
„	1.000861*	Dulong and Petit.
Copper	1.001722	Lavoisier and Laplace.
„	1.001712	
„	1.001716	Daniell.
Brass	1.001867	Lavoisier and Laplace.
„	1.001890	„ „
„ (standard scale) .	1.001855	Roy and Ramsden.
„ (English plate in a rod 5 feet long)	1.001893	„ „
„ (English plate in a trough of 5 feet)	1.001895	„ „
Iron, soft (forged) . .	1.001220	Lavoisier and Laplace.
„ „ (drawn) . . .	1.001235	„ „
„ wrought . . .	1.001182*	Dulong and Petit.
„	1.001156	Borda.
Steel (untempered) . .	1.001079	Lavoisier and Laplace.
„ „ . .	1.001080	„ „
„ (tempered yellow) .	1.001240	„ „
„ rod 5 feet . . .	1.001145	Roy and Ramsden.
Cast iron (prism length 5 feet) . .	1.001109	„ „
„ „	1.001072	Daniell.
Lead	1.002848	Lavoisier and Laplace.
„	1.002788	Daniell.
Tin (East Indies) . . .	1.001938	Lavoisier and Laplace.
„ (Falmouth) . . .	1.002173	„ „
„	1.001767	Daniell.

* Obtained from the cubical dilatation of these solids (see Art. 41).

Name of substance.	Length at 212° of a rod whose length at 32° = 1.000000.	Name of observer.
Silver (fine)	1.001910	Lavoisier and Laplace.
„ (standard of Paris)	1.001909	„ „
„	1.001951	Daniell.
Gold (de dèpart)	1.001466	Lavoisier and Laplace.
„ (standard of Paris, not annealed) . .	1.001552	„ „
„ (standard of Paris, annealed) . . .	1.001514	„ „
„	1.001230	Daniell.
Platinum	1.000884*	Dulong and Petit.
„	1.000857	Borda.
Zinc	1.002976	Daniell.

38. Remarks on the preceding table. If we suppose that by means of the methods already described a great amount of accuracy of measurement may be obtained, yet there is an uncertainty regarding the real temperature of the experimental bar, and this becomes very great for temperatures above the boiling point of water. In such cases, where a bath is used, it is not only very difficult to keep this at a constant temperature, but it is also very difficult to estimate accurately the temperature by means of a thermometer. This uncertainty with regard to estimation applies still more strongly to higher temperatures. But for the range between freezing and boiling water, which is that of the above table, it may perhaps be assumed that the determinations are very good. Whence then proceed the differences between the results of different observers, and even between those of the same observer when estimating the dilatation of different specimens of the same substance? This is probably due to two causes. In the first place, substances which bear the same name are not always of precisely the same chemical composition. Of these, glass may be mentioned as a prominent example, and accordingly we find the dilatation of this substance ranging in the table from .000918 to .000776. Brass, cast iron, and steel are likewise compounds of which the composition is variable. But besides this, the commercial varieties of those substances which when pure are elementary, such as iron, lead, silver, gold, &c., often contain a very appreciable amount of impurity, so that the composition of different specimens is by no means uniform. Very often too a comparatively small impurity causes a very great alteration in some of the properties of a metal. In the next place, it ought to be observed that two solids may have precisely the same chemical composition, while yet their molecular condition may be different, owing to a difference in the treatment which they have experienced. Thus steel heated and suddenly cooled is a very different substance from steel which has not been treated in this manner; and accordingly we find that while steel tempered yellow has for its expansion .001240, untempered steel has .001080. Glass also will behave in a different manner according as it is annealed or unannealed, and in certain cases it is almost impossible to obtain two bars, although made of precisely the same material, which shall in all their properties be precisely alike.

39. Cubical dilatation of solids. To determine the cubical dilatation of a solid we may either, first, weigh the substance at different temperatures in a liquid of which the absolute dilatation is known, or we may, secondly, enclose it in a glass vessel the remainder of which is filled with mercury or water; and if the absolute dilatation of either of these liquids is known, that of the glass envelope and of the enclosed solid may be easily determined. To illustrate this second method let us in the meantime regard the dilatation of mercury as known, and suppose that the following experiment has been made.

A glass bottle thoroughly cleansed, so as to admit of being well filled with mercury without air specks, is found to hold at 32° Fahr. 10169.3 grains of this fluid, while at 212° it only holds 10011.4 grains. Now it is known from Regnault's experiments (see Art. 52) that the dilatation of mercury between 32° and 212° = .018153, that is to say, a quantity of this fluid occupying a volume equal to unity at 32° will at 212° occupy a volume = 1.018153. Hence the weight of mercury occupying a given volume at 212° will bear to that occupying the same volume at 32° the proportion of 1 : 1.018153, and hence (had the bottle not dilated) the weight of mercury filling it at 212° would have been $\frac{10169.3}{1.018153}$ = 9987.9 grains. But the glass envelope having expanded, the bottle holds 10011.4 grains, or 23.5 grains more than it would have held had there been no expansion. The volume of the expanded bottle will therefore bear to that of the same bottle at 32° the ratio of 10011.4 to 9987.9, or of 1.00235 to 1 ; and hence *the expansion of this bottle between* 32° *and* 212° *will be* .00235.

Let us now suppose that this bottle contains a piece of iron weighing 2000 grains, and that the remainder of it is filled with 6707.8 grains of mercury at 32°, while at 212° the mercury filling it only weighs 6599.4 grains. There is thus the loss of 108.4 grains of mercury between the two temperatures. Had there been no expansion either of the bottle or of the iron the amount of mercury sufficient to fill the bottle at 212° would have been $\frac{6707.8}{1.018153}$ = 6588.2 grains, and there would thus have been the loss of 119.6 grains of this fluid. But we have already seen that the expansion of the bottle enables it to contain 23.5 additional grains of mercury, and hence, had the bottle expanded but not the iron, the loss would only have been 119.6 — 23.5 = 96.1 grains. The difference between this and the actual loss (108.4 grains) must therefore have been caused by the expansion of the iron, and this must be such that a piece weighing 2000 grains will expand between 32° and 212°, so as to occupy an additional volume equal to that occupied by 12.3 grains of mercury at 212°.   If we assume that the specific gravities of mercury and of iron at 212° are 13.2 and 7.8, we shall find that this additional volume is that occupied by 7.26 grains of iron.   Hence of the whole 2000 grains of iron at 212°, 7.26 grains are occupying an additional volume, while the remaining 1992.74 occupy the same volume as that originally occupied by the 2000 grains at 32°.   Hence also $\dfrac{7.26}{1992\ 74}$ = .00364 denotes, according to this experiment, *the cubical dilatation of iron between* 32° *and* 212°.

40. This example is sufficient to give an idea of the process employed, which may be used for such substances as do not act chemically upon mercury, and even for those metals which do so, provided that they are protected by a thin film of their oxide.

The following table exhibits the cubical dilatations obtained after this method by different observers; of these MM. Dulong and Petit, and also M. Regnault, employed mercury as their fluid, while, on the other hand, Kopp made use of a flask filled with water.

Table of cubical dilatations of solids.

Substance.	Mean coefficient of expansion for 1°C between 0°C and 100°C.	Mean coefficient of expansion for 1°C between 0°C and 300°C.	Observer.
Glass	.00002584	.00003039	Dulong and Petit
,, (ordinary) ..	.00002761	.00003056	Regnault
,, (crystal) ..	.0000228	.0000233	,,
Copper	.00005155	.00005650	Dulong and Petit
,, ...	.000051	....	Kopp
Iron	.00003546	.00004405	Dulong and Petit
Lead	.000089	....	Kopp
Tin	.000069	....	,,
Zinc..........	.000089	....	,,

Other substances besides those mentioned in the above table have engaged the attention of observers. M. Brunner (fils) has made experiments on the cubical dilatation of ice. His method consisted in determining the specific gravity of this substance at different temperatures. From these experiments he concludes that, while at $0°$C ice has a density of 0.91800, at $-19°$C its density has increased to 0.92013. This would give a cubical dilatation for $1°$C of .000122.

41. Remarks on the above tables. Relation of cubical to linear expansion. In comparing this last table with the preceding one of linear expansion we obtain the following result.

Comparison of linear and cubical expansions.

Substance.	Mean linear expansion between 32° and 212° Fahr.	Observers.	Mean cubical expansion between 32° and 212° Fahr.	Observers.
Glass	.000837	Lavoisier and Laplace, Roy and Ramsden.	.00254	Dulong and Petit, Regnault.
Copper....	.001716	Lavoisier an Laplace, Daniell.	.005127	Dulong and Petit. Kopp.
Lead	.002882	Lavoisier and Laplace, Daniell.	.0089	Kopp.
Tin	.001959	Lavoisier and Laplace, Daniell.	.0069	,,
Zinc..	.002976	Daniell.	.0089	,,
Iron......	.001204	Lavoisier and Laplace, Borda.	.003546	Dulong and Petit.

From this it will be seen that the cubical expansion is in every case equal to about three times the linear expansion of the same substance. The reason of this relationship between the two follows at once from the fact that when an uncrystallized solid expands it does so in such a manner that its figure at one temperature is similar to that at another. Universal experience demonstrates the truth of this statement; and it can be very easily shewn that assuming it to be correct the cubical dilatation of a substance will then be as nearly as possible three times as great as its linear dilatation.

For let a represent the coefficient of linear expansion, and a' that of cubical expansion of the same substance for a rise of $1°$ Fahr. above $32°$; also let L and V represent the length and volume of the substance at $32°$. Then $L (1 + a)$ and $V (1 + a')$ are its length and volume at $33°$. But since similarity of figure is preserved, we shall have by a well-known proposition in geometry,

$$V : V (1 + a') : : L^3 : L^3 (1 + a)^3;$$
$$1 : 1 + a' : : 1 : (1 + a)^3;$$
$$1 + a' = (1 + a)^3 = 1 + 3\,a + 3\,a^2 + a^3.$$

Now since a is a very small fraction we may dispense with the last two terms of the right hand member of this equation, and hence $1 + a' = 1 + 3\,a$, or $a' = 3\,a$ nearly; that is to say, the cubical is equal to three times the linear dilatation.

42. Increase of the coefficient of expansion with the temperature. It will be seen by comparing the mean coefficient of expansion between $0°$ and $100°C$ with that between $0°$ and $300°C$, that the latter is greater than the former for each of the substances given in the above table; it would appear, however, that in the case of hardened steel the coefficient of expansion diminishes as the temperature increases; but this is probably due to the fact that heat deprives the steel of part of its temper, and that it thus becomes more like soft steel, which has a smaller coefficient of expansion than hard steel, as may be seen from the table of linear expansion already given.

DILATATION OF CRYSTALS.

43. It is found that many crystals do not expand under heat equally in all directions so as to preserve their similarity of figure. Mitscherlich has investigated at great length the' action of heat upon crystals, and has obtained the following laws :—

1. Crystals of the regular system which do not cause double refraction dilate uniformly in all directions in the same manner as uncrystallized bodies.

2. Crystals that are optically uniaxal are differently affected by heat in the direction of the principal axis and in the direction of the three secondaries, but in the direction of the latter they are similarly affected.

3. Crystals that are optically biaxal dilate unequally in all directions.

Mitscherlich believes he has determined, as the result of his investigations, that the tendency of heat in crystals is to increase the mutual distance of the molecules in that direction in which this is least, so as to equalize the distances in different directions and bring the axes into a state of equality.

REMARKS ON THE DILATATION OF SOLIDS.

44. The general law connected with the dilatation of solids is that enunciated at the commencement of this chapter, which states that such bodies expand when heated, but regain their original volume when they are restored to their original temperature.

Neither of these statements is, however, universally true, and a singular exception to the first occurs in the case of Rose's fusible metal. Erman, and afterwards Kopp, have found that there is for this body in the solid state a point of maximum expansion through heat, after which, if the temperature be increased, it contracts instead of expanding. According to Kopp something of the same kind takes place in sulphur.

45. In the second place, the statement regarding the recovery by a solid of its original volume when it resumes its original temperature is by no means absolutely correct. For if a solid be cooled very suddenly, in most cases its particles have not had time to bring themselves into the condition proper to the reduced temperature, and in consequence the substance is in a state of constraint, which continues often for a very long time. This is probably the cause of the change of zero in a mercurial thermometer (Art. 22). For when such an instrument is made, or filled, the bulb is heated and suddenly cooled, and hence its particles have not had time to approach so near to one another as they would have done had the process of cooling been very gradual. The bulb is therefore abnormally dilated, and only recovers from this state after a considerable time, during which a slow contraction takes place and the mercury is pushed up in the tube, or the zero appears to rise.

In like manner when such an instrument is exposed to the temperature of boiling water and suddenly cooled, the bulb remains somewhat dilated, or the zero appears to have fallen, and only recovers its former position after ten days or a fortnight have elapsed.

Magnus, and afterwards Phipson, have noticed a similar behaviour in certain specimens of the idocrase and garnet family. These have their density considerably diminished after they have been heated to a red heat, but in the course of time they recover their former volume.

Other instances of this behaviour might be mentioned, and the knowledge of the fact is of much importance in many of the arts. It is accordingly well known to workers in the metals and in glass that the utensils which they form from the molten material require to be very carefully and slowly cooled in order that the particles may have had time to assume their most stable position, otherwise the structure is fragile and comparatively useless. The process by which this is accomplished is called annealing.

It thus appears that time is an important element in the cooling of bodies; and with this reservation it may not perhaps be erroneous to assert that a solid body heated and very slowly cooled will regain its original volume on regaining its original temperature.

CHAPTER III.

Dilatation of Liquids.

46. Apparent dilatation and real dilatation. The cubical dilatation of a liquid may be either apparent or real. By apparent dilatation is meant the apparent increase of volume of a liquid confined in a vessel which expands but in a less degree than the liquid which it contains. By real or absolute dilatation is meant the true change of volume of the liquid without reference to the containing vessel.

In order to find the real dilatation of liquids one of the following processes is employed.

47. (I) Method by thermometers. In this method the liquid under experiment is made to fill the bulb of a thermometer of which the internal volume or capacity is supposed to be known at the various temperatures of observation. This bulb is attached to a graduated stem, and the internal capacity of each division of this stem is likewise supposed to be known.

When this instrument has been filled with the liquid under examination it is exposed to different temperatures, and for each of these the position which the extremity of the liquid occupies in the stem is accurately noted. It is clear that by this means the volume of the liquid for each temperature becomes known, and hence the amount of its dilatation may be easily deduced.

48. (II) Method by specific gravity bottle. Here a vessel, the internal volume of which is accurately known for all temperatures, is separately filled at each temperature with the liquid under examination, and the whole is then weighed. The weight of the vessel when empty is also ascertained, and thus the *weight* of liquid which it contains at each temperature becomes known. But the *volume* of this liquid is also known; hence its density, or the weight of unity of volume, becomes known, and thus the dilatation may be determined. In this method the kind of bottle generally used is one made of glass, having a glass stopper which fits it accurately. This stopper is ground out of a capillary tube, such as that used for the stem of a thermometer, and hence, when the bottle is filled with liquid and the stopper pushed home, any excess of liquid is forced out through the capillary orifice. The bottle ought to be filled in this manner at a temperature lower than that of observation, so that, when it is subjected to the higher temperature and the liquid expands, the excess may escape by the orifice of the stopper and yet leave the bottle quite full.

49. (III) Method by weighing a solid in the liquid, or the areometric method. In this method a solid whose volume is accurately known for each temperature of observation is weighed immersed in the liquid at these temperatures. The difference between the weight of this solid in vacuo and its weight in the liquid will give us the means of determining the relative density of the latter at the various temperatures. This will be seen from the following example : —

Let us suppose that the volume of the solid at 32° Fahr. is denoted by unity, but at 212° Fahr. by 1.006.   Suppose also that the apparent loss of weight of the solid when weighed in the liquid at 32° is 1800 grains, while at 212° the same is only 1750 grains: 1800 grains is therefore the weight at 32° of a volume of the liquid equal to unity, while 1750 grains is the weight at 212° of a volume of the liquid equal to 1.006.   Hence 1739.56 grains will denote the weight of unity of volume of the liquid at 212°; and hence also 1800 grains, which at 32° occupied a volume equal to unity, will at 212° occupy a volume $= \dfrac{1800}{1739.56} = 1.0347$; or the dilatation between these two temperatures is represented by .0347.

50. Absolute dilatation of mercury.   In all these methods the capacity of the vessel or the volume of the solid employed must be known at the various temperatures of observation, or, in other words, we must know its cubical dilatation.

But the remarks in the preceding chapter (Art. 38) lead us to conclude that in order to determine accurately the cubical dilatation of a solid it is hardly sufficient to determine the linear dilatation of another specimen of the same material and to multiply this by three, but the cubical dilatation ought, if possible, to be obtained by direct experiment.   We have already seen (Art. 39) that in order to accomplish this it is necessary to know the absolute dilatation of some one fluid, such as water or mercury.

The problem before us is thus reduced to the determination of the absolute expansion of some one liquid, after which that of other liquids may be easily derived.   This therefore is a determination of much importance ; and since mercury has been chosen for the purpose, we shall now proceed to shew how the absolute expansion of this liquid may be found.

51. The method about to be described was first employed by MM. Dulong and Petit. It consists in filling a U-shaped tube with mercury, one limb being kept at a low and the other at a high temperature. The portion of the liquid which is heated will of course be specifically lighter than the other, and hence the hot column must be higher than the cold one, since the two balance each other hydrostatically. Thus if D, D' are the two densities, and H, H' the corresponding heights, we shall have $D : D' : : H' : H$, or the heights will vary inversely as the densities. This method is perfect in principle, but it is almost impossible to keep a column of mercury at a constant high temperature and at the same time be able to observe accurately the position of the top of the column. Regnault has however improved the apparatus so as to overcome this obstacle, and the following sketch will give an idea of the arrangement which he employed. $ab, a'b'$ are the two vertical tubes to be filled with mercury, and these are connected together near the top by a horizontal tube aa'. At the bottom they are not connected together, but ab is connected with the horizontal tube bc, and $a'b'$ with $b'c'$. To the extremities of these horizontal tubes two vertical glass tubes $cg, c'g'$ are attached, and these are both connected with a tube hi leading to a large reservoir f supposed to be filled with gas whose temperature is constant; hence the pressure of this gas in the tubes cg, $c'g'$ is also constant. Heat is applied to the tube ab, and by means of an agitator every part of this tube, including the mercury which it contains, may be brought to the same temperature throughout, and the value of this temperature is accurately ascertained. On the other hand, the tube $a'b'$ is exposed to a current of cold water of a known constant temperature.

The tubes ab, $a'b'$ are supposed to be filled with mercury until above the level aa', but we will shew in the sequel that it is not necessary to know the height of the fluid above this level.

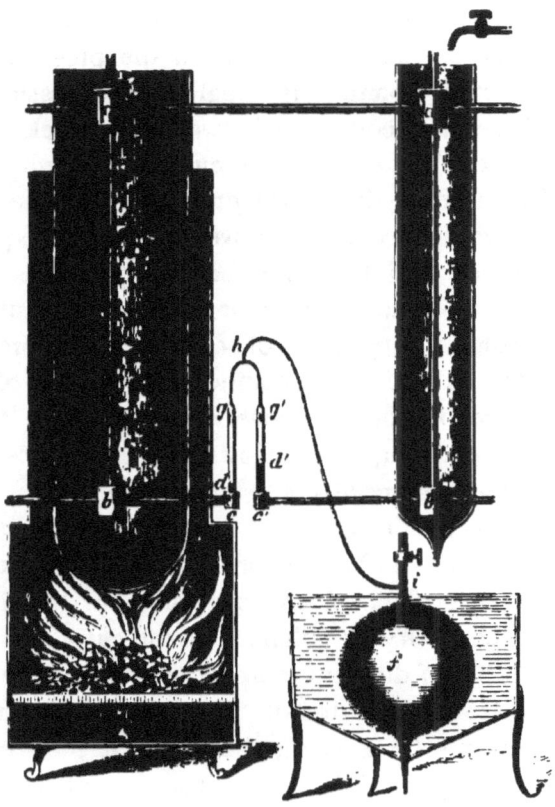

Fig. 11.

Now let p denote the whole pressure due to the left hand column of mercury, and p' the whole pressure due to the right hand column. The pressure at c is evidently p, while that at c' is p'. Hence the pressure at $d = p -$ pressure of column cd, and in like manner pressure at $d' = p' -$ pressure of column $c'd'$. But the pressure at d is equal to that at d', both being equal to the pressure of the gas in the reservoir f: hence we have

p — pressure of $c\,d = p'$ — pressure of $c'\,d'$,

and therefore

$p' - p$ = pressure of column $(c'\,d' - c\,d) \ldots$ (1)

that is to say, the difference between the pressures of the two great vertical columns is equal to the pressure of the column of mercury contained between the levels d' and d. Now since the tubes $a b$, $a'\,b'$ communicate together by $a\,a'$, it is evident from hydrostatical principles that the portions of the two vertical columns above $a\,a'$ are in equilibrium with each other, and therefore that the pressures of these two portions are equal. But p, or the whole pressure of the left hand column, = pressure of column $a b$ + pressure of portion above a; and in like manner p' = pressure of column $d'\,b'$ + pressure of portion above a'. Now since the pressures above $a\,a'$ are equal, it follows that

$p' - p$ = pressure of $a'\,b'$ — pressure of $a b$, $\ldots$ (2)

and equating (1) with (2),

pressure of $(c'\,d' - c\,d)$ = pressure of $a'b'$ — pressure of $a b$.

We have thus obtained an expression for the difference in pressure between two columns of mercury $(a b, a'\,b')$ of equal length but of different temperatures, and since there is no occasion to view the top of the column, we can perfect our arrangements for keeping the whole at the same temperature throughout, while by the insertion of an air thermometer alongside of $a b$ this temperature may be measured with great exactness. By this means therefore the relative density of mercury at various temperatures may be determined, and its dilatation thence easily deduced.

52. Using this method, and also a modification of it, Regnault obtained results which enabled him to construct a table giving the dilatation of mercury for every ten degrees Centigrade from 0°C to 350°. But before exhibiting this table let us explain the distinction between the *mean* and the *true* coefficient of dilatation, as it is quite necessary to know this in the case of liquids which change their rate of expansion from one temperature to another.

In general language, if we take a quantity of liquid whose volume at 0°C is equal to unity, then the true coefficient of dilatation of this liquid at any point is the *rate of increase* in volume of the liquid at that point, as the temperature goes on *regularly increasing*.

On the other hand, the mean coefficient of dilatation for 1°C of the liquid between 0° and any point is the mean rate of increase in volume of the liquid between these two points, that is to say, it is the whole expansion divided by the number of degrees included between the two points.

Thus we see in the following table, 2nd column, that the whole dilatation of mercury between 0° and 100°C is .018153 ; that is to say, a volume of this fluid equal to unity at 0° will at 100° be equal to 1.018153. Now .018153 is the increase for 100°, and hence the mean increase for 1° will be the hundredth part of this or .00018153, which accordingly will be found in the third column opposite 100°, as denoting the mean coefficient of dilatation of mercury between 0° and that point.

On the other hand, the true coefficient of dilatation of mercury at 100° is found by the fourth column to be .00018405 ; that is to say, if the temperature rises through a very small distance such as 1° and becomes 101°C there will be an increase of volume represented by .00018405.

Table of the absolute dilatation of mercury*.

True temperature as determined by an air thermometer (t).	Whole dilatation from 0° to t°C of a volume of mercury equal to unity at 0°.	Mean coefficient of dilatation between 0° and t°C.	True coefficient of dilatation at t°C.
0	. . . .	. . . .	.00017905
10	.001792	.00017925	.00017950
20	.003590	.00017951	.00018001
30	.005393	.00017976	.00018051
40	.007201	.00018002	00018102
50	.009013	.00018027	.00018152
60	.010831	.00018052	.00018203
70	.012655	.00018078	.00018253
80	.014482	.00018102	.00018304
90	.016315	.00018128	.00018354
100	.018153	.00018153	.00018405
110	.019996	.00018178	.00018455
120	.021844	.00018203	.00018505
130	.023697	.00018228	.00018556
140	.025555	.00018254	.00018606
150	.027419	.00018279	.00018657
160	.029287	.00018304	.00018707
170	.031160	.00018329	.00018758
180	.033039	.00018355	.00018808
190	.034922	.00018380	.00018859
200	.036811	.00018405	.00018909
210	.038704	.00018430	.00018959
220	.040603	.00018456	.00019010
230	.042506	.00018481	.00019061
240	.044415	.00018506	.00019111
250	.046329	.00018531	.00019161
260	.048247	.00018557	.00019212
270	.050171	.00018582	.00019262
280	.052100	.00018607	.00019313
290	.054034	.00018632	00019363
300	.055973	.00018658	.00019413
310	.057917	.00018683	.00019464
320	.059866	00018708	.00019515
330	.061820	.00018733	.00019565
340	.063778	.00018758	.00019616
350	.065743	.00018784	.00019666

It will be seen from this table that the true coefficient of dilatation of mercury increases with the temperature.

* The accuracy of Regnault's determination of the absolute expansion of mercury has been confirmed by experiments very recently made by Dr. A. Matthiessen by a quite different method.

53. Dilatation of water. The determination of the dilatation of water is also a point of much importance; but before proceeding to this subject it will be necessary to notice a very striking peculiarity which this fluid exhibits with reference to its change of volume through heat.

If ice-cold water, or water at 32° Fahr., be heated, it does not at first expand as might be supposed, but contracts for about 7° Fahr., and after that begins to expand. It thus exhibits a point of maximum density. This behaviour was illustrated by Hope by means of the following ingenious apparatus.

Fig. 12.

Fig. 12 represents a glass cylinder filled with water at an ordinary temperature, and having holes made for the insertion of two thermometers, one near the top and the other near the bottom. The middle of the cylinder is surrounded by an envelope filled with a freezing mixture. At first, as the temperature falls, the lower thermometer is very much affected, while the upper one falls but slowly. This continues until a temperature about 39° Fahr. is reached, when the lower thermometer ceases to fall, remaining stationary for some time. On the other hand, the upper one begins to fall more rapidly, and continues doing so until it reaches the freezing point. This behaviour is explained by supposing that water attains a point of maximum density at about 39° Fahr., below which it expands instead of contracting. At first therefore the particles of water contiguous to the freezing mixture becoming denser descend, and are replaced by warmer particles from beneath: and this process goes on until the water below *A* is reduced to 39° Fahr.; while, on the other hand, that above the freezing mixture is not so cold. But as the action proceeds, the water contiguous to the freezing mixture having already attained its point of maximum density, becomes specifically lighter instead of heavier, and rising upwards rapidly cools the upper thermometer: all this while the lower thermometer remains stationary at the point which corresponds to the maximum density of water. Many observers have made experiments with the view of determining the temperature corresponding to the maximum density of water, and by the mean of all their determinations this appears to be as nearly as possible equal to 4°C, or 39°.2 Fahr. Various watery solutions also possess their own points of maximum density; but a very extensive series of researches made by M. Pierre tends to shew that for other liquids such points do not exist.

54. Having made these remarks on this peculiarity of water and watery solutions, let us now exhibit a table framèd by M. Despretz, in which the volume and density of water is given at the various temperatures from − 9° to 100°C. It may appear anomalous that this table should descend below the freezing point of water, but we shall afterwards see (Art. 98) that this liquid, if kept perfectly still, may be brought to a lower temperature than its usual freezing point without assuming a solid state.

These experiments were made according to the method first described in this chapter, or the method by thermometers (Art. 47).

Table of the density and volume of Water, from −9°C to 100°C, according to M. Despretz (the density and volume at 4° taken as unity).

Tempe- rature.	Volume.	Density.	Tempe- rature.	Volume.	Density.
−9°	1.001 631 1	0.998 371	15°	1.000 875 1	0.999 125
−8	1.001 373 4	0.998 628	16	1.001 021 5	0.998 979
−7	1.001 135 4	0.998 865	17	1.001 206 7	0.998 794
−6	1.000 918 4	0.999 082	18	1.001 39	0.998 612
−5	1.000 698 7	0.999 302	19	1.001 58	0.998 422
−4	1.000 561 9	0.999 437	20	1.001 79	0.998 213
−3	1.000 422 2	0.999 577	21	1.002 00	0.998 004
−2	1.000 307 7	0.999 692	22	1.002 22	0.997 784
−1	1.000 213 8	0.999 786	23	1.002 44	0.997 566
0	1.000 126 9	0.999 873	24	1.002 71	0.997 297
1	1.000 073 0	0.999 927	25	1.002 93	0.997 078
2	1.000 033 1	0.999 966	26	1.003 21	0.996 800
3	1.000 008 3	0.999 999	27	1.003 45	0.996 562
4	1.000 000 0	1.000 000	28	1.003 74	0.996 274
5	1.000 008 2	0.999 999	29	1.004 03	0.995 986
6	1.000 030 9	0.999 969	30	1.004 33	0.995 688
7	1.000 070 8	0.999 929	40	1.007 73	0.992 329
8	1.000 121 6	0.999 878	50	1.012 05	0.988 093
9	1.000 187 9	0.999 812	60	1.016 98	0.983 303
10	1.000 268 4	0.999 731	70	1.022 55	0.977 947
11	1.000 359 8	0.999 640	80	1.028 85	0.971 959
12	1.000 472 4	0.999 527	90	1.035 66	0.965 567
13	1.000 586 2	0.999 414	100	1.043 15	0.958 634
14	1.000 714 6	0.999 285			

55. Dilatation of other liquids. The dilatations of a great many liquids have been carefully determined by M. I. Pierre, and he has embodied his results in expressions of the following kind—

$$\delta_t = 1 + at + bt^2 + ct^3;$$

where δ_t represents the dilatation of unit volumes from 0° to *t*°C, and where *a*, *b*, *c* are constants depending on the nature of the substance. This expression, he finds, generally represents the expansion of a liquid with considerable accuracy. We derive from his results the following table, in which the approximate temperature of the boiling point of each liquid is compared with its coefficient of dilatation at 0°C.

Name of liquid.	Approximate temp. of boiling point in Centigrade degrees.	Coefficient of dilatation for 1°C at the temperature o°C.
Chloride of ethyle	11.0	.001575
Oxide of ethyle (sulphuric ether) .	35.5	.001513
Bromide of ethyle	40.7	.001338
Iodide of methyle	43.8	.001200
Sulphuret of carbon . . .	47.9	.001140
Formiate of oxide of ethyle . .	52.9	.001325
Terchloride of silicon	59.0	.001294
Acetate of oxide of methyle . .	59.5	.001296
Bromine	63.0	.001038
Methylic alcohol	66.3	.001186
Iodide of ethyle	70.0	.001142
Acetate of oxide of ethyle . . .	74.1	.001258
Alcohol	78.3	.001049
Terchloride of phosphorus . . .	78.3	.001129
Butyrate of oxide of methyle . . .	102.1	.001240
Bichloride of tin	115.4	.001132
Amylic alcohol	131.8	.000890
Terchloride of arsenic	133.8	.000979
Bichloride of titanium	136.0	.000943
Terbromide of silicon	153.4	.000953
Terbromide of phosphorus . .	175.3	.000847
Mercury (*Regnault*)	350.0	.000179

56. It will be gathered from this table that in general liquids with high boiling points expand less at the temperature o°C than volatile liquids which boil at a low temperature, and it may be inferred that there is some connexion between the coefficient of expansion of a liquid and its volatility. This leads us to consider the dilatation of very volatile liquids.

57. Dilatation of volatile liquids. When we come to liquids, such as carbonic acid, which can only exist in this state at ordinary temperatures under very great pressure, we have reason to think that their coefficient of dilatation is extremely great. Thilorier in 1835 had made the curious remark that liquid carbonic acid presents the anomaly of a liquid more dilateable than any gas, and he concluded from his observations that its dilatation was four times greater than that of air. M. Drion has since made very careful experiments upon several volatile liquids, and among them liquid sulphurous acid and chloride of ethyle. From these he has constructed the following table.

True coefficient of expansion for 1°C.

Tempe- rature.	Chloride of ethyle.	Sulphurous acid.	Tempe- rature.	Chloride of ethyle.	Sulphurous acid.
0	.001482	.001734	70	.002390	.003176
10	.001588	.001878	80	.002625	.003608
20	.001699	.002029	90	.002910	.004147
30	.001811	.002192	100	.003250	.004859
40	.001919	.002371	110	.003690	.005919
50	.002045	.002585	120	.004306	.007565
60	.002202	.002846	130	.005031	.009571

We may perhaps conclude that the coefficient of expansion of a liquid is very great at those temperatures at which the substance can only exist in the liquid state under very great pressure.

58. **Contraction of liquids from their boiling points.** Views perhaps analagous to those we have just mentioned induced Gay Lussac to compare the contraction of different liquids reckoned from their respective boiling points, and he obtained the following result for alcohol and sulphuret of carbon.

Table of the contraction of alcohol and sulphuret of carbon for successive intervals of 5°C, reckoned from their boiling points, the volumes at these points being equal to 1000.

Tempe- rature interval.	Alcohol.	Sulphuret of carbon.	Tempe- rature interval.	Alcohol.	Sulphuret of carbon.
5	5.55	6.14	35	40.28	40.48
10	11.43	12.01	40	45.68	45.77
15	17.51	17.98	45	50.85	51.08
20	24.34	23.80	50	56.02	56.28
25	29.15	29.65	55	61.01	61.14
30	34.74	35.06	60	65.96	66.21

It thus appears that the contractions of alcohol and sulphuret of carbon, reckoned in this way, are as nearly as possible the same. Pierre and Kopp have both verified this law of Gay Lussac, and the former has shewn—

1. That amylic, ethylic, and methylic alcohol follow nearly the same law of contraction, or, in other words, equal volumes of these liquids at their respective boiling points will preserve their equality at all temperatures equidistant from these points.

2. That the same law holds true for the bromides and iodides of ethyle and methyle;

3. And in one or two other cases: but that in general two liquids formed by the combination of a common principle with two different isomorphous elements follow different laws of contraction starting from their respective boiling points.

59. In conclusion, if we compare this chapter with the preceding we shall be led to the following result :—

1. *Solids have a much smaller coefficient of expansion than liquids.*

2. *The coefficient of expansion of liquids increases with the temperature.*

3. *The coefficient of expansion of a liquid which only preserves its state under intense pressure is probably very great.*

CHAPTER IV.

Dilatation of Gases.

60. Before commencing the subject of this chapter it may be well to draw attention to the following experiment and law.

Let there be a tube shaped as in the accompanying figures, of a uniform bore throughout, and let it contain at the atmospheric pressure (equal, let us say, to 30 inches of mercury) a volume of air *AB*. If this air be shut out from the atmosphere by mercury, then the surfaces *B* and *D* of the mercury in the two limbs of the tube will be at the same

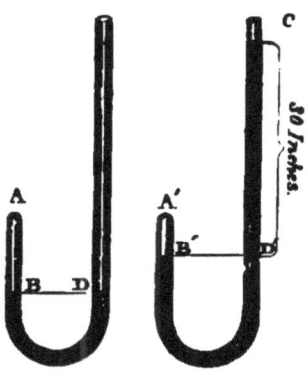

Fig. 13.   Fig. 14.

level, since the pressure upon the surface at *B* is supposed equal to that of the atmosphere pressing at *D*. Now if additional mercury be poured into the tube until there is a difference of 30 inches between the levels *B'* and *C'*, then it is evident that the air *A'B'* exists under the pressure of two atmospheres; for we have not only the column of mercury *C'D'* = 30 inches tending to press this air into less volume, but we have in addition the pressure of the atmosphere upon the surface *C'*, which is also equal to 30 inches of mercury. Hence we have the air in Fig. 14 existing at a pressure double of that in Fig. 13. Now it is a well-known fact that the space occupied by the air in Fig. 14 will be one-half of that occupied by it in Fig. 13; and generally, "*provided the temperature remains the same, the* volume *which a gas occupies is* inversely proportional *to the pressure under which it exists ; or, in other words, its* density *is* proportional *to its pressure."*   This is known as the law of Boyle or Marriotte.

61. But if the temperature be increased, the air will on this account alone tend to expand, and one of two things will happen.   1. If we wish to keep the air always occupying the same space we must employ additional pressure; 2. If we wish to keep it exerting the same pressure we must allow it to occupy additional space.   Our subject thus naturally divides itself into two parts.   In one of these we determine the relation between the pressure and temperature of a gas whose volume is constant, and in the other we determine the relation between the volume and temperature of a gas whose pressure is constant.

If we imagine Boyle's law to hold rigidly for gases, then the two cases are connected with each other in a very simple manner.   For if a gas whose volume is V and pressure P at o°C has at $t°$ and under the same pressure the volumn V', then it is clear that were it constrained to occupy its old volume its pressure would be $P \times \dfrac{V'}{V}$.

Either of the methods would in this case present us with precisely the same proportional change for increase of temperature, this being in the one case *change of volume*, and in the other *change of elasticity ;* but it has been deemed right to determine the change by both methods, and we shall see in the sequel that the two values thus found are not precisely the same.

62. The fact of the dilatation of gas may be easily proved by filling a bladder nearly full of air, tying its orifice, and heating it; it will then soon appear to be quite full, the contained air having expanded by heat under the constant pressure of the atmosphere.

Dalton in this country and Gay Lussac in France were the first who investigated the law` of expansion of gases with any considerable success, and they were both led to the conclusion that all gases expand equally for equal increments of temperature. With regard, however, to the precise law which connects together volume and temperature, there was a difference in the result obtained by these two philosophers. According to Gay Lussac, the augmentation of volume which a gas receives when the temperature increases 1° is a certain fixed proportion of *its initial volume at o°C;* while according to Dalton, a gas at any temperature increases in volume for a rise of 1° by a constant fraction of *its volume at that temperature.*

Gay Lussac's law may be expressed as follows.

Let V_o, V_t denote the volumes at o°C and t° of a certain quantity of gas existing at the pressure P, then these two volumes are connected with one another by means of the following formula—

$$V_t = V_o \{ 1 + a t \} ;$$

where a is the coefficient of expansion, nearly the same for all gases, which it is the object of experiment to determine. From this equation we derive at once the relation between the temperature and the density (density being represented by the mass contained in unit of volume) of air whose pressure remains constant. For let D denote the mass of air that occupies unit of volume at o°C; this mass will at t° occupy a volume equal to $1 + a t$, and hence the mass of unit volume or the density at this temperature will be $\dfrac{D}{1 + a t}$.

The dilatation of gases has since been investigated by Rudberg, Dulong and Petit, Magnus, and Regnault, and the result of their labours leaves little doubt that Gay Lussac's method of expressing the law is much nearer the truth than Dalton's. It has also been ascertained that the coefficient of dilatation is not precisely, although very nearly, the same. for all gases. The experiments of Regnault were conducted with very great care, and we shall now shortly describe, in the first place, his method of ascertaining the increase of elasticity of a constant volume of air between 0°C and 100°, and, in the second place, his method of ascertaining the increment of volume between the same limits of air of which the elasticity remains constant.

68. Relation between elasticity and temperature of air whose volume remains the same. The following description of an apparatus, nearly the same as Regnault's, and used by the author of this work for the same purpose, will enable the reader to understand the method pursued in this investigation.

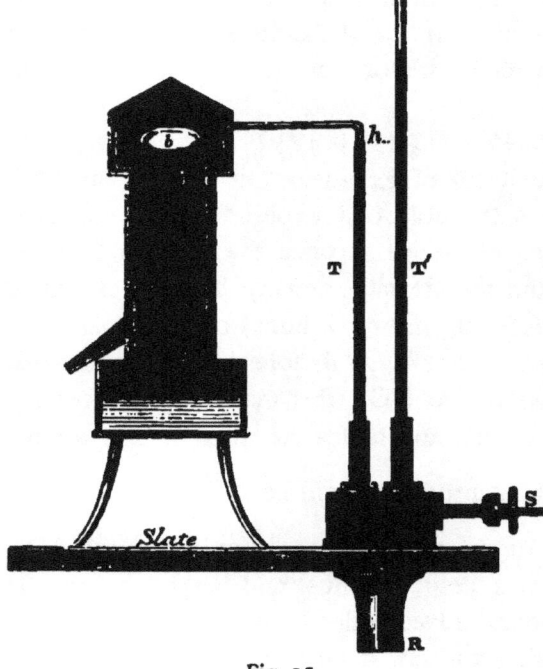

Fig. 15.

A bulb *b* had its volume at 32° and 212° Fahr. accurately determined by being gauged by mercury at these temperatures, as described in Art. 39; and the contained air was also thoroughly dried by being passed through a desiccating apparatus. The capillary termination of the bulb was then attached to a tube T, connected with another tube T'', which was open to the atmosphere.

The lower terminations of these tubes were fitted into a reservoir R containing mercury, and this reservoir might be enlarged or contracted at pleasure by means of a screw S which moved a piston out or in.

The whole apparatus was made to rest firmly on a slab of slate. The experiment consisted of two parts: the bulb b was first of all surrounded by melting ice, and by means of the screw S the mercury was forced to the height h in the tube T, and the difference of level between the surface of mercury in the two tubes was read by means of a catheto-meter, or instrument for measuring vertical heights. Adding this to the height of the barometer, which was observed at the same moment, the whole pressure under which the air in the bulb existed at the temperature of melting ice was thus ascertained. Let us call this P. The bulb b was next attached to a boiling-water apparatus, as in the figure, and by means of the screw S the mercury was forced up to the *same height h* in the tube T. Since the elasticity of air increases with the temperature, it is evident that the pressure will now be greater, and that in consequence the mercury will be pushed high up in the tube T''. Taking the difference of level as before, noting the barometer, and adding the two heights together, we get the whole pressure under which the air now exists at the temperature of boiling water. Let this pressure be called P'. It is now very easy to construct the formula which must be applied.

Let the temperature of the atmosphere around, including the mercury in the two tubes, be $t°$ C, and let $T°$ denote the temperature of boiling water at the present atmospheric pressure.

Further, let V denote the internal volume at $0°$C of the bulb b and of that portion of the capillary tube which is subjected to the heating and cooling agents, and let v denote the internal volume at o°C of that portion of the tube T above the mercury which is not subject to the influence of these agents, but which contains air having the temperature t.

Also let κ denote the coefficient of expansion for 1°C of the glass, and let a denote the corresponding coefficient of increase of elastic force of dry air whose volume remains constant—this being what we wish to determine; and, finally, let us denote by D the mass of air which occupies unit volume under unit of pressure at the temperature o°C.

Then DPV (according to Boyle's law) will denote the mass of that portion of the enclosed air existing in the bulb (volume $= V$) at the temperature o°C and under the pressure P when the bulb is surrounded by melting ice; also (Art. 62) $\dfrac{DPv(1+\kappa t)}{1+at}$ will denote the mass of that portion of the enclosed air existing at the same time in the tube (volume $= v(1+\kappa t)$) at the temperature of the atmosphere ($= t$) and pressure P. Hence the whole mass of enclosed air will be denoted by

$$DP\left\{ V + \frac{v(1+\kappa t)}{1+at} \right\}. \tag{1}$$

Now let the bulb be subjected to the temperature of boiling water ($= T$). The volume of the bulb then becomes $V(1+\kappa T)$, and hence the mass of air existing in the bulb at this temperature and under the pressure P' will be $\dfrac{DP'V(1+\kappa T)}{1+aT}$, while that existing in the tube (vol $= v(1+\kappa t)$) at the temperature of the atmosphere ($= t$) and pressure P' will be $\dfrac{DP'v(1+\kappa t)}{1+at}$.

Hence the whole mass of enclosed air will be denoted by

$$DP'\left\{ \frac{V(1+\kappa T)}{1+aT} + \frac{v(1+\kappa t)}{1+at} \right\}. \tag{2}$$

But since the *mass* of air remains unchanged, being enclosed, we have (1) = (2); and hence, since D is a common factor,

$$P\left\{ V + \frac{v(1 + \kappa t)}{1 + a t} \right\} = P'\left\{ \frac{V(1 + \kappa T)}{1 + a T} + \frac{v(1 + \kappa t)}{1 + a t} \right\};$$

where every thing is known but a, which may thus be easily determined. By a similar means Regnault found that if unity denote the elasticity of a given volume of dry air at 0°C, its elasticity at 100°C if confined to the same volume will be 1.3665. The author of this work has obtained a somewhat larger increase, but we may probably assume the above number to represent the increase of elasticity of air of constant volume with great exactness.

64. Dilatation of air between 0°C and 100°C under constant pressure. A slight alteration in the apparatus of Fig. 15 enabled Regnault to make this experiment. Here the air will of course expand and occupy part of the tube T, and it will therefore be necessary to surround the two tubes T, T' with water of a constant temperature, since nearly a fourth part of the enclosed air will exist in T, and its temperature must therefore be accurately known. By means of the screw S the mercury in the two tubes is brought as nearly as possible to the same level, both when the bulb is in melting ice and when it is in the boiling apparatus, so that in both these cases the pressure will be as nearly as possible equal to that of the atmosphere. Any small difference of level between the two tubes is read by means of a cathetometer, and the barometer is noted so that the whole pressure under which the air exists in the two cases is accurately known; but these pressures will in this experiment be very nearly the same in both. By calibrating the tube the additional volume occupied by the air at the high temperature may be determined, and thus the coefficient of expansion becomes known.

From these and other experiments Regnault has concluded

that while the dilatation of air between 0°C and 100°C is equal to .3665 of its volume at 0° when this dilatation is calculated by means of the law of Boyle from the change of *elastic force* of air of which the *volume* is constant; yet when the dilatation is deduced directly from the change of *volume* while the *elasticity* remains constant this coefficient is somewhat increased and becomes .3670.

Dividing these results by 180 we find the coefficient which denotes increase of *elasticity* for 1° Fahr. of air whose *volume* is constant = .002036.

Also, the coefficient which denotes increase of *volume* for 1° Fahr. of air whose *elasticity* is constant = .002039.

65. Dilatation of other gases at ordinary pressures. Regnault has investigated this subject minutely, and has found that different gases have notably different coefficients, and that the coefficient of the same gas differs according as it has been determined by the method of constant pressure or by that of constant volume. He gives the following results :—

Dilatation between 0°C *and* 100°C.

	Under constant pressure.	Under constant volume.
Hydrogen	0.3661	0.3667
Atmospheric air	0.3670	0.3665
Nitrogen	....	0.3668
Carbonic oxide	0.3669	0.3667
Carbonic acid	0.3710	0.3688
Protoxide of nitrogen	0.3719	0.3676
Sulphurous acid	0.3903	0.3845
Cyanogen	0.3877	0.3829

It will be noticed in this list that sulphurous acid and cyanogen, which have the greatest coefficients, are gases which may easily be liquefied; while, on the other hand, the three permanent gases which have never been liquefied have small coefficients.

66. Dilatation of gases existing under different pressures. The following law has been deduced by Regnault : "*Air and all gases except hydrogen have coefficients of dilatation which increase to some extent with their density.*"

Regnault has likewise enunciated the following very important law : "*The coefficients of dilatation of the different gases approach more nearly to equality as their pressures become feeble, in such a manner that the law which is expressed by saying that all gases have the same coefficient of dilatation ought strictly to be considered as a law which applies only to gas in a state of extreme tenuity, but which is departed from as gases become compressed, or, in other words, as their molecules approach each other.*"

A gas whose molecules are so far apart as not to exert any sensible influence upon each other may be called a *perfect gas.*

67. Air Thermometer. The present is a suitable opportunity to discuss the air thermometer, to which in our first chapter we promised to return.

If we have a series of thermometers with different liquids, such as mercury, alcohol, water, &c., and all enclosed in envelopes of the same description, and if each instrument has been accurately pointed off and graduated in such a manner that $1°C$ denotes the one hundredth part of the capacity of the capillary tube between $0°$ and $100°$, nevertheless these instruments, if plunged into the same liquid, will not all register precisely the same temperature.

But if we restrict our choice to thermometers with the same liquid, as, for instance, to mercurial thermometers made of the same kind of glass, we obtain instruments strictly comparable one with another, and which if plunged into the same liquid will all indicate the same temperature.

But though such instruments are comparable with each

other, we are not yet sure if their common reading accurately represents the true temperature; for there is no obvious reason why we should prefer a mercurial to an alcohol or water thermometer, which we have seen would both give slightly different indications.   The mercurial thermometer stands therefore in the following position:—different instruments of this kind may be made to give identical indications, but yet we cannot rely upon these for accurately measuring temperature; nevertheless we cannot suppose that they are very far wrong.

Let us now employ a gas or air thermometer, and confine in envelopes of the same material different gases of sufficient tenuity and not liable to be easily condensed, and let us suppose that we have the means of ascertaining accurately the pressure which they exert upon their envelopes; and let us also in the meantime disregard the expansion of these envelopes.   Now if all these gases have a common pressure at 0°C they will all have a common pressure at 100°C, or at any other temperature.   If we make use of this pressure to determine the temperature, we have thus obtained different instruments whose indications are comparable with each other, *even although the gases with which they are filled are different.*   Gases, if of sufficient tenuity, are therefore in this respect superior to liquids; and it only now remains for us to determine the precise law which connects together the temperature and pressure of a gas in order to make a perfect thermometer.   We have various reasons for imagining the law announced by Gay Lussac to be correct, at least in the case of perfect gases.   This law, taken in connexion with that of Boyle, asserts that if the pressure of a constant volume of gas be unity at 0°C and 1.3665 at 100°C, then the pressure at 50°C will be the mean between these two numbers, or 1.18325.   Strictly speaking, it is impossible to prove this law experimentally with precision, for to do so implies the previous possession of an accurate instrument for measuring temperature. Now we have seen that the mercurial thermometer is not reliable, while for the purpose of this proof it must be presumed that the air thermometer does not yet exist, since in order to use it we must have a knowledge of this very law which we wish to prove. The case stands thus; if we employ mercurial thermometers (which we cannot imagine to be far wrong), Gay Lussac's law is found to give a near approximation to the experimental result. There is, however, a small difference, and the cause of this may be either that mercurial thermometers are not quite right, or that Gay Lussac's law itself is only an approximate expression of the truth. Now, in the first place, we know very well that mercurial thermometers are not absolutely correct, and in the next place, with regard to Gay Lussac's law, its extreme simplicity is in its favour, and we shall afterwards see that there are perhaps theoretical reasons for supposing it to be correct, at least for perfect gases.

In fine, we apprehend that a perfect gas obeys Gay Lussac's law, and may be made to furnish us with a perfect thermometer, and if we cannot procure a gas that is quite perfect, yet atmospheric air deprived of moisture and carbonic acid is a substance sufficiently good for all practical purposes.

Although the air thermometer is in principle peculiarly fitted for the determination of very high temperatures, yet there are considerable mechanical difficulties in the employment of the instrument in such cases. Regnault has lately invented two modifications of this instrument in order to render it suitable to measure the temperature of furnaces (see Annales de Chimie for September 1861). In one of these vapour of mercury is the gas employed, and the instrument is constructed as follows. There is a kind of flask, either cylindrical or spherical, which may be either of cast or wrought iron, of platinum or of porcelain: the mouth is closed by a plate containing a small aperture. From 15 to 20 grammes of mercury are added to this flask, which is then placed in that part of the furnace the temperature of which we desire to know. The mercury soon boils, its vapour expels the air by the orifice, and the excess of mercurial vapour goes off by the same means. When the apparatus has acquired the temperature of the furnace the flask is withdrawn and made to cool rapidly, and the mercury which remains in the flask is weighed. It may be weighed directly, or, if it contains impurity, it is dissolved in acid and estimated as a precipitate. This weight is that of the vapour of mercury which filled the flask at the temperature of the furnace, and the volume of the flask as well as the density of mercurial vapour being known this temperature may thus be determined.

In conclusion, we append the results of a comparison made by M. Regnault between an air thermometer and a mercurial thermometer with an envelope of crown glass.

Temperature given by air thermometer.			Temperature given by mercurial thermometer with envelope of crown glass.
100°C.	...	...	100°
120	...	...	119.95
140	...	...	139.85
160	...	...	159.74
180	...	...	179.63
200	...	...	199.70
220	...	...	219.80
240	...	...	239.90
260	...	...	260.20
280	...	...	280.52
300	...	...	301.08
320	...	...	321.80
340	...	...	343.00
350	...	...	354.00

CHAPTER V.

Applications of the Laws of Dilatation.

68. Since all the bodies around us are subject to continual change of volume owing to their varying temperature, it is necessary to take account of this in very many operations and investigations whether of a scientific or strictly practical nature. Let us, in the first place, proceed to describe the influence which change of temperature exerts on our standards of length, weight, density and time.

STANDARDS OF LENGTH.

69. Supposing that a yard is taken to denote a certain absolute distance, and that the length of a bar is precisely one yard at the temperature 62° Fahr., it is clear that, owing to the expansion of the material of the bar, its length will be greater than a yard for temperatures higher than 62°, but less than a yard for temperatures below 62°.

If now we employ this bar as a standard by means of which to measure the absolute distance between any two points in terms of the yard as a unit of length, and if it be inconvenient or impossible to make this comparison at 62° Fahr., it will be necessary to know the precise temperature of our standard bar in order that we may know its real length.

The formation of a standard of length is an object of national importance, and we shall now shortly describe the respective standards authorised by the Governments of England and France.

70. English standard. The English standard of length was formerly the parliamentary standard yard executed by

Bird in the year 1760. A yard was defined to be the straight line or distance between the centres of the two points in the gold studs in the brass rod formerly in the House of Commons, whereon the words "Standard yard 1760" were engraved, the temperature of the standard being 62° Fahr.

On October 16, 1834, a fire occurred in the Houses of Parliament, in which the standards were destroyed. The bar of 1760 was recovered, but one of its gold pins having a point was melted out, and the bar was otherwise injured.

A committee was therefore formed to reproduce this standard yard in the best manner possible, and this was admirably accomplished chiefly through the labours of the late Mr. Sheepshanks. A new standard and four authorised copies were made and lodged at the office of the Exchequer, the Royal Mint, the Royal Society of London, the Royal Observatory, Greenwich, and the new palace at Westminster; and it was enacted (July 30, 1855), "that the straight line or distance between the centres of the two gold plugs in the bronze bar deposited in the office of the Exchequer shall be the genuine standard yard at 62° Fahr., and if lost it shall be replaced by means of its copies." Many other copies of this standard have since been made, the errors of which have been very accurately ascertained. When the length of a substance has to be measured with precision it is necessary to compare it either with the standard or one of its copies of which the error is known. It is here that a knowledge of the laws of dilatation becomes of importance, for to make the comparison accurately we must know

  1. The precise temperature at which the comparison is made.
  2. The coefficient of expansion of the standard used.

Suppose, for instance, that our standard is of brass, that we are comparing a platinum scale with it at the temperature of 72° Fahr., and that we find the length of our scale to be

35.998 inches as read by the standard at this temperature; then in order to find the true length of our platinum scale at this temperature we must know the coefficient of expansion of the brass standard. Suppose this to be .00001 for 1° Fahr., then if the standard is right at 62°, its length, or the true value of 36 apparent inches, will be = 36 inches × 1.0001 at 72°, = 36.0036 inches; and hence the true length of our platinum scale (which is .002 inch less than 36 apparent inches) will be as nearly as possible 36.0016 inches at the temperature 72° Fahr.

If we now wish to ascertain its length at 62° we find the co-efficient of dilatation for platinum for 10° Fahr. to be .000048. Hence its length at 62° will be as nearly as possible $\dfrac{36.0016}{1.000048}$ = 35.9999 inches. Thus we see that the two scales agree almost exactly at 62°, but they differ sensibly at 72°: this is owing to the one scale being made of brass and the other of platinum.

71. French standard. The French standard of length is the mètre which represents with considerable accuracy the 10,000,000th part of a quadrantal arc of a meridian on the earth's surface. The French standard platinum mètre made by Borda represents a mètre at 0°C, and all the copies of this standard are made so as to denote mètres and parts of a mètre at this temperature. One mètre is equal to 39.37079 English inches; that is to say, the length of the French standard platinum mètre at 32° Fahr. bears to the length of the English standard bronze yard at 62° Fahr. the proportion of 39.37079 : 36; but this will not be the proportion between these standards if compared together at any common temperature. The French standard is sub-divided and multiplied according to the decimal scale, and the relation between our measures and those of France will be seen from the following tables.

	In English inches.	In English feet = 12 inches.
Millimètre	0.03937	0.003281
Centimètre	0.39371	0.032809
Décimètre	3.93708	0.328090
Mètre	39.37079	3.280899
Décamètre	393.70790	32.808992
Hectomètre	3937.07900	328.089920
Kilomètre	39370.79000	3280.899200

In like manner we have

Centiare, or square mètre	=	10.764299 English square feet;
Are, or 100 square mètres	=	1076.429934 „ „
Hectare, or 10,000 square mètres	=	107642.993418 „ „

Also

Millilitre, or cubic centimètre	=	0.06103 cubic inches;
Centilitre, or 10 cubic centimètres	=	0.61027 „ „
Decilitre, or 100 cubic centimètres	=	6.10271 „ „
Litre, or cubic décimètre	=	61.02705 „ „
Decalitre, or centistère	=	610.27052 „ „
Hectolitre, or decistère	=	6102.70515 „ „
Kilolitre, or Stère, or cubic mètre	=	61027.05152 „ „

STANDARDS OF WEIGHT.

72. These are at the same time standards of mass, since the weight of a body at the same point of the earth's surface is proportional to its mass.

If all weighings could be made in vacuo, temperature would exercise no influence upon our measures of weight. But since weighings must be made in air, and since a substance weighed in air is apparently lighter than in vacuo by the weight of air which it displaces, and since the weight of a certain bulk of air of given pressure depends upon its temperature, it is necessary to know this temperature in very accurate determinations: the effect is however very small. We shall now shortly describe the standards of weight or mass authorised by the Governments of England and France.

73. English standard. Formerly in this country the standard of weight was the double pound Troy made by

Mr. Bird, and it was resolved that the pound Troy should contain 5760 grains, and that 7000 such grains should make one pound avoirdupois. This standard was destroyed at the burning of the Houses of Parliament, but was restored in a very accurate manner by Professor W. H. Miller of Cambridge, with this difference, that whereas the old standard denoted one pound Troy, the new one represents one pound avoirdupois. Accordingly a standard and four authorised copies, all made of platinum, were constructed by this gentleman and deposited in the same places with the standard yard and its copies; and it was enacted, "that the platinum weight deposited in the Exchequer shall be denominated the imperial standard pound avoirdupois, and that the $\frac{1}{7000}$th of 'it shall be a grain, while 5760 such grains shall denote one pound Troy."

74. French standard. In France the weight of a décimètre cubed of distilled water at the temperature of its greatest density (supposed equal to 4°C) is adopted as the standard of weight, and is called the Kilogramme, while the gramme is a centimètre cubed of distilled water at the same temperature*. The following table exhibits the relation between French and English measures of weight:—

	In English grains.
Milligramme . . .	0.01543
Centigramme . . .	0.15432
Décigramme . . .	1.54323
Gramme	15.43235
Décagramme . . .	154.32349
Hectogramme . . .	1543.23488
Kilogramme . . .	15432.34880.

* It will thus be noticed that considerations of temperature enter into the fundamental conception of the French standard of weight, and in so far it is different from the English pound, which is merely an arbitrary standard. We shall afterwards take occasion to make some remarks on the comparative merits of the French and English systems.

STANDARDS OF DENSITY.

75. In this country it was formerly the practice to determine the comparative density or specific gravity of solids and liquids by comparing them at 60° Fahr. with distilled water, also at 60°, reckoned as unity *, but usage is now divided, and the French practice is very much adopted. For gas also the practice is usually stated to be a comparison at 60° with dry air under a barometric pressure of 30 inches of mercury at 60°, but here also the practice is changing.

In France the comparative density or specific gravity of solid and liquid bodies is determined with reference to that of water at its point of maximum density (supposed to be 4°C), and the comparison is always made at 0°C. Gases, again, are compared at 0°C with dry air at 0°C under the barometric pressure of 760 millimètres of mercury reduced to 0°C. The following examples will exhibit the effect of temperature upon determinations of density.

Example I.—It has been determined by Regnault that the weight of a litre of dry air at 0°C, and under the reduced pressure of 760 millimètres of mercury at Paris, is 1.29318 gramme; find what is the weight at London of 100 cubic inches of dry air at 60° Fahr. and 30 inches barometric pressure of mercury reduced to 60° Fahr. Now a litre is equal to 61.02705 cubic inches (Art. 71), also we have already seen (Art. 21) that 760 millimètres of pressure in Paris are equal to 29.914 inches in London at 32° Fahr., while (by the table of Art. 52) we find that 29.914 inches of mercury at 32° are equivalent in weight to 29.914 × 1.00278 = 29.997 inches of mercury at 60° Fahr. or 15°.5C. Also 1.29318 gramme is equal to 19.9568 grains (Art. 74), and finally the comparative

---

* A cubic inch of distilled water in vacuo at 60° Fahr. opposed to weights, also in vacuo, weighs 252.769 grains.

densities of gas existing under the same pressure at 32° and at 60° will be (Art. 64) in the proportion of

$$(1 + 28 \times .00204) : 1 \text{ or of } 1.057 : 1.$$

Hence the required weight will be—

$$19.9568 \times \frac{100}{61.02705} \times \frac{30}{29.997} \times \frac{1}{1.057} = 30.940 \text{ grains;}$$

where the first factor is on account of the difference between the capacities of the two measures, the second on account of the difference of pressure, and the third on account of the difference of temperature.

Example II.—It has been determined at Kew Observatory that the weight in vacuo at 62° Fahr. of a given volume of purified mercury is to that of the same volume of water in the proportion of 13590.86 to 1001.62 grains ; what is the specific gravity of mercury at o°C according to the French method of computation ? We find by the table of the absolute dilatation of mercury (Art. 52) that a unit of volume of this liquid at o°C will become 1.00298 at 62° Fahr., or 16°.6C. Hence the weight of the above volume of mercury would at o°C be 13590.86 × 1.00298 = 13631.361 grains.

In like manner we find by the table of dilatation of water (Art. 54) that a volume of this fluid equal to unity at 4°C will at 16°.6C be 1.0011437.

Hence the weight of the above volume of water would at 4°C be—

$$1001.62 \times 1.0011437 = 1002.766 \text{ grains;}$$

and hence the specific gravity of mercury according to the French method will be—

$$\frac{13631.361}{1002.766} = 13.594:$$

a determination by Regnault gives 13.596.

REMARKS ON THE ENGLISH AND FRENCH SYSTEMS OF STANDARDS.

76. The English standards of length and weight are arbitrary; that is to say, a yard and a pound do not bear any recognized relation to any natural constant.

On the other hand, the French chose their standard of length, or mètre, as that distance which was supposed to represent the ten millionth part of a quadrantal arc of a meridian of the earth's surface, while their standard of weight, or kilogramme, professed to be the weight of a décimètre cubed of distilled water at the temperature 4°C. On these principles Borda constructed the platinum mètre and platinum kilogramme, which have become the authorized standards of France.

But whatever conception presided at the construction of these standards, it is evident *that when once made and authorized they may to all intents be regarded as arbitrary standards.* For if future and accurate investigations should determine that one ten millionth of the earth's quadrantal arc is not exactly Borda's mètre, and that a décimètre cubed of distilled water at 4°C is not exactly Borda's kilogramme, the French nation would yet adhere to Borda's platinum métre and kilogramme as their standards; and were these standards destroyed, it is probable they could best be replaced by means of copies.

Nevertheless it is of importance to connect the authorized standards of a nation, always bearing in mind that they are in practice arbitrary, with certain natural constants supposed to be invariable: thus, for instance, to connect the standard of length with the length of a pendulum, vibrating seconds, or with an arc of a meridian, and also to connect the standard of weight with that of length, after the manner of the French.

For it may be inferred from what we have said in Art. 45, that a standard of length, however carefully constructed and well annealed, may possibly in the course of time alter its length to a small but yet an appreciable extent.

But we cannot perhaps so readily suppose that any such change can take place in the length of the second's pendulum or in that of an arc of the meridian, and hence any change in the length of the standard, if such occurred, might be detected by occasional comparisons with these natural constants.

In like manner a standard weight might ultimately become altered by slight abrasion of particles through frequent use, and it would therefore be of importance to connect it from time to time with the standard of length.

Another safeguard might be the construction of a standard made of granite or marble, or of some substance which has probably become cooled by a very slow natural process, and which may therefore be supposed to be thoroughly annealed.

We remark, in conclusion, that the French system has some obvious advantages. In the first place, their standards of length and weight are divided and multiplied in accordance with the decimal system, by which means calculation is greatly simplified. Secondly, the mètre becomes their standard of length at 0°C, which is the most convenient temperature. Again, although the kilogramme may not exactly denote the weight of a cubic décimètre of distilled water at 4°C, yet it does so very nearly, and hence the French chemist when he knows the specific gravity of any substance knows also the weight of one cubic décimètre of that substance. For instance, if a substance have the specific gravity 2.5 at 0°C, it means that a cubic décimètre of that substance will at the temperature 0°C weigh 2.5 kilogrammes.

On this, and other accounts, the French or metrical system of weights and measures is very widely adopted by scientific chemists.

EFFECT OF TEMPERATURE UPON MEASURES OF TIME.

77. The rate of a clock depends upon the time in which its pendulum vibrates, and that of a watch upon the time of oscillation of its balance-wheel. Now the time of vibration of a pendulum depends upon its length; and since change of temperature alters the length of a pendulum it likewise alters its time of vibration, the general effect being that the higher the temperature the longer does the pendulum become and the more slowly does it vibrate. In like manner a change of temperature, by altering the dimensions of the balance-wheel of a watch and the force of the spring, will alter its time of oscillation in such a manner that it will vibrate more slowly in hot weather than in cold.

All good clock-makers endeavour to obviate these sources of error by means of certain compensations which we shall now describe.

78. Graham's mercurial pendulum. The first who attempted to compensate for change of length of a pendulum was Mr. Graham, an English clockmaker. The rod of his pendulum, Fig. 16, was made of glass, to the lower extremity of which was attached a cylindrical vessel containing mercury. As the glass rod expands by heat the bottom of the vessel which contains the mercury will of course be rendered more distant from the point of suspension, but since the column of mercury resting on this base expands upwards its centre of gravity is raised, or brought nearer the point of suspension. The lowering of the centre of gravity due to the expansion of the glass may thus be counteracted by the rise of the same due to the expansion of the mercury. The correction for imperfect compensation is made by raising or lowering the cylinder of mercury by means of a screw.

Fig. 16.

79. Harrison's gridiron pendulum. Shortly after Graham Mr. Harrison invented the arrangement in Fig. 17, which from its form is called the gridiron pendulum. The dark lines represent iron, the lighter lines brass or zinc; and it is evident that the former being attached to the upper cross-pieces will expand downwards, while the latter, being attached to the lower cross-pieces, will expand upwards. Hence the change of position of the bob due to a change of temperature will be denoted by the difference between the upward and the downward expansions. Let L be the length of iron expanding downwards, and κ its coefficient of expansion, also let L' denote the length of the other metal expanding upwards, and let κ' be its coefficient of expansion, then if $L\kappa - L'\kappa' = 0$ it is evident that the position of the bob will remain unaltered, even though the temperature change.

Fig. 17.

The correction for timing the pendulum is made by the screw d, while that for imperfect compensation is effected by shifting one of the cross traverses.

In some respects this pendulum is better than the mercurial one, for should any cause render the bob of the latter somewhat warmer or colder than the rest of the pendulum, it is evident that this would produce its full effect upon the mercury, while the length of the pendulum rod would be little altered. The gridiron pendulum, on the other hand, is not liable to this imperfection. But here, as in other things, it is better to avoid the source of error than to trust too much to the perfection of the compensating arrangement; and some astronomers, in order to procure the greatest possible regularity in their clock-rates, have removed the clocks themselves to a place where the change of temperature is extremely small.

80. Compensation balance for chronometers. If a ribbon or bar be made of two metals of different expansion firmly attached to one another, and if the temperature rise, then one of these metals will expand more than the other. Under these circumstances the ribbon will bend so that the most expansible metal will form the outside or convex surface of the curve, and the least expansible the concave. In like manner should the temperature fall the most expansible will form the inner or concave surface.

Now if the balance-wheel of a chronometer be formed as in Fig. 18, not with one continuous rim, but with a broken rim of several separate pieces, all of which are fixed at one end and free at the other, the free ends being loaded; and further, if each piece be composed of two metals, of which the most expansible is placed without; then it is evident, from what we have just said, that

Fig. 18.

on a rise of temperature the loaded ends will approach the centre. This may be so arranged as to counteract the effect produced on the rate of the chronometer by the matter of the wheel being thrown from the centre on account of the radius being lengthened through expansion. In practice, however, this method of compensation is very seldom perfect, and the rate of the best chronometer probably varies a little from one temperature to another. In the Greenwich and Liverpool Observatories the temperature corrections of chronometers are ascertained; and Mr. Hartnup, of the Liverpool Observatory, has given some very interesting examples of his method of applying a temperature correction to these instruments.

OTHER APPLICATIONS OF THE LAWS OF DILATATION.

81. Breguet's metallic thermometer. A very sensitive thermometer has been made by M. Breguet on the principle just mentioned. It consists of a spiral (Fig. 19) composed of silver, gold, and platinum rolled together so as to form a very fine ribbon. In this state it is sensitive to an exceedingly small change of temperature, becoming coiled or uncoiled, owing to the different expansion of the metals of which the compound ribbon is made. A

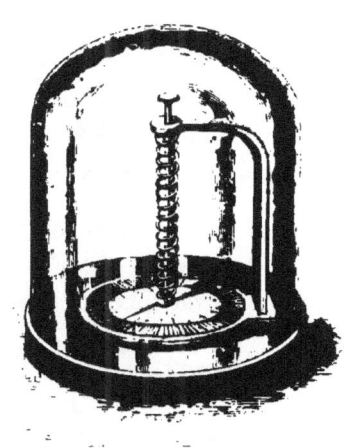

Fig. 19.

needle attached to one extremity of the coil points to a scale which is graduated experimentally by the aid of an ordinary thermometer.

82. Reduction of barometric column. When the pressure of the atmosphere is expressed in the number of inches of mercury which it is capable of supporting, in order to render the statement complete it is necessary to know the temperature of the mercury, since this fluid has a different density at different temperatures. Thus we find (Art. 52) that one inch of mercury at 0°C will denote the same atmospheric pressure as 1.005393 inches at 30°C.

Another thing to be noted is that the scale, by aid of which we read the column of mercury, even if correct, yet only denotes true inches and parts of an inch at 62°Fahr., if it be of English make, so that at any other temperature allowance must be made not only for the change in density of the mercury but for the change in length of the divisions of the scale.

Example.—Suppose that an English barometer with a brass scale, correctly graduated, reads 30 inches at 45° Fahr., what is the pressure in true inches of mercury reduced to the specific gravity it has at 32° Fahr.?

Since the scale is only correct (Art. 70) at 62° Fahr., and since brass expands very nearly .00001 for 1° Fahr., it follows that 30 apparent inches at 45° Fahr. $= \dfrac{30}{1.00017} = 29.995$ true inches. Also the density of mercury at 32° Fahr. (or 0°C) is to its density at 45° Fahr. (or 7°.2C) as 1.001294 to 1. Hence the atmospheric pressure in mercury at 32° Fahr. will be $\dfrac{29.995}{1.001294} = 29.956$ inches.

In French barometers, on the other hand, the indications of the scale are correct at 0°C, the same temperature to which the mercurial column is reduced, while the scale itself represents millimètres.

In comparing an English and a French barometer together it is therefore necessary to reduce the indications of each to 32° Fahr.; that is to say, to find by the one the pressure of the air in inches of mercury at 32° Fahr., and by the other the same in millimètres of mercury at 0°C. If both instruments are correct, their indications should then bear to one another the same proportion as inches to millimètres.

83. Expansion and contraction of metals. It requires the application of very intense pressure to produce the same change of volume in a solid or liquid body as that which is occasioned by a very small change of temperature. It follows from this that the forces exerted by solids in contracting or expanding, or by liquids in expanding, must be very great. If a strong vessel be entirely filled with a liquid and then sealed tightly, the vessel will burst if there be a considerable rise of temperature.

In like manner it has been calculated, that a bar of wrought iron whose temperature is 15° Fahr. above that of the surrounding medium, if tightly secured at its extremities, will draw these together with a force of one ton for each square inch of section on cooling down to the surrounding temperature.

In the arts it is of great importance to bear in mind the intensity of this force, sometimes with the view of guarding against its action, and sometimes in order to make it useful. Thus bars of furnaces must not be fitted tightly at their extremities, but must at least be free at one end. In making railways also a small space must be left between the successive rails.

Allowance must also be made for expansion and contraction in the case of tubular and lattice bridges. The reader who has visited the Menai tubular bridge will recall the arrangement made for this purpose.

For a similar reason water or gas pipes are fitted to each other by telescopic joints; and, generally speaking, the effects which may follow change of temperature must always be present before the mind of the constructor or engineer.

As an instance of the advantage which may be derived from the force of contraction, we may mention the familiar method by which tires are secured on wheels;—the tire is put on hot, when it fits loosely, but when it has contracted on cooling, it grasps the wheel with very great force.

It is probably also owing to the sudden change of volume from rapid cooling that tempered steel acquires that hardness which renders it so invaluable in the arts.

CHAPTER VI.

Change of State.—Liquefaction and Solidification.

84. Very many of the substances with which we are acquainted may be made to appear before us, either in the solid, the liquid, or the gaseous condition; but there are others that cannot be made to change the state in which we find them, or can only be compelled to do so with very great difficulty.

Thus we have not yet been able to freeze pure alcohol, nor have we been able to liquefy atmospheric air.

Heat is the well-known agent which causes change of state; and it always acts in such a manner that a substance passes from the solid to the liquid, and from the liquid to the gaseous state, by the addition of heat, and back again in the reverse direction by the withdrawal of this agent. This law is quite universal, and the order is never reversed; so that, although we cannot as yet solidify alcohol, we are quite sure that our only chance of success lies in abstracting heat from this liquid; and in like manner, although we have not as yet succeeded in melting some substances, we are sure that if we ever succeed it will be by the application of great heat.

85. Let us in the first place study the passage of bodies from the solid to the liquid state.

The characteristics of these states are too well known to need description. We are all acquainted with the rigidity and permanence of form which denote a solid, and with the excessive mobility of a liquid which enables it readily to assume the form of the vessel in which it is placed; nevertheless, although nothing is more marked than the difference between the characteristic properties of solidity and liquidity, there are a set of bodies that possess properties intermediate between these two states, and receive the name of viscous bodies. Treacle is an instance of a body of this kind.

86. If a substance be capable of assuming the viscous state, we find that it does so before it begins to melt, and that it passes gradually from a solid state through a semi-solid viscous state to that of a liquid of evident mobility. Sealing-wax is a very good example of a substance of this nature; when cold it is brittle, when heated it first of all grows plastic and finally melts. In like manner, before fluidity iron loses its hardness and becomes soft in such a manner that pieces may be easily welded together or moulded into any form; and this property of iron greatly enhances its value in the arts. Other substances might be mentioned, and a gradual passage from the solid to the liquid state characterises a large number of bodies. Furthermore, certain substances even after they have become unmistakeably solid acquire certain properties, such as hardness and brittleness, in greater perfection as the temperature continues to fall. Indeed, most of our hard bodies have high melting points, and the diamond, which is the hardest, is not susceptible of fusion even at a very high temperature.

With many substances, however, the change from the solid to the liquid state is very abrupt, and such substances afford the means of indicating with very great precision, by their altered appearance, the attainment of a certain temperature. Thus the temperature at which ice begins to melt is, under ordinary circumstances, a constant point, and is so used in the construction of thermometers.

87. But while there is a marked difference between bodies in the abruptness with which they change their state, there is also a class of substances which change their composition in the act of changing their state. Such are saline solutions. In many of these a greater quantity of salt is retained in solution at a high temperature than at a low one, so that, when they are left to cool, crystals of salt are deposited.

With weak saline solutions, such as sea salt, we have however a phenomenon of a somewhat different nature when the temperature is lowered. At a certain point which is constant for a solution of the same strength, the water solidifies as nearly pure ice, leaving the salt behind.

In what follows we shall distinguish between those substances which do not, and those which do, change their composition in changing their state.

PASSAGE FROM THE SOLID TO THE LIQUID STATE, OR LIQUEFACTION.

88. Fusion. Substances which do not change their composition in passing from the solid to the liquid state. The following laws are observed by all such when melting.

1. *Each substance begins to melt at a certain temperature, which is constant for the same substance if the pressure be constant.*

2. *The temperature of the solid remains at this constant point from the time when fusion commences until it is complete.*

3. *If a substance expands in congelation its melting point is lowered by pressure, but if a substance contracts in congelation its melting point is raised by pressure.*

89. The following table contains the melting points of various substances under the ordinary atmospheric pressure.

Table of melting points.

Name of substance.	Temp. of melting point in degrees Fahr.	Observer.
Mercury	−37.9	Stewart.
Oil of vitriol	−30	Regnault.
Bromine	+ 9.5	Pierre.
Ice	32	
Phosphorus	111.5	Schrötter.
Potassium	136	Regnault.
Sodium	207.7	,,
Sulphur	239	Person.
Tin	451	,,
Bismuth	512	,,
Lead	623	,,
Zinc	680	Pouillet.
Antimony	810	,,
Siver (pure)	1832	,,
Gold (pure)	2282	,,
French wrought iron . .	2732	,,
English wrought iron .	2912	,,

The higher points in this table are subject to considerable uncertainty.

90. Change of density produced in the act of melting. It is probable that most substances expand in the process of melting, so that the liquid is of smaller specific gravity than the solid; but there are some which contract. Ice is a familiar instance of this last class, being considerably lighter, bulk for bulk, than water. According to M. Brunner (fils), (Art. 40), the specific density of ice at 0°C is only 0.91800, that of water at 4°C being reckoned equal to unity. The force with which water expands when it becomes ice is very great. Cast iron, bismuth, and antimony are examples of the same class. On the other hand, mercury, phosphorus, gold, silver, copper, and many other substances, contract as they become solid; and this is the reason why coins of these three last mentioned metals cannot be cast, but require to be stamped.

91. Latent heat of fusion. When heat is applied to a pound of ice at the temperature of 32° Fahr., it is not instantly converted into water, but the process is a very gradual one. The reason of this is that a large amount of heat must first enter into the pound of ice at 32° before it becomes water at 32°. This heat is called latent, because it is absorbed by the ice without producing any rise of temperature; and we may represent the process of liquefaction to ourselves by the following formula:—

Water at 32° = ice at 32° + latent heat.

All substances in passing from the solid to the liquid state absorb heat, and we shall afterwards shew how the amount of this may be measured;—that absorbed by water is very great. The doctrine of latent heat was first taught by Dr. Black of Edinburgh. The great latent heat of water serves to retard the melting of snows. If snow or ice at 32° were suddenly to be converted into water by the smallest addition of heat the inhabitants of valleys would be exposed to terrific inundations, whereas by the gradual melting of ice this is prevented, and by the same means also these inhabitants are furnished with a continuous supply of water.

92. Influence of pressure upon the melting point. Professor James Thomson of Belfast anticipated theoretically the truth that the melting point of a body which expands in congelation would be lowered by pressure, while that of a body which contracts in congelation would be raised by it. We shall afterwards give the reasoning by which this conclusion was arrived at; in the meantime we will content ourselves with stating that his brother's idea was verified experimentally by Professor W. Thomson of Glasgow, who shewed that by a pressure of 16.8 atmospheres the freezing point of water (a substance which expands when freezing) was reduced 0°.232 Fahr.

Bunsen afterwards found that the melting points of paraffin and spermaceti, both of which contract when freezing, were raised by the application of pressure. Thus spermaceti

solidified at 117°.9 Fahr. under the atmospheric pressure, but
under a pressure of 156 atmospheres it solidified at 123°.6 Fahr.

Hopkins made similar experiments, not only on spermaceti,
but also on wax and stearin; and finally, Mousson, by the
enormous pressure of 13000 atmospheres, was able to lower
the temperature of freezing water from 0° to −18°Cent.

93. Alloys and Fluxes. The fusing point of a mixture
of bodies is often considerably lower than that of either of its
components: thus, for instance, an alloy of five parts of tin
and one of lead fuses at 194°C. In like manner Rose's fusible
metal, consisting of four parts of bismuth, one of lead, and one
of tin, fuses at 94°C, a temperature lower than that of boiling
water. Alloys are much used in soldering and in taking casts.

Similar results are produced by mixing salts together:
thus a mixture of the chlorides of potassium and of sodium
melts at a lower temperature than either of its constituents.
A mixture of equivalent quantities of carbonate of sodium
and carbonate of potassium melts below the fusing point
of either salt separately, and is used to facilitate the fusion
of certain minerals in analysis. In like manner, fluxes
are substances which, when added to an ore, promote the
formation of a fusible medium.

**94. Solution. Substances which change their com-
position in passing from the solid to the liquid state.**
If we have a saturated solution of any salt at the bottom of
which are crystals of the same salt, as long as the temperature
remains the same there will be no change in the aspect of
these crystals; but in most cases a rise of temperature will
cause some of them to dissolve and assume the liquid state.

95. Freezing mixtures. In solution, just as in fusion,
a certain quantity of heat becomes latent; and this is sometimes taken advantage of to produce intense cold. If two
solids, or at least one liquid and one solid, on being mixed
together produce a compound which is not solid but liquid,

we have generally the production of cold. The following table exhibits some of the best known freezing mixtures :—

Substances.	Parts by weight.	Reduction of temperature in Centigrade degrees.
Sulphate of soda	8	} $+10°$ to $-17°$.
Hydrochloric acid	5	
Pounded ice or snow	2	} $+10°$ to $-18°$.
Common salt	1	
Sulphate of soda	3	} $+10°$ to $-19°$.
Dilute nitric acid	2	
Sulphate of soda	6	
Nitrate of ammonia	5	} $+10°$ to $-26°$.
Dilute nitric acid	4	
Phosphate of soda	9	} $+10°$ to $-29°$.
Dilute nitric acid	4	

If the substances used and the apparatus have both been previously cooled down, still lower temperatures may be obtained.

96. Influence of pressure upon solution. Mr. Sorby (Proceedings of the Royal Society, vol. xii., April 30, 1863) has found that pressure exercises upon the solubility of salts an influence analogous to that which it exerts upon the melting points of bodies. Thus, when the united volume of the water and of a salt after solution is less than that of the water and salt separately before solution, or, in other words, where solution has diminished the volume, he finds that the effect of pressure is analogous to that which takes place where ordinary fusion diminishes the volume. In this case the solubility is increased by pressure, just as in the corresponding case the liability of ice to melt is increased by pressure (see Art. 92). Again, where solution has increased the volume (as, for instance, where sal-ammoniac is dissolved in water), pressure lessens instead of increasing the solubility.

PASSAGE FROM THE LIQUID TO THE SOLID STATE,
OR SOLIDIFICATION.

97. Substances which do not change their composition in passing from the liquid to the solid state.

We have here two laws of the same nature as those which regulate fusion.

1. *Every substance under ordinary circumstances solidifies at a fixed temperature, which is the same as that of fusion.*

2. *The temperature of the liquid remains at this constant point from the time when solidification commences until it is complete.*

If a liquid be allowed to cool very slowly, in becoming solid it often assumes the crystalline form, but most frequently we have the vitreous or amorphous state. The crystalline is, however, the most natural condition, and it will always be assumed when the particles have sufficient time to fall into their proper place; and even after substances have become solid molecular change in the direction of crystallization often takes place. Thus brass or silver if repeatedly heated and cooled becomes brittle, and exhibits a crystalline structure. In like manner, a cannon that has been often fired will at last burst in consequence of a change of this kind; and the vibrations to which the axles of railway carriages are liable gradually destroy the fibre and toughness of the iron, rendering it crystalline and brittle.

98. It is possible to lower the freezing point by various means. Thus pressure acts in lowering the freezing point of water just as it acted (Art. 92) in lowering the melting point of ice.

Again, water deprived of air and allowed to cool very slowly and without agitation may be reduced to $-6°C$ while still retaining its fluid state, and if it be enclosed in a tube, its surface covered with a film of oil, and the pressure of the atmosphere withdrawn, it may be reduced to $-12°C$: but under these circumstances the smallest agitation or the presence of a crystal of ice produces solidification. Very frequently a glass vessel filled with water may be found in this state on a cold morning, when the addition of a bit of ice in a very few seconds changes èntirely the appearance of the liquid.

This sudden formation of ice is accompanied by a rise of temperature of the whole liquid, which mounts to the freezing point of water. The reason of this is, that ice requiring much less heat than water, leaves a quantity of heat free to raise the temperature of the whole liquid.

A very rapid agitation, or any other cause which, exerting an action upon the molecules, hinders them from assuming the requisite arrangement, retards the formation of ice. Capillary attraction acts in this way; and M. Despretz has found that in fine capillary tubes water may be lowered to — 20°C without solidification. This circumstance probably explains why the sap is not oftener frozen in the capillary vessels of plants.

99. The great amount of the latent heat of water, combined with the fact that ice is lighter than water, are facts of great importance in the economy of nature. To make this clear let us see what occurs when a lake is frozen, supposing that the cold influence or abstraction of heat takes place over the surface of the lake. As the upper layer of water is cooled down it becomes heavier and sinks to the bottom, being replaced by a warmer and lighter layer from below: this process will go on until the whole water of the lake is reduced to 39° Fahr., the point of maximum density of water. When this temperature has been reached the process above described is at an end, and any further cooling of the upper strata will not cause them to sink, since they become specifically lighter below 39°.

When the surface of the lake has been cooled down to 32° Fahr. it will begin to freeze, but the process of freezing will go on very slowly, since a great quantity of heat must be taken from water before it becomes ice.

Again, when a layer of ice is once formed it does not sink

to the bottom, but remains on the top, so that the cooling influence can only freeze a second layer through the substance of the first, and so on. The ice formed thus protects the water below, which remains at 39°, a temperature which is not destructive to animal life.

100. Regelation. Faraday was the first to observe a very curious property of ice. Two pieces of thawing ice if put together adhere and become one; and this adhesion will take place in air or in water, or in vacuo. It would also seem to be independent of the application of pressure; and, provided the surfaces be smooth, when they are brought into the slightest contact, regelation ensues. Nor is it necessary that both surfaces be ice, for wool may be made to adhere to a block of thawing ice after the manner of regelation. The same thing takes place when a snowball is formed.

101. Probably the true explanation of this phenomenon is that advanced by Professor Forbes. He adopts the idea of the gradual liquefaction of ice which was deduced by Person from Regnault's experiments on latent heat, and supposes that true hard ice does not pass at once into water, but that there are intermediate stages in the process of liquefaction. The temperature of true hard ice is by this hypothesis essentially somewhat less than that of ice-cold water, and the substance corresponding to the intermediate temperature is supposed to appear in a slightly viscous or plastic state, being as yet neither quite solid nor quite liquid, and also to possess probably less than the latent heat of perfectly fluid water. In fact, ice in melting is here supposed to be similar to sealing-wax or wrought iron, both of which substances require a considerable range of temperature in order to pass from the solid to the liquid state, while we may imagine that the whole latent heat is not required until perfect fluidity is reached. The difference between ice and wrought iron in melting would therefore be one of abruptness of transition.

In ice the change is accomplished throughout a very small temperature range, in iron it requires a very large one. The subjoined figure will approximately represent the state, as regards temperature, of a cubical block of thawing ice on this hypothesis.

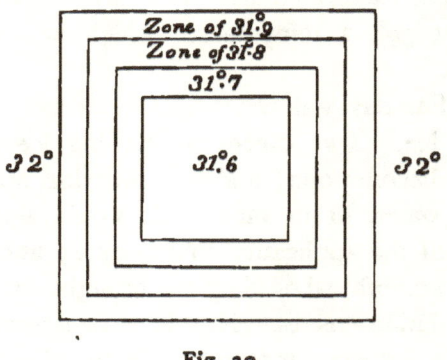

Fig. 20.

102. Our conception of latent heat (Art. 91) will require to be somewhat modified in order to suit the hypothesis of gradual liquefaction, and we may represent to ourselves what takes place by means of the following diagram (Fig. 21).

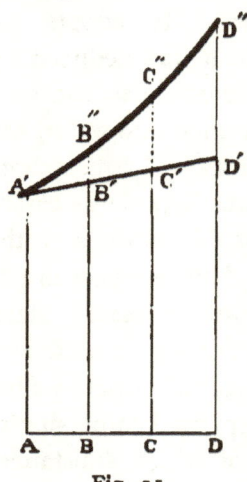

Fig. 21.

Let the whole range of temperature between the commencement and the end of the process of liquefaction be denoted by AD, and subdivided into equal parts AB, BC, CD; also let AA' denote the whole heat of the body at temperature A; and supposing there were no such thing as latent heat, let BB' denote the heat of the body at temperature B, CC' its heat at temperature C, and DD' its heat at temperature D. The latent heat will however have to be added to these heats, in order to express the total heat of the body at the various temperatures. Expressing this latent heat, which is supposed to increase gradually between the two temperatures A and D, by $B'B''$, $C'C''$, $D'D''$, we have the whole lines BB'', CC'', DD''

denoting the whole heat, sensible and latent together, of the substance at the respective temperatures B, C, D.

103. If now it be assumed that hard ice is essentially colder than ice-cold water, we can easily see why two wet pieces of ice will have the water between them frozen when they come into contact. For the ice *on both sides* of the layer of water will now be colder than it, and hence a new distribution of heat will take place, the consequence of which will be that the water will be frozen, becoming as it were the centre of the block.

104. It might be said that the laws of conduction are against this hypothesis, and that we cannot conceive a piece of ice entirely surrounded for a considerable length of time by water at 32°, or a little over it, to have in its interior a temperature lower than 32°, however small we may imagine this difference to be; but we think this objection must vanish if it be assumed that the supposed intermediate states between ice and water correspond to intermediate quantities of latent heat. For in this case the heat which is conducted from the outside into the body of a block of ice is not altogether influential in adding temperature, since in each small addition of temperature a certain quantity of heat becomes latent. Let us consider, for instance, what would take place if a large mass of sealing-wax were to be gradually melted by agitation in a pan of liquid sealing-wax over the fire. As the heat was conveyed to the lump of wax, envelope after envelope would become liquid and drop off, mixing with the liquid mass until a very small solid nucleus was left: but as long as there was left a solid nucleus, however small, we should surely be entitled to assume that the temperature of the centre of this nucleus was lower than that of the melted wax.

We imagine that there is no impossibility in conceiving that something of the same kind takes place in ice. Heat will no doubt be conveyed into the interior of a block of ice that is left for a long time in water a little above 32°, but this heat (as remarked by Professor Forbes) will exhibit its action rather in diminishing the size of the block of ice than in completely equalizing its temperature throughout.

105. If we imagine this objection to be obviated by these remarks, there are three questions started by the hypothesis which can only be decided by experiment.

1. Is the interior of a block of ice in fact colder than the exterior ?

2. Is the interior of such a block harder than the exterior ?

3. Does soft ice possess more latent heat than hard ice ?

With regard to the first of these points certain experiments made by Professor Forbes would seem to indicate that the interior of a block of ice is slightly colder than the exterior. For, in the first place, he found that a thermometer buried in the heart of a block of ice fell decidedly below 32° Fahr., and he also found that rapidly-pounded ice was colder than melting ice. This last experiment has been tried by the author of this work with the same result. With regard to the second point, Professor Forbes has remarked that the surface of a block of ice is much softer than hard cold ice. With respect to the third point, Person's deductions from Regnault's experiments are in favour of the view that soft ice possesses more latent heat than hard ice. On the whole, we think the gradual liquefaction of ice is a view which appears not only to be supported by analogy, but to be the best explanation of observed facts : nevertheless it would be desirable that this view should be confirmed by further experiments.

106. Substances which change their composition in passing from the liquid to the solid state. When a solid is dissolved in a liquid until it refuses to dissolve any further, we have what is termed a saturated solution. But what is a saturated solution at one temperature will not be so at another. In general, a hot liquid dissolves more than a cold liquid. The consequence is that, if the temperature of a saturated solution be diminished, we have a deposition of solid matter in the shape of crystals, and the liquid which is left behind is saturated for the reduced temperature. If the solution contain two salts of unequal solubility, of different crystalline forms, and having no chemical action upon each other, a greater or less separation of these two salts may be produced by crystallization; by this means nitre is purified from common salt.

107. Solutions are subject to the same anomalies as water and the like liquids. Thus if we have a solution of Glauber's salt at a high temperature, and if it be allowed to cool gradually and at rest without the admission of air, it will retain the salt in solution, even though the temperature be much reduced. But if it be agitated, or if air be admitted, or, better still, if a crystal of Glauber's salt be dropped into it, crystallization will immediately commence, attended, as in the case of water, with a rise of temperature.

108. If instead of a saturated solution we have a weak solution of certain salts, such as sea water, this, when lowered in temperature, will change its state in a different way. At a temperature which is always lower than the freezing point of water such a solution will freeze, producing nearly pure ice and leaving the salt behind. Mr. Walker, who accompanied Sir L. McClintock in the "Fox," made numerous experiments on sea water: he used cold as a means of separating the salt from the water, but was by this means unable to obtain water of less density than 1.002.

Rudorff has made many experiments on this subject, and finds that in saline solutions generally the freezing point is below 32° Fahr., but the extent to which it is lowered depends upon the nature of the salt.

CHAPTER VII.

Change of State.—Production of Vapour and its Condensation.

109. When sufficient heat is applied to a body it generally assumes the gaseous state; unless it be of such a nature that it will under ordinary circumstances be decomposed before assuming this state. By means of a certain application of electricity, it is probable that the most refractory substances, such as carbon, can be made to appear as gases, although only in very small quantity.

Generally when a solid passes into a gas it first assumes the intermediate state of a liquid, but sometimes its passage into a gas is completed without the intermediate form of liquidity being assumed. This is called *sublimation;* while the passage of a liquid to the gaseous state goes under the general name of *vaporization.* In whatever way the gaseous condition is produced it always requires a considerable amount of latent heat. Thus a pound of water at 212° Fahr. will absorb a great quantity of heat before it is entirely converted into steam, although the steam does not possess a higher temperature than 212°. In the same manner as before we may apply the following formula, and say—

Steam at 212° = water at 212° + latent heat of steam.

The latent heat of gases is greater than that of liquids, and we will afterwards shew how it may be measured. This latent heat has to be disposed of in some sensible form, when the gas which possesses it is reconverted into a liquid, and thus the latent heat of gases is of great service in retarding the change from the liquid to the gaseous or from the gaseous to the liquid state, which, but for the great latent heat of gases, would be inconveniently sudden.

Elastic fluids have been divided into gases and vapours, but the distinction between these is merely conventional. A vapour denotes a substance in the gaseous form which at ordinary temperatures appears as a liquid or solid, while a gas denotes a substance which under ordinary circumstances appears in the gaseous form, and which can only be reduced to the solid or liquid form by intense pressure or intense cold. Our subject may be divided into the following parts.

1. Vaporization, or the conversion of a liquid into a gas ; and sublimation, or the conversion of a solid into a gas.

2. Liquefaction and solidification of vapours and gases.

3. Elasticity and density of vapours and gases, with a few remarks upon hygrometry.

VAPORIZATION AND SUBLIMATION.

110. Vaporization is the general name for a process of which there are three varieties, namely—

1. *Evaporation*, where a liquid is converted into a gas quietly, and without the formation of bubbles.

2. *Ebullition*, where bubbles of gas are formed in the mass of the liquid itself.

3. Vaporization in the *spheroidal condition*, where a liquid evaporates slowly, although in apparent contact with a very hot substance.

111. Vapours are formed in vacuo more readily than in air. The presence of air or of any foreign gas retards the formation of vapours, but in vacuo a liquid is very quickly converted into vapour. If a small quantity of water, alcohol, or ether be introduced up through a barometer tube into the Torricellian vacuum at the top, as soon as it reaches this it is converted into vapour, which shews itself by lowering the column of mercury by means of its elastic force. This column, which originally denoted the pressure of the atmosphere, now denotes the pressure of the atmosphere *minus* the pressure of the vapour of the liquid.

112. Maximum of pressure in vacuo. If we continue to introduce an additional quantity of the volatile fluid into the Torricellian vacuum of a barometer, we shall at first probably perceive an additional depression; but as we go on we shall find that the depression does not increase beyond a certain limit, or, in other words, the elastic force of the vapour we have introduced has reached a maximum, and the introduction of more liquid will not increase the density of the vapour. We shall further find that the maximum of pressure is regulated by the temperature in such a manner that the higher the temperature the higher is the maximum pressure, so that we are enabled to deduce the following law, first discovered by Dalton : *In space destitute of air the vaporization of a liquid goes on only until the vapour has attained a determinate expansive force dependent on the temperature, so that in every space void of air which is saturated with vapour determinate vapour pressure corresponds to determinate temperature.*

The tension of vapour corresponding to a given temperature differs of course with the nature of the substance which is vaporized. Thus the tension of the vapour of water at ordinary temperatures is much greater than that of the vapour of mercury, while the vapours of alcohol and ether have still higher tensions.

113. Mixtures of gas and vapour in a confined space. The experiments of Dalton lead to the following law : *In a space filled with air the same amount of water evaporates as in a space destitute of air ; and precisely the same relation subsists between the temperature and the expansive force of the vapour, whether the space contains air or not.*

Thus if a closed space contain air of the pressure of 30 inches at a temperature for which the tension of aqueous vapour is 2 inches, and if a little water be introduced, the pressure will rise to 32 inches; while if the same space be void of air the pressure of the aqueous vapour will of course be 2 inches. This law of Dalton has been verified by Gay Lussac. More lately, Regnault has made experiments on this subject, and has investigated the tensions of the vapours of water, ether, bisulphide of carbon, and benzole, both in vacuo and in air. He has found that the tension in air is always slightly less than it is in vacuo, the difference being greater for volatile liquids; but he is inclined to believe that Dalton's law is true in principle, and that the differences which he observed are caused by the hygroscopic properties of the sides of the chamber which contained the vapours.

114. Mixed liquids in a confined space. Where a mixture of liquids is allowed to evaporate in a closed space, Gay Lussac inferred that the tension of the mixed vapour was equal to the sum of the tension of the two vapours taken separately.

Magnus and Regnault have found that this holds for a mixture of bisulphide of carbon and water, or of benzole and water, of which the components do not dissolve each other; but in other cases it does not hold.

Thus for a mixture of ether and water the tension is scarcely higher than for ether alone. If the liquids mix readily together in all proportions, then the vapour tension is generally less than that of the one liquid and greater than that of the other.

115. Effect of chemical affinity upon evaporation. If water be put into a confined space along with some substance which has a great attraction for it and does not readily part with it, the vapour density may be much diminished. Thus if a small quantity of water be mixed with a large quantity of sulphuric acid, the acid will retain the water and will not suffer any of it to evaporate.

On the other hand, if we have a large quantity of water and an exceedingly small quantity of acid, we shall have very nearly the usual tension of vapour.

Between these two extremes we may prepare solutions of intermediate strength which will diminish to a greater or less extent the tension of aqueous vapour corresponding to the temperature of observation.

A similar rule will hold for other solutions ; and if the substance mixed with the liquid whose tension in a state of gas is sought be a fixed and not a volatile body, its tendency will generally be to prevent the liquid from evaporating, and thus to diminish the tension due to vapour.

116. Tension when two vessels at different temperatures are in communication with each other. In Figure 22, let us first suppose that the stop-cock at *C* is shut, and that two similar vessels *A* and *B* are entirely filled with water and vapour of water to the exclusion of air or any other gas. Also let *A* be surrounded with ice, and let heat be applied to *B*, so that we may suppose *A* to be at the temperature of melting ice and

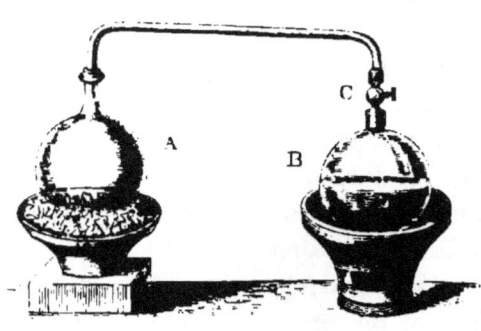

Fig. 22.

B to be at 212° Fahr. In this case the tension of the vapour in *A* will hardly be one-fifth of an inch, while in *B* it will be 30 inches. Now on opening the stop-cock, there will of course be a rush of vapour from *B* to *A*, and we may suppose that for a moment the pressure of the vapour will be the mean between the two original pressures, but the effect of the cold surface of *A* will be to condense this vapour and to render it as nearly as possible equal to the tension at 32°, viz. one-fifth of an inch. If there be water in *B* more vapour will rise and pass to *A*, there to be condensed as before. In fact, the apparatus will now act as a still, and the water of *B* will be gradually transferred to *A*. The latent heat, set free by the large quantity of vapour which is condensed at *A*, will of course tend to raise the temperature of *A*; but provided this temperature be kept steadily at or near 32° by a sufficiently powerful application of cold, the pressure in *A* will by this arrangement be kept very low, while the pressure of vapour in *B* will be somewhat higher than in *A*, and the dynamical effect of this inequality of pressure in these two vessels will be represented by the rush of vapour from *B* to *A*. The intensity of this rush will depend on the intensity of the source of heat : if the heat which enters *B* be sufficient to produce a large quantity of vapour in a short time, this vapour will rush very fast towards *A*, and a powerful freezing mixture will have to be applied in order to keep down the temperature of *A*, but if the source of heat be feeble the rush will be feeble also; in fact, by this arrangement the vapour of water may be regarded as a vehicle for transferring the heat from the source at *B* to be spent in liquefying the ice or freezing mixture, or to be otherwise disposed of at *A*.

If in the first part of this experiment, when the cock *C* is shut, the vessel *B* contains no water in a liquid form, but is entirely filled with the vapour of water at 212°, then when *C* is opened this vapour will be almost immediately condensed at *A*, and an approximate vacuum will be formed. We shall afterwards see how this principle has been applied by Watt in the steam-engine.

It will be evident that the perfection of vapour as a vehicle for carrying heat, as described above, depends upon the absence of air in the arrangement of the experiment.

For if *A* and *B* be filled with air, each particle of vapour which is carried from *B* to *A* must pass through all this air, and the transmission of vapour will in this case be very difficult.

There are various useful applications of the process described above. The first we shall mention is—

117. Distillation. The subjoined figure will represent this process. The liquid to be distilled away is contained in *A*. It generally exists combined either with some fixed impurities or with some other liquid less volatile than itself, and the object of distillation is to separate it from these. This is done by applying heat to *A* and by attaching to it a

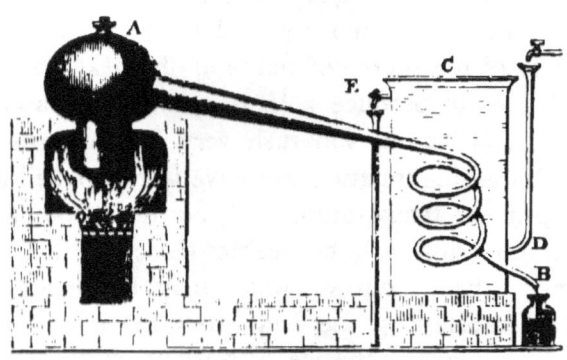

Fig. 23.

tube, as in Fig. 23, the other extremity of which passes in coils through a vessel of cold water. The liquid is vaporised by the applied heat, and is then driven through this tube, but as it passes through the coils immersed in the cold water (technically called *the worm*), a comparatively large surface is exposed to the cooling agent, and the vapour is rapidly condensed, passing in drops from B into a bottle prepared to receive it. The vessel C through which the worm of the still passes must be kept cool: this is done by constantly supplying it at a low level with cold water by means of a tube at D, and by withdrawing the hotter and therefore lighter layers of the water at C; a constant current of cold water is thus made to circulate through the vessel.

118. Cold due to evaporation. Freezing apparatus. Whenever vapour is produced a quantity of heat is rendered latent. This heat is necessary to the formation of vapour, and must be supplied either from some foreign source, or, if this be not available, from the very liquid which is being evaporated. In this last case the temperature of the liquid falls in order to supply the heat necessary to the existence of vapour.

Leslie was the first to freeze water by means of the drain of heat caused by its own evaporation.

In his experiment a vessel containing strong sulphuric acid is placed under the receiver of an air-pump, and above it a thin metallic vessel containing a little water. As the receiver becomes exhausted the water evaporates more and more rapidly, and the vapour, as fast as it is formed, is absorbed by the sulphuric acid. The vapour thus becomes a vehicle for carrying heat from the metallic vessel, and the consequence is a diminution in temperature until ice is formed.

An instrument called the cryophorus, or frost carrier (κρύος *frost*, φορὸς *bearing*), very similar to that of Fig. 22, is sometimes used to shew the freezing of water from its own evaporation. Thus if we suppose all the water to be in B, and only vapour of water without air in A, and if A is cooled by a powerful freezing mixture, while B is not exposed to a source of heat, then rapid evaporation of the water in B will take place, and this vapour will go to A and be condensed there as fast as it is formed.

Heat is thus carried, as before, from *B* to *A*, but as there is now no source of heat at *B* the water there must part with its own heat in order to furnish that which is necessary for evaporation, in consequence of which it will be frozen. In this experiment it is well to protect *B* from the influence of currents of air.

When other liquids and mixtures more volatile than water are used in this manner, a very intense cold may be produced. Thus by the evaporation of liquid sulphurous acid a degree of cold is obtained sufficiently strong to freeze mercury.

By a mixture of solid carbonic acid and ether Faraday obtained a degree of cold which he estimated at − 166° Fahr.; and more recently, Natterer, by mixing liquid nitrous oxide with bisulphide of carbon, and placing them both in vacuo, has obtained − 220° Fahr.

In hot climates porous vessels called alcarazas are used for cooling water. The water reaches the outside through the pores, and hence a continual evaporation is going on, especially when the vessels are placed in a current of air.

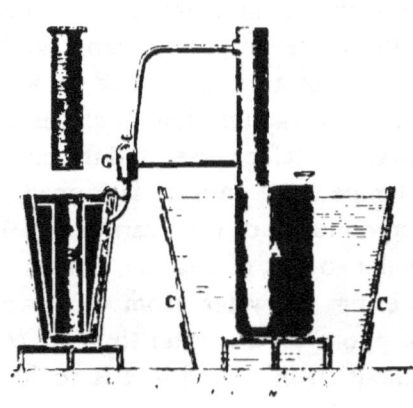

Fig. 24.

MM. Carré and Co. of Paris have invented a very ingenious freezing machine, which was exhibited in London at the International Exhibition of 1862.

This apparatus is represented in Figs. 24 and 25. *A* is a strong vessel of wrought iron three-quarters filled with a concentrated solution of ammonia. *B* is a strong wrought iron circular condenser having a central space sufficiently large to receive the vessel

D. The pipes are so arranged as to prevent the liquid from boiling over into the condenser. Before using the instrument it is laid upon its side, boiler downwards, for about 10 minutes, so as to allow any liquid that may be in the condenser to drain back into the boiler, and this is facilitated by heating the condenser slightly with a lamp. The process consists of two parts. In the

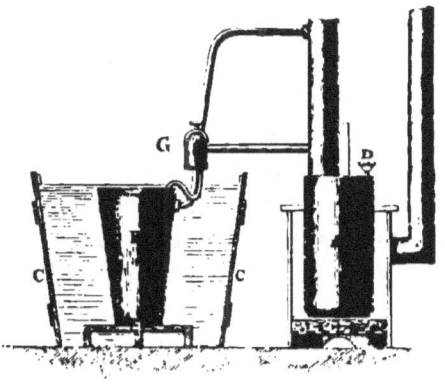

Fig. 25.

first of these, Fig. 25, the boiler is heated very gradually by a charcoal chauffer, or other source of heat, while the condenser *B* is kept in a vessel through which a. stream of cold water is constantly flowing. As the result of this process, the ammoniacal gas separates from the water and is condensed by its own pressure in *B*, and the heating is allowed to go on until a thermometer attached to the boiler indicates about 270° Fahr., at which temperature it is presumed that nearly all the ammoniacal gas is condensed in *B*, while all the water remains behind in *A* : the second part of the process next begins.

The apparatus is now withdrawn from the fire ; the water is allowed to run out of the orifice *B* through a hole in the bottom; this orifice is then stopped with a cork, and the cylinder *D* containing the liquid to be frozen is put into *B*, a little alcohol having been previously introduced in order to establish a liquid communication between the sides of *B* and *D*; the vessel *A* (Fig. 24) is now plunged into water which is kept cool, while the condenser is wrapped round with flannel

—a non-conductor. The temperature of *A* now falls very rapidly, and as the water in *A reacquires* its power of absorbing ammoniacal gas, this gas rises very abundantly from *B*, and is condensed in *A*.

In consequence of this rapid evaporation *B* becomes intensely cold, and if it contains water this will be frozen. Mercury may also be frozen by this means.

As the success of this instrument depends upon its being devoid of air, there is an arrangement of the following kind, by which any air can be got rid of. *G* is a small cup which is always kept full of water, and in it works a screw, so that when relaxed it opens up an exceedingly small entrance into the interior. When the temperature of the boiler has risen to about 140° Fahr. the screw is slightly loosened, and the disengaged ammoniacal gas is rapidly absorbed by the water in *G*. If any air be present, this will be seen by its rising to the surface, and the channel must be kept open so long as such an appearance of air continues, but when the gas is wholly dissolved by the water, the screw must be again tightened and the operation of heating continued.

A portion of the boiler at *D*, Fig. 25, is made of metal which will fuse below that temperature at which the pressure of the steam would burst the boiler. This arrangement acts therefore as a safety-valve.

119. Tension in communicating vessels filled with air. Dalton, as we have already mentioned, was the first to shew that in a space filled with air the same amount of water evaporates as in a space destitute of air; and that precisely the same relation subsists between the temperature and the maximum vapour tension whether the space contains air or not. Unfortunately there has been based upon this experimental result a theory which is *only a possible but not a necessary* result of these experiments. It has been supposed that no mutual relation whatever exists between vapour and air, and that they remain near each other without producing the slightest mechanical effect upon one another. This theory has come to be too much regarded as a necessary result of Dalton's experiments, although certain observations made by Bessel, Broun, Welsh, and others seemed to be incapable of explanation by it. Dr. Lamont of Munich has devised a crucial experiment, the result of which has been to refute this hypothesis. The arrangement adopted was of the following nature. A glass tube, bent as in Fig. 26, had at one end a globe K, while the other end e is left open to the atmosphere. q is a drop of quicksilver, which is

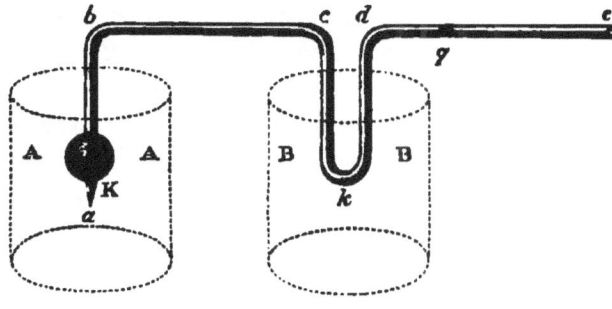

Fig. 26.

capable of moving backwards and forwards along de. The curved part ckd of the tube is plunged into a vessel BB filled with cold water, while into the vessel AA, in which the globe K is placed, cold and warm water can alternately be poured. The experiment was of the following nature: suppose that before commencing it the temperature of the whole apparatus as well as of the water in BB is 32° Fahr., and suppose also that the globe and tube are filled with dry air of the pressure of 30 inches.

First raise the temperature of the globe K to 100° Fahr. by pouring warm water into AA, while the temperature of $bcde$ remains as before. Owing to the increased elasticity of the dry air, the quicksilver q is pushed toward e ;—notice how far.

Next cool down the globe to its former temperature (32°), and introduce a little water into K by breaking off the fine point a, which is then sealed on again, and repeat the previous experiment—that is to say, heat the globe to 100° Fahr. as before, and again notice how far the quicksilver is pushed towards e.

The result of this experiment will be a test of the truth of this hypothesis. Let us see, in the first place, what ought to take place if these views are correct; that is to say, if the vapour and air are quite independent of each other. For simplicity's sake we may imagine the second heating of the globe to take place not a very long time after the intro-duction of the water, in which case the vapour will not yet have penetrated to q (in Lamont's experiment there was no trace of vapour at this part of the apparatus). If these views be correct, there being no tension of vapour at q, the pressure there will be entirely due to dry air. No doubt there is pressure of vapour in the globe K, but by this hypothesis it has no effect on the particles of dry air, and cannot therefore be communicated to q. The drop of quicksilver at q ought therefore to move, for a given heating of the ball, precisely the same distance whether the air of the globe be dry or whether it contain vapour.

Let us now suppose, instead of this hypothesis, that the air exerts a pressure upon the vapour and the vapour upon the air. Then the globe K will have a tension of vapour corresponding to 100° Fahr. = 1.9 inches nearly; this has to be added to the tension of dry air, and the sum will be communicated through the dry air of the tube to the quick-silver at q, which will, on this hypothesis, be pushed much further when there is vapour than when there is only dry air. On the other hypothesis, however, as we have seen, the quicksilver will be pushed equally far in both cases. Now Lamont found that the quicksilver was pushed much farther when there were air and vapour together than when there was only dry air, and he therefore concluded that the first hypothesis is incorrect.

120. Various modes of vaporisation. Our attention has hitherto been directed to certain laws which have no special reference to the particular modes in which vaporisation is accomplished.

Let us now consider the peculiarities of these various modes. We have already (Art. 110) stated that there are three such—viz. *evaporation, ebullition, and vaporisation in the spheroidal state.* Let us begin with the first of these.

121. Evaporation. Evaporation denotes the quiet production of vapour at the surface of a liquid, and is subject to the following laws.

1. It varies with the temperature.

2. It varies with the extent of surface exposed.

3. It goes on very rapidly in vacuo, but much more slowly in a space filled with air.

4. It goes on more rapidly in dry air than in air containing vapour.

5. It is assisted by any agitation tending to renew the particles of air over the evaporating surface.

The reason of the fourth and fifth laws is very evident. When vapour forms above the surface of a liquid in still air, it rises so slowly that the air above the liquid soon becomes saturated with vapour, or nearly so, and hence the evaporation, if not quite stopped, yet proceeds very slowly. But when new and comparatively dry particles of air are constantly brought into contact with the liquid the process is greatly facilitated.

This process is constantly going on in nature, and forms one of the means by which the surface of the earth is rendered fit for the maintenance of living beings; it is also of very extensive application in chemistry and in the arts, being employed to separate a volatile from a fixed substance.

122. Ebullition. When a liquid is heated in an open vessel it gradually gets hotter and hotter, and the evaporation more and more rapid. After some time the layers of liquid in contact with the sides of the vessel become changed into vapour, which begins to rise, but is condensed by the colder strata before it reaches the surface. This is the cause of the singing noise of liquids before they begin to boil. Soon, however, the bubbles of vapour are able to reach the surface, and the process of ebullition has begun. The temperature now ceases to rise, and remains stationary until the whole of the liquid has been boiled away.

The temperature of ebullition depends, (1) on the external pressure; (2) on the nature of the vessel; (3) on the substance dissolved in the liquid; (4) on the nature of the liquid.

123. Influence of pressure upon the boiling point. It may be easily shewn, by an arrangement like that of Figures 1 and 2, that the elastic force of vapour during ebullition is equal to the external pressure, for it will be found that the level of the liquid is the same on both sides of the gauge. We see now what takes place when a liquid is heated in the open air. Its temperature will continue to rise until that point for which the corresponding vapour tension is equal to the external atmospheric pressure. The temperature of the boiling point will thus be low when the pressure of the air is low, and high when this is high. The following experiments will illustrate the effect of pressure.

First experiment.—Let a flask half filled with water be boiled until all the air has been driven out of the upper part of it, which is filled with steam instead. If it now be corked tightly and inverted, it will very soon cease boiling; but if cold water be poured upon it ebullition will commence anew: the reason being that the cold water by condensing the vapour with which the upper part of the flask is filled withdraws the pressure from the water, which is thus enabled to boil at a comparatively low temperature.

Second experiment.—Put a vessel containing ether under the receiver of an air-pump. Exhaust the receiver, and the ether will begin to boil at the ordinary temperature.

It follows from these experiments that at the top of a lofty mountain, where the pressure of the atmosphere is much diminished, the temperature of the boiling point of water will be much reduced. At the top of Mont Blanc, for example, water boils at about 185° Fahr. The temperature of boiling water at high elevations is often too low for culinary purposes, and those who live in such places are therefore compelled to heat water in a closed vessel under a pressure greater than that of the atmosphere in order to prepare their food.

This is done by means of an apparatus invented by Papin, a French physician, and which bears the name of Papin's Digester. It consists simply of a strong closed vessel to contain the water to which heat is applied. When the pressure rises too high the vapour escapes by means of a safety-valve. There is thus a limit depending on the strength of the vessel, beyond which the pressure and temperature cannot mount, but this limit is sufficiently high to permit of the contained water doing great service in culinary operations. This apparatus is often used at the level of the sea, since water is much more efficient in extracting gelatine from bones at a high temperature than at the ordinary boiling point.

Boiling-point thermometers are sometimes used for indicating, by means of the temperature of ebullition, the pressure of the air, and thus determining the heights of mountains. Such instruments perform the part of a barometer, while they are more portable. Their scale embraces a temperature range generally extending only from about 30° below 212° to a few degrees above this point; it is thus very open, and the temperature of the boiling point may be very accurately observed. Mountain thermometers are accompanied by an apparatus similar to that of Fig. 1, devised by Regnault, and fitted in this case with telescopic joints, in order to make it easily portable.

124. Influence of the nature of the vessel upon the boiling point. Gay Lussac was the first to observe that water has a higher boiling point in a glass vessel than in a metal one. He attributed this to the adherence of the molecules of water to the glass. M. Marcet and others have since made many experiments on this subject. It is found as the result of these that the boiling point of water in a glass vessel under the pressure of 760 millimètres may be raised as high as 102°C. If the interior of the vessel be varnished with shell-lac the temperature may even rise to 105°C before the water begins to boil : ebullition will then take place in bursts, each burst causing the temperature to fall. If, however, iron filings be dropped into the glass vessel, the temperature of the boiling point is lowered ; and if the vessel itself instead of being glass be made of metal, the temperature is reduced nearly to 100°C. On the other hand, the temperature of the vapour arising from the water is as nearly as possible the same in all these cases.

Hence we see that while the temperature of the vapour remains constant, that of the liquid varies according to the nature of the vessel; we ought also to state that in all cases the temperature of the vapour of water is below that of boiling water.

125. Influence of substances dissolved upon the boiling point. Magnus, Marcet, and others have made experiments on saline solutions of different kinds and strengths, from which it appears that the general effect of the salt is to raise the temperature of ebullition. In this _case also (just as in the case of pure water), the temperature is highest in glass vessels and lowest in metallic ones. According to these experiments the salt has the effect of raising the temperature of the vapour as well as that of the liquid. Regnault, who has investigated this subject, concludes that the vapour is at first in temperature equilibrium with the boiling solution, but that it is quickly cooled, so that the results obtained by Rudberg, who found that the vapour of a solution possesses the same temperature as if it were disengaged from pure water at the same pressure, may be considered correct. In practice the temperature of the vapour of moderately pure water in an apparatus similar to that of Fig. 1 may be considered to be regulated entirely by the atmospheric pressure.

126. Influence of air dissolved upon the boiling point. Magnus had made the observation that if water could be boiled in a vessel formed as it were of water itself, or in a vessel the sides of which would retain the water everywhere with the same force as that which its particles exert upon each other, we should then know the true boiling point of water, and he calculated that under such circumstances water would not boil until about 105°C, so that the difference between the elastic force of vapour at this temperature and that due to 100°, or about one-fifth of an atmosphere, is the measure of the cohesive force of the particles of water.

M. Donny was afterwards led to conclude that the boiling point of perfectly pure water is considerably above that determined by Magnus, and that the cohesion of the particles is very great. By depriving the water of air as far as possible by long continued boiling and by enclosing it in a peculiarly shaped vessel, he was able to raise its temperature to 135°C without ebullition, and even higher temperatures have since been obtained. Mr. Grove has recently made experiments on this subject, and has found that even after water has been long boiled it is not quite deprived of all traces of nitrogen; and he has gone the length of saying that no one yet has seen the phenomenon of *pure water* boiling, that is, of the disruption of the liquid particles of the oxy-hydrogen compound, so as to produce vapour, which will condense into water, leaving behind no permanent gas.

127. Influence of the nature of the liquid upon the boiling point. Some liquids, such as ether and sulphurous acid, have very low boiling points, while others, such as mercury, have very high ones. The following table of boiling points and specific gravities has been constructed by Dr. W. A. Miller, and is derived chiefly from the labours of Pierre and Kopp.

Table of boiling points and specific gravities of liquids.

Name of Substance.	Boiling point, Fahr.	Specific gravity at 32° Fahr.	Observer.
Sulphurous anhydride	17.6	....	Pierre
Chloride of ethyle........	51.9	0.9214	,,
Bromide of methyle	55.5	1.6644	,,
Aldehyde	69.4	0.8009	Kopp
Formiate of methyle	92.1	0.9984	,,
Ether....................	94.8	0.7365	,,
Bromide of ethyle........	105.8	1.4733	Pierre
Iodide of methyle	111.4	2.1992	,,
Bisulphide of carbon	118.5	1.2931	,,
Formic ether............	127.7	0.9357	,,
Acetone..................	133.3	0.8144	Kopp
Acetate of methyle	133.3	0.9562	,,
Chloride of silicon........	138.2	1.5237	Pierre
Bromine.................	145.4	3.1872	,,
Wood-spirit	149.9	0.8179	Kopp
Iodide of ethyle..........	158.5	1.9755	Pierre
Acetic ether	164.9	0.9069	,,
Alcohol..................	173.1	0.8151	,,
Terchloride of phosphorus..	173.4	1.6162	,,
Benzole	176.8	0.8991	Kopp
Dutch liquid	184.7	1.2803	Pierre
Butyrate of methyle	204.6	0.9209	Kopp
Water	212.0	1.0000	,,
Formic acid	221.5	....	,,
Butyric ether............	238.8	0.9041	,,
Perchloride of tin	240.2	2.2671	Pierre

Name of Substance.	Boiling point, Fahr.	Specific gravity at 32° Fahr.	Observer.
Valerate of methyle	241.1	0.9015	Kopp
Acetic acid	243.1	......	,,
Fousel oil	269.8	0.8271	Pierre
Bromide of ethylene	270.9	......	,,
Terchloride of arsenic ...	273.0	2.2050	,,
Perchloride of titanium....	276.6	1.7609	,,
Bromide of silicon	308.0	2.8128	,,
Butyric acid	314.6	0.9886	Kopp
Sulphurous ether	320.0	1.1063	Pierre
Terbromide of phosphorus	347.5	2.9249	,,
Sulphuric acid	640.0	1.8540	Marignac
Mercury	662.0	13.5960	Regnault

Kopp, as far back as 1841, pointed out that in analogous compounds the same difference of chemical composition frequently involves the same difference of boiling points, and he has more particularly endeavoured to shew that in a very extensive series of compounds (alcohols, acids, and compound ethers) the elementary difference $C H^2$ (new notation) is attended by a difference of 19°C in the boiling point. Kopp has also made comparisons of the specific volumes $\left(\text{sp. vol.} = \dfrac{\text{atomic weight}}{\text{sp. gravity}}\right)$ of different liquids, and finds that when these are compared at the respective boiling points of the liquids, or points of similar vapour tension, one arrives at very simple results.

128. Leidenfrost's Phenomenon. Spheroidal state. Leidenfrost was the first who scientifically examined the curious phenomenon which bears his name. He found that if a drop of water or other liquid be thrown upon a surface of high temperature, the liquid does not adhere to the surface but forms an ellipsoidal mass, which, if the heat be kept up, oscillates and moves about, evaporating meanwhile without boiling.

This phenomenon, which has been named the caloric paradox, has of late years been the subject of much attention, and experiments have been contrived with the view of rendering its peculiarities as prominent as possible. Thus, for instance, M. Boutigny poured liquid sulphurous acid upon a platinum capsule heated to a white heat, and although this liquid ordinarily boils at a very low temperature there was no appearance of ebullition and the rate of evaporation was very slow. In this state some water poured into the sulphurous acid was instantly frozen. Faraday went even further, and by pouring on a red hot platinum capsule some ether and solid carbonic acid he formed a spheroidal mass which evaporated very slowly, but nevertheless solidified some mercury brought into contact with it.

In connexion with these experiments we may remark the very singular fact, that the skin of the hand, if slightly moistened, may be brought into contact with molten metal at a very high temperature without being sensibly affected or injured in the least. This may explain some of the tales which have reached us from the middle ages, in which accused persons went through the ordeal of fire with impunity.

129. The following are the experimental laws of this phenomenon.

1. It has been found by M. Boutigny that the lowest temperature of the hot surface capable of producing this state varies with the liquid, being higher for liquids of high boiling points. M. Marchand has shewn that it also varies with the temperature of the projected liquid and with the nature of the surface.

2. The spheroid seems not to touch the surface. If this surface be a plane, M. Boutigny has found that the eye may see the light of a taper through the space between the liquid and the surface. He has also found that a drop of nitric acid has in this state no action on a silver or copper surface, nor one of dilute sulphuric acid on iron or zinc. Professor Poggendorff has also shewn that if the hot plate be metallic and connected with one pole of a galvanic

battery, while the spheroid is connected with the other, no current will pass; thereby proving the interruption of contact between the spheroid and the plate.

3. M. Boutigny and M. Boutan have shewn that liquids in the spheroidal state remain at a temperature inferior to that of ebullition.

130. An experiment made by M. Buff will serve to connect together the second and third of these experimental laws, and to shew their dependence on one another. He placed a clean silver spoon filled with water over a lamp, and found that it might be held by the hand with impunity, until the water was all vaporised; the reason being that the heat which entered the spoon was transferred to the water in contact with it, and hence no part of the spoon had a higher temperature than 212°. There was in fact equilibrium of temperature between the spoon and the water. He then covered the inside of the spoon with a coating which was not moistened by water, and found that the spoon became very hot before the water began to boil. When however the coating was capable of being moistened by water the result was the same as with the clean spoon. We see from this that the establishment of ordinary thermic equilibrium in such a case depends upon the liquid moistening the spoon, and thus being brought into intimate contact with it. We have thus also a very simple explanation of the spheroidal condition; for we have seen that the existence of this state at a given temperature depends, among other things, on the nature of the plate, and Buff's experiment shews us that any coating which diminishes the adhesive force of the liquid to the plate is favourable to the production of this phenomenon. These facts, along with Boutigny's observation of a want of contact between the liquid and the plate, enable us to connect the separation between the two surfaces with the very small transmission of heat which forms the leading feature of this phenomenon. There is probably, however, a layer of vapour between the two surfaces.

131. Vaporization of liquids at a very high temperature and in a limited space. When a liquid is enclosed within a limited space, and heat is applied, each increment of heat produces a certain quantity of vapour, which thus accumulates, and by its pressure prevents the liquid from boiling, the temperature of the liquid meanwhile rising considerably above its ordinary boiling point. M. Cagniard de la Tour pushed his observation of this process to an extreme limit by enclosing certain liquids in a space not much larger than their own volume. On the application of heat he found that the liquids at a certain temperature passed completely and instantaneously into the state of vapour. The apparatus which he employed for this experiment had within it some atmospheric air shut out from the liquid by a drop of mercury. As the liquid became heated its vapour pushed the mercury before it along a tube, compressing, by this means, the air into a very small volume. Thus, if the volume finally occupied by the air was one-fiftieth of that which it would have filled under the ordinary pressure, it might be concluded that the pressure was equal to fifty atmospheres, and so on. M. Cagniard de la Tour made experiments on ether, alcohol, bisulphide of carbon, and water, and obtained the results given in the following table.

Nature of liquid.	Pressure in atmospheres.	The whole became gaseous at temperature (Fahr.)
Ether	37.5	369.5
Alcohol	119.0	497.7
Bisulphide of carbon .	66.5	504.5
Water	......	773.0

There was considerable difficulty in performing the experiment with water, as at the high temperature to which it was raised its power of dissolving glass was very great.

It thus appears that at a certain temperature a liquid under the pressure of its own vapour becomes changed into a gas. Faraday has imagined that at this temperature, or one a little higher, no pressure that we are likely to produce would convert the gas into a liquid, and he also thinks that the temperature of 166° Fahr. below zero is probably above this limiting point for the gases oxygen, hydrogen, and nitrogen; so that, apply what pressure we may, we shall not be able to liquefy these gases unless we can at the same time produce intense cold.

Dr. Andrews has recently noticed that when a vessel containing liquid carbonic acid is raised to 88° Fahr. the surface of demarcation between the liquid and gas becomes gradually fainter, loses its curvature, and at last disappears *. The space is then occupied by a homogeneous fluid, which exhibits, when the pressure is suddenly diminished or the temperature slightly lowered, an appearance of moving or flickering striæ throughout its entire mass. At temperatures above 88° no apparent liquefaction of carbonic acid could be effected even under the pressure of 300 or 400 atmospheres. He obtained similar results with nitrous oxide.

If we consider capillary curvature to be one of the characteristics of a liquid, the gradual diminution of curvature in the foregoing experiment would seem to imply a gradual transition from the liquid to the gaseous state, and to lead to the belief that there may be an intermediate condition of matter between the liquid and the gaseous, just as we have in a viscous fluid a link between a solid and a liquid.

132. Sublimation. There are some solids which under ordinary circumstances appear to assume the gaseous state at once instead of passing through the intermediate state of liquidity. Of these arsenic and solid carbonic acid are

---

* A similar change of curvature has been noticed for other liquids by Wolf, and also by Drion.

examples. It is well known too that snow slowly evaporates, and thus to some extent appears to assume the gaseous form, even although the temperature is decidedly below that of the melting point of ice.

Again, some substances, such as chalk, are decomposed before fusion, the gaseous element going off. Nevertheless it has been found that if chalk be heated under intense pressure it melts and assumes the appearance of marble when it becomes solid.

CONDENSATION OF VAPOURS AND GASES.

133. Distillation, or the condensation of vapours. This process has already been described in Art. 117.

134. Condensation of gases. Sometimes gases are compelled to assume the liquid form by their affinity for some liquid. Thus, for instance, if ammoniacal gas is brought into contact with water it is immediately dissolved. The same result takes place with hydrochloric acid and other gases. This condensation of gas renders sensible a large quantity of latent heat, and it is therefore necessary to keep the vessel in which it takes place surrounded by cold water.

It is much more difficult to condense gases by themselves and without the aid of a chemical solvent. The auxiliaries employed in this condensation are, as might be imagined, pressure and cold. A number of gases have yielded to the joint effect of these two agents, but there are nevertheless six substances which we have not yet been able to obtain either in the liquid or the solid form—these are oxygen, hydrogen, nitrogen, nitric oxide, carbonic oxide, and marsh gas.

Faraday was one of the first who succeeded in liquefying gases by the joint application of cold and pressure. Others have since joined in these attempts, and carbonic acid gas is now condensed in large quantities, forming in this shape a very convenient source of cold. An instrument invented by Thilorier, somewhat modified, is very much used for the purpose of liquefying this gas—it acts on the following principle :—The gas is generated in a strong iron vessel called the *generator*, into which the materials necessary for making the gas are put. This generator is connected with an equally strong iron vessel called the *receiver*, which is kept cool, and when sufficient gas has been generated it condenses in the receiver. The two vessels are now separated and a fresh charge introduced into the generator, and the gas is condensed in the receiver as before, until at last a large quantity of liquefied gas has been obtained.

Fig. 27.

It will be seen from Fig. 27 that in the interior of the receiver there is a tube which descends below the level of the liquid. When the cock is opened the pressure of the gas drives the liquid with great force up the tube and out through the fine nozzle in which it terminates.

The liquid as it issues evaporates with such rapidity that part of it is frozen, and if on its way out it be made to play into a cylindrical box the solidified gas may be collected in the form of a snow-white powder. This powder evaporates very slowly, and may therefore by proper precautions be preserved for a considerable length of time. It may also be handled with impunity, and may even be laid upon the tongue without a disagreeable sensation of cold being produced, although the temperature of the solid is extremely low, perhaps even — 106° Fahr. The reason of this absence of the feeling of cold is want of contact between the two. If·however this solid acid be mixed with ether, for which it has a great attraction, the mixture will now be in contact with the containing vessel, and will be felt to be intensely cold, while a rapid evaporation of carbonic acid will take place, thereby preserving the low temperature by drawing off the heat.

By means of a mixture of this description from 20 to 30 pounds of mercury may readily be frozen. If the bath of carbonic acid and ether be placed in vacuo the evaporation is accelerated, and a still greater degree of cold is produced. Faraday by this means has reached the temperature — 166° Fahr. A still lower temperature has been obtained by Natterer, who by means of a bath of liquid nitrous oxide and bisulphide of carbon in vacuo has reached the temperature — 220° Fahr.

ELASTIC FORCE AND DENSITY OF VAPOURS AND GASES.

135. Before discussing the laws which regulate the elastic force of gases and vapours we must first of all bear in mind what takes place when we condense a gas or vapour into smaller volume. Let us suppose this condensation to be performed slowly and at a constant temperature. As it proceeds the pressure will of course increase, until at last, if the gas be condensable, liquid will begin to make its appearance. The pressure and density have now attained the greatest possible value which they can have for this temperature and for this kind of gas, and if the condensation be pushed further the only result will be the formation of more liquid, but without a further increase of pressure. Our inquiry must therefore be divided into two parts. We must consider, in the first place, the laws which regulate the pressure of gas or vapour not in contact with the liquid which produces it; and, secondly, those which regulate the pressure of gas or vapour in contact with its own liquid.

136. Pressure of gas or vapour not in contact with its own liquid. We have already had occasion (Chap. IV. Art. 60) to advert to Boyle's law, which gives the relation between the pressure and volume of a gas, the temperature remaining constant, and we have seen that in this case the pressure varies inversely as the volume. We have also seen (Art. 62) that Gay Lussac was the first to state the true connexion between the volume and temperature of a gas of which the pressure remains constant, and that this law may be expressed as follows :—

Let V denote the volume of a gas under given pressure at the temperature $0°$C, then $V(1 + at)$ will be its volume under the same pressure at the temperature $t°$C, where $a = .00367$ nearly.

Neither of these laws is however absolutely correct under all circumstances. With regard to Gay Lussac's law it has been found by Regnault, as we have already seen (Art. 66), that it only holds absolutely in the case of a perfect gas; that is, of a gas very far removed from its point of maximum density; and in like manner Boyle's law ceases to be perfectly true when this same point is approached, for the density is then found to increase more rapidly than the pressure. But if the gas be sufficiently attenuated it is probable that both of these laws are exactly true, and in this case it is very easy to solve all problems in which it is sought to connect the pressure of a gas with its temperature and volume.

Thus, let $V_{(p, t)}$ denote the volume occupied by a gas at pressure p and temperature $t°$C, and let it be required to find the volume of this gas at pressure p' and temperature $t°$.

Calling $V_{(p, 0)}$ the volume at pressure p and temperature $0°$C, we find by Gay Lussac's law,

$$V_{(p, t)} = V_{(p, 0)}\{1 + at\}; \qquad \therefore \quad V_{(p, 0)} = \frac{V_{(p, t)}}{1 + at}.$$

Also, by the same law combined with that of Boyle, we find,

$$V_{(p', t)} = V_{(p, 0)}\{1 + at'\}\frac{p}{p'};$$

and finally, substituting for $V_{(p,\,o)}$ its equivalent $\dfrac{V_{(p,\,t)}}{1+at}$, we find

$$V_{(p',\,t')} = V_{(p,\,t)}\,\frac{1+at'}{1+at}\cdot\frac{p}{p'}\,.$$

Example. Let the volume of a gas be 5 cubic feet at the pressure of 30 inches and at 15° C, what will be its volume at the pressure of 35 inches and at 72°C?

Here we have

$$V_{(p,\,t)} = 5,\quad p = 30,\quad p' = 35,\quad t = 15°,\quad t' = 72°;$$

hence

$$V_{(p',\,t')} = 5 \times \frac{1+.00367\times 72}{1+.00367\times 15} \times \frac{30}{35} = 5.1355 \text{ cubic feet.}$$

Other problems of a similar kind will easily suggest themselves.

137. Pressure of gas or vapour in contact with its own liquid. Since a gas or vapour in contact with its own liquid always possesses the greatest pressure possible at the temperature, there is consequently only one such pressure corresponding to each temperature; and hence for a given substance this maximum pressure will only vary when the temperature is made to vary, and it will vary in such a manner that the higher the temperature the greater the corresponding maximum pressure (Art. 112).

In mathematical language, the pressure of gas in contact with its liquid will be a function of the temperature; and what we wish to know is the nature of this function for each substance; that is to say, the relationship in each case subsisting between such pressure and temperature. As this has been most extensively and accurately investigated for the vapour of water we shall commence with it.

138. Pressure of aqueous vapour. Many experimentalists have engaged in this research, and yet it is only lately that great exactness has been obtained.

In 1823 the subject was referred to a Commission of the Academy of Paris, and the experiments undertaken in consequence were made by MM. Dulong and Arago.

The object of these was to determine the pressure of the vapour of water at high temperatures, and the experiments ranged between 1 and 24 atmospheres of pressure and between the temperatures 100° and 224° C.

About the same time the same subject was taken up by a Committee of the Franklin Institute of Pennsylvania, their experiments ranging from 1 to 10 atmospheres.

The apparatus of the French Commission consisted of a manometer, or pressure measurer, having a detached column of atmospheric air cut off by mercury, which by its volume served to denote the pressure; the Commission having previously ascertained by direct experiment the correctness of Boyle's law for air up to a pressure of 27 atmospheres.

Very nearly the same apparatus was employed by the American Committee. Unfortunately, however, there was a considerable difference between the results of the two investigations. One cause of this discrepancy may have been the employment of mercurial thermometers composed of different kinds of glass, since we have seen (Art. 25) that at high temperatures the indications of two instruments of this kind, both accurately graduated but made of different kinds of glass, will not agree together. On this account Regnault resolved to make a full set of experiments on the subject, extending to high pressures but also embracing low ones, and he has recently completed these with very satisfactory results.

139. Regnault divides his research into three parts.

The first of these relates to his experiments on the pressure of aqueous vapour at low temperatures; that is to say, from −32° to +50°C.

The second part comprehends all his experiments at higher temperatures, or from 50° to 230°C.

Finally, in his third part he treats of the *graphic representation* of his experiments, and discusses various *formulæ of interpolation.*

In the first place, as regards his experiments at low temperatures, Regnault employed various methods, and even repeated those made use of by former experimentalists, in order, as he tells us, to see if when used with proper precautions they would all lead to the same result; and if this be not the case, to point out by direct experiment the causes of error in the defective methods.

The general plan underlying the various methods made use of by him in this branch of his investigation, is that of comparing together two barometers placed side by side, one having a dry vacuum chamber, and the other a chamber filled with the vapour of water at a determinate temperature; the difference between the heights of the two giving the tension of aqueous vapour at the temperature of the experiment. He found that when sufficient precautions were adopted the various methods employed by him agreed together very well.

140. In the second part of his research, which had reference to high temperatures, Regnault employed another kind of apparatus, founded on the principle that the vapour of water boiling in a large space filled with air has a tension equal to the atmospheric pressure.

In order to secure all the advantages of this method Regnault constructed the following apparatus. A strong retort *A* (Fig. 28) contains the water to be heated, and has arrangements for holding four mercurial thermometers, two of them being plunged in the water, and two in the vapour of water: these arrangements are such that the bulbs of the thermometers are not exposed to the pressure of the vapour. In order to ensure correctness Regnault employed an air thermometer in addition to the mercurial ones. The retort A is connected by means of a long neck CC with a balloon or reservoir B, into which air may be pumped or

Fig. 28.

from which it may be extracted, so that the internal pressure of the air may be regulated at pleasure. The balloon is enclosed in water of the temperature of the surrounding medium, by which means change of pressure due to change of temperature of the balloon is avoided. The neck CC, connecting the balloon B with the retort, is kept cool by a stream of water constantly flowing through a cylinder which surrounds it. By this means the vapour is condensed as fast as it is formed, and trickles back into the retort, its pressure being equal to that of the artificial atmosphere in B.

It only remains to state that the air of the balloon B communicates with one column of a manometer M, the other column being open to the atmosphere.   It is evident from the arrangement in the figure that the pressure of air in B is equal to that of the external atmosphere *plus or minus* (as the case may be) the pressure of a column of mercury equal in length to the difference between the levels of this fluid in the two limbs of the manometer.   By this method Regnault was enabled to measure accurately the temperature of the vapour, and also to keep the pressure of the artificial atmosphere (and in consequence the temperature of ebullition) very nearly constant ; lastly, this pressure might be accurately measured by means of the attached manometer.

141. The third part of Regnault's memoir relates to the *graphic construction* of his experiments, and to *formulæ of interpolation.*   The following considerations will suffice to shew the necessity for this.

There are two kinds of errors which make their appearance in physical research.   The first of these is due to a defect in the process employed, or to a defect of the observer. Thus in the particular problem under consideration, namely, that of finding the maximum pressure of aqueous vapour corresponding to a given temperature, the methods employed by the earlier observers were defective to some degree.   But the course pursued by Regnault in his investigation got rid of this source of error to a very great extent ; for he worked out the various methods of his predecessors after having discovered and corrected their defects, and he then found that the results obtained agreed very well together.   We may therefore imagine that in his experiments errors due to defective apparatus or observation have been to a very great extent eliminated.   There is however another description of error which cannot be entirely got rid of.   If, for instance, we make the same observation with the same instrument under the same conditions several times in succession, we shall find that none of the results obtained agree exactly together, although they all lie within a very narrow range. Under these circumstances men of science are agreed upon a certain mathematical treatment, which when applied to a set of observations obtains the best result; and it will always be found that results thus obtained from sets of observations agree together much better than the results of individual observations.

We see now the distinction between the two classes of errors. The one is an error of apparatus or observer that affects all the observations alike, and which cannot be got rid of by multiplying observations; the other is an error which will manifest itself with the most perfect instruments, but which may be got rid of by multiplying observations.

Let us now return to the case in hand, and suppose that Regnault had found a number of values for the pressure of aqueous vapour at 100°C, all slightly different from one another; having previously rendered his apparatus and method of observing as accurate as he could, he would then group them together so as to obtain the most probable result. The same thing will apply to an observation at any other temperature, so that at last we may suppose that the observer has obtained the most probable values of the pressure of aqueous vapour at the various temperatures of experiment. These results are not *absolutely* free from either of the two kinds of error we have described, but only as nearly free as he can get them. It will however be borne in mind that in this process, as we have described it, each different temperature is considered apart by itself, and the result obtained gives the most probable value of the pressure for any given temperature, the observations for this temperature being considered as quite unconnected with those for any other temperature. The question then arises, can we combine together and compare the various values thus obtained for different temperatures so as to make them mutually correct each other's errors? This is to a great extent accomplished by the method of graphic representation.

Let us, for instance, reckon the temperatures along a line of abscissæ, after the manner represented in the figure, and raise at the various temperatures of experiment ordinates proportional to the observed pressures; and finally, connect the extremities of our ordinates together by a line. We shall find that this line, while it approaches very nearly to a regular curve, has yet a great many sinuosities, and a little considera- tion will convince us that these irregularities do not denote any law of nature, but are merely due to the residual error in our observations; and that the most probable line de- noting the true law of nature, which we are seeking, will be a curve passing midway between these points and leaving

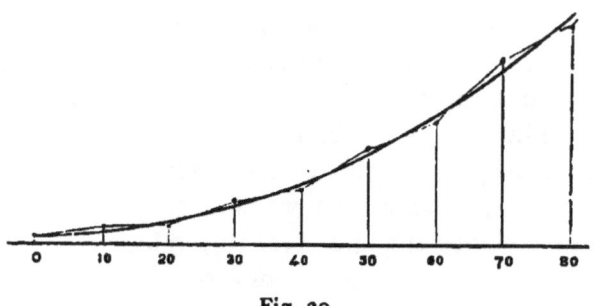

| o | 10 | 20 | 30 | 40 | 50 | 60 | 70 | 80 |

Fig. 29.

as many above it as below. Now suppose that when we have traced such a curve the eye yet detects an abnormal bend of considerable extent at some region where we can imagine no natural cause for any deviation in the regular sweep of the curve, then we may very justly suspect that some error has crept into our determinations at that region, and we ought, if possible, to repeat our experiments.

We thus see the value of this process in detecting errors,

and it is one which is very generally employed by experimentalists.

In the present case, Regnault, having constructed such a curve with great care, adopted it as the most probable representation of the law connecting together the pressures and temperatures of aqueous vapour, as shewn by the experiments which he had made.

142. After we have constructed a curve of this kind, something more yet remains to be done in order to make the experiments as serviceable as possible. For this purpose it is necessary to know the pressure for each exact degree from $-32°$ to $230°$ C, and even for each tenth of a degree throughout part of this range. This may of course be determined at once from the curve by raising ordinates at the points denoting these various temperatures and measuring their lengths with great exactness. In practice, however, another method is preferred. Our observations have furnished us with a curve, but we do not know the exact equation between the abscissæ and ordinates which represent this curve ; if we knew this equation we might at once find the ordinate corresponding to any abscissa, that is to say, the pressure corresponding to any temperature. But while we are ignorant of the exact equation we may try different equations, and we shall no doubt be able to find formulæ that will represent the progress of the curve with very great exactness, one formula suiting one part best and another another part. And thus by means of these, which are called formulæ of interpolation, we may readily find the value of the pressure corresponding to each exact degree and decimal of a degree between the limits of the experimental research.

143. Correction for latitude and height above sea level. In the results of Regnault's experiments the elastic force is expressed in the length of a column of pure mercury at 0°C at the latitude of Paris ($48°\ 50'$), and at the height of

60 mètres above the level of the sea which it will sustain. But we have already remarked (Art. 21) that the absolute pressure of a column of mercury of given length varies with the latitude, and we may add that it varies, although but slightly, with the height of the place of observation above sea level; in fact its absolute pressure varies with the force of gravity at the place of experiment. If, therefore, Regnault had made his experiments at another latitude and height he would have obtained lengths of the mercurial column to denote his pressures different from those which he obtained in Paris.

The following is the formula by means of which the results at one latitude and height are made comparable with those at another. Let g denote the intensity of gravity at the latitude $45°$ and at the level of the sea, R the mean radius of the earth = 6366198 mètres = 20886852 feet, also let λ' denote the latitude of the place of observation, and h' the height above the level of the sea; then if g' denote the intensity of gravity at this locality, we have—

$$g' = g \left\{ 1 - .002837 \cos 2\lambda' \right\} \frac{R^2}{(R + h')^2}.$$

Hence the force of gravity at Paris (*latitude* 48° 50′) at the height of 60 mètres above the level of the sea will be denoted by

$$g \left\{ 1 - .002837 \cos 2(48° 50') \right\} \frac{(6366198)^2}{(6366258)^2} = g \times 1.00036.$$

Also the force of gravity at Greenwich, near London (*latitude* 51° 28′), at the level of the sea = $g \times 1.000635$.

We see now that the pressure denoted by 760 millimètres or 29.922 inches of mercury at 0°C at Paris will correspond to $29.922 \times \dfrac{1.00036}{1.000635} = 29.914$ inches of mercury at 32° Fahr. at London, and this is in accordance with what we have already stated (Art. 21).

If, therefore, we adhere to centigrade degrees it is very easy to convert Regnault's table into one expressing the pressure of vapour at any temperature in inches of mercury at o°C at the place of observation, but if we use degrees Fahrenheit we shall find that Regnault's tables do not give us the pressure at our precise points of temperature, and we shall have to calculate these as Regnault himself did, by adapting his formulæ of interpolation to our case. In this adaptation it must be borne in mind that 212° Fahr. is not *exactly* 100°C.

The Rev. Robert Dixon, in his work on Heat, has made the requisite adaptation with great care, and we cannot do better than present to our readers in an abbreviated form the tables he has calculated.

They are adapted to the latitude 53° 21′, which will answer very well for any station in Great Britain or Ireland.

These tables, along with an abbreviation of Regnault's table, will be found at the end of this work; they comprise—

Table I. Shewing the elastic force of aqueous vapour in inches of mercury at the latitude 53° 21′ for each degree Fahr. from − 30° to 432°.

Table II. Shewing the elastic force of aqueous vapour in inches of mercury at the same latitude from 0° to 100° Fahr. for every two-tenths of a degree.

Table III. Shewing the elastic force of aqueous vapour in millimètres of mercury at the latitude of Paris (48° 50′) for each degree Centigrade from − 32°C to + 230°C.

144. Pressure of other vapours. Signor Avagadro and M. Regnault have both determined the tension of the vapour of mercury at various temperatures, but their results can only be considered an approximation. Regnault has also determined the tension of other vapours at various temperatures, and the following table gives the results of some of his experiments.

Pressure of vapour in millimètres of mercury.

Temp. Cent.	Alcohol.	Ether.	Sulphuret of Carbon.	Chloroform.
−20	3.34	68.90	47.30	. . .
−15	5.10	89.31	61.64	. . .
−10	6.47	114.72	79.44	. . .
− 5	9.09	146.06	101.29	. . .
0	12.70	184.39	127.91	. . .
+ 5	17.62	230.89	160.01	. . .
10	24.23	286.83	198.46	. . .
15	32.98	353.62	244.13	
20	44.46	432.78	298.03	160.47
25	59.37	525.93	361.13	200.18
30	78.52	634.80	434.62	247.51
35	102.91	761.20	519.66	303.49
40	133.69	907.04	617.53	369.26
45	172.18	1074.15	729.53	446.01
50	219.90	1264.83	857.07	535.05
55	278.59	1481.06	1001.57	637.71
60	350.21	1725.01	1164.51	755.44
65	436.90	1998.87	1347.52	889.72
70	541.15	2304.90	1552.09	1042.11
75	665.54	2645.41	1779.88	1214.20
80	812.91	3022.79	2032.53	1407.64
85	986.40	3439.53	2311.70	1624.10
90	1189.30	3898.26	2619.08	1865.22
95	1425.13	4401.81	2966.34	2132.85
100	1697.55	4953.30	3325.15	2428.54
105	2010.38	5556.23	3727.19	2754.03
110	2367.64	6214.63	4164.06	3110.99
115	2773.40	6933.26	4637.41	3501.03
120	3231.73	7719.20	5148.79	3925.74

145. The change of condition from liquid to solid is without influence on vapour tension. From experiments made by Gay Lussac and Regnault it would appear that *the passage of a substance from the liquid to the solid state is without influence upon the vapour densities*, so that in the curve which embodies M. Regnault's observations on the elasticity of aqueous vapour there is no break at the freezing point.

146. Dalton's hypothesis regarding vapour tensions. Dalton supposed that the tensions of all vapours would be equal at equal distances from their respective boiling points. Thus, for example, water boils at 212° Fahr. and alcohol at 173°. Of course at these temperatures the tension of both vapours is equal, being represented by one atmosphere, or 30 inches of mercury. According to Dalton the tensions of these two vapours will also be equal at

$$212 - 10 = 202° \text{ and } 173 - 10 = 163°.$$

This hypothesis of Dalton does not generally hold, but for short distances on either side of the boiling point it holds approximately in a large number of instances.

147. Density of gases and vapours. When substances are compared together in the state of gas at the same temperature and pressure, a very simple relation is found to subsist between their density and their combining chemical equivalent. This was first discovered by Gay Lussac, who found that *when gas or vapours combine together, the volumes in which they combine bear a very simple ratio to one another*. The following table, kindly furnished by Dr. Williamson, will serve to illustrate this law, which is generally called the law of volumes. The new notation is used.

Vapour volume of compounds.		Vapour volume of elements liberated from them.
Hydrochloric acid	(H Cl) 2 vols. ...	1 vol. hydrogen + 1 vol. chlorine.
Hydrobromic acid	(H Br) 2 vols. ...	1 vol. hydrogen + 1 vol. bromine.
Hydriodic acid	(H I) 2 vols. ...	1 vol. hydrogen + 1 vol. iodine.
Steam	(H^2O) 2 vols. ..	2 vols. hydrogen + 1 vol. oxygen.
Ammonia	(N H^3) 2 vols. ...	1 vol. nitrogen + 3 vols. hydrogen.

We see from this table that equal volumes of chlorine and hydrogen, for instance, combine together without change of volume to form hydrochloric acid gas, which contains one atom of hydrogen united to one of chlorine. Equal volumes of chlorine and hydrogen contain therefore an equal number of atoms of these elements.

There are thus three laws which bear immediately upon the density of gases. 1. The above law of volumes, in which the density of a gas at a *given temperature and pressure* is shewn to depend upon its chemical constitution; 2. Boyle's law, in which the density of a gas of a *given constitution and temperature* is shewn to depend upon its pressure; 3. Gay Lussac's law, in which the density of a gas of a *given constitution and at a given pressure* is shewn to depend upon its temperature.

148. Many experiments have been made with a view to determining whether these three laws hold for all gases and vapours, and we shall now very briefly indicate the various methods pursued in these investigations.

In the first place, Gay Lussac's method in his researches consisted in ascertaining the volume occupied by a known weight of liquid when entirely converted into vapour at a certain temperature and pressure.

It is, however, essential to this method that the whole of the liquid should be converted into vapour, and hence it is inapplicable to a gas at its maximum density and in contact with its own liquid. It only applies to these cases when the density is considerably inferior to that of saturation. No doubt the density of saturation might be calculated from an experiment of this kind, if we supposed Boyle's law to hold good; but one great object of such experiments is to determine whether this law holds accurately for gases near their point of saturation.

In order to obviate this objection M. Despretz introduced a method which consists in filling with gas or vapour at different temperatures and pressures a balloon of known weight screwed on the top of a barometer tube.

Afterwards Dumas, in order to experiment upon gases that act upon mercury, and to obtain results at high temperatures, used a glass balloon, which he arranged so as to be filled with the vapour of a liquid at a temperature 20° or 30° above the boiling point of the liquid, and under the ordinary atmospheric pressure.

More lately Regnault has made several series of experiments on this subject.

1. His first series was on the density of aqueous vapour *in vacuo* at the temperature of boiling water, and under a pressure not exceeding half an atmosphere, and he found that both Boyle's and Gay Lussac's laws were applicable within the limits of his experiments, but when the pressure approached more nearly to its maximum, he found that the density increased more rapidly than the elastic force.

2. His second series was on the density of aqueous vapour *in vacuo* at temperatures not very far removed from that of the surrounding medium, and from these he concludes that the density of aqueous vapours in vacuo and under feeble pressures may be calculated according to Boyle's law, provided that the fraction of saturation does not exceed 0.8, but that this density is notably greater when we approach more nearly to the state of saturation. He adds, however, that this latter circumstance may be owing to one or both of two causes; either aqueous vapour really suffers an anomalous condensation on approaching its point of saturation, or a portion of the vapour remains condensed on the surface of the glass, and does not assume the aëriform state until the mass of vapour is at some distance from the point of saturation.

3. Regnault has also examined the density of aqueous vapour *in air* at its maximum value for the temperature of experiment between the limits 0° and 25°C, and he concludes that the density of aqueous vapour in air, in a state of saturation and under feeble pressures, may be calculated, without much error, from Boyle's law.

Messrs. Fairbairn and Tate have lately made experiments to determine the density of steam at different temperatures, and to find the law of expansion of superheated steam.

The general plan of their method of ascertaining the density of steam consists in vaporizing a known weight of water in a large glass globe with a stem, of known capacity and devoid of air, and observing the exact temperature at which the whole of the water is just vaporized.

In the following table the authors exhibit the relation between the specific volume, pressure, and temperature of saturated steam as determined from their experiments. Specific volume denotes the number of times the volume of steam exceeds the volume at 39°.1 Fahr. of the water from which it is raised.

Pressure in inches of mercury.	Maximum temperature of saturation. in degrees Fahr	Specific volume of steam.
5.35	136.77	8275.3
8 62	155.33	5333.5
9.45	159.36	4920.2
12.47	170.92	3722.6
12.61	171.48	3715.1
13.62	174.92	3438.1
16.01	182.30	3051.0
18.36	188.30	2623.4
22.88	198.78	2149.5
53.61	242.90	943.1
55.52	244.82	908.0
55.89	245.22	892.5
66.84	255.50	759.4
76.20	263.14	649.2
81.53	267.21	635.3
84.20	269.20	605.7
92.23	274.76	584.4
90.08	273.30	543.2
99.60	279.42	515.0
104.54	282.58	497.2
112.78	287.25	458.3
122.25	292.53	433.1
114.25	288.25	449.6

With regard, in the next place, to superheated steam, the results of these experiments shew that for temperatures within about ten degrees from the maximum temperature of saturation, the rate of expansion on account of heat greatly exceeds that of air, whereas at higher temperatures from this point the rate of expansion approaches that of air, so that as the steam becomes more and more superheated, the coefficient of expansion approaches that of a perfect gas, while at or near the maximum temperature of saturation the coefficient of expansion greatly exceeds that of a perfect gas.

We thus perceive that near their points of saturation gases and vapours would appear to depart both from Boyle's and from Gay Lussac's law, while probably if the pressure under which they exist be far inferior to that of saturation these laws are obeyed.

Generally speaking we may presume that *the three laws to which we have before alluded as regulating gaseous density (namely the law of volumes, Boyle's law, and Gay Lussac's law), only hold accurately in the case of perfect gases.*

149. Regnault has furnished us with the following determination of the weight of a litre of the most important gases.

Weight of one litre (61.02705 cubic inches) of air, oxygen, hydrogen, nitrogen, and carbonic acid gas.

Name of gas.	Density.	Weight at o°C and under the pressure of 760 millimètres of mercury reduced to o°C at the latitude of Paris. (= 29.914 inches of mercury at 32° at London.)
Air	1.0000	1.293187 grammes.
Oxygen	1.1057	1.429802 ,,
Hydrogen......	0.0693	0.089578 ,,
Nitrogen	0.9714	1.256167 ,,
Carbonic acid ..	1.5291	1.977414 ,,

We have also the following densities of vapours.

Air	1.0000	
Vapour of water	0.6235	Gay Lussac and Thenard.
„ alcohol ..	1.6133	Gay Lussac.
„ ether	2.5860	Gay Lussac.

150. Hygrometry. Hygrometry is that branch of science which treats of the state of the air with regard to moisture. As this is one of the elements which form the climate of a place, and as the human body is very much affected by the hygrometric state of the air, the subject is one of much practical importance.

There are several facts regarding the vapour present in the air which it is very desirable to know.

151. One of these is its Tension. Suppose that we were to isolate in a vessel a cubic foot of air, allowing it to remain at its present temperature and pressure, and then to introduce into the vessel containing it a substance which absorbs moisture; the air by this means will be rendered dry, and its tension will be diminished by an amount representing the tension of aqueous vapour present in the air.

It is of importance to know what this tension is, for upon this, among other things, depends the behaviour of the air when it is cooled down. If, for instance, at the higher temperature there be present nearly as much aqueous vapour as the air can contain at that temperature, then if the air be cooled down only a few degrees, some of this vapour will be deposited in the liquid or solid state. The temperature at which this takes place is called the *dew-point.* We thus see that if the tension of vapour in the air at its existing temperature be great the dew-point will be high, but if this tension be small, the dew-point will be low in the thermometric scale.

152. Another object of research is the relative humidity of the air. Of course all substances exposed to the air will be affected by the deposition of moisture when the dew-point is reached, but many substances will be affected long before this takes place; our bodies, for instance, will experience the wetness of the air long before. On the other hand, if the present temperature be far above that of deposition, we pronounce the air dry. It ought here to be observed that the sensation of dryness or wetness does not depend upon the *absolute* amount of aqueous vapour present in one cubic foot of air. For if the temperature be very low, although the air may not contain much aqueous vapour, yet this vapour may approach very nearly to the maximum amount which can be retained at the temperature, and the air will be pronounced wet. But if the very same mixture of air and vapour be heated up many degrees, the vapour will represent only a small fraction of the total amount which can be retained at the higher temperature, and hence it will feel very dry. If this high temperature be produced by a stove, it may even be necessary to place near the stove a vessel containing water in order to increase the amount of aqueous vapour present in the air.

We see now what is meant by the dryness or wetness of the air, and all that remains is to express it numerically. This is done by the conception of *relative humidity*, which may be thus defined. *Relative humidity* is the fraction expressing the ratio between the tension of vapour actually present in the air at a given temperature and the greatest amount of vapour which it can contain at that temperature. The greatest amount, representing complete saturation, is generally reckoned equal to 100, and on this principle 50, 40, 30, &c. will denote that the air contains 50, 40, 30, &c. per cent. of the maximum amount which can be contained at that temperature.

153. The weight of vapour present is another object of

interest. In order to know completely the state of the air, it is necessary to know the weight of vapour present in a given volume of air, and also the entire weight of a given volume of air, or its specific gravity. This last element is necessary on another account, for a body weighed in air is lighter than if weighed in vacuo by the weight of its own bulk of air; in very delicate weighings, therefore, it is necessary to find the exact weight of the air displaced by the body; and in order to obtain this information it is not sufficient to know the temperature and pressure of the air, but we must also know the weight of vapour contained in a given volume of air.

154. Having now mentioned the objects sought in hygrometry, let us proceed to describe shortly the various instruments made use of in this science. We may state at the commencement that there are various means of ascertaining in a general way the dryness or wetness of the air. We may, for instance, use some substance which has a great affinity for water and readily deliquesces. Such a substance, if the air be very dry, will remain a long time comparatively unaffected, but if the air be moist it will rapidly deliquesce. In the next place, various substances have the property of becoming elongated when moist and of contracting again when dry; a hair, for instance, possesses this property, and Saussure has used it in his hair hygroscope. Other bodies, such as catgut, untwist when moist and twist when dry; and a toy has been made in which there are two figures, a man and a woman, suspended by catgut in such a manner that the man comes out when the air is wet and the woman when it is dry. All these methods, however, *indicate* rather than *measure* the hygrometric state of the air—they are *hygroscopes* rather than *hygrometers*—and we proceed from these to instruments by which the state of the air with regard to moisture may be determined with precision.

155. Dew-point instruments. Daniell's dew-point hygrometer. This instrument (Fig. 30) is composed of two glass bulbs. The one A is more than half filled with ether, and contains a delicate thermometer plunged in the ether; the space above is void of air and of everything but the vapour of ether. The bulb B is covered with some fine fabric, such as muslin, upon which ether is dropped; the evaporation of the ether produces intense cold, in consequence of which the ether

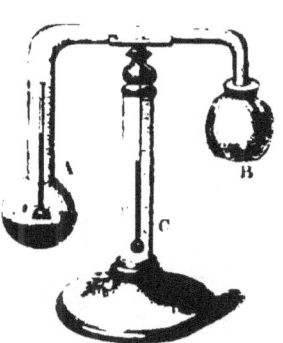

Fig. 30.

vapour inside B is rapidly condensed, and of course the ether in A as rapidly evaporates. The evaporation of the ether at A cools the bulb until the air in contact with it sinks below the dew-point. Dew is therefore deposited on the outside of A, which is made of black glass in order that this deposition may be more readily observed. At the moment of deposition the thermometer in A is read. When the dew disappears, as the temperature rises, the same thermometer is also read, and the mean of these two readings is taken to indicate the dew-point. The thermometer C gives the temperature of the air.

156. Regnault's dew-point hygrometer. Regnault has invented a dew-point hygrometer which is free from some of the objections to which Daniell's is liable. It consists (Fig. 31) of two tubes of polished silver having glass tubes fixed to them. The tube A is half filled with ether. It contains a thermometer t' with its bulb in the ether, and also a fine glass tube C open at both ends, the extremity C being open to the atmosphere, and the other open end being plunged below the ether of A. The bulb B also contains a thermometer t, the object of which is to indicate the temperature of the air. There is a communication between the air in *A* and the tube *DE*, and to the end *E* of this tube is attached an aspirator.   By means of this aspirator the air

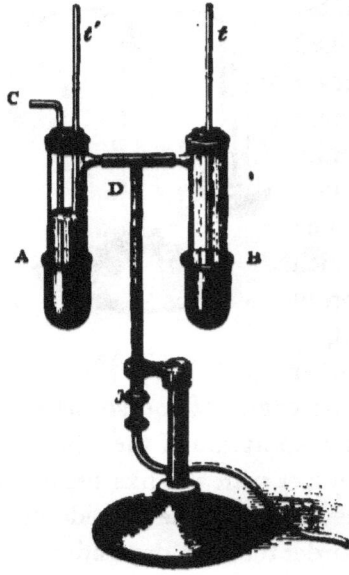

from *A* is drawn through the tube *DE*, and its place supplied by new air entering at *C* and bubbling up through the ether. This continual current of air passing through the ether causes it to evaporate rapidly, and a diminution of temperature is thus produced, until at last dew is deposited on the polished silver of *A* ; the exact moment of deposition may easily be observed, and if the temperature of *t'* be immediately noticed, we obtain the dewpoint with great exactness, since the agitation of the

Fig. 31.

ether renders it certain that the temperature of this thermometer is precisely the same as that of the polished silver. The moment of the disappearance of the dew may also be noted, but we have not in this case the same certainty that the thermometer and the polished silver are of the same temperature.

157. Wet and dry bulb hygrometer.   This instrument was devised by Mason, and consists of two thermometers (Fig. 32) placed alongside of each other, one having a dry bulb and the other a bulb covered with muslin, kept moist by an arrangement similar to that in the figure.   Owing to the evaporation from the latter its temperature will be generally below that of the former, and this difference will be greatest when the air is very dry, while in a very wet atmosphere the two temperatures will nearly coincide; the reason of this being that evaporation (Art. 121) is more rapid in dry air.

It might at first sight appear that the difference between the two instruments
would depend, not only on
the dryness of the air, but
also upon its velocity, since
we have seen (Art. 121) that
agitation of the air is favourable to evaporation. Unques-
tionably the withdrawal of heat
by evaporation is greater when
there is a current of air, but
then it must be remembered
that the difficulty of keeping
a thermometer at a temperature below that of the air is
increased by the same cause
and very nearly in the same
proportion.

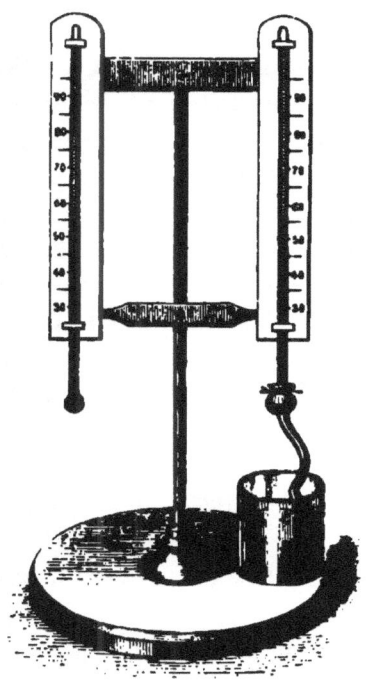

Fig. 32.

This arrangement may be
advantageously employed as a
simple method of ascertaining the hygrometric state of the
air with considerable accuracy, and for this purpose the following formula, devised by Dr. Apjohn, is employed.

Let f' denote the maximum elasticity of vapour corresponding to the temperature of the wet thermometer, and f'' the
elasticity of the vapour present in the air which it is wished
to find. Also let d denote the difference in Fahrenheit
degrees between the two thermometers, and let h be the
height of the barometer : then—

$$f'' = f' - \frac{d}{87} \times \frac{h}{30}$$

for temperatures of evaporation above 32° Fahr., and

$$f'' = f' - \frac{d}{96} \times \frac{h}{30}$$

for temperatures of evaporation below 32° Fahr.

Having found f'', or the elasticity of the vapour present in the air, we have only to look in our table for the temperature of which the saturation elasticity is f'' in order to obtain the dew-point. Now it has been found, as the result of numerous experiments, that the dew-points obtained by this simple method agree very well with those determined by *direct observation* with Daniell's or Regnault's dew-point hygrometer.

158. Weight of vapour present in air. Specific gravity of air. We can easily calculate the weight W of a litre of dry air at temperature $t°$C, and of elasticity P millimètres, by the formula (see Arts. 136, 149)—

$$W = 1.293187 \text{ grm.} \times \frac{P}{760} \times \frac{1}{1 + .00367 \times t}.$$

In like manner if we wish to know the weight W' of a litre of aqueous vapour at temperature t' and elasticity P', we have (Art. 149)—

$$W' = 0.6235 \times 1.293187 \text{ grm.} \times \frac{P'}{760} \times \frac{1}{1 + .00367 \times t'}.$$

Suppose now it is wished to know the weight of one litre of air at temperature 15°C, and pressure equal to that of 750 millimètres of mercury reduced to 0°C at Paris, the dew point being 10°C.

By Table III., at the end of this work, we find that the vapour pressure corresponding to 10°C is 9.165 millimètres. Hence 740.835 millimètres will represent the pressure of dry air, and 9.165 millimètres the vapour pressure at the time of

observation. Now the weight of the dry air in one litre
will be—

$$W = 1.293187 \text{ grm.} \times \frac{740.835}{760} \times \frac{1}{1 + .00367 \times 15} = 1.19480 \text{ grm.};$$

also the weight of the vapour in one litre will be—

$$W' = 1.293187 \text{ grm.} \times .6235 \times \frac{9.165}{760} \times \frac{1}{1 + .00367 \times 15} = 0.00921 \text{ grm.}$$

Hence the whole weight of one litre of air will be
1.20401 gramme.

159. Correction for weighing in air. This will be
best understood by an example. Suppose, for instance,
that a substance of the approximate specific gravity 2.5
weighs 100 grammes in the air of which the weight was
determined in last article, and that the approximate specific gravity of the weights against which it is compared
is 9.0.

Now since the specific gravity of the substance is 2.5, we
see from Art. 76 that the weight of a cubic décimètre or litre
of the substance will be 2.5 kilogrammes, or 2500 grammes;
and hence, since it only weighs 100 grammes, its volume will

be $\frac{100}{2500} = .04$ litre.

In like manner the volume of the weights against which it

is weighed will be $\frac{100}{9000} = .01$ litre.

The weight of air displaced by the substance will therefore be—

$$1.204 \text{ gramme} \times .04 = .04816 \text{ gramme},$$

and that displaced by the weights will be .01324 gramme,
nearly.

Hence the substance will weigh heavier in vacuo than in
air by .04816 gramme.

In the next place it must be remembered that the *real*
weight of the body in air is somewhat less than 100 grammes,

for the weights against which it is balanced denote 100 grammes in vacuo, and hence in air they will denote—

$$100 - .01324 = 99.98676 \text{ grammes, nearly.}$$

Therefore—

$$99.98676 + .04816 = 100.03492 \text{ grammes}$$

will be the true weight of the body.

—————————————————————

CHAPTER VIII.

Effect of Heat upon other Properties of Matter.

160. In what has preceded we have investigated the effects of heat upon bodies, chiefly as regards their volume and condition ; but this agent affects bodies in many other ways, and to these we shall now allude : but in the first place it may be well to recapitulate very shortly the leading results of the preceding chapters.

We have seen that as the temperature of a solid rises it almost invariably expands in volume, and also that the co-efficient of expansion is greater at a high temperature than at a low one.   If we continue to heat the solid it will ultimately assume the liquid state.   In some bodies this change of state takes place very abruptly, but in others very gradually, so that they require a very considerable range of temperature in order to complete the change and become perfectly liquid. Sealing - wax is an example of the latter class, and ice probably of the former.

In many cases there is an increase of volume as a body passes from the solid to the liquid state, but in others, such as ice, there is a considerable diminution.   In all cases a quantity of heat is rendered latent by the change. When the liquid state has been *completely* assumed any further increase of temperature will generally increase the volume of the liquid also. The coefficient of increase of volume is greater in liquids than in solids, and, just as in the case of solids, it is greater at a high temperature than at a low one.

If we continue to heat the liquid it will ultimately assume the gaseous state, and during the process of change a great quantity of heat will be rendered latent, and a very considerable expansion will under ordinary circumstances take place. There is some reason to think that, just as in the previous case so here, the state of a perfect gas is not instantaneously assumed, and that a vapour in contact with the liquid which produces it is not a perfect gas. If however this vapour, separated from the liquid, be allowed to expand in volume while its temperature is not diminished, it will approach more and more to the state of a perfect gas.

161. We shall afterwards see, when we come to treat of the conduction of heat, that the thermal conductivity of a body becomes lessened as its temperature increases : and, under the head of specific heat, we shall also find that this quality of a body becomes altered by change of temperature. In the meantime let us endeavour to shew how the other properties of a body are altered by increase of temperature.

EFFECT OF TEMPERATURE UPON REFRACTION AND DISPERSION.

162. One of the first experiments on this subject was that made by Jamin, who gradually cooled down water to the freezing point, and found that as it cooled its index of refraction went on gradually increasing even after the point of maximum density (4°C) had been reached. This observation was afterwards confirmed by Messrs. Dale and Gladstone, who however found that the reversion at 4°C of the behaviour of water was not without influence on the refraction, and the following table exhibits the result of their inquiries regarding the refractive index of water at different temperatures.

Temperature of the water.	Refractive index for line A of the solar spectrum.	Refractive index for line D of the solar spectrum.	Refractive index for line H of the solar spectrum.
0°C	....	1.33374	....
1	1.32913	....	1.34377
2	1.32913	....	1.34377
3	1.32913	....	....
4	1.32902	1.33367	1.34366
6.5	....	1.33356	1.34366
9	1.32882	1.33342	1.34337
11	1.32879	....	1.34331

Messrs. Gladstone and Dale have since examined a great many different liquids; their mode of research being to use the liquid as a fluid prism by which to obtain a solar spectrum; and they have found—

1. *That the refraction uniformly diminishes as the temperature increases.*

2. *That the solar spectrum given by the substance diminishes in length as the temperature increases.*

EFFECT OF TEMPERATURE UPON THE ELECTRICAL PROPERTIES OF BODIES.

163. Thermo-electric currents. It was discovered by Seebeck that *if a circuit composed of two different metals soldered together have one of its junctions heated, an electric current will be produced.* Thus in Fig. 33, if the lower plate be made of bismuth and the sides and upper plate of copper, and if one of the junctions be heated, then a current of electricity will be made to circulate. The direction of this current will be represented by the arrow-head, that is to say, there will be at the heated junction a flow of positive electricity from the bismuth through the copper to the cold junction. The existence of this current may be easily rendered evident, for we have only to place the compound circuit with its length in the magnetic meridian, so that a magnetic needle inside will take the direction *C C*, when by heating the junction *C* by means of

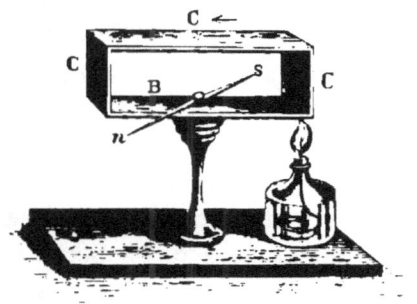

Fig. 33.

a lamp the north pole of the needle will be deflected as in the figure. The current so produced is called the thermoelectric current.

164. Thermo-electric series. If a compound circuit be made with any two metals in the following list, the positive current will go across the heated junction from the metal nearest the top to that nearest the bottom of the list :—

Bismuth	Silver
Nickel	Zinc
Lead	Iron
Tin	Antimony
Copper	Tellurium.
Platinum	

It will be seen that bismuth and antimony are nearly at opposite extremities of this table, and as both these metals are easily obtained they are generally employed in thermoelectric combinations.

165. Thermo-pile. It was formerly assumed that the quantity of electricity set in motion by heating the junction of a compound circuit is proportional to the difference in temperature of the two junctions. It will be afterwards seen (Art. 166) that when the heating is very great this law does not hold, but if the junction be only heated slightly it will represent the truth. In this latter case, if we can find means to measure the strength of the current we obtain at the same time a measure of the difference in temperature of the two junctions, and thus the combination will be equivalent to a differential thermometer.

In adapting a thermo-electric arrangement to this purpose three things have to be borne in mind, if great delicacy be desired. In the first place, it will be necessary to produce as strong an electric current as possible; in the second place, we ought to render this current as effective as possible in deflecting a magnetic needle; and in the third place, we ought to magnify the smallest motion of the needle so as to make it visible.

In order to produce as strong a current as possible, a number of pieces of antimony and bismuth are soldered together, as in Fig. 34, and when the heat is applied above we have the united effect of all the currents at the hot junctions passing though the circuit, including the galvanometer, in the direction of the arrow-heads.

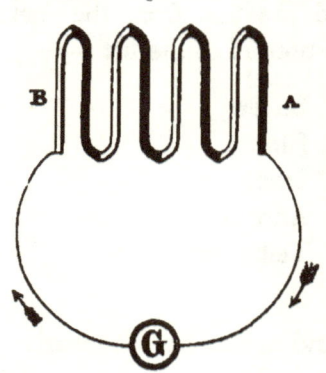

Fig. 34.

In practice a square block, containing altogether 25 couples of bismuth and antimony, is generally employed—such an arrangement is called a thermo-pile. This instrument is however incomplete without a galvanometer, and we shall now shortly describe Professor William Thomson's reflecting galvanometer, which is admirably adapted for use with the thermo-pile. In this galvanometer a small magnet *m* (Fig. 35) acts as the magnetic needle; it is attached to the back of a small flat circular mirror which is delicately suspended by a fine thread. The needle is surrounded by coils of the wire which conveys the current of the thermo-pile, and when the current is passing, the needle and attached mirror will of course be deflected out of their previous position. But the needle *m* is under the influence

Fig. 35.

of the earth's magnetism, and under ordinary circumstances a very weak current coming from the thermo-pile would be able to turn this needle only a very little distance out of the magnetic meridian before it would be stopped by the earth's magnetic force tending to bring it back. A rather large magnet *M* (Fig. 36*) is however placed in

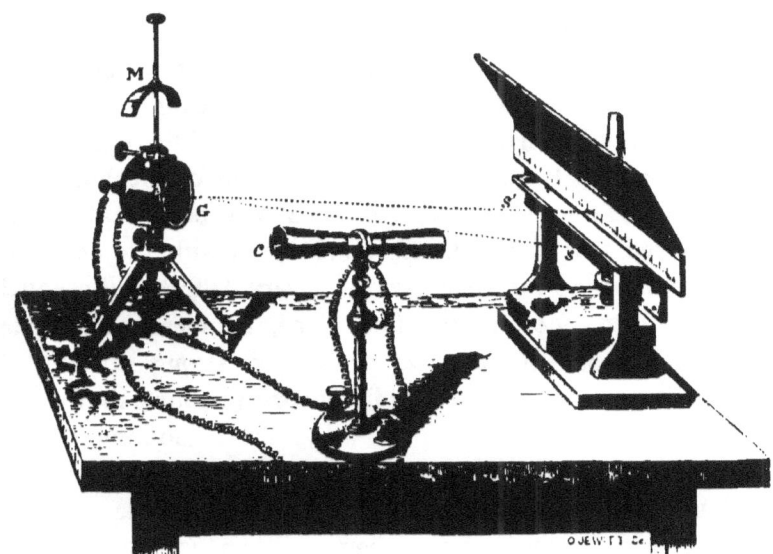

Fig. 36.

* This figure is due to the kindness of Mr. C. Becker of Messrs. Elliott, Brothers, London.

such a position as to counteract as nearly as possible the earth's magnetic force upon the needle *m* which is inside *G*. The consequence of this arrangement will be that whereas without *M* the earth's magnetic force would overcome the current when the magnet *m* had been deflected but a little way; now, by means of *M*, the earth's magnetic force on *m* being very nearly counteracted, the magnet *m* will behave as if it were astatic, and will describe, when acted on by the current, a very much larger arc before it is checked.

In the next place, a small motion of *m* is rendered visible by the following means. Since the needle is attached to the back of a freely-suspended mirror, any motion of the needle will of course be followed by an angular deviation of the mirror. Now the light from an illuminated slit *s*, having first been made to pass through a small lens in the galvanometer *G*, falls upon the mirror and is reflected back in the line *Gs'* so as to throw an image of the luminous slit upon a graduated scale. It is evident from this arrangement that a comparatively small change in the plane of the mirror will produce a very large change in the position of the luminous image on the scale. Also, from what has been said it will be inferred that this instrument combined with the thermo-pile will have all the requisites of a very delicate differential thermometer. For, in the first place, by means of a pile with a number of pairs we produce a strong current of electricity; secondly, the needle is very sensitive to the influence of this current; and thirdly, small motions of the needle are magnified so as to be rendered easily visible, being at the same time strictly proportional to the strength of the current which causes them. When used to indicate the presence of radiant heat the pile is generally furnished with a brass cone *c*, the interior of which is polished; by which means not only the heat which reaches the pile itself but that which falls upon the cone is ultimately reflected upon the face of the pile, and its sensibility is thereby greatly increased. In the figure there are two brass cones, but in the experiment we are describing only one of these is exposed to the source of heat, the other being shut by a brass cover. The junctions of the pile are also usually covered with lamp-black, a substance which absorbs every kind of radiant heat. So delicate may an arrangement of this description be made, that if a substance be presented before the cone *c* one degree Fahr. hotter than the pile itself, the *mere radiation* from this substance, by very slightly heating the one face of the pile, will in some instruments cause a change in the position of the reflected luminous image equal to 50 or 60 divisions of the scale.

On account of its great delicacy an arrangement of this kind is eminently adapted to researches on radiant heat —as we shall see when we come to that branch of our subject.

166. Thermo-electric inversions. It was at first supposed that the current produced by heating one junction of a compound-circuit would prove to be proportional to the difference in temperature between the two junctions. This, however, is not the case. Cumming was the first to shew that in a circuit of certain metals, if one junction is kept cool while the other is gradually raised in temperature, the current, instead of going on regularly increasing, begins to diminish, then comes to a stop, and ultimately sets in the opposite direction. This observer found that if gold, silver, copper, brass, or zinc wires be heated with iron the direction of the current becomes changed at a red heat.

167. Pyro-electricity. Certain minerals when heated acquire electrical properties. One of these is tourmaline, in which this effect of heat was originally discovered by observing that when brought into contact with hot ashes it first attracted and then repelled them. It was found by Canton that it is not the absolute temperature but change of temperature which renders a tourmaline electric. Suppose, for instance, we have a tourmaline whose poles we call A and B. If this tourmaline be kept sufficiently long in a medium of constant temperature it will exhibit no electric manifestations. If it be transferred into a warmer medium, A will exhibit positive and B negative electricity; while if transferred into a colder medium, A will exhibit negative and B positive electricity.

A similar property is possessed by other crystals, and Haüy was the first to remark that those crystals are pyro-electric which are deficient in symmetry.

168. Effect of temperature upon the electric conductivity of bodies. Pure metals. This subject was first studied by Sir H. Davy, but the latest and probably the most accurate research is that of Dr. A. Matthiessen and M. Von Bose, who have obtained the following result:—

Electric conductivity.

Name of substance.	At 0°C. Silver at 0°C = 100.	At 100°C. Silver at 0°C = 100.	Silver at 100°C = 100.
Silver (hard drawn)....	100.00	71.56	100.00
Copper (hard drawn) ..	99.95	70.27	98.20
Gold (hard drawn)....	77.96	55.90	78.11
Zinc	29.02	20.67	28.89
Cadmium	23.72	16.77	23.44
Tin	12.36	8.67	12.12
Lead	8.32	5.86	8.18
Arsenic	4.76	3.33	4.65
Antimony	4.62	3.26	4.55
Bismuth	1.245	0.878	1.227

We thus see by comparing together the first and third columns of this table that the proportion between the electric conductivity of the different metals is very nearly the same at 100°C as at 0°, while by the second column we see that the decrement between 0° and 100° is nearly 29 per cent. for each metal.

A later research by Dr. Matthiessen and C. Vogt shews that thallium and iron are exceptional in their behaviour, and that for thallium the decrement between 0° and 100°C is 31.42 per cent. In like manner the decrement for pure iron between the same limits was found to be 38.26 per cent.

169. Liquids. Marianini was the first to shew that an increase of temperature exalts the electric conductivity of liquids, and his results have since been confirmed by Becquerel, who made experiments on solutions of sulphate of copper and sulphate of zinc, and on the nitric acid of commerce. From these it appears that a difference of from 20 to 30°C suffices to double the conductivity of these liquids, probably by facilitating electrolysis.

170. Bad conductors. Heat converts many insulating solids into conductors by making them liquid, and of these ice is a notable example, which insulates when solid, but conducts electricity in the fluid state; also glass, resin, and wax, which insulate at ordinary temperatures, become conductors at a temperature sufficient to soften them, and their conductivity is still more increased when they assume the liquid state. There are, nevertheless, many substances in which igneous fusion does not develope conducting power, and of these sulphur, phosphorus, and camphor may be quoted as examples.

Finally, the loss of electricity in dry air increases very sensibly with the temperature.

EFFECT OF TEMPERATURE ON MAGNETISM.

171. If we heat a magnetised bar of hard steel we produce a diminution in its magnetism, but if the heating be not too great, when again cold it will recover its former state. In such a magnet, therefore, the intensity will be a function of the temperature. But if this bar be brought to a white heat it will totally lose its magnetism, and will not recover it when again cooled.

In like manner a soft iron bar when it is brought to a red heat is no longer attracted by the magnet. Nickel also ceases to be magnetic at the temperature of boiling oil, or about 600° Fahr., and cobalt at an extremely high temperature.

EFFECT OF TEMPERATURE ON CHEMICAL AFFINITY.

172. An increase of temperature in a great many instances promotes chemical combination. Thus phosphorus, if slightly heated in oxygen or air, takes fire; and, generally speaking, a large number of bodies which do not combine together at ordinary temperatures do so when the temperature is increased.

Sometimes, however, heat promotes chemical decomposition, especially when the products of such decomposition are gaseous. Thus, if limestone be heated it parts with its carbonic acid gas and is converted into lime. Many substances, too, which possess little chemical stability, decompose on the application of heat, often with explosive violence. The terchloride of nitrogen, and the various fulminates, are examples of this class. The effect of heat upon the solvent powers of bodies has been already alluded to.

EFFECT OF TEMPERATURE ON OTHER PROPERTIES OF MATTER.

173. It is well known that an increase of temperature alters the behaviour of a liquid in a capillary tube. M. Wolf and also M. Drion have lately made some interesting experiments on this subject, in which the capillary tubes containing the liquids were heated very considerably under pressure. M. Drion has come to the following conclusions :—

1. That for the liquids studied the capillary meniscus remains concave until the moment of complete evaporation; its form at that instant being plane.

2. That for the same liquids the capillary ascension and curvature diminish as the temperature rises, until the moment of complete conversion of the liquid into vapour.

An increase of temperature affects also the extensibility of bodies. Wertheim has made numerous experiments on this subject, and he finds that in general metallic threads offer more resistance at a low than at a high temperature to a force tending to elongate them, so that the proportional elongation produced by a given weight is smaller in the first case than in the second.

To this law, however, iron and steel present an exception, their resistance to elongation augmenting from —15° to 100°C, while at 200° it is not only smaller than at 100°C but sometimes even smaller than at ordinary temperatures.

In like manner the tenacity of a metallic wire, as estimated by its breaking charge, is altered by increase of temperature. This subject has been studied by Wertheim and also by Baudrimont, by whose researches it appears that the effect of heat is to some extent irregular, tending sometimes to diminish and sometimes to increase the tenacity if one does not go above 200°C. At a red heat, however, the tenacity of iron is very much diminished.

According to the experiments of M. Grassi the compressibility of water under pressure diminishes as the temperature increases, while heat, on the contrary, appears to augment the compressibility of ether, alcohol, and chloroform.

In like manner the cohesion and the hardness of bodies is diminished by heat, their crystalline form is altered, and indeed there is no property of matter that is not affected by this agent, although it is only in a few cases that its effects have been accurately examined.

BOOK II.

CHAPTER I.

Radiant Heat. (Preliminary.)

174. IT has already been stated on a previous occasion (Art. 5) that a body parts with its heat in two ways, namely,—

    1. By contact with a cold body,

    2. By radiation through space;

and in order to render this distinction very evident it is only necessary to mention a familiar instance of each method.

When one end of a poker is heated in the fire the heat is gradually conveyed to the other end through the substance of the poker. This is an instance of communication of heat by contact, the cold particles receiving heat from the warmer ones next them, and in their turn conveying it away to still colder particles, until *after a considerable time has elapsed* it reaches the other extremity of the poker.

Now in this case it is evident that the particles at the cold end are not *immediately and directly heated* by those at the hot end, but only through the agency of the intervening particles, and the great characteristic of this process is its exceeding slowness. It is very clear that this cannot be the method by which we receive heat from the sun, and indeed we have no reason to think that there is matter capable of retaining heat between the earth and our luminary. The effect in this instance is certainly not due to the heating of the intervening regions, but, on the contrary, it is as powerful in a very cold atmosphere as in a warm one, and may even be felt behind a screen of ice. We know, too, that light, and doubtless also heat, reach us from the fixed stars, although these bodies are vastly more distant than the sun.

It is this heating emanation which we term radiant heat, and in its character and distribution it is subject to certain laws, which we shall now proceed to describe. In the first place—

175. Radiation of heat takes place in vacuo as well as in air. For it takes place between the sun and the earth and between the fixed stars and the earth, and we have no reason to think that all space is filled with some kind of air.

176. Radiation takes place equally on all sides. If a sphere be heated and very delicate thermometers be placed on different sides of such a sphere at equal distances from the centre, they will always give the same indications. Such a sphere will also appear equally luminous from all sides.

177. Radiant heat traverses void space in straight lines and with the same velocity as light, that is to say, at the rate of about 190,000 miles in a second. The best proof of this statement is derived from the great probability, if not certainty, that heat and light are varieties of the same physical agent. This will be investigated at a subsequent part of this book.

178. Radiant heat is capable of passing through

certain substances without sensibly heating them.
If a plate of rock salt be placed between us and the sun, we
shall yet feel to a very great extent the effect of his beams;
few of his rays will be stopped, and the screen will not be
heated to a perceptible extent.

We may therefore infer that radiant heat passes through
certain substances without being perceptibly absorbed or
heating them to a sensible extent.

It is, however, probable that no substance is perfectly
transparent with respect to heat (or diathermanous, as it is
termed), and that all bodies are heated to a greater or less
extent by the passage through them of calorific rays.

**179. Radiant heat is probably not a substance
emitted by a hot body, but an undulatory motion
conveyed through a medium which pervades all
space.** Apart from the difficulty of conceiving space to be
traversed by excessively minute particles all moving with the
uniform velocity of 190,000 miles per second, the following experiment has been performed by Mr. Bennet. The
light and heat of the sun have been concentrated upon a
substance swung so delicately that the slightest momentum
would cause it to change its position, but no such change
has been observed. If we infer that light and heat do not
consist of particles emitted by a hot body, our natural al-
ternative is to suppose that they are undulations of a medium
pervading space. This hypothesis furnishes by far the
best explanation of many very curious phenomena in light
and heat, and is now very generally received.

It will be convenient here to define the various terms connected with this hypothesis. If a stone be dropped into a
pool of water, a series of undulations consisting of crests
and hollows succeeding one another will spread outwards
from the centre of disturbance. Now the distance between
two contiguous crests or between two contiguous hollows is

termed the *wave length*, because in this distance is embraced the whole variety of motions which together constitute a wave. When the ocean is agitated by a storm we have also waves, but here the wave length is obviously much greater than in the case above mentioned. We thus see that the same substance may be the medium of propagating waves of different lengths. In these instances the direction of disturbance is up and down, while the direction of propagation is horizontal; and thus the displacement of a particle is in a direction at right angles to that of transmission of the wave.

In air we have another substance capable of conveying undulations of different wave lengths. These undulations constitute musical sounds, the *wave length* defining the *pitch* of the note. Thus if one note be an octave lower than another, its wave length will be double that of the other. The waves of sound are, however, different from those of water, inasmuch as they are not waves made up of crests and hollows, but of condensations and rarefactions succeeding one another; in fact, the direction of displacement of the air instead of being at right angles to that of transmission of the wave, is in the same direction. We have thus two varieties of waves—

1. Waves of crests and hollows, where the direction of displacement is perpendicular to that of transmission.

2. Waves of condensation and rarefaction, in which the direction of displacement coincides with that of transmission.

Now whether light and heat rays consist of undulations of the first or of the second description, in either case we are entitled to expect that difference of wave length will denote some important difference in the quality of the ray. There are many considerations which induce us to imagine that difference of *colour* is denoted by difference of *wave length*, and that red, yellow, orange, green, blue, indigo, and violet have all their peculiar wave lengths.   There are other considerations which induce us to imagine that these wave lengths are very small, being for violet rays no longer than .0000167, and for red rays .0000266 of an inch, while for heat rays we shall afterwards see that the wave length is some-what larger than for red rays.

But again, there are strong reasons for believing that waves of light consist of crests and hollows, while sound waves consist of condensations and rarefactions.   There is this important distinction between the two cases.   If we hold a string somewhat tightly in a horizontal direction and strike it from above downwards, we perceive speeding along it a crest and hollow wave for which the direction of displacement is in a vertical plane.   And if we strike it from the side we perceive a similar wave, for which the direction of displace-ment is in a horizontal plane.   We can have thus two sets of crest and hollow waves proceeding in the same direction along the string, the plane of vibration of the first being at right angles to that of the second; but it is evident that we can have no such distinction in waves of condensation and rarefaction.   Now when the vibrations of a crest and hollow wave are always confined to the same plane, that wave is said to be *polarized*.   Thus in a wave proceeding in a horizontal direction if the vibrations of the particles be confined to a vertical plane, the wave is polarized; and if they be confined to a horizontal plane it is also polarized, but in a direction at right angles to the former: but if these vibrations have no reference to any particular plane, then the wave is unpolarized.

Now there are certain processes by which a ray of ordinary light may be broken up into two rays that appear to have reference to planes at right angles to one another. By such a process the ray is said to be polarized.   And this fact entitles us to assume that waves of light are crest and hollow waves and not waves of condensation and rarefaction, since these last from their nature cannot have a reference to any particular plane.

180. The intensity of radiation varies inversely as the square of the distance from the radiating body. It would appear that this law ought theoretically to hold good whether we consider radiant heat to be particles ejected by a heated body, or to be an undulatory movement of an etherial medium proceeding outwards from this body. In either case the amount of *vis viva* which at one moment, and at the distance (say) of one mile from the centre, covers the surface of a sphere of which the radius is one mile, will at another moment and at the distance of two miles from the centre cover the surface of a sphere of which the radius is two miles; that is to say, the same amount of *vis viva* or *heat* will have spread itself over a surface four times as large, and hence the amount of *vis viva* or *heat* corresponding to unit of area, that is to say the intensity, will be diminished four times, and will therefore vary inversely as the square of the distance.

The following ingenious experimental verification of this law was first given by Melloni. Suppose, in the first place, that we have a large red-hot wall before us and that we view it through a small tube, blackened in the inside, held close to the eye. The opening of this tube furthest from the eye will appear to be red hot, and it will appear so whether we approach the eye and tube close to the wall or withdraw them to a distance, always *provided that the wall be large enough to fill up the field of view from the eye.* If the eye and tube be far from the wall we embrace in the field of view a much larger extent of the wall, but we view it from a greater distance, so that what is gained in extent is lost in distance, seeing that in this arrangement the same amount of light reaches the eye at all distances. Now we know that the *extent* of heated surface viewed in this manner varies *directly as the square of the distance,* therefore we see that *rate of diminution* must be *inversely as the square of the distance.*

Melloni applied a tube of this kind not to the eye but to a thermo-pile, (which is very sensitive to heat rays, just as the eye is to those of light,) and he found that the indication of the galvanometer, and hence the amount of heat acquired by the pile, was the same whether the pile was near the hot wall or far from it, provided always that the wall was sufficiently large to fill up the field of view from the pile.

CHAPTER II.

Reflection, Refraction, &c. of Radiant Heat.

181. The laws of radiation which have been stated in the preceding chapter are sufficient to exhibit the great similarity between radiant light and heat, and even to render it probable that both these effects are due to the same physical agent.

Our belief in this is greatly strengthened by observing that the various phenomena of optics are reproduced in radiant heat, and it is to a consideration of these that the present chapter will be devoted. We shall mainly direct attention to the following properties of radiant heat—

1. Reflection.
2. Refraction.
3. Absorption.
4. Polarization and double refraction.

But, in the first place, we shall make a few preliminary remarks on the spectra of heated bodies.

182. Newton was the first to prove that a ray of sunlight really contains, blended together, a very great number of simple rays, each exhibiting a different colour; and his fundamental experiment may be shortly described as follows.

Let us take a glass prism, and place it in a vertical position, and let a ray of sunlight strike obliquely against its side. As this ray passes through the prism it will be bent in such a manner that its line of exit will differ very much in direction from that of incidence. But, besides this, each simple coloured ray of which the compound ray is composed will be bent by the prism in a different manner, so that the rays which entered the prism in the same direction will leave it in different directions, and we shall thus obtain in a separated condition all those variously coloured rays which together form a beam of white light. It is easy now to shew what is meant by the term 'Spectrum.' Suppose, for instance, that by an arrangement similar to the ordinary photographic camera we were to throw upon a screen the image of a vertical line of light. Under ordinary circumstances this image would be a vertical *line*, but if a prism were interposed in the path of the rays each constituent of the light from the slit would be bent by it in a different direction, and we should have the vertical image of the slit due to one of these constituent rays thrown upon one part of the screen, and that due to another constituent ray thrown upon another part, and so on. We should thus obtain not *one* image of the slit *but a very great number of these* contiguous to one another, so as to form an oblong space illuminated by various colours. This space is called the spectrum of the line of light, and if the light be that of the sun we thus obtain the solar spectrum.

183. This oblong space, we have observed, is differently coloured throughout. The following diagram (Fig. 37), in which the left side represents the least and the right the most refrangible rays, will give an idea of the colour and comparative luminosity of the different parts of the solar spec-

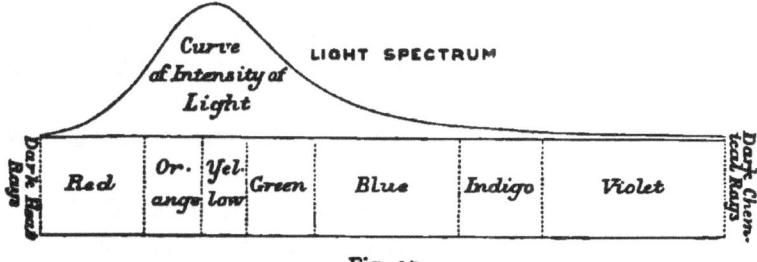

Fig. 37.

trum. The ordinates of the curve denote the luminosity for each part, and it will be seen that the greatest intensity of light is in the yellow.

If now we obtain the solar spectrum by means of a prism, or set of prisms, which we are sure do not absorb any of the rays, or do so only to a very small extent, (and for this purpose we must use rock salt,) and if we estimate the heating effect of each portion of the spectrum by means of a thermopile or otherwise, we shall have an exceedingly curious result, which is roughly sketched in the following diagram (Fig. 38).

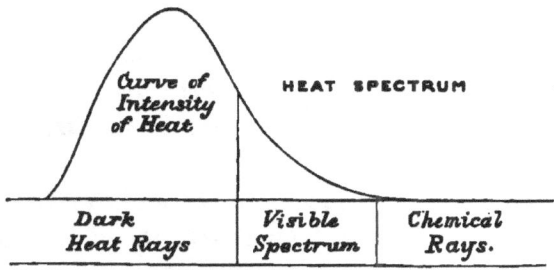

Fig. 38.

From this it appears that the maximum heating effect is a good deal beyond the red, and that the rays which produce it are invisible to the eye. If our instrument for measuring heat be delicate enough, we shall also find that the heating effect extends to the right as well as to the left of the visible spectrum, although in the former direction it is extremely feeble.

Besides the illuminating and heating powers of rays they have a third property, namely that of producing chemical action. Chloride of silver, it is well known, becomes blackened under the influence of light, and it is by making use of this property that we are enabled to obtain photographic pictures of bodies.

But the action of certain rays upon chloride of silver is much more energetic than that of others; this being most intense for the violet, or more refrangible rays, and even extending much beyond the visible extremity of the spectrum towards the right.

We have thus three things—

1. A luminous spectrum with a maximum of light in the yellow.

2. A heat spectrum with a maximum to the left of the visible spectrum.

3. A chemical spectrum with a maximum probably in the violet, and a great intensity of chemical action beyond the violet, to the right.

184. If we now proceed to consider the spectra of other luminous solid bodies, we shall find that these are very analogous to that of the sun, except in respect of dark lines, which we may for the present dismiss from our consideration.

If the temperature of the source be high, we have, besides a great deal of dark heat, a good amount of luminosity and a smaller amount of chemical action; but as the temperature decreases we perceive a very considerable diminution in the amount of light and a still greater falling off in the chemical rays, until below a red heat both chemical action and light have entirely disappeared and the whole of the radiation consists of dark heat.

Thus if the temperature of the source be low, the whole radiation is of the nature of that portion of the solar spectrum which lies in the diagram to the left of red. (We shall afterwards see what experimental grounds we have for this assertion.)

If the temperature be moderately high we get in addition a little light, and if it rise still higher, a little chemical action, until, when it becomes very high, we have a good deal of light and somewhat less chemical action, but we have reason to think that in all cases the light and chemical action bear but a small proportion to the dark heat.

185. Dismissing in the meantime the chemical rays from our consideration we may separate radiant heat into two kinds, the first embracing those rays which by means of the prism can be separated from light and which lie to the left of the visible rays in the spectrum, while the second denotes that heating effect which accompanies light and which cannot be separated from it by prismatic analysis. With regard to these we must now answer the two following questions :—

1. Is the dark heat beyond the red composed of rays similar in physical constitution to those of light?

2. In the portion of the spectrum which is visible is the heating effect produced by the very same rays which produce the luminous effect, or are there two sets, the one heating and the other luminous, mixed together?

We shall best answer these questions by proceeding at once to state the various properties of radiant heat which have been experimentally proved, and then using these as a means of comparing together the two agents heat and light.

REFLECTION OF HEAT.

186. Dark heat is capable of reflection. The following experiment will exhibit the reflection of heat.

Suppose that we have two concave metallic reflectors facing one another (as in Fig. 39), and let *A* be the focus

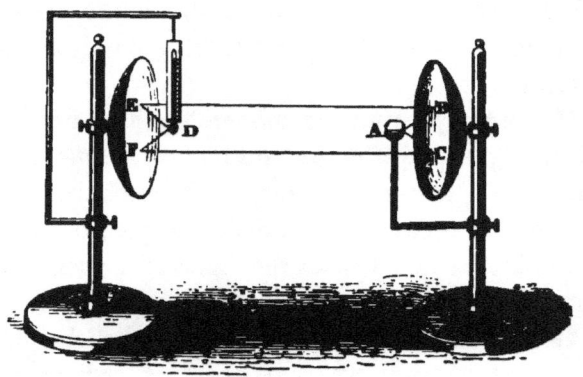

Fig. 39.

of the one and *D* that of the other. Let an iron ball, heated to a temperature somewhat below redness, be placed at *A*; if we place a piece of phosphorus at *D* it will probably take fire, or if we place a thermometer there its temperature will rise much more than if we placed it in any other position in the neighbourhood. The reason is, that the rays which leave the ball *A*, such as *A B, A C*, are reflected at *B* and *C* from the polished metallic surface of the one mirror in parallel lines *B E, C F*, while at *E* and *F* these are again reflected by the other mirror in the directions *E D, F D*, and thus converge upon the point *D*, the focus of that mirror.

In the heating of the thermometer placed at *D* we have thus a proof of the reflection of dark heat from a metallic surface.

Leslie has made numerous experiments with regard to the reflecting powers of bodies for dark heat. The following was the arrangement which he adopted at a time when the thermo-pile was yet unknown. In Fig. 40, *m* is a concave metallic mirror, and the source of heat is a cube containing hot water, the rays of heat proceeding from which would, if left to themselves, converge to a focus at f'; but in consequence of a reflecting plate ab being

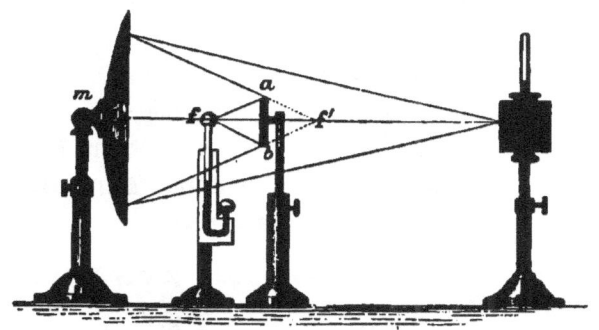

Fig. 40.

placed in their path their focus is at f. It is clear that if the plate ab be taken away and another plate substituted in its place which reflects only half as many of the rays which fall upon it, then the heating effect at f will be reduced to one-half of its previous amount; in fact, this heating effect will be proportional to the reflecting power of the surface ab. Leslie measured this effect by means of his differential thermometer, an instrument which we have already described (Art. 29). By this means he obtained not the absolute reflecting power of any body or the number of rays which it reflects out of every hundred which fall upon it, but only the comparative reflecting power of different surfaces. Calling that of brass 100, he obtained by these means the following result—

Brass	100	Lead	60
Silver	90	Amalgamated tin	10
Tin	80	Glass	10
Steel	70	Lamp-black	0

It will be seen from this list that metals which reflect light most copiously are also the best reflectors of obscure heat..

187. The heat which belongs to light is reflected in the same manner as the light.   M. Jamin has shewn that if we take certain elementary rays, or, which is the same thing, a certain small portion of the spectrum, the reflecting power of any substance with respect to the light of this portion will be as nearly as possible the same as its reflecting power for the heat.   We thus obtain the following table, in which any small difference between heat and light may be attributed to error of experiment.

Metal used for reflecting.	Green of the spectrum. Reflecting power for		Red of the spectrum. Reflecting power for	
	heat.	light.	heat.	light.
Platinum......	59	...	60	...
Zinc	65	62	60	58
Metal of mirrors	58	62	65	69
Brass	63	62	75	72

188. Variation of the reflecting power with the angle of incidence.   It has been proved by MM. de la Provostaye and Desains that the reflecting power of glass for heat increases very rapidly with the angle of incidence, and that the law which regulates this augmentation is, as nearly as we can perceive, the same as that which holds for light.

These observers have also found that the reflecting power of metallic surfaces for heat varies very slowly with the incident angle, a peculiarity which metals also possess with regard to light.

189. Diffuse reflection of heat.   MM. Provostaye and Desains, and also Knoblauch, have made experiments on this subject, and they find that as in the case of light some of the rays are scattered about by the surface and reflected in an irregular manner, so also with regard to heat there is a diffuse reflection or scattering about of the rays.   The laws of this are not exactly known, but what is known tends to strengthen the argument in favour of the identity of light and heat.

190. As the result of the experimental researches made with regard to the reflection of heat, we find :—

1. Dark heat in the same manner as light is reflected very copiously by metals.

2. Heat, whether reflected from a surface of glass or from one of metal, is subject to laws precisely similar to those of light, whereby the intensity of the reflected beam is connected with the angle of incidence.

3. Heat, in the same manner as light, suffers a scattering or diffuse reflection from the surface of bodies.

4. If we confine our experiments to a part only of the spectrum, we find that the light of this portion is reflected by a surface precisely in the same manner as the heat.

We are therefore disposed to conclude that, *as far as reflection is concerned, dark heat is subject to the same laws as light*, and also that, *if we take any region of the visible spectrum, its illuminating and heating effects are caused by precisely the same rays.*

REFRACTION OF HEAT.

191. When Sir W. Herschel first noticed that there was a heating effect beyond the red of the visible solar spectrum, this observation implied the refraction of heat. But Melloni was the first to prove experimentally that the heat which emanates from a non-luminous source is capable of refraction. His success in these experiments was due to two very important aids.

In the first place, he found that a plate of rock salt allows almost every sort of dark heat to pass readily through it, while every other substance powerfully absorbs this kind of heat.

By using a rock-salt prism he was thus sure that the heat would not be stopped by the substance of his prism. Furthermore, Nobili and Melloni were the first to employ

the thermo-pile for investigations of this nature, and by an
improved arrangement of this instrument the latter was.
enabled to detect the presence of an exceedingly small
amount of radiant heat.   (This instrument has been already
described, Art. 165.)   By means of these two important
experimental adjuncts Melloni was able to render manifest
the concentration of dark heat upon the focus of a rock-salt
lens, and also to shew that it is bent by a rock-salt prism;
thus proving conclusively the refrangibility of such heat.

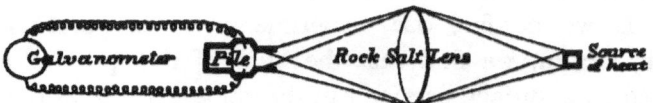

Fig. 41.

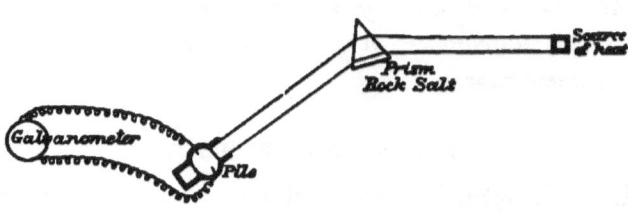

Fig. 42.

The method of experiment is illustrated in Figs. 41 and 42.
The subject was afterwards taken up by Professor Forbes, who
shewed that the refrangibility of dark heat is inferior to that
of the luminous rays.   By a method founded on the total
reflection of heat he obtained the following indices of refraction, the substance being rock salt.

		Indices of refraction.
Heat from Locatelli lamp	. . .	1.571
„ from incandescent platinum	.	1.572
„ from brass at 700° Fahr.	. .	1.568
Mean luminous rays	. . . . .	1.602.

It is important to compare this result with that obtained by Sir W. Herschel, who found dark rays beyond the red of the visible spectrum, and consequently less refracted than light. We thus see that dark rays of a less refrangibility than light belong alike to sources of heat of low temperature, and to those of high temperature, such as the sun; the difference being, as we have already remarked, that bodies of low temperature give out only dark rays, whereas those of high temperature give out luminous rays as well. Pursuing his researches on this subject, Professor Forbes found that the wave length of the heat rays was most probably considerably greater than that of the light rays, a result in accordance with the optical determinations of Fraunhofer and others, who have found the wave length of the red rays greater than that of the more refrangible rays of the spectrum. We thus see that *both as regards refrangibility and wave length the dark spectrum appears to be the appropriate prolongation of the luminous one.*

ABSORPTION OF HEAT.

192. The discovery by Melloni, that rock salt is a body which transmits heat freely, sufficiently indicates that most substances which are transparent for light are not so with regard to heat. In the language adopted by scientific men this is expressed by saying that most substances are *athermanous*, and that rock salt is almost the only *diathermanous* substance, these two words corresponding to the terms *opaque* and *transparent* in the science of optics. There are two facts regarding the absorption of heat that may with advantage be discussed here. In the first place, *when the heat which radiates from a hot body has passed through one screen it is more easily able to penetrate another screen of the same material.* This was originally observed by De la Roche, and his observations have since been abundantly confirmed by Melloni, Forbes, and others. They have expressed it as a sifting of the radiant heat by its passage through the first screen; certain rays being stopped and only those allowed to proceed which are of a nature easily able to penetrate the material of the screen. It will be observed that this is quite analogous to the action of a red screen upon light, which stops the blue rays but allows the red to pass, nor will these red rays be much diminished by a second screen of the same material.

There is thus exercised by solid and liquid bodies a selective absorption both for heat and light, in virtue of which certain rays are set apart to be stopped while certain others are allowed to proceed.

It may be remarked that besides *selective* absorption of rays by substances there is probably also a more *general* absorption, which may conveniently be kept separate from the former. We have some grounds for believing that very thick strata of air, water, glass, or any substance seemingly transparent, will ultimately stop light, possibly at a rate not greatly differing for the different rays.

But to return to *selective* absorption. We have reason to think that this property, as regards both light and heat, is exceedingly marked in gases; indeed the vapour of sodium is found to be quite transparent for every kind of light except for that from a salt flame, for which it is quite opaque, and Professor Tyndall has also observed a similar action of gases with respect to radiant heat.

We remark, in the second place, *that most substances, including those that are transparent for light, are generally opaque for dark heat of great wave length and small refrangibility.* Rock salt has been mentioned as an exception, but even this is not perfectly diathermanous. Provostaye and Forbes have both found that it passes a smaller proportion of heat rays than of light rays, and the author of this work has attempted to shew that the rays which it stops are those of very great wave length. Forbes has also shewn that transmission in general raises the index of refraction of the transmitted heat; in other words, a screen stops in preference those rays which have the lowest index of refraction or greatest wave length. But this rule, though very general, is not universal; for it has been found by Melloni and Forbes that smoked rock salt and mica, split by heat into a bundle of thin pellicles, pass in preference dark rays; and by Tyndall that a solution of iodine in bisulphide of carbon has the property of completely stopping the light rays, while it allows dark heat to pass in great quantity. Tyndall found that a fluid lens formed of this solution and enclosed in rock salt will stop all the light from an electric lamp, but permit the dark rays to pass in sufficient abundance to produce incandescence. We shall on a future occasion return to the subject of absorption, which is a very important one.

POLARIZATION OF HEAT.

193. We have seen that there is an analogy between light and heat as regards reflection, refraction, and absorption; and it might be expected that the same should hold as regards polarization. Malus and Berard were the first to shew that the heat accompanying solar light is capable of polarization. In 1834 Professor Forbes took up the inquiry; but before describing his experiments it may be well to describe the action of tourmaline and glass with respect to light. If a plate of tourmaline be cut with its plane surface parallel to the axis of the crystal, and if a ray of ordinary unpolarized light be allowed to fall upon it, it divides the ray into two parts, one polarized in the plane of the axis, and the other in a plane perpendicular to the axis, and the former of these is absorbed while the latter is allowed to pass. The light transmitted through such a plate will therefore be polarized in a plane perpendicular

N

to the axis of the crystal. If now a similar plate of tour-maline be placed behind the first, but with its axis at right angles to the axis of the first, then the light transmitted by the first will be absorbed by the second, so that the com-bination will be virtually opaque; if, however, we turn the second plate round until the axis of both plates coincide, then the combination will be transparent. Again, if a bundle of plates of glass or any similar substance, such as mica, be held together, and if a ray of light be allowed to strike obliquely at a certain angle upon them, part of this will be reflected back, and part will be transmitted through the plates. Now it is found that the reflected part is very nearly polarized in one plane, and the transmitted part in a plane perpendicular to that of the reflected light; and furthermore, if the reflected or the transmitted ray be again reflected or transmitted by a similar bundle of plates, but with its plane of incidence perpendicular to that of the first bundle, then the rays that have been reflected by the first bundle will not be reflected by the second, nor will those that have been transmitted by the first bundle be transmitted by the second. But if the plates are parallel, so that the planes of incidence coincide, then they will reflect or trans-mit the rays.

Now if radiant heat be similar to light, we should expect phenomena similar to the above; and accordingly Professor Forbes, by using two plates of tourmaline cut with their planes parallel to the axis, proved that there was a marked additional stoppage of heat (just as there is of light) when the axes of the two plates were crossed, whether the source of heat were a lamp or brass heated below luminosity. He also proved that heat, like light, is polarized in the pro-cesses of reflection and refraction. In his refraction ex-periments he employed mica split by heat, and therefore acting like a bundle of plates. In this state the substance, ordinarily transparent, assumes a glossy silvery appearance, and, though nearly opaque to light, allows nevertheless a large portion of heat to pass; and if the rays of heat make a proper angle with the surface they are found to be polarized to a considerable extent, and hence two such screens placed in opposite directions are found to stop a large portion of the incident heat. This result was found to hold for all kinds of heat, including that from the blackened surface of a vessel containing boiling water. In addition to these results Professor Forbes was able to prove the circular polarization and depolarization of heat. Circular polarization was proved by using a rhomb of rock salt, while by interposing a film of mica between his polarizing and analyzing plates, which had their planes of incidence inclined at right angles to one another, and observing whether any difference of heating effect appeared when the principal section of the plate was parallel to the plane of primitive polarization or inclined 45° to it, he shewed the depolarization of heat.

Other observers have confirmed these results, and have furthermore shewn that *very many of the phenomena of optics can be reproduced by dark heat. Indeed, the analogy between these two agents is as complete as our experiments are capable of shewing.* Our instruments are doubtless very delicate, but it ought to be borne in mind that the most refined apparatus is far less sensitive for dark heat than the eye is for light.

CONCLUDING REMARKS.

104. The facts detailed in this chapter all tend to shew that radiant light and heat are only varieties of the same physical agent, and also that when once the spectrum of a luminous object has been obtained, the separation of the different rays from one another is physically complete; so that if we take any region of the visible spectrum, its illuminating and heating effect are caused by precisely the same rays. We may extend this observation to that region of the spectrum near the violet, or most refrangible extremity, which possesses not only a luminous but also a chemical effect, and assert that these two effects are caused by the same rays. The solar spectrum, it is well known, is intersected with dark lines, of which more hereafter; in the meantime suffice it to say that these lines have done good service in shewing that there is only one agent at one part of the spectrum. Thus towards the left extremity, or the red, we have at the same time a heating and a luminous effect. Now whenever a dark line occurs this of course denotes that a certain ray of light is absent, but by means of very delicate investigations with the thermo-pile it has been found that heat as well as light is absent from the spaces occupied by these lines.

So also towards the right extremity, or violet, we have at the same time a luminous and a chemical effect, and we may therefore obtain a map of this region either from eye observations or by means of photography. Now when two maps obtained by these two different methods are compared together, it is found that the same dark lines occur in both, or, in other words, an absence of luminosity implies at the same time an absence of chemical effect.

Furthermore, we have reason to suppose that the physical distinction between different parts of the spectrum is one of wave length, and that rays of great wave length are in general less refracted than those of small wave length.

We would remark, in conclusion, that while the effects produced by different rays are generally divided into their heating, luminous, and chemical effects, yet there is a material distinction between the first of these and the other two. The luminous effect depends upon the constitution of the eye, and may be possessed by certain rays and by those alone; the chemical effect also, as it depends upon the nature of the substance and of the change which it undergoes, may be possessed by certain rays but not by others. But we are led to think that the heating effect of a ray is the true physical measure of its power, so that by making (as we can make) any portion of the spectrum wholly available in heating a body and by estimating exactly the heating effect which is produced, we shall at once be able to know the amount of energy or *vis viva* of which this portion of the spectrum is possessed. .

CHAPTER III.

Theory of Exchanges.

195. At an early stage in the history of radiant heat the following question arose. A hot body, we all know, radiates heat towards those bodies that are of a lower temperature than itself, but does it also radiate when surrounded by bodies of a temperature equal to its own or of a higher temperature? In other words, is the radiation of a given body at a given temperature dependent upon the bodies that surround it, or is it independent of them?

Either hypothesis will serve to explain the fact that bodies of the same temperature neither gain nor lose heat by virtue of each other's presence, for we may either suppose that such bodies do not radiate at all to one another, or else that each one radiates and receives back as much heat as it gives out. Upwards of seventy years ago Professor Pierre Prevost, of Geneva, introduced this latter idea, and ever since that time it has been gaining ground, and is now very generally received.

Prevost's theory was called by its author that of a *moveable equilibrium of temperature*, and according to it bodies at all temperatures are constantly radiating heat to one another, while those of a constant temperature get back as much heat as they give out. The equilibrium suggested by Prevost is not therefore a statical or tensional equilibrium or one of repose, but it is essentially an equilibrium of action; and viewed in this light it would seem to flow naturally from the dynamical hypothesis which views all heat as a species of motion.

Let us take, for instance, a thermometer: this, according to the theory of exchanges, is constantly giving out heat at a rate depending on the temperature of the bulb and independent of that of the surrounding enclosure. On the other hand, it is receiving heat from this enclosure at a rate depending upon the temperature of the enclosure and independent of that of the bulb. Thus its heat expenditure depends upon its own temperature, its heat receipts upon that of the enclosure, and there is equilibrium of temperature when its expenditure is exactly balanced by its receipts.

196. A curious experiment by Pictet was probably the means of leading Prevost to this theory. Pictet, reversing the experiment of Art. 186 (Fig. 39), put ice, or a freezing mixture, in the focus of one of the reflectors and a thermometer in that of the other. And in consequence of this the temperature of the thermometer was found to fall. This fall would be at once explained if we could suppose cold to be a principle susceptible of radiation. It was probably his conviction of the inadmissibility of this explanation that led Prevost to frame the theory of exchanges, and a very little consideration will shew that this phenomenon can be easily explained by this hypothesis. Referring to Fig. 39, let us first take the case in which the bulb of the thermometer at D is of the same temperature as the substance at A. According to the theory of exchanges, rays DE, DF, &c. will proceed from the bulb D, and ultimately, by virtue of the laws of reflection, will be concentrated upon the substance at A. In order therefore that the bulb D may not lose heat, it is necessary that the place of these rays be supplied by other rays of equal intensity, that is, by AB, AC, &c. which proceed from A and ultimately fall upon D.

It thus appears that when D and A are of the same temperature both sets of rays are of equal intensity, and hence the thermometer will remain stationary.

Again, when A is warmer than D the rays which reach D from A are more intense than those which reach A from D, and hence D will gain heat, or the thermometer will rise ;—this is the ordinary experiment.

But, on the other hand, when A is colder than D the rays which leave D for A will be more intense than those which reach D from A, and hence D will be deprived of heat, or the thermometer will fall ;—this is Pictet's experiment.

We see therefore that the theory of a moveable equilibrium explains very well the apparent reflection of cold, and that according to this theory, the same cause which in the one case makes the thermometer peculiarly sensitive to an increase in the temperature of the opposite body (that is to say, the reflection from the concave mirrors), will in the other make it equally sensitive to a diminution of the same temperature.

107. Besides this happy explanation the hypothesis of Prevost has consistently vindicated its claims to represent the truth, not only by explaining very many experiments, but also by suggesting new truths which have afterwards received an experimental verification.

This theory, since its proposal by Prevost, has been developed by Provostaye and Desains, and more recently by the author of this work and by Kirchhoff. It will, perhaps, best conduce to clear conception if we assume at first the truth of this hypothesis, then deduce its legitimate conclusions, and shew at the same time that these are all supported by experiment. Deferring until next chapter a proof in favour of the theory derived from the laws of cooling as ascertained by Dulong and Petit, let us for our present purpose imagine to ourselves a chamber of the following kind.

198. Let the walls which surround this chamber be kept at a constant temperature, say 212° Fahr., and let them be covered with lamp-black—a substance which reflects no heat, or at least very little;—also let there be a thermometer in the enclosure. It is well known that this thermometer will indicate the temperature of the surrounding walls, and that it will be a matter of indifference whether it be hung in the middle of the enclosure or at one of the sides; in whatever part of the enclosure this instrument is placed its indication will be precisely the same, namely 212° Fahr. (In what follows it ought to be *clearly borne in mind* that we are now supposing the theory of exchanges to be true, according to which bodies even of the same temperature are always giving and receiving radiant heat.)

EQUILIBRIUM OF HEAT-RAYS.

199. Heat equilibrium of surfaces. Suppose that the outside of the bulb of this thermometer is covered with tinfoil, so that its reflecting power is considerable. Now according to the theory of exchanges this thermometer is constantly radiating heat towards the lamp-black, but it is receiving back just as much as it radiates. Let us call the radiation of lamp-black 100, and suppose that 80 of these 100 rays which strike the thermometer are reflected back from its tinfoil surface, while the remaining 20 are absorbed. Since therefore the thermometer is absorbing 20 rays, and since nevertheless its temperature is not rising, it is clear that it must also be radiating 20 rays, that is to say, *under such circumstances its absorption and radiation must be equal to one another*.

If we now suppose the outside of the bulb to be blackened instead of being covered with tinfoil, the thermometer will absorb nearly all the 100 rays that fall upon it, and just as in the previous case, since its temperature is not rising, it must be radiating 100 rays.

Thus we see that when covered with tinfoil it only radiated 20 rays, but when blackened it radiates 100. The radiation from a reflecting metallic surface ought therefore, if our theory be true, to be much less than from a blackened one. This has been proved experimentally by Leslie, who shewed that *good reflectors of heat are bad radiators*.

200. Again, we have seen that in the case of the bulb covered with tinfoil 80 of the 100 rays which fell upon it were reflected back, and we have also seen that 20 rays were radiated by the bulb. Hence the heat reflected *plus* the heat radiated by this thermometer in the imaginary enclosure will be equal to 100, that is to say, it will be equal to the lamp-black radiation from the walls of the enclosure. We may generalise this statement by saying that *in an enclosure of constant temperature the heat reflected* plus *the heat radiated by any substance will be equal to the total lamp-black radiation of that temperature*, and this will be the case, whether the reflecting substance be placed inside the enclosure or whether it form a part of the walls of the enclosure. In fact, we may conceive the walls of such an enclosure to be formed of a large variety of substances from polished metal to lamp-black, and yet the total flow of radiant heat coming from one portion will be the same as that coming from another portion, the only difference being that in the case of a reflector, such as the thermometer with tinfoil, this heat is partly radiated and partly reflected, while in the case of lamp-black it is altogether radiated, the reflection being insensible.

The statement that the heat reflected *plus* the heat radiated by any substance in an enclosure of constant temperature will be equal to the total lamp-black radiation of that temperature has been experimentally verified by MM. Provostaye and Desains, who found—

Radiation from polished silver at a given temp. =   2.2

Reflection by silver of rays from lamp-black

    at this temperature represented by 100   = 97.0

                                Sum = 99.2

Now 99.2 comes very near the lamp-black radiation or 100.

They also found that the sum of the reflected and radiated heat from glass at different angles was equal to 93.9 (lamp-black radiation being equal to 100); the difference between 93.9 and 100 they supposed to be due to diffuse reflection.

201. Let us now once more return to our chamber of constant temperature, and imagine the thermometer carried from one part of the chamber to another where the surface is of a different shape.

We may, for instance, pass from Fig. 43, where the thermometer T is at the centre of a sphere, to Fig. 44, where it is within an acute angle. In the first case, the rays which reach the instrument will be those which have been emitted by the surrounding spherical envelope in a direction perpendicular to the surface; but in the latter case, most of the rays reaching the thermometer will have been

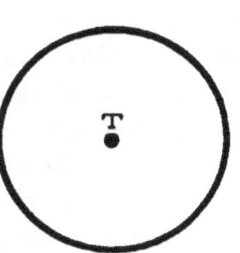

Fig. 43.

Fig. 44.

emitted in an oblique direction. · Yet the thermometer receives precisely the same amount of heat in both cases, and will always do so, whatever be the shape of the surrounding enclosure.

In fine, in such an enclosure streams of heat may be supposed to be passing and repassing in every possible direction, and to be equally intense in all directions, without the least regard to the shape or substance of that part of the enclosure from which they come.

Thus the stream of radiant heat impinging upon the surface AB (Fig. 45) in the direction CA perpendicular to AB will be the same whether it be supposed to proceed from a surface CD parallel to AB or from a surface CE inclined to AB. It thus appears that in our hypothetical enclosure of

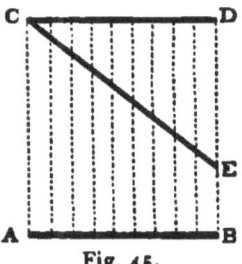

Fig. 45.

constant temperature the heating effect of a stream of heat is solely dependent upon its cross section, that is to say, upon the extent of surface AB perpendicular to its direction which it will exactly cover. This result has been verified experimentally by Provostaye and Desains; these observers having found, as we have already said, that the sum of the reflected and radiated heat from glass at different angles is a constant quantity.

When the source of the rays is a non-reflecting substance such as lamp-black, the statement of this law is very simple. We see from Fig. 45 that the heat which leaves the surface CD in the direction CA is precisely equal to that which leaves the surface CE in the same direction.

Hence the heat which radiates from a surface of lamp-black in any direction is proportional to and may be represented by the projection of this surface upon a plane perpendicular to the direction of the rays.

This result has been experimentally proved by Lambert

of Berlin and also by Leslie, who made observations upon the heat from blackened surfaces at different angles.

The method of observation is very simple. Fig. 46

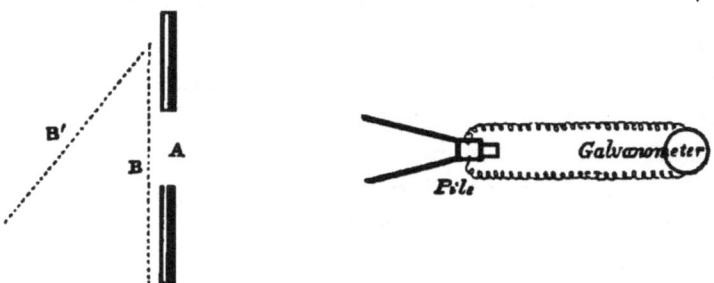

Fig. 46.

represents the arrangement, where *A* is an aperture behind which the heated body is placed. Now if this body be a blackened surface, it is quite immaterial whether it be placed in the position *B* or *B'*, provided it be large enough to fill up, in the latter position, the field of view from the cone; in both cases the galvanometer attached to the pile will give the same indication. Undoubtedly, when the surface is in the position *B'*, a greater extent of this will be viewed by the cone; but as far as radiant heat is concerned, we may imagine the surface to be projected upon the aperture *A*, so that if the field behind this aperture be filled up by the blackened surface its inclination or curvature is of no consequence.

202. We have seen that the stream of radiant heat which beats upon the thermometer in our enclosure of constant temperature is independent both of the materials and of the shape of the walls of the enclosure, so that if the instrument be carried from one part to another, there will be no change in the amount of radiant heat falling upon it. Something more however is necessary, for we must not only have the *quantity* of heat which falls upon the thermometer the same throughout, but the *quality* of this heat must also remain the same. It will be necessary to give a short explanation of the word '*quality*.' It is well known that different kinds or qualities of light affect the same substance in different ways, thus red glass will absorb green light while it will allow red light to pass. In like manner there are a great many different kinds of dark heat, and the same substance will absorb some of these much more rapidly than others. So also heat as well as light may be polarized, and we have already seen (Art. 193) that a substance such as tourmaline absorbs heat polarized in one plane with greater avidity than heat polarized in a plane perpendicular to the former.

Now the word '*quality*' is here taken to denote *any difference, whether of wave length or polarization*, which causes rays of heat to be differently absorbed by any substance.

When we say therefore that two pencils of heat are of the same quality, we mean that the mixture of wave lengths in the one is precisely the same as in the other, and also that the polarization of both is the same.

Suppose now that our thermometer is covered with some substance which displays this selective absorption for certain kinds of heat, and that we carry it about from one part of the enclosure to another. It will not only be necessary that the *quantity* of radiant heat which beats upon our thermometer shall be the same throughout the enclosure, in order that the instrument may preserve its constancy of temperature, but the *quality* of this heat must also be the same; for if not, we might suppose that in one place the heat is of a kind that is greedily absorbed by the coating of the bulb, and that in another place it is of a kind that is reflected back from this coating; thus although the quantity of heat falling on the bulb might be the same in both places, yet the thermometer would absorb more in the first case than in the second, and its constancy of temperature would be destroyed. It is therefore clearly necessary that the stream of radiant heat

which beats against the thermometer as it is carried about
in the enclosure should be the same at all places, both as
regards *quantity* and *quality*.

Various experiments go to prove this uniformity both in
the quantity and quality of the heat from different parts of
an enclosure of constant temperature. Perhaps the most
striking of these is that when an enclosure is heated to
a red or white heat the luminous rays from the different
parts of this enclosure will be the same both in quantity
or luminosity, and in quality, or colour, and will depend only
on the temperature, and not on the nature of the materials
composing the walls of the enclosure.

Again, as regards polarization, certain experiments by
Provostaye and Desains appear to shew that the stream of
heat in an enclosure of constant temperature is unpolarized,
and that if there be a reflecting substance in the enclosure,
so that the reflected portion of the heat from it is polarized,
then the radiated heat from this substance will be polarized
in the opposite way, so that the whole heat reflected and
radiated together is unpolarized.

203. We are now in a position to extend the remark
already made (Art. 199) with regard to the equality of the
absorption and radiation of a surface in our hypothetical
enclosure. Such a surface must not only give back by
radiation to the general stream of heat as much as it withdraws by absorption, but what it gives back must be of the
same quality as that which it withdraws. The absorption
of such a surface will therefore be equal to its radiation,
and this equality will hold for every individual kind of heat
of which the whole heterogeneous radiation is composed.

204. We deduce therefore, as the result of our inquiries,
both theoretical and experimental, in this branch of our
subject, that in an enclosure of constant temperature—

1. *The stream of radiant heat is the same throughout,*

both in quantity and quality; and while it depends on the temperature it is entirely independent of the materials or shape of the enclosure.

2. *This stream is unpolarised.*

3. *The absorption of a surface in such an enclosure is equal to its radiation, and this holds for every kind of heat.*

205. Heat equilibrium of plates. Returning once more to our chamber of constant temperature, let us suspend in it a thin plate of rock salt. Now since the temperature of this plate remains constant, the plate must radiate just as much heat as it absorbs. But rock salt (Art. 191) absorbs very little heat, hence also it will radiate very little. Moreover, a thick plate will absorb more than a thin one, and hence also it will radiate more. Both of these conclusions have been verified by the author of this work. By making use of the thermo-pile he has found that the radiation from a thin plate of rock salt is only 15 per cent. of the total lamp-black radiation for the same temperature, and that the radiation from a thick plate of rock salt is greater than from a thin one.

206. Suppose, however, that instead of rock salt we had suspended two plates of glass of unequal thickness. Since this substance is extremely athermanous, either of these plates would probably absorb nearly all the heat which fell upon it, and hence the radiation of both plates (radiation being equal to absorption) would be sensibly the same, and would be very great—in fact it would be much the same as if they stopped the whole heat, or were covered with lamp-black.

207. From this we see what it was that misled the early experimentalists on this subject, and induced them to think that radiation was confined, if not to the surface of a body, at least to a very small depth beneath it. They found that when a metallic surface was coated with varnish its radiative power was very much increased, but that very soon this increase attained its maximum, after which an additional coating produced no further effect. But the reason of this was, not that radiation is in all cases confined to a very small distance beneath the surface, but that these coatings were of a very athermanous substance, so that a very small thickness was practically equivalent to a surface of lampblack. Could it have been possible to apply a coating of transparent rock salt, the result would have been very different.

208. Let us now take our thermometer and cover its bulb once more with a substance having a selective absorption for heat, and, further, let us hang up before it in the enclosure a plate of rock salt. No change in its indication will take place; but in order that the temperature of this thermometer may remain without change it is obviously necessary that this plate of rock salt should change neither in quantity nor in quality the stream of heat which impinges against the bulb; that is to say, this stream after it has passed through the salt must be precisely the same both in quantity and in quality as before it entered it. In order that this may be the case it is necessary that the absorption of the rock salt should be equal to its radiation for every kind of heat.

This result has also been verified experimentally by the author of this work. If the kind of heat which rock salt radiates be the same as that which it absorbs, it would follow that a cold plate of rock salt ought to be exceedingly opaque to the radiation from heated rock salt. This was found to be the case. A moderately thick plate of this substance was found to stop at least three-fourths of the heat from a thin plate of heated rock salt, whereas it will only stop a small proportion of ordinary heat.

209. This affords an explanation of the fact that two plates of rock salt placed the one behind the other, or a single plate of double thickness, do not radiate twice as much as a single plate. For let *EF* be the front surface of such a double plate, of which *CD* represents a line midway between the two surfaces. Now, while as much heat will cross the line *CD* from the hinder half of the plate as would be radiated from the single

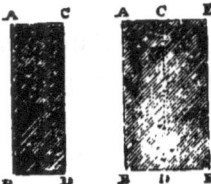

Fig. 47.

plate *ABCD*, a great proportion of this heat (probably three-fourths) will be absorbed by the front half in its passage through it, since we have seen that rock salt absorbs intensely the heat which it radiates. Hence, if the radiation of the single plate be $= 1$, that of the double plate, instead of 2, will probably not be more than $1\frac{1}{4}$.

210. Our readers will thus be prepared to see that radiation is a thing which goes on in the interior of a plate just as much as near the surface; and they will also see that it does not necessarily follow from this that the radiation of a plate should be proportional to its thickness, but very much the reverse;—indeed, had the substance of the plate in Fig. 47 been glass instead of rock salt, the single plate would have given out sensibly the same amount of heat as the double plate, since in the latter the heat from *ABCD* would all have been stopped by *CDEF*. We are thus prepared to see that *in the interior of substances, as well as in air or vacuo, a stream of radiant heat is constantly passing and repassing in all directions, and in the case of constant temperature, as this stream of heat passes any layer of particles it is just as much diminished by the absorbing action of these particles as it is recruited by their radiation, so that the stream flows on virtually unchanged* *both in quantity and quality until at last it reaches the surface.*

211. Amount of internal radiation. We have now to consider a more difficult question, which may be thus stated. Supposing we have several different substances all remaining at the same constant temperature, will the streams of radiant heat continually passing and repassing in the interior of these substances be equal to each other? In the first place, and before attempting to answer this question, we must shew how the intensity of a stream of radiant heat may best be measured. For this purpose let us suppose a small square surface representing unity of area to be placed in the interior of an enclosure, or of a substance surrounded by an enclosure kept at an uniform temperature. In accordance with our views, streams of radiant heat will be continually passing through this surface in all directions; let us confine our attention to these rays, which are as nearly as possible perpendicular to the plane of our square unit. But it may be said, why not confine our attention to rays strictly perpendicular to this plane? In answer to this, we remark that in our present investigation (the reason will afterwards appear) we must regard a ray in the sense in which a straight line is regarded. And just as a line is in reality always part of the boundary of a solid, so a ray is always in reality part of the boundary of a beam or pencil of light. We may satisfy ourselves that this is the case in nature by considering the light which reaches the eye from a star or other object apparently very small; this would seem to be the nearest approach to a geometrical line of light, whereas since a star has a certain real though very minute angular diameter, the light from it is in reality a converging pencil, although no doubt the angle of convergence is very small.

We will confine our attention therefore to rays as nearly

as possible perpendicular to our unit area. Let B (Fig. 48) represent this area, and let CBD be a very small pencil or cone of rays nearly perpendicular to the plane of B, the central line AB being strictly perpendicular to this plane. Now if we suppose the angle CBD as well as our unit area to remain constant while we pass from one substance to another, then the quantity of heat radiated in unit of time upon this unit area B through directions comprised within the small cone CBD will denote the intensity of internal radiation of the substance in question.

212. The circle CAD may in fact be compared to the disk of a small star whose diameter CD subtends with the eye the angle CBD

Fig. 48.

(greatly exaggerated in the diagram for the purpose of demonstration), and from which a beam or pencil of light represented by the cone CBD reaches the eye of the terrestrial observer at B. Now imagine, for the sake of demonstration, that it is possible to place the eye in the interior of a substance of constant temperature, and also that the eye is sensible to all the rays which compose, according to our hypothesis, the entire radiation of the substance, then it is evident that if the eye look in the direction of CAD, the *brightness* of the field of view in front of the eye or of any given detached portion of it, such as the area CAD, will indicate the internal radiation; so that, if the eye be now removed to the interior of another substance of greater internal radiation, more rays will strike it in front from CAD in one second of time, and the field of view will therefore appear brighter in the very same proportion in which the internal radiation is increased.

213. Let us now direct our attention to an enclosure, such as a sphere (Fig. 49), kept at a uniform temperature, and suppose the lower half of this enclosure to be filled with an uncrystallized solid or liquid (index of refraction = μ) while the upper half is a vacuum. Let us also suppose that the external boundary of this upper half of the sphere is covered with lamp-black, and let the area B be now placed on the surface of the solid or liquid, while the area CAD is a very small circle approximately coinciding with the

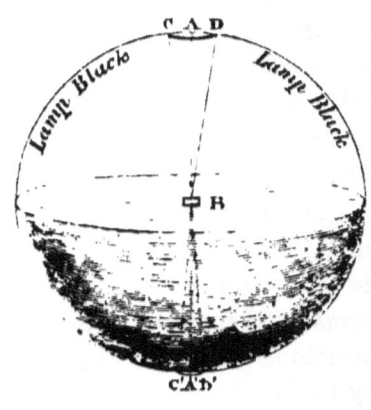

Fig. 49.

lamp-black boundary of the sphere. Let us denote by R the radiation of lamp-black, that is to say, R will represent the number of heat rays which *reach* the unit area B through the directions of the cone CBD in one second of time.

214. Part of these rays *reaching* B will be reflected back; let us call this reflected portion aR; then $R-aR$, or $(1-a)R$, will denote the amount of these rays which *really penetrate* the medium in one second of time. But these rays will be bent by refraction towards the perpendicular, after entering the medium, and will therefore be comprised in a cone $C'BD'$ with a smaller angle than CBD.

The angle $C'BD'$ may very easily be found;—for

$$\frac{\sin CBA}{\sin C'BA'} = \mu;$$

or, since these angles are very small,

$$\frac{CBA}{C'BA'} = \mu, \quad \text{or} \quad \frac{CBD}{C'BD'} = \mu.$$

We thus see that of the rays under consideration a portion

equal to $(1-a)$ R *enters* the substance, and is after its entrance embraced in a cone of which the angle

$$C'BD' = \frac{CBD}{\mu}.$$

215. But since the substance we are considering, being of constant temperature, gains as much heat as it loses in all of its parts, it follows that as much heat must *pass out* by B along lines embraced within the cone $C'BD'$ as *passes into* the substance through these same directions. Hence the quantity of heat which will *pass out* of the substance by B along lines embraced within a cone having the angle $C'BD'$ will (for one second of time) be $(1-a)$ R.

216. Now let R' be the unknown internal radiation for the medium; that is to say, let R' denote the quantity of heat rays which will in one second reach B from the interior in directions comprised within a cone which has a constant standard angle equal to CBD (Art. 211). We must find what fraction of this radiation will reach B if the angle be $C'BD'$ instead of CBD. It is evident that the amount of heat reaching B through the directions of the cone CBD will be proportional to the area CAD, and this area will be proportional to the square of CD, and very nearly to the square of the angle CBD. Hence—

Heat through $C'BD'$: heat through CBD $(=R')$: : $(C'BD')^2$: $(CBD)^2$.

Therefore—

Heat from interior through $C'BD' = R' \times \left(\dfrac{C'BD'}{CBD}\right)^2 = \dfrac{R'}{\mu^2}$ by Art. 214.

We thus see that a quantity of heat $= \dfrac{R'}{\mu^2}$ will in one second of time reach B from the interior through the cone $C'BD'$. But of this heat we know from the laws of optics that the amount a $\left(\dfrac{R'}{\mu^2}\right)$ will be reflected back into the interior, and hence $(1-a)\dfrac{R'}{\mu^2}$ will be the heat which *passes out* through B through the cone $C'BD'$.

217. We have thus obtained two expressions, one for the heat which enters the substance through B and diverges through the directions of the cone $C'BD'$, namely $(1-a)\,R$ (Art. 214), and the other for the heat which passes out through B through the same cone, namely $(1-a)\dfrac{R'}{\mu^2}$; and we have seen (Art. 215) that these two expressions must be equal to one another.

$$\text{Hence } (1-a)\,R = (1-a)\,\frac{R'}{\mu^2};$$

$$\therefore \qquad R' = \mu^2 R.$$

That is to say, the internal radiation in a substance of which the index of refraction is μ will be $\mu^2 R$, R denoting the radiation of lamp-black corresponding to the temperature of the experiment.

It is also clear from what we have said that this relation will hold for every individual description of heat of which the whole radiation is composed.

EQUILIBRIUM OF LIGHT RAYS.

218. It is of importance to extend these observations to radiant light, or to those rays which affect the eye, and this extension has been made both by Professor Kirchhoff of Heidelberg and by the author of this work.

We have already endeavoured to accumulate evidence in favour of the opinion that radiant light and heat are only varieties of the same physical agent, differing from one another simply in wave length; but during the progress of this branch of science many inquirers have been inclined

to think that light and heat are physically distinct, although
possessing many properties in common, and it has even
been imagined that some kinds of light are entirely destitute
of any heating effect.

But if it can be shewn thàt the consequences of Prevost's
theory extend to radiant light, we are furnished with very
strong evidence in favour of that hypothesis which regards
heat and light as varieties of the same agent.

219. Prevost's theory consists of the three following
statements.

1. If an enclosure be kept at a uniform temperature, any
substance surrounded by it on all sides will ultimately attain
that temperature.

2. All bodies are constantly giving out radiant heat, at a
rate depending upon their substance and temperature, but
independent of the substance or temperature of the bodies
that surround them.

3. Consequently when a body is kept at uniform temperature it receives back just as much heat as it gives out.

From these statements follow all the laws that have been
deduced for radiant heat.   But in the process of argument
it is essential to regard the rays under consideration as being
capable of heating the bodies on which they fall and by
which they are absorbed.

Hence, if this theory extend to light, it follows that
uminiferous rays are capable also of heating more or less
the bodies by which they are absorbed.

The following experiments exhibit the extension of the
theory of exchanges to rays of light.

220. Light equilibrium of surfaces.   It has been
shewn with respect to Heat (Art. 199) that good reflectors
are bad radiators, and a similar experiment may be made
for light.   Thus if a pot of red-hot lead or tin be carried
into a dark place and the dross scummed aside by a red-hot

iron ladle, the liquid metal will appear less luminous than the surrounding dross.   Also if a piece of platinum partly polished and partly tarnished be held above the flame of a Bunsen's burner in a dark room, the tarnished portion will shine much more brilliantly than the polished.   Finally, if we take a piece of stoneware of a black and white pattern, heat it to redness and then view it in the dark, the black will shine much more brightly than the white, presenting a very curious reversal of the pattern, which we have endeavoured to delineate in Figures 50 and 51.

Fig. 50.   Fig. 51.

221. Light equilibrium of thin plates. *Experiment I.*—If a piece of colourless transparent glass be heated to redness in the fire, removed to the dark, and then viewed, it will be found to give out very little light; but if the glass be coloured, its light radiation will be more copious, the amount of light given out depending upon the depth of colour.   This is an experiment analogous to that with rock salt, and it is evident that colourless glass gives out but little light because it absorbs but little.   A stratum of heated air may likewise be instanced as a substance which neither absorbs nor emits light or heat to a sensible degree.

222. *Experiment II.*—It has been shewn that the heat radiated by a thin plate of any substance at a given temperature is precisely that kind of heat which the plate absorbs when heat of that temperature is allowed to fall upon it. Now the same thing holds with regard to light. With respect to the rays proceeding from an ordinary fire, all coloured glasses may be divided into two groups, those which redden and those which whiten the fire as we look through them. The first group comprises red and orange glasses, and these absorb the whiter descriptions of light; the second group comprises green and blue glasses, and these absorb the redder kinds of light. We should therefore expect red and orange glasses to give out, when heated, a peculiarly white light, and green and blue glasses a peculiarly red light. Now this is found to be the case. A red glass coloured by gold, when heated to redness, removed, and viewed in the dark, gives out a milky-white or even greenish light, and the orange glasses used by photographers do the same. On the other hand, green and blue glasses give out, when thus heated, a reddish kind of light. This experiment is analogous to that wherein it is shewn that a cold plate of rock salt stops a large proportion of the heat from a hot plate of the same substance.

223. *Experiment III.*—Again, we know (Art. 193) that when a ray of ordinary light falls upon a plate of tourmaline cut parallel to the axis, it absorbs nearly all that resolved portion of the rays which is polarized in a plane parallel to the axis of the crystal, while it allows to pass a considerable portion of those which are polarized in a plane perpendicular to the axis. Now it can be shewn that if such a plate be heated red hot, the rays of light which it gives out are partially polarized in the same direction as those which it absorbs, viz. in a plane parallel to the axis. This experiment may best be tried by a method devised by Professor Stokes, in which a hollow cast-iron bomb is heated to redness. This bomb is represented in Figures 52 and 53. In Figure 52 we see it

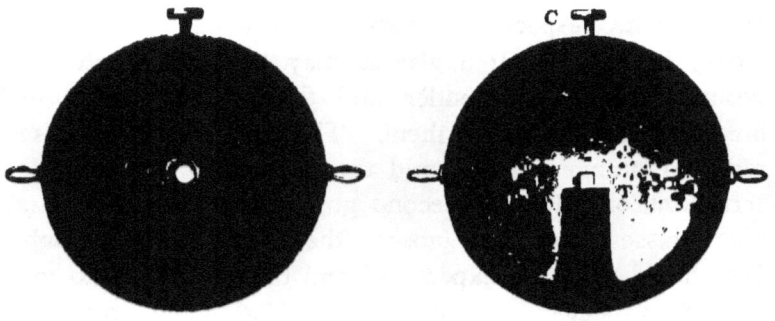

Fig. 52.   Fig. 53.

as it appears from the outside, with a small hole by which we can see through it. Fig. 53 represents a cross cut through the centre of the bomb, shewing the tourmaline *T* attached to a stand, *C* denoting the moveable lid. This tourmaline is in the very centre of the bomb, and hence in looking through the bomb, by means of the small hole, the eye encounters the plate of tourmaline. Now let this bomb be heated to redness, having the tourmaline inside of it, and then taken out of the fire and placed in the dark. The tourmaline will cool very slowly in this position, since it is (with the exception of the small hole) entirely surrounded by a red-hot enclosure, viz. the interior of the bomb, which, if the iron be sufficiently thick, will remain hot for some time. Now the eye in looking through the bomb by means of the small hole will encounter the radiated light from the heated tourmaline, and by means of a polariscope it is easy to ascertain in what plane this light is polarized. It will be found to be polarized in a plane at right angles to that in which light is polarized as it passes through the same tourmaline when cold and similarly placed.

224. *Experiment IV.*—We have seen that in an enclosure of uniform temperature the flow of radiant heat is the same in all directions, both as regards quantity and quality, whatever be the substances with which the enclosure is filled. Now with regard to light a good coal fire may be viewed as an enclosure of approximately uniform temperature, and accordingly we ought to find that, whatever substances be put into this fire, when these ultimately become of the same temperature as the fire, they will not alter the nature of the light which is given out. We may prove this by throwing coloured glasses into the fire, and when these become sufficiently heated they will be found to have lost all their colour. The red glass, for instance, which we have thrown in will, as we have already seen, give out a greenish light on its own account; but it will pass red light from the coals behind it in such a manner that the light which it radiates precisely makes up for that which it absorbs; so that we have *virtually a coal radiation* coming partly from and partly through the glass.

225. We cannot conclude this subject without alluding to a very interesting experiment first made by Foucault, but afterwards revived and extended by Kirchhoff, in which the equality between radiation and absorption is extended to individual rays of the spectrum.

Foucault found that the voltaic arc formed between charcoal points often emits the ray D of the solar spectrum on its own account, and at the same time absorbs it when it comes from another quarter. Kirchhoff, again, found that coloured flames, in the spectra of which bright sharp lines present themselves, weaken rays of the colour of these lines when such rays pass through the flames. We thus see that the same media which in a heated state emit rays of a certain refrangibility in great abundance have also the power of stopping these rays when they fall upon them from another source.

CONCLUDING REMARKS.

226. We have thus arrived both theoretically and experimentally at a law which may be enunciated as follows:—

Bodies when cold absorb the same rays which they give out when hot. The reader will at once be struck with an analogy between sound and light in this respect. A musical string when at rest takes to itself and therefore absorbs the very note (given out by another instrument) which it will itself give out when in a state of vibration.

Reasoning from this analogy Professor Stokes had suggested beforehand the probability of a connexion between the absorption and radiation of bodies for particular rays of the spectrum, and he also imagined that this suggestion would account for the dark lines in the solar spectrum.

The prediction of this philosopher has been abundantly confirmed by the labours of Kirchhoff; but the striking conclusions with regard to the constitution of the sun and stars which Kirchhoff has experimentally arrived at must be deferred till another chapter.

We cannot, however, refrain from remarking that the law developed in this chapter affords a valuable confirmation by analogy of the truth of the undulatory theory of light. The likeness between a vibrating string and a heated particle has been remarked above, and we have seen that a particle (just as a string with regard to sound) absorbs the same kind of ray which it gives out. It is, perhaps, allowable to infer that light, like sound, consists of undulations which are propagated in a medium surrounding bodies, and that when heat or light is absorbed by a particle, the motion is conveyed from the medium to the particle, just as when a string takes up a note passing through the air the motion is conveyed from the air to the string; and that, again, when heat or light is radiated by a particle it is similar to the giving out by a string of its note to the air.

CHAPTER IV.

Radiation at Different Temperatures.

227. It has already been shewn (Art. 204) that the stream of radiant heat continually proceeding through an enclosure of which the walls are kept at a constant temperature depends only on the temperature of the walls, and not on the nature of the various substances of which they are composed; the only difference being that for metals this stream is composed partly of radiated and partly also of reflected heat, while for lamp-black it is composed wholly of radiated heat. This may be expressed by saying that this stream depends upon or is a function of the temperature, and of it alone; but there is the following very important difference between a reflecting and a lamp-black surface, as representing this stream of radiant heat.

It is only when a reflecting surface forms part of a *complete enclosure* of the same temperature as itself, that the radiated and reflected heat from this surface together represent the whole stream of heat; for if we bring it for a moment into another enclosure of lower temperature, the reflected heat is altered, and although the radiation will for a short time continue nearly constant, yet this radiation will not represent the whole stream of heat due to the temperature of the surface.

On the other hand, if a lamp-black surface be placed in the above position, since the stream of heat which flows from it is entirely independent of the reflection due to neighbouring bodies, the heat which it radiates when brought for a moment into an enclosure of lower temperature than itself will truly represent the stream of radiant heat due to the temperature of the lamp-black.

228. Suppose now that we have a thermometer with a blackened bulb, and that this is placed in a blackened enclosure of a lower temperature than itself, the heat which it radiates will represent the total radiation due to the temperature of the bulb, while that which it receives will represent the total radiation due to the temperature of the enclosure, and the difference between these two will thus be represented by the loss of heat experienced by the thermometer.

Thus, if θ be the temperature of the enclosure, and $t + \theta$ that of the bulb, then, since the stream of radiant heat (Art. 204) is a function of the temperature only, we shall have this stream represented by $F(t + \theta)$ and $F(\theta)$ for these two temperatures, and the rate at which the thermometer loses heat will be denoted by $F(t + \theta) - F(\theta)$.

This is the rate at which the instrument loses radiant *heat*, and it will also represent the rate at which it loses *temperature*, or the velocity of cooling, as this is termed, if we suppose that the specific heat (or heat required to produce a change of 1°) of the mercury of the thermometer remains the same for all the temperatures of the experiment. This, though not precisely, is very nearly the case, and hence the velocity of cooling of a thermometer placed in these circumstances may be regarded as representing with great accuracy the intensity of radiation.

With these remarks we shall now discuss the experiments that have been made on velocity of cooling.

VELOCITY OF COOLING; VARIATION WITH TEMPERATURE
OF *QUANTITY* OF RADIATION.

229. Newton was the first to enunciate his views on the
cooling of bodies. He supposed that a heated body exposed to a certain cooling cause would lose at each instant
a quantity of heat proportional to the excess of its temperature above that of the surrounding air. It was, however,
soon found that this law was not exactly followed, and
several philosophers made experiments on the subject with
more or less success, until the time of MM. Dulong and
Petit, who made a very complete and successful investigation
of the velocity of cooling of a thermometer both in vacuo
and in air. It is with their experiments in vacuo that we
have now to do.

230. The apparatus used by these experimentalists consisted of a hollow globe of thin copper with the interior
blackened, which could be immersed in a vessel of water
of known temperature. Through an orifice in this globe
a thermometer could be inserted, so as to have its bulb in
the centre of the globe. The temperature of this thermometer was always higher than that of the globe, and the
number of degrees that the mercury would sink in a minute,
supposing the cooling to be uniform during that time, was
taken to denote the velocity of cooling.

A preliminary set of experiments was first made, from
which it appeared that the *law of cooling* of a liquid mass is
independent of the nature of the liquid and of the form and
size of the vessel which contains it. Having determined this,
MM. Dulong and Petit proceeded to make their final experiments with a thermometer containing about 3 lbs. of mercury. In the first instance this thermometer preserved its
natural vitreous surface, but since glass is exceedingly opaque
towards the heat radiated at all the temperatures of the

experiment, the results may be regarded as being nearly identical with those which a thermometer with a blackened bulb would have given.

The following were the results obtained where the temperature of the enclosure was that of melting ice.

Excess of temperature of the thermometer. °C.	Velocity of cooling. °C.
240	10.69
220	8.81
200	7.40
180	6.10
160	4.89
140	3.88
120	3.02
100	2.30
80	1.74

We see at once from this table that the law of Newton does not hold, for according to it the velocity of cooling for an excess of 200° should be precisely double of that for an excess of 100°: now we find that it is more than three times as much.

231. In Dulong and Petit's experiments both the excess of temperature of the thermometer and also the absolute temperature of the enclosure were made to vary, that is to say, both t and θ varied; and they obtained the following results.

Excess of temperature of thermometer. (t)	Velocity of cooling, for various temperatures of enclosure.				
	$\theta = 0°C.$	$\theta = 20°C.$	$\theta = 40°C.$	$\theta = 60°C.$	$\theta = 80°C.$
240	10.69	12.40	14.35	...	...
220	8.81	10.41	11.98	...	...
200	7.40	8.58	10.01	11.64	13.45
180	6.10	7.04	8.20	9.55	11.05
160	4.89	5.67	6.61	7.68	8.95
140	3.88	4.57	5.32	6.14	7.19
120	3.02	3.56	4.15	4.84	5.64
100	2.30	2.74	3.16	3.68	4.29
80	1.74	1.99	2.30	2.73	3.18
60	...	1.40	1.62	1.88	2.17

Now if we divide the numbers of the third column by the corresponding numbers of the second—for instance, 12.40 by 10.69—we find the quotient to be 1.16; and continuing the process for the other numbers in these columns, we find :—

$$\frac{\text{3rd column}}{\text{2nd column}} \text{ gives as quotients, } 1.16, 1.18, 1.16, 1.15,$$

1.16, 1.17, 1.17, 1.18, 1.15.

In like manner

$$\frac{\text{4th column}}{\text{3rd column}} \text{ gives as quotients, } 1.16, 1.15, 1.16, 1.16,$$

1.17, 1.16, 1.17, 1.15, 1.16, 1.16.

$$\frac{\text{5th column}}{\text{4th column}} \text{ gives as quotients, } 1.15, 1.16, 1.16, 1.15,$$

1.17, 1.16, 1.18, 1.16.

$$\frac{\text{6th column}}{\text{5th column}} \text{ gives as quotients, } 1.15, 1.15, 1.16, 1.17,$$

1.16, 1.17, 1.17, 1.15.

These numbers are all nearly the same, and their mean is 1.165. Hence we see that corresponding numbers in the various columns form a geometrical progression, so that if we denote a number in the second column by unity we shall have

$$1, \ 1.165, \ (1.165)^2, \ (1.165)^3, \ (1.165)^4,$$

as representing the velocities of cooling for the same excess of temperature for the cases where the temperature of the enclosure is denoted by 0°, 20°, 40°, 60°, and 80°.

We are thus entitled to say that *the velocity of cooling of a thermometer in vacuo for a constant excess of temperature increases in a geometrical progression when the temperature of the surrounding medium increases in an arithmetical progression, and the ratio of this progression is the same whatever be the excess of temperature.*

232. MM. Dulong and Petit soon saw that this remark would enable them to find the law of cooling.

In the first place, it ought to be observed that the results already given are in accordance with the theory of exchanges, and that they form an additional proof of the truth of that theory. The theory of exchanges asserts that the loss of heat experienced by a thermometer cooling in vacuo is represented by the difference between the radiation due to the temperature of the thermometer and that due to the temperature of the enclosure. Hence, according to this theory, if A, B, C denote the absolute radiation at the temperatures a, b, c, of which a is the highest and c the lowest, then

$A - B$ will represent the rate of cooling of a thermometer of temperature a in an enclosure of temperature b:

$B - C$ will represent the rate of cooling of a thermometer of temperature b in an enclosure of temperature c:

$A - C$, or $(A - B) + (B - C)$, that is to say, the *sum of the two preceding rates will represent the rate of cooling of a thermometer of temperature (a) in an enclosure of temperature (c) if Prevost's theory is true.* Testing this by the table of Art. 231, we find that if $a = 140°$ and $b = 80°$ ($l = 60°$, $\theta = 80°$), then the velocity of cooling is 2.17. Again, if

$$b = 80° \text{ and } c = 20° \ (l = 60°, \ \theta = 20°),$$

the velocity of cooling is found to be 1.40. Hence the sum of these two rates will be

$$2.17 + 1.40 = 3.57.$$

Once more : if $a = 140°$ and $c = 20°$ ($l = 120°$, $\theta = 20°$), we find from the same table that the velocity of cooling is 3.56. Now this is as nearly as possible equal to the sum of the two preceding rates, which was 3.57; so that the evidence derived from these experiments is decidedly in favour of the theory of exchanges.

Assuming therefore the truth of this theory, MM. Dulong and Petit supposed that the velocity of cooling of a thermometer in vacuo may be represented by the function $F(t+\theta)-F(\theta)$, where the first term represents the absolute radiation of the thermometer whose temperature is $t+\theta$, and the second term the counter-radiation of the enclosure whose temperature is θ.

233. Now we have seen (Art. 231) that for an excess of temperature of 200° of the thermometer above that of the enclosure the velocity of cooling may be denoted thus—

Temperature of enclosure	= 0°C.	20°	40°	θ°
Velocity of cooling ($t = 200°$) =	7.40	7.40(1.165)	7.40(1.165)^2	. . .
—	—	= 7.40	7.40(1.0077)^{20}	7.40(1.0077)^{40} 7.40(1.0077)$^{\theta}$.

In like manner if t, or excess of temperature, = 180°, we shall have—

Temperature of enclosure	= 0°C.	20°	40°	θ°
Velocity of cooling ($t = 180°$) =	6.10	6.10(1.0077)^{20}	6.10(1.0077)^{40}	6.10(1.0077)$^{\theta}$.

It thus appears that for an excess = 200° we have 7.40 as a constant multiplier of the various terms, while for an excess = 180° this multiplier becomes 6.10. This multiplier varies therefore with the excess of temperature, or t, but not with the absolute temperature of the enclosure, or θ, if only the excess remains constant; it is therefore a function of t, and we may represent it by $\phi(t)$, according to the usual notation. Hence we see that the velocity of cooling for any values of t and θ may be represented by

$$\phi(t) \times (1.0077)^{\theta}.$$

But the velocity of cooling (Art. 232) is also represented by $F(t+\theta)-F(\theta)$.

Hence these two expressions must be equal to each other, or

$$F(t+\theta)-F(\theta) = \phi(t) \times (1.0077)^{\theta}.$$

Dividing by $(1.0077)^\theta$ we have

$$\frac{F(t+\theta)-F(\theta)}{(1.0077)^\theta} = \phi(t);$$

and expanding in terms of t we find

$$\frac{\left\{ F(\theta) + \frac{dF(\theta)}{d\theta}t + \frac{d^2F(\theta)}{d\theta^2}\frac{t^2}{1.2} + \&c. \right\} - F(\theta)}{(1.0077)^\theta} = A + Bt + Ct^2 + \&c.,$$

or $\quad \dfrac{dF(\theta)}{d\theta}\dfrac{t}{(1.0077)^\theta} + \dfrac{d^2F(\theta)}{d\theta^2}\dfrac{t^2}{1.2(1.0077)^\theta} + \&c. = A + Bt + Ct^2 + \&c.$

Now since this equation must hold good for all values of t we may equate corresponding coefficients; and hence

$$\frac{dF(\theta)}{d\theta}\frac{1}{(1.0077)^\theta} = B = \text{a constant quantity,}$$

$$\text{or} \quad \frac{dF(\theta)}{d\theta} = B(1.0077)^\theta.$$

Hence integrating

$F(\theta) = m(1.0077)^\theta + \text{a constant quantity} \left(\text{if } \dfrac{B}{\log 1.0077} = m \right);$

and hence also

$$F(t+\theta) = m(1.0077)^{t+\theta} + \text{a constant quantity.}$$

The velocity of cooling of the thermometer in vacuo will therefore be represented by

$$F(t+\theta) - F(\theta) = m(1.0077)^\theta (1.0077^t - 1);$$

where $t+\theta$ is the temperature of the thermometer, and θ that of the enclosure in Centigrade degrees.

The value of m in the present case is 2.037, as may be easily found from the table of results.

When the bulb of the thermometer was covered with silver it was found that the velocity of cooling might be expressed by the same formula, only with a change in the value of m. Here it was necessary to suppose $m = 0.357$.

234. We are thus induced to suppose that the expression

one substance to another, will represent the absolute radiation corresponding to the temperature θ; but this expression must nevertheless be considered as an empirical formula satisfying observation, but which we are unable to deduce as a consequence from any known properties of matter. In truth our knowledge of the forces concerned in radiation is very small.

MM. Prevostaye and Desains have since made experiments on the cooling of bodies, which tend to confirm the accuracy of the results obtained by Dulong and Petit.

235. Absolute measure of radiation. While the experiments of Dulong and Petit were admirably adapted to give the law of cooling, they are not so well fitted to determine in absolute measure the radiation from a heated body. This has since been done approximately by Mr. Wm. Hopkins. Mr. Hopkins represents by unity the quantity of heat required to raise 1000 grains of water one degree Centigrade, and in terms of this unit he measures R, or the amount of radiant heat, which would emanate in *one minute* from a *square foot* of a given surface. He thus obtained as the radiation in vacuo for

Glass,
$$R = 9.566\, a^\theta(a^t - 1).$$
Dry Chalk,
$$R = 8.613\, a^\theta(a^t - 1).$$
Dry New Red Sandstone,
$$R = 8.377\, a^\theta(a^t - 1).$$
Sandstone (Building Stone),
$$R = 8.882\, a^\theta(a^t - 1).$$
Polished Limestone,
$$R = 9.106\, a^\theta(a^t - 1).$$
Unpolished Limestone (same block),
$$R = 12.808\, a^\theta(a^t - 1).$$

Where *a* retains the value given in Dulong and Petit's experiments, viz. $a = 1.0077$, and θ denotes the temperature of the enclosure, while t denotes the excess of temperature of the hot surface.

VARIATION WITH TEMPERATURE OF QUALITY OF HEAT.

236. Having now considered the law of cooling as representing with much accuracy the *quantity* of heat given out by a black substance at different temperatures, we come next to the relation between the temperature and the *quality* or nature of the heat given out. And here we may remark that the laws which connect the radiation of a black body with its temperature, both as regards the quantity and the quality of the heat given out, hold approximately for bodies of indefinite thickness which are not black,—thus, for instance, they would hold for a metallic surface, which would represent very nearly a lamp-black surface, with the radiation diminished a certain number of times.

These laws would not, however, hold exactly for a white surface, such as chalk; for this substance behaves like lamp-black with respect to rays of low temperature, while it is white for rays of high temperature, and the consequence of this will be that its radiation will increase less rapidly than that of a lamp-black surface. In like manner, these laws will not hold exactly for coloured surfaces.

Now with regard to a lamp-black surface, which, as we have seen, is the proper representative of heated surfaces, we have reason to believe that the following laws hold.

1. *The spectrum of the radiant heat or light given out by a lamp-black surface is a continuous one, embracing rays of all refrangibilities between certain limits on either side.* Thus the spectrum of an ordinary fire is a continuous one, and in like manner that of the electric light, or of carbon at a very high temperature, is also continuous.

2. *We have reason to believe, that as the temperature rises the spectrum of a black substance is extended in the direction of greatest refrangibility, so as to embrace more and more of the violet and photographic rays.*

This extension of the spectrum is also very perceptible to the eye, for a body at first emits only dark rays or rays of low refrangibility, then it becomes red hot, after which it is of a yellow heat, and finally it becomes white hot.

There is thus a very apparent change with increasing temperature in the refrangibility of the radiation; and this is produced in the first place, as we have seen, by the addition of rays of a high refrangibility, which are (at least as far as we can judge) absent from the radiation of lower temperature. But besides this, we are induced to believe that each individual ray of the low temperature is increased for the high temperature, only a ray of high refrangibility is increased in a greater proportion than one of low refrangibility, so that perhaps the average refrangibility is augmented at the same time that the total amount of radiation of any given refrangibility is also increased. Thus, the radiation from a piece of coal just below redness consists entirely of dark rays, while that from the sun embraces a large proportion of luminous and chemical rays, and is probably of a much higher average refrangibility than the radiation from the coal; but the dark rays common to both bodies likewise occur in greater amount in the solar radiation, where they form, in fact, a spectrum of great heating power towards the left of the red.

237. It thus appears that the rays proceeding from a heated body do not sensibly affect the human eye until the body has attained the temperature of redness, after which the body rapidly increases in luminosity. Thus, for a range of at least 500° Fahr. above the temperature of the eye the rays of heat emitted by a body are invisible. The cause of this invisibility is rather a physiological than a physical question; nevertheless, the suitableness of this arrangement is at once apparent, for if any other law were to hold— if, for instance, the eye were affected by each substance in proportion to the difference between its radiation and that due to the temperature of the human body—it is difficult to conceive how we could either enjoy the advantages of darkness, or experience that variety of shade and colour which is one of the chief pleasures of vision. It is also worthy of remark that by the present arrangement our safety is secured, for the eye is generally able to detect the presence of combustion when it occurs.

RADIATION OF A PARTICLE; RADIATION OF GASES.

238. Having discussed the radiation from heated surfaces, that from thin plates or particles comes next to be considered. Take, for instance, a glass plate at a low temperature: this will stop nearly all the rays corresponding to this temperature, and therefore it will behave very much like a lamp-black surface. But at a high temperature (above redness, for instance) it will pass a great many of the rays of this temperature; and hence, its proportional absorption being less, its proportional radiation compared to lamp-black will also be less. The radiation of such a plate will not therefore increase with the temperature as fast as that from a lamp-black surface. Many other bodies beside glass possess the property of being more opaque to heat of low than to that of high temperature, and for all these the radiation will not increase with the temperature so fast as that from a black surface.

The thinnest plates of solid or liquid substances which we can obtain will not, however, afford us the means of studying the radiation from a particle; in order to do this recourse must probably be had to a gas, each of whose particles we may perhaps suppose acts for itself, and is not fettered by the neighbouring particles in the way in which it would be in the solid or liquid state.

239. In studying the radiation of gases we are led to some very peculiar laws.

1. In the first place, we may say that *the general absorption and radiation of gases are often small, while on the other hand the selective absorption and radiation of many of them are very strong.* The feeble radiation from heated air was observed by Melloni, and the feeble absorptive power of it (and of many other gases) for light is familiar to every one. Nevertheless, by aid of electricity we are enabled to heat a portion of any gas or vapour to a very high temperature, so as to obtain a visible spectrum from it, which we may then analyze by means of the spectroscope. Such spectra when obtained are always discontinuous, that is to say, they consist of a very intense radiation of certain disconnected spectral rays, while the intervening spaces are totally, or nearly, dark. It matters not what gas be subjected to analysis, the result obtained is of this nature in all cases. The spectra of all gases are thus characterised by a few bright lines on a dark background.

2. In the next place, *as far as we know at present, the bright lines given out by any one gas have not been found to coincide in spectral position with those given out by any other gas.* One or two coincidences of this kind have been suspected, but these have not been confirmed by results of a more searching analysis. Elaborate researches on the spectra of gases have been made by various philosophers.

3. In the third place, *the spectra of gases probably remain of the same character, with certain limitations to be afterwards mentioned, throughout a very wide range of temperature.* Thus we know that the vapour of metallic sodium, as soon as it has attained a yellow heat, will give out exclusively the

double line D in the yellow, and it will continue to radiate this kind of heat up to the highest temperature we can produce. The same law holds for other gases and vapours, only we must make the following exception. If, for instance, one of the bright lines given out by a heated vapour be in the blue of the spectrum, and if this vapour be capable of existing at a red heat, we must not expect that it will give out the blue line at this heat, nor until the temperature rises to such a degree that blue becomes one of the constituent rays of that temperature. When this is reached the blue line will be given out, and when once given out it will probably continue for all higher temperatures.

240. These laws of gaseous radiation have lately become of great practical importance. Let us recapitulate them.

In the first place, the spectrum of an ignited gas consists of a few bright lines of definite refrangibility.

Secondly, these lines are probably not the same for any two substances.

Thirdly, the lines peculiar to any substance remain the same throughout a great range of temperature.

If to these three laws we add the following chemical one, namely, that at a very high temperature most substances are decomposed, we shall soon readily perceive the great practical importance of this combination of facts.

For if we already know the spectra of the various chemical elements, and if we heat a specimen of any substance presented to us for analysis sufficiently to resolve it into its elements and to drive these into the state of vapour, then will the position of the bright lines of the spectrum of the flame obtained enable us to ascertain what elements were present in the substance, since each element will furnish its own peculiar lines, which are supposed to be known and recognizable. It was first remarked by Professor Swan that by means of the well-known and peculiar double line

D the presence of a salt of sodium may be detected in a most delicate manner; and Bunsen and Kirchhoff, who have done much more than any one else to introduce and perfect this method of analysis, remark that by means of the spectroscope the presence of less than $\frac{1}{200,000,000}$ of a grain of sodium may probably be detected. Bunsen has also by this means discovered two new metals, namely *cæsium* and *rubidium.* Our countryman Crookes has discovered *thallium,* and Messrs. Reich and Richter *indium,* by the same means.

An apparent exception to the law that the nature of the spectrum of a gas remains constant throughout a great temperature range, ought to be remarked in the case of nitrogen, which changes the nature of its spectrum at a very high temperature. This is viewed by some as an indication that nitrogen is in reality a compound body, since the same change takes place in the spectra of some other gases which we know to be compound.

241. Before concluding this chapter we ought to allude to the beautiful discovery of Kirchhoff, by which it has been proved that substances with which we are here familiar exist also in the atmospheres of the sun and stars. It had been observed, first by Wollaston and after him by Fraunhofer, that the solar spectrum contains a number of dark lines, while it is in other respects a continuous spectrum, and the latter observer extended his remarks to the spectra of many of the fixed stars. The origin of these lines for a long time remained a mystery, nor was this mystery diminished when it was found by Fraunhofer that a bright band corresponding in refrangibility to the double dark line D of the solar spectrum was produced by the light of a flame containing sodium. Sir D. Brewster was the first who prepared the way for the solution of this problem, by shewing that analogous (not identical) lines might be artificially produced by interposing a jar of nitrous acid gas in the path of a ray of light. The inference naturally drawn from this experiment was, that the lines of the solar spectrum do not denote rays originally wanting in the light of the sun, but are due to the absorption of his light by some substance interposed between the source of light and the spectator. It was doubtful, however, whether this stoppage of light occurred in the atmosphere of the sun or in that of our earth, until the matter was finally settled by Kirchhoff, not however before the true explanation had been divined by Professor Stokes.

Kirchhoff found that a sodium flame which gives out on its own account the double line D absorbs a ray of the same refrangibility when it is given out by a body of a higher temperature than the sodium flame, thus producing a dark line D instead of a bright one, and he therefore conjectured that the dark line D in the light of our luminary was occasioned by the presence of the vapour of sodium in the solar atmosphere, and at a lower temperature than the source of light. This belief was strengthened by his finding that many of the dark solar lines correspond in position with the

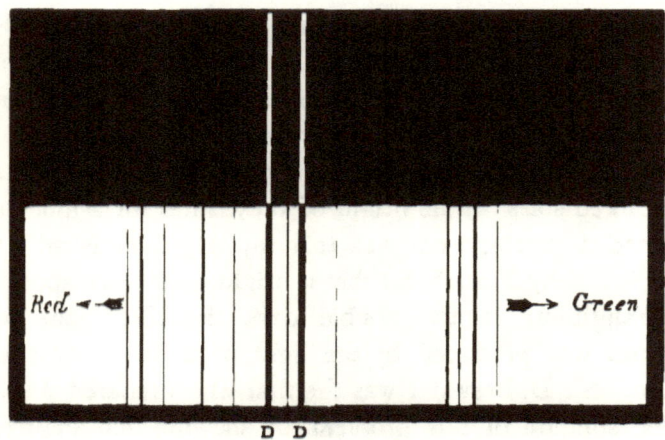

Fig. 54.

bright lines given out by metallic vapours, and by this means he detected the presence not only of sodium but also of iron, nickel, calcium, magnesium, barium, copper, and zinc, in the atmosphere of our luminary. In Fig. 54 we have a sketch of the appearance presented when the sun's spectrum is compared with that of the vapour of sodium.

By a similar process Messrs. Miller and Huggins have detected the presence of sodium, magnesium, hydrogen, calcium, iron, bismuth, tellurium, antimony, and mercury in Aldebaran, and other elements in other stars.

More lately Mr. Huggins, in directing his spectroscope to certain nebulæ, was surprised to find that their light resolved itself into bright lines with a dark background, thereby indicating from analogy that these bodies are vast masses of incandescent gas. The position of these lines appeared to indicate that the composition of these curious bodies was a mixture of nitrogen and hydrogen, but about this there is some uncertainty.

A still more recent experiment of Donati would appear to indicate that the constitution of comets is similar to that of the nebulæ above mentioned, and that these erratic visitants are likewise composed of incandescent gas. This, however, is not yet well proved *.

It would thus appear that through the laws of radiation we are likely to attain much information regarding the structure of the universe, both as regards the constitution and materials of celestial systems, and perhaps also as regards the internal structure of material molecules.

* While this work is being printed Mr. Huggins has successfully directed his spectroscope to Comet I, 1866, and he finds that the light from the nucleus consists of bright lines, appearing thus to indicate ignited gas ; on the other hand, the coma has a continuous spectrum.

CHAPTER V.

Radiant Heat.

Further Remarks on Absorption.

242. It has already been stated (Art. 183) that the spectrum of a radiant body may be divided into three, according to three effects which rays produce. The first of these is the heating, the second the luminous, and the third the chemical, spectrum.

The absorptive behaviour of substances with regard to the different rays of the spectrum is exceedingly varied in character, and forms at the same time a subject well worthy of our study both from its theoretical and practical importance.

With regard to light, we know that the absorption of a substance for certain rays produces the colour of the substance, and sometimes enables us to determine its composition by means of its peculiarity of colour; but if we were able to study the behaviour of a substance not only with respect to light but also with respect to dark heat and chemical action, it is quite clear that we should both extend our knowledge of the relation which substances bear to various kinds of rays, and also add largely to our means of discriminating between different substances.

We shall now shortly study the behaviour of bodies with respect to dark heat and to light, reserving for another chapter their behaviour with regard to chemical rays.

ABSORPTION OF DARK HEAT BY DIFFERENT BODIES.

243. Delaroche was the first to shew that bodies exercised a selective absorption for dark rays, or sifted a stream of dark heat passing through them; and from this he argued that such heat consists of different kinds of rays mingled together, just as white light consists of a mixture of differently coloured rays; and these conclusions of Delaroche

Melloni. The method of analysis adopted by Melloni will be seen from the following table, although the heat is not strictly dark, being the rays from a Locatelli lamp.

Transmission of 100 incident rays.

Names of substances interposed; thickness, unless mentioned, 2.6 millimètres.	Rays from lamp.	Rays from alum, thickness 2.6 millimètres.	Rays from sulphate of lime, thickness 2.6 millimètres.	Rays from chromate of potash, thickness 2.6 millimètres.	Rays from green glass, thickness 1.85 millimètres.	Rays from black glass, thickness 1.85 millimètres.
Rock salt	92	92	92	92	92	92
Fluor spar	78	90	91	88	90	91
Iceland spar	39	91	89	56	59	55
Glass, thickness 0.5 mm.	54	90	85	68	87	80
„ „ 8 mm.	34	90	82	47	56	45
Rock crystal	38	91	85	52	78	54
Acid chromate of potash	34	57	53	71	28	24
Sulphate of baryta	24	36	47	25	60	57
White agate	23	70	78	30	43	17
Feldspar	23	23	58	43	50	23
Yellow amber	21	65	61	20	13	·8
Opaque black mica, thickness 0.9 mm.	20	0.4	12	16	38	43
Yellow agate	19	57	64	24	35	14
Aigue marine	19	60	57	26	20	21
Borate of soda	18	23	33	23	30	24
Green tourmaline	18	1	10	14	24	30
Common gum	18	61	52	12	6	4
Sulphate of lime	14	59	54	22	9	15
„ thickness 12 mm.	10	56	45	17	5	0.4
Carbonate of ammonia	12	44	34	11	6	5
Citric acid	11	88	52	16	3	2
Tartrate of potash and soda	11	85	60	15	2	1
Alum	9	90	47	15	0.5	0.3
Glass, white	40	90	83	50	67	55
„ violet	34	76	72	42	56	47
„ red	33	74	69	41	54	45
„ orange	29	65	58	36	48	39
„ apple green	25	3	20	22	25	50
„ mineral green	23	1	15	19	52	58
„ yellow	22	49	46	27	35	30
„ blue	21	47	42	26	34	29
„ opaque black	16	0.5	18	11	42	52
„ indigo	12	27	26	14	20	17

244. If we refer to alum in the first column of this table we find that only 9 per cent. of the heat from the naked lamp passes through a screen of this material, while 90 per cent. of heat which has already passed through one screen of alum is capable of passing through a second. So in like manner, choosing sulphate of lime from the first column, we find that it only passes 14 per cent. of naked heat, but 54 per cent. of heat which has already passed through the same material. The same thing may be remarked for chromate of potash, green glass, and black glass, so that. all of these substances are capable of sifting heat in such a manner that a second plate will pass a greater proportion of the heat which has already passed through one plate of the same material than it will of naked heat.

We see occasionally, too, evidences of athermanous combinations in the above table, just as red and green glass together produce an opaque combination. Thus rays which have passed through alum will scarcely pass at all through black mica or black glass, through green tourmaline or green glass. It appears that in particular black glass and alum are antagonistic combinations, and the reason is supposed to be that alum is exceedingly opaque for all rays below the red and transparent to those above it, while black glass, on the other hand, is comparatively diathermanous for rays up to red, but opaque for those above it.

Thus we know in a general way that there are different varieties of dark heat, but how these are distributed in the spectrum, or what are the positions of the absorption bands produced by a screen which exhibits a selective absorption for dark heat, we do not know. By no device have we as yet been able to render visible in an unexceptionable manner this region of the spectrum.

245. More lately Professor Tyndall has made some very interesting experiments on the absorption of bodies, but especially gases for dark heat. These were made by means of a very delicate thermo-electric apparatus, and from them we learn that the absorptive power of the three permanent simple gases for dark heat is exceedingly small. He has also shewn that where aqueous vapour is present in the atmosphere on a day of average humidity its absorption is upwards of sixty times that of the air itself. We derive the following table from Professor Tyndall's memoir on the subject.

Comparative absorption of various gases, each of the tension of 1 *inch.*

Air	1	Carbonic oxide	750
Oxygen	1	Nitric oxide	1590
Nitrogen	1	Nitrous oxide	1860
Hydrogen	1	Sulphide of Hydrogen	2100
Chlorine	60	Ammonia	7260
Bromine	160	Olefiant gas	7950
Hydrobromic acid	1005	Sulphurous acid	8800

246. The results of this table are very remarkable, and Professor Tyndall deduces from it the fact that for the heat experimented on, the absorption of the simple gases is much less than that of the compound ones. It would also appear that the same chemical change which renders chlorine and bromine more transparent to light renders them more opaque to obscure heat. Professor Tyndall has likewise shewn that the absorptive power of scents for dark heat is very strong, as also that of ozone. With regard to the action of vapours, that of bisulphide of carbon he found to be very small; and he also found that a solution of iodine in liquid bisulphide of carbon formed a medium which might be rendered perfectly opaque for light while it was very transparent for dark heat. Enclosing this substance in rock salt, so as to form a lens, he was enabled by this means to cut off all the luminous rays from the electric light, while he condensed the dark rays so powerfully as to produce ignition in the focus of his fluid lens.

ABSORPTION OF LIGHT BY DIFFERENT BODIES.

247. It is a well-known fact that a coloured body, such as red glass, absorbs one kind of light more than another; but even when bodies are apparently of the same colour their power of absorbing certain rays of light may be very different. In order, therefore, to analyze completely the relation of a substance to light, a pure spectrum must be formed by means of a narrow luminous slit·lighted up by the sun or by the electric light, and the substance to be examined must be held in front of the slit ;—in this way certain rays will either be entirely wanting in the spectrum or at least be partially stopped, being absorbed by the substance in front of the slit.

The following example will serve to shew that bodies very similar in colour have nevertheless a very different selective absorption for certain rays of light. Port wine and blood are two fluids very similar in appearance, but the former merely causes a general absorption of the more refrangible rays of the spectrum, while the latter produces two dark bands in the yellow and green. These bands were first observed by Hoppe. Professor Stokes has chosen this very example in order to shew the value of selective absorption for light as a discriminating test of the presence of certain substances. He remarks that the colouring matter of blood contains a large quantity of iron, and that it might therefore be supposed that the colour is due to some salt of iron, more especially as some salts of the peroxide of iron have a blood-red colour. But there is found to exist a strong general resemblance, or family likeness, between salts of the same metallic oxide as regards the character of their absorption. Now none of the salts of iron give absorptive lines at all similar to those of blood, and Professor Stokes remarks that the assemblage of the facts with which we are acquainted seems to shew that the colouring matter of blood is some complex compound of the five elements, oxygen, hydrogen, carbon, nitrogen, and iron. This example is sufficient to shew the great importance of absorption as an auxiliary in chemical analysis. But in examining the selective absorption of bodies it is not necessary to have a solution. Thus, for example, if a spectrum be thrown upon a screen of paper painted with blood, the same dark bands are seen in the yellow and green as when the light is transmitted through a solution of blood. We thus see that the colour of a paper screen so painted is really caused by absorption, even although the paper is viewed by reflected light, and that it is not in reflection that the preferential selection for certain rays is generally made. The light, in fact, which is irregularly reflected from such a surface of paper has first of all to pass through a film of blood, and it is in this passage that the selective absorption is accomplished which produces the red colour.

248. Metallic reflection. There are, however, some very curious exceptions to this rule. Gold, for instance, reflects yellow light most abundantly, while a very thin leaf of gold transmits blue and green but absorbs yellow. Haidinger was the first to notice this fact in a general way, which he expressed by saying that the reflected and transmitted light from gold are complementary to each other. Professor Stokes was, however, the first to examine the subject in a complete manner. The substance he used was permanganate of potash. Crystals of this substance have a metallic appearance and reflect a greenish light. When this green reflected light is analyzed by the prism, bright bands are observed, denoting a maximum of reflecting power; and these bright bands correspond in position to dark bands in the light transmitted by a solution of the same crystal.

This is an exceedingly remarkable phenomenon, and it is the more interesting as it appears to be entirely confined to metallic and quasi-metallic bodies.

There are yet other peculiarities exhibited by bodies in. their action upon different rays, but these must be reserved until next chapter.

CERTAIN PRACTICAL CONSEQUENCES.

249. Suppose we have a large heated globe, as in Fig. 55 : and in the first place, let us suppose there is no en-

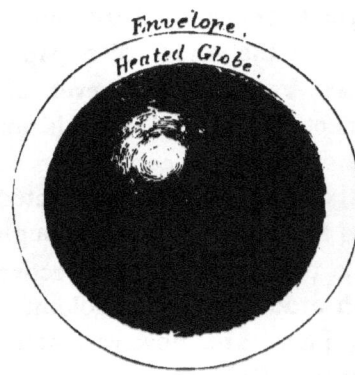

velope round it, but that it is free to radiate its heat into space without receiving back any in return. Let its velocity of radiation be denoted by R. Suppose now that this sphere is closely surrounded by a very thin envelope, opaque as regards the heat from the sphere; and let us imagine that there is no heat conveyed from the sphere to the envelope either by con-

Fig. 55.

vection or conduction, or in any other way than by radiation. Now let R' denote the radiation of this envelope outwards into space, then R' will also approximately denote the radiation of the envelope inwards towards the sphere, since as the envelope is very thin, both its surfaces may be imagined to be of the same temperature.

Hence the radiant heat which leaves the envelope will be $2R'$, while that which reaches it from the globe will be R.

But if the globe be very large and cool very slowly, the envelope will, it is clear, settle down into a state of equilibrium of temperature, and therefore its absorption will be equal to its radiation; that is to say,

$$R = 2R', \quad \text{or} \quad R' = \frac{R}{2}.$$

We see, therefore, that by an arrangement of this nature

the uncompensated radiation of the globe is diminished by one half, and by additional envelopes it would be still more diminished. The envelope has thus served to retain the heat of the globe by diminishing its uncompensated radiation into free space.

If we imagine the globe to be a body of comparatively low temperature, an envelope of a substance like glass will be sufficiently opaque for such heat to answer the purpose above indicated.

Let it be further supposed that the direct rays of the sun are the source of heat which keeps up the temperature of the globe. These rays, proceding from a source of very high temperature, will pass through the glass envelope with great facility, so that while this envelope will diminish the radiation from the sphere it will yet allow most of the rays from the source of heat to reach the sphere. Now imagine the sphere to be the bulb of a thermometer, and surround this with a thin glass envelope with a vacuum between, and it will be easily seen that by this means, even without the aid of a burning lens, the bulb may be heated by the rays of the sun to a considerable extent.

If we now suppose the source of heat, that is to say the sun, to be withdrawn, it is evident that the globe will cool more slowly with the envelope than without it, so that we may imagine the effect of such an envelope to tend in the first place to increase the temperature of the globe while the sun is present, and in the next to diminish the velocity of cooling when he is absent. But this twofold action of such an envelope in such a case will depend, it is evident, upon its being more opaque to heat of low than to heat of high temperature. Glass is one substance of this kind, but it has already been mentioned that this property is very common, so much so indeed that very few substances are transparent to heat of low temperature.

250. It has long been imagined that the earth's atmosphere is a body of this kind, and that while it stops a comparatively small portion of the sun's rays in their progress to the earth, it stops a very large portion of those which are given out from the surface of the earth.

That this is a property of our atmosphere has been rendered very probable by the experiments of Professor Tyndall upon the absorptive power of aqueous vapour for heat of low temperature, which he finds to be very great;—greater probably than we can suppose it to be for heat of high temperature, such as the sun's rays.

From the known presence of aqueous vapour in our atmosphere we may therefore infer that we are surrounded by an envelope which passes with comparative freedom the rays of the sun, while it absorbs most of the dark heat from the surface of the earth. Whatever we may suppose to be the whole effect both as regards radiation and convection of such an atmosphere during the day, there can be little doubt that during the night the absorptive nature of the atmosphere for dark heat diminishes the rate of cooling of the earth and thus perhaps serves to render it a fit habitation for living beings.

251. Rapid refrigeration in central Asia and in the African desert. Professor Tyndall has remarked the effect which an absence of aqueous vapour exerts upon the climate of certain portions of central Asia, and on that of the great African desert of Sahara. Owing to this absence the cooling of the earth after sunset is exceedingly rapid. Accordingly in central Asia the nights are very cold, and the winters almost unendurable. In the African desert, again, during the day the air is intensely heated, owing perhaps amongst other causes to the absence of evaporation; but during the night the refrigeration is so rapid that ice may sometimes be produced.

252. Formation of Dew. These remarks lead naturally to the subject of Dew. For the true theory of this phenomenon we are indebted to Dr. Wells, a London physician, who published an account of his experiments in 1818. By these he ascertained the following laws :—

1. Dew is most copiously deposited under a clear sky ;

2. And with a calm state of the atmosphere.

3. It is most copiously deposited on those substances which have a clear view of the sky ;

4. And which are good radiators (thus a gilded thermometer is less liable to be covered with dew than one ungilt) ;

5. And which are placed close to the earth.

6. The deposition of dew is always accompanied with a lowering of temperature; and at those places where dew falls most copiously the temperature sinks lowest.

Dr. Wells soon saw that the deposition of dew was owing to radiation. A solid substance which is a powerful radiator and is exposed to the clear sky gives off a great deal of its heat by uncompensated radiation into space, and is thus reduced below the temperature of the surrounding air. The particles of air in contact with the substance share in this reduction until they reach a temperature at which they can no longer retain their aqueous vapour, but must deposit it on the solid body.

We thus see why dew is most copious under a clear sky ; and if we reflect that the solid body is colder than the surrounding air, and can only obtain dew by cooling the particles of air in contact with it, we see the necessity for calmness of atmosphere. We see also why the substance must have a clear view of the sky.

Since the deposition of dew is the effect of cooling, we see why it is always accompanied with a fall of temperature; and the hypothesis that the lowering of temperature is caused by radiation is also quite in accordance with those experiments in which Dr. Wells found that dew was most copiously deposited on good radiators.

It is not at first sight so obvious why a substance suspended a little above the earth should have less dew than one at the earth's surface; but Dr. Wells' explanation is no doubt the correct one; he remarks that, in the case of a substance above the earth, when the air in contact with it becomes cooled it also becomes heavier and sinks down, its place being supplied by warmer air. The cooling in this case, just as in that in which there is a horizontal movement of the air, is not sufficiently intense to produce dew.

253. Artificial formation of ice. Dr. Wells by means of this theory was able also to explain the formation of ice in Calcutta, where shallow pans containing water are during night exposed to the clear sky, and are often in the morning covered with a layer of ice.

Professor Tyndall has justly remarked that the formation of ice under these circumstances, while it is due to radiation, demands nevertheless an absence of aqueous vapour from the air; and he quotes in favour of this view the remark of Sir Robert Baker, who, speaking of the formation of ice in Bengal, says that the nights most favourable for its production are those which are clearest and most serene, *and in which very little dew appears after midnight.*

CHAPTER VI.

Radiant Heat.—Phosphorescence and Fluorescence.

254. Phosphorescence. In the preceding chapters it has been attempted to shew that the radiation of a heated body is, both in quantity and quality, dependent upon the temperature of the body, and on it alone; and this law may be regarded as a very accurate expression of a great number of facts. Accordingly, if a thermometer were raised to 100° Fahr., either by exposure to the direct rays of the sun, or by immersion in hot water, we should expect to find its radiation precisely the same in both cases, and we should be right in our expectation.

Nevertheless, there are certain substances in which the nature of the radiation depends not altogether on their present temperature, but to some extent upon the kind of radiant heat to which they have recently been exposed.

Such bodies are said to be *phosphorescent.* It has been shewn by E. Becquerel that the property of becoming phosphorescent belongs to a great number of substances. Thus, if we take a tube containing powdered sulphide of calcium, or sulphide of strontium, and expose it to sun light or the electric light, if viewed afterwards in the dark it will remain luminous for several hours. Evidently this luminosity is not due to the temperature of the powder; and since this appearance takes place whether the powder be in vacuo or in air, it cannot be due to chemical action, and is probably rather due to a modification in the molecular state of the body caused by the action of light.

The same phenomenon may be observed in many diamonds, in fluor-spar, arragonite, chalk, heavy spar, and a number of other minerals; also among organic substances, in dry paper, silk, cane-sugar, &c.

255. In many instances this exhibition of light lasts for a considerable time after the exposure of the substance to the exciting source; but in some cases it disappears in a few seconds, or even in a very small fraction of a second. In order to investigate the duration of this effect Becquerel has invented an instrument called a phosphoroscope. In this instrument two disks are placed alongside of one another, having the same axle, and the substance to be tried for phosphorescence is placed in a fixed support between these disks; there are apertures in these disks, but the aperture in the one does not correspond to that in the other, so that it is impossible to see through the disks. Suppose now that on the other side of that disk which is further from the eye there is a source of light, such as the sun or the electric light, and that the disks by means of a suitable train of wheels are made to revolve with great rapidity; then at the time when the aperture of the disk further away exposes the substance in the support to the rays of light it will be hidden from the eye of the observer by the nearer disk, but a moment afterwards the opening of this disk will reveal it, and if phosphorescent it will then appear luminous. It is clear that by this arrangement the length of time elapsing between the exposure of the substance to the source of light and afterwards to the eye of the observer will depend upon the rapidity of rotation, and may therefore be made as small as possible. The observations must be made in a dark chamber. Becquerel found by this means that compounds of uranium are luminous only if viewed .003 or .004 of a second after exposure.

256. Fluorescence. Sir David Brewster was the first to remark that when the sun's light is condensed by a lens and admitted into certain solids or fluids, there appears to be an internal dispersion of the rays. Some time afterwards, in 1845, Sir J. Herschel began to study a very curious phenomenon connected with sulphate of quinine—which is in reality a colourless liquid—namely, that under certain aspects a solution of this substance exhibits a beautiful blue colour. This may be readily verified by viewing by daylight a solution of this substance placed in an ordinary test tube. Sir J. Herschel shewed that the incident light, after passing through a small thickness of the fluid, although not sensibly enfeebled or coloured, had lost its power of producing this effect. In a solution of quinine therefore there is a copious dispersion of light, which takes place near the surface, while there is also a feeble dispersion for a long distance within the fluid; and Sir D. Brewster was led to the belief that the dispersion produced by sulphate of quinine was only a particular case of internal dispersion.

257. Professor Stokes has since explained this phenomenon with great success. The circumstance to which he directed his attention was the fact that a very thin stratum of the fluid is sufficient to deprive the light of the power of again producing the same effect. The rays producing dispersion, he was led to see, are very quickly absorbed; but he remarked that the dispersed rays themselves are able to travel many inches of the fluid with great freedom. The rays producing dispersion are therefore of a different nature from the dispersed rays.

Professor Stokes was thus led to recognize a change in the refrangibility of the rays when they become dispersed. If it further be supposed that the rays causing dispersion are the invisible rays beyond the violet, this will account for the circumstance that the visible appearance of the light is not changed when it is deprived of its power of producing this phenomenon; and it will also account for the fact that the blue appearance can hardly be seen by candle light, which is deficient in chemical rays beyond the violet.

258. In order to prove this change of refrangibility Professor Stokes instituted a very extensive series of experiments, from which he deduced the following results: —

1. In the phenomenon of true internal dispersion the refrangibility of light is changed.

2. The refrangibility of the incident light is greater than that of the dispersed light to which it gives rise.

3. The nature and intensity of the light dispersed by a solution appear to be strictly independent of the state of polarization of the incident rays. The dispersed light is unpolarized, and appears to emanate equally in all directions, as if the fluid were self-luminous.

4. The phenomenon proves to be extremely common, especially in the case of organic substances.

5. It furnishes a new chemical test of a remarkably searching character, which seems likely to be of great value in the separation of organic compounds.

Professor Stokes has given a list of highly sensitive substances, of which the following is an extract:—

Glass coloured by peroxide of uranium.

A solution of the green colouring matter of leaves in alcohol.

A weak solution of the bark of the horse-chestnut.

A weak solution of sulphate of quinine, namely a solution of the common disulphate in very weak sulphuric acid.

Certain varieties of fluor-spar.

Red sea-weeds of various shades.

Various solutions obtained from archil and litmus.

Safflower red, scarlet cloth, and various other dyed articles in common use.

259. It is important to notice the very striking likeness between the phenomena of fluorescence and those of phosphorescence, noticed in the preceding part of this chapter: *in both cases it is found to be the most refrangible rays of the spectrum that produce the effect, and the dispersed rays appear always to have a lower refrangibility than the rays producing dispersion.*

In fact, it is now generally believed that the only difference between the two phenomena is one of *duration*, and that whereas in phosphorescence the acquired luminosity may last for a considerable time, in fluorescent substances, or at least in fluorescent solutions, the effect vanishes almost instantaneously when once the exciting ray is withdrawn.

260. In conclusion, it ought to be observed that the phenomena of fluorescence and phosphorescence afford peculiar facilities for the study of the invisible rays of the spectrum beyond the violet, and also for the study of the effects of the rays on different substances.

In order to obtain all the information which these phenomena can give, it is necessary to form the spectrum by means of a prism of rock crystal, and to use likewise a rock crystal lens, as this substance allows the more refrangible rays to pass, while they are absorbed by glass. If a spectrum so formed be thrown upon a screen, any substance to be examined for fluorescence or phosphorescence ought to be placed at the more refrangible end of the spectrum, and if it is found to become luminous in that position it may be assumed that it is fluorescent or phosphorescent.

If the object of the observer be to study the fixed lines in the invisible ultra violet portion of the spectrum, a screen of paper washed with a moderately strong solution of sulphate of quinine may be employed. The screen will thus be fluorescent, and will shine when exposed to the invisible rays, except for that part of it which corresponds to a dark line. The position of the dark line is thus obtained, and by this means Professor Stokes has been able to represent the spectrum far beyond the violet. It is needless to mention that a spectrum so obtained will agree in the position of the dark lines with one obtained by any other process.

CHAPTER VII.

Conduction of Heat.

261. If one end of a poker be thrust into the fire and
allowed to remain there, the other end will in course of
time become hot; the heat is thus conveyed to the further
end of the poker by means of the particles of the poker
itself, and this mode of conveyance is termed the conduction
of heat.

Many simple experiments might be mentioned in illustration of this property possessed by bodies of conveying heat
by means of their particles.   Thus if a silver spoon be held
in the flame of a candle or thrust into hot water, the end
which is held in the hand will soon become inconveniently
hot, while if a wooden or stone-ware spoon be used instead,
no inconvenience will be felt by the hand, for in this case
the particles have not the same facility for conducting
heat.

We thus perceive a difference between the conducting
power of different substances, and indeed it is well known
that the faculty of conducting heat is possessed by metals
much more than by other bodies; gems and hard stones
come next in order: while certain organic substances, such
as wool, feathers, &c., and gases, such as air, possess this
property to a very limited extent.   Another familiar experiment is to wrap a handkerchief tightly round a polished ball
of metal; this may be held for some time in the flame
of a candle before the handkerchief is burned, the heat being

conducted rapidly into the substance of the metal. If however the ball be of wood instead of metal, the handkerchief will very soon take fire.

262. Conduction of heat, it will at once be seen, is a very different thing from radiation; and yet there is this bond of union between the two, that they both tend to diffuse heat in such a manner as ultimately to produce equality of temperature. Thus it has already been stated, that a thermometer placed in an enclosure of constant temperature will ultimately attain the temperature of the inclosure, and it is no less true that in a pot of melted metal the thermometer will attain the temperature of the metal; a good conductor therefore, such as a metal, distributes heat by conduction very rapidly, a bad conductor very slowly.

263. The conducting power of a body may be roughly recognized by the touch: thus if the temperature of a bar of metal be much higher than that of the hand, on touching it, heat is rapidly conveyed from the metal to the hand, and the sensation of heat is felt. Again, if the metal be much colder than the hand, heat is rapidly conveyed from the hand to the metal, and the sensation of cold is felt.

If, however, the substance be a very bad conductor, such as a woollen texture, we can handle it with impunity, even although it be considerably hotter or considerably colder than our body, and we can use it as clothing to protect us from the cold, since although the outer surface of such a texture may be exposed to a low temperature, yet the interior does not rapidly carry off the heat from our body; in like manner, if we touch anything hot we do it through a similar medium, and if we wish to preserve ice we keep it wrapt up in woollen cloth; in fine, the state of a substance with regard to temperature, whatever this may be, can best be preserved unaltered when the substance is surrounded by a non-conductor, such as wool or feathers. We shall now proceed to discuss the conduction of heat: first in solids, and secondly in fluids, including liquids and gases.

CONDUCTION OF HEAT IN HOMOGENEOUS SOLIDS.

264. The difference in the conducting power of different solids may be recognized by a very simple experiment. Let two bars, one of copper and one of iron, be fixed as in Fig. 56, and let them be heated equally by the flame of a

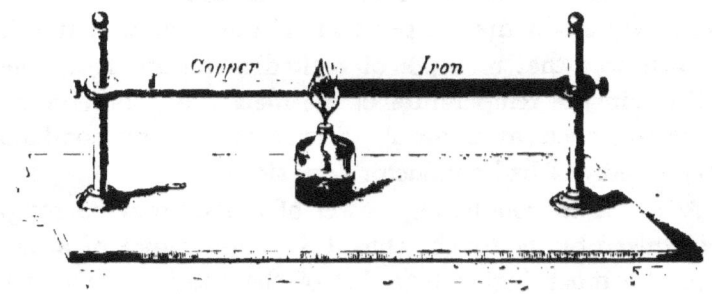

Fig. 56.

spirit lamp placed between them. In the course of time heat will be propagated along both bars, and they will both ultimately settle down into a state in which those parts of the bars nearest the flame will be hotter than those more remote from it.

The copper bar will however be hotter than the iron one at the same distance from the source of heat, so that a piece of phosphorus will take fire or wax will melt on the copper bar at a greater distance from the flame than on the iron one. Hence we infer that the conducting power for heat, or *thermal conductivity* as it is termed, is greater for copper than for iron.

265. Flow of heat across a wall. Fourier was the first to obtain a clear conception of this property of bodies, so as not only to define it precisely, but by applying to it mathematical calculation to bring the whole subject under the domain of accurate experiment.

In order to conceive a clear idea of conductivity, let us imagine a large vertical wall, one foot in thickness, made of some conducting substance, and let us suppose that the one side of this wall is constantly kept at the temperature 0°C by means of melting ice, while the other side is kept at a temperature 1°C higher; all the particles of such a wall will, it is clear, ultimately settle down into a permanent state with respect to temperature. Let *AB* (Fig. 57) denote the hotter side of this wall and *CD* the colder, the wall being perpendicular to the plane of the paper; also imagine *AC* to be a horizontal line, and let *AB* represent the temperature of the one side of the wall according to some fixed scale of temperature, while *CD* denotes that of the other side according to the same scale; and, finally, imagine the dotted line

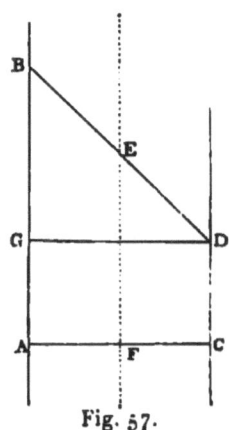

Fig. 57.

EF to represent an imaginary cut parallel to the sides of the wall and half way between them.

266. Now, in the first place, it is evident that there will be a regular diminution of temperature from the one side of the wall to the other, so that the temperature of this half-way section will be the mean between the temperatures of the two sides. On the same scale of temperature as that before used the dotted line *EF* will therefore denote the temperature of this half-way section.

267. It is clear also that there is a certain quantity of heat continually flowing from the wall *AB* to the wall *CD*, so that if we cut the wall by imaginary sections similar to *EF* there will be a flow of heat across all these sections in the direction of AC; and further, it is evident that this flow of heat will be the same across all the various sections; for if it were greater across a section near AB than across one near CD, then the space between these two sections would be receiving a greater amount of heat than it is giving out, and hence it would be rising in temperature. But by our hypothesis all parts of the wall have settled down into a permanent state with respect to temperature, and thus we see that the flow of heat must be the same across the different sections.

268. Again, were the difference in temperature between the one side and the other double of what it is, it is reasonable to suppose that the flow of heat would also be doubled, so that for two walls of the same substance and equal thickness the flow of heat will be proportional to the difference in temperature between the two sides.

269. If we now suppose the wall in the above figure to be split up into two equal sections, each six inches thick, by the imaginary plane EF, we see that the *very same* flow of heat may be regarded either as taking place across the wall of the entire thickness of one foot, the difference of temperature between the two sides being $1°C$, or as taking place across the section six inches thick, the difference of temperature between the sides being only $\frac{1}{2}°C$; that is to say, the flow of heat for a wall one foot thick and one degree Centigrade temperature difference between the sides is the same as that for a wall six inches thick and one half degree temperature difference between the sides.

This result may be put in the following tabular form :—

Thickness of wall.	Temp. difference between the sides.	Flow of heat.
One foot	$1°$ Cent.	1
Six inches	$\frac{1}{2}°$ Cent.	1

But by Art. 268 the flow of heat across a wall one foot

thick and one degree temperature difference is double of that across a wall of the same thickness with half a degree temperature difference. Hence—

Thickness of wall.	Temp. difference between the sides.	Flow of heat.
One foot	$\frac{1}{2}°$ Cent.	$\frac{1}{2}$

We see at once from this that the flow of heat across a wall one foot thick with half a degree of temperature difference is only half of that across a wall of half the thickness and the same temperature difference; or in other words, the flow of heat for the same temperature difference is inversely proportional to the thickness of the wall: and combining this with the result previously obtained (Art. 268), we may say that the flow of heat varies directly as the temperature difference, and inversely as the thickness. This may also be expressed in the following manner. Draw the line GD in Fig. 57 parallel to AC, then BG and GD represent the temperature difference and thickness of the wall, and hence—

$$\text{Flow of heat varies as } \frac{BG}{GD}; \text{ varies as } \tan BDG.$$

This law has been experimentally verified by M. Peclet.

270. Definition of conductivity. We are now in a position to define what is meant by thermal conductivity. *Supposing that we have a wall a unit in thickness, then by the conductivity of this wall we mean the quantity of heat referred to some constant unit which passes in unit of time across unit of surface of such a wall, the difference of temperature between the two sides being unit of our thermometric scale.* To make this still plainer, let us adopt as our unit of heat the quantity necessary to raise one pound of water from 0°C to 1°C, and as our units of space, time, and temperature difference, let us adopt one foot, one minute, and one degree Centigrade, then will the conductivity of the wall be denoted in this case by the number of pounds or fractional parts of a pound of ice-

cold water, which will be raised in temperature one degree
Centigrade by the heat which passes in one minute across one
square foot of this wall one foot thick, the difference of temperature between its two sides being one degree Centigrade.

If the substance of the wall be changed, so that while
other conditions remain the same, twice as much heat passes
across it in one minute, then we say that the second substance has twice the conductivity of the first.

Let C denote the conductivity of such a wall and F the
flow of heat across unity of surface in unity of time: then
if in Fig. 57 we denote our different units by equal lines, we
have—

$$F = C \times \frac{BG}{GD} = C \times \tan BDG = C \times \text{rate of decrement of temperature.}$$

271. Flow of heat along a bar. It is not, however,
by such a wall that we can best ascertain the conductivity of
a substance; for this purpose it is preferable to employ
a bar heated at one end. The principle by which the conductivity may be deduced from the temperature conditions
of such a bar was indicated by Fourier, and has been applied with more or less success by various experimentalists.
Professor (now Principal) Forbes was, however, the first who
conducted his research in such a manner as to get rid of
certain theoretical assumptions not strictly accurate, and to
leave his results to be decided entirely by experiment. We
shall now proceed to describe the course which he pursued
in his investigation.

A bar AB (Figs. 58, 59) is exposed at its extremity A to
a source of heat of constant temperature: in these experiments this extremity was fixed into a vessel full of molten
lead. If this bar be sufficiently long, its other extremity B
will virtually be of the same temperature as the surrounding
atmosphere; that is to say, it will be unaffected by the source
of heat at A.

When things have been left for a sufficiently long time, the bar will have settled down into a permanent state as regards

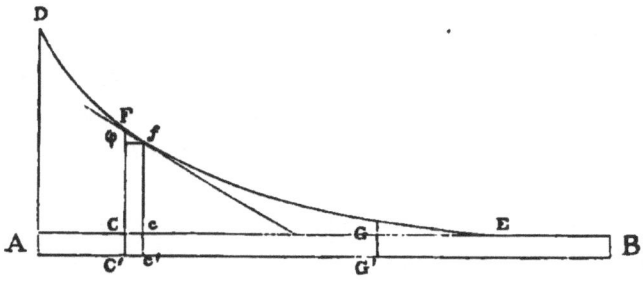

Fig. 58.

temperature, and in this state there will be a gradual decrease of temperature outwards from the extremity *A* of the bar.

Fig. 59.

By practice it was found possible to keep the extremity *A* of the bar at a nearly constant temperature, and it ought to be

of immersion must be defended by means of screens (Fig. 59) from the influence of the source of heat, so that the bar beyond A may be heated by conduction of heat, and by nothing else.

By means of thermometers plunged into small holes drilled in the bar, and kept by some fluid metal in metallic contact with the bar itself, the temperature of each part of the bar was accurately ascertained. An auxiliary bar LM, hung in the room sufficiently far from the source of heat, served to determine the temperature of the room. Deducting this from the temperature of the various parts of the bar AB, the difference will represent the excess of temperature of each part of AB due to the source of heat at A, and by having a sufficient number of thermometers a curve of temperature DE may be obtained, of which the ordinate AD represents the excess of temperature at A, the ordinate CF the excess at C, and so on. At the point E, where this curve cuts the bar, there is no excess of temperature; that is to say, E and all points beyond it are virtually unaffected by the source of heat at A.

272. Now it is clear that heat is constantly flowing outwards across any section of the bar CC', but since by hypothesis all parts of this bar have attained a constant state with respect to temperature, the flow of heat across CC' does not increase the temperature of the bar beyond CC'; what then does it do? A little consideration will shew that it is all spent in radiation and convection of hot air from the heated surface of the bar beyond CC'.

If, therefore, we are able to estimate the value of this radiation and convection for each portion of the bar beyond CC', the integral of this effect will represent the flow of heat across CC', which, as we have just now seen, is entirely carried off by radiation and convection.

273. Suppose that by this means we have been able to

ascertain the flow of heat across *CC'*. Now let *cc'* represent another cross section of the bar a little (but very little) further off than *CC'* from the source of heat, and let *CF* denote the temperature of the first section, and *cf* that of the second, the difference between these two temperatures is therefore ϕF, while the distance between the two sections is ϕf; our units of temperature and length being denoted by equal lines.

Hence if we imagine the sectional area of the bar to be denoted by unity, according to Art. 270, we shall have—

Flow of heat across *CC'* = conductivity $\times \dfrac{\phi F}{\phi f}$ = conductivity $\times \tan Ff\phi$ = conductivity $\times$ tangent of the angle denoting the downward slope of the temperature curve at the point *F*;

and hence—

$$\text{conductivity} = \frac{\text{flow of heat across } CC'}{\tan Ff\phi}. \qquad (1)$$

274. In this experimental investigation it is therefore necessary to determine two things: in the first place, we must have the means of drawing a true temperature curve; and secondly, we must be able to estimate the whole loss of heat due to radiation and convection united past any section *CC'*, since this, as we have seen, will represent the flow of heat outwards past the same section.

We have already stated how, in this investigation, the curve of temperature was determined by means of thermometers plunged into small holes in the bar, and we shall now proceed to shew how the amount of heat carried off by radiation and convection united past any given cross section *CC'* was determined. For this purpose a smaller but otherwise similar bar *LM* (Fig. 59) was heated to a temperature at least equal to the highest temperature of the bar *AB*. A thermometer *P* plunged into a small hole in the centre of this bar gave the velocity of cooling at the various temperatures of the bar.

It is clear from what we have already said (Arts. 228, 229) that the velocity of cooling of such a bar really denotes the rate at which heat is momentarily carried off by radiation and convection united from the bar at the various temperatures of observation, and a little reflection will convince us that by making use of these observed velocities of cooling we may be able to estimate the amount of heat carried off momentarily from all portions of the similar bar AB by radiation and convection united, since we know by the curve we have drawn the temperatures of the various parts of this bar.

Having thus estimated the amount of heat carried off by convection and radiation united from the surface of the bar AB past any cross section CC', we can find at once its equivalent or the flow of heat past this same section.

Knowing therefore this flow of heat, and being able to determine by means of the curve of temperatures the tangent of the angle denoting the downward slope of the temperature curve at any point F, we are able at once from the expression (1) Art. 273 to determine the conductivity at any section CC'.

275. It will be observed that this process is entirely devoid of any theoretical assumption with regard to the laws of radiation and convection, and that it may even be employed for the purpose of finding whether the conductivity of the bar AB varies from one point to another, or whether it is constant throughout. If this be constant throughout, then the expressions for the conductivity found by the process above described for two different sections CC', GG' will be the same. On the other hand, if the conductivity be not constant, but vary with the temperature, then the expression found for one cross section CC' will be different from that found for another section GG', since the temperatures of these two sections are different.

276. It was mainly with the view of ascertaining whether the thermal conductivity of wrought iron varies with the temperature that Professor Forbes made these experiments, and we will state the result obtained in a future paragraph. In the meantime, let us state the results obtained by other observers for the comparative thermal conductivity of the various metals.

M. Despretz was one of the first to make experiments on the subject, his instrument of research being a bar with thermometers plunged into it at different intervals from the source of heat. After him MM. Wiedemann and Franz investigated very carefully the relative conductivity of several of the most important metals. They operated with thin bars, and the temperature of these bars at the various points was ascertained by means of a thermo-electric arrangement.

Their results are embodied in the following table.

Metal.	Relative Thermal Conductivity obtained from experiments.	
	in air.	in vacuo.
Silver	100.0	100.0
Copper	73.6	74.8
Gold	53.2	54.8
Brass	23.6	24.0
Tin	14.5	15.4
Iron	11.9	10.1
Steel	11.6	10.3
Lead	8.5	7.9
Platinum	8.4	9.4
Palladium	6.3	7.3
Bismuth	1.8	

We are probably furnished in this table with very good determinations of the relative conductivity of these different metals. The same remark ought however to be made here that was made on a former occasion, when a table of the linear dilatations of different metals was given, namely, that difference in quality makes probably a very considerable difference in conductivity; and there is reason to think that the relative conductivity of pure copper is considerably greater than that here given.   This table gives however only the *relative* conductivity, and to complete our information we require to know the *absolute* conductivity of some one metal.   One or two observations of absolute conductivity have been made.   M. Peclet has determined the absolute conductivity of lead by finding how much heat was conveyed across a plate of this substance whose two sides were kept at unequal temperatures.

Principal Forbes, in connection with the experiments already described, has likewise determined the absolute conductivity of wrought iron.   In his experiments conductivity was expressed in terms of the amount of heat as unity which is required to raise the temperature of one cubic foot of water by one degree Centigrade.   It expresses the amount of heat reckoned in such units which would traverse in one minute across an area of one square foot a plate of iron one foot thick with the two surfaces maintained at temperatures differing by $1°$ Centigrade.   According to these experiments, the conductivity at $0°$ Centigrade of one of his bars was .01337, while that of another bar was only .00992.   This discordance was probably due to a difference in the quality of the iron of the two bars.

277. Variation of thermal conductivity with temperature. We have already mentioned that the main object of Principal Forbes in his research was to ascertain if the conductivity of an iron bar varies with its temperature.   The method employed has already been described; it only now remains to mention the results.   There were two square bars; the side of the one being $1\frac{1}{4}$ in., while that of the other was 1 in.

The following table exhibits the thermal conductivity of these bars at the various temperatures of experiment.

Temperature Cent.	Conductivity (units, foot—minute—degree).	
	1¼ in. bar.	1 in. bar.
0	.01337	.00992
25	.01235	.00943
50	.01144	.00904
75	.01070	.00865
100	.01012	.00835
125	.00966	.00813
150	.00934	.00795
175	.00904	.00779
200	.00876	.00764
225	.00851	.00749
250	.00826	.00736
275	.00801	.00724

It thus appears that in each case the conductivity diminishes as the temperature increases, the per-centage decrement of conductivity between 0° and 100°C being 24.5 for the large and 15.9 for the small bar of iron.

278. Similarity of bodies as regards their thermal and electric conductivity. Forbes was the first to shew that metals follow each other in the same order as conductors whether of heat or of electricity.

The following table, confirming this remark, was drawn up by MM. Wiedemann and Franz when they were engaged in determining the thermal conductivity of metals.

Names of metals.	Electric conductivity.			Thermal conductivity.
	Riess.	Becquerel.	Lenz.	
Silver	100.0	100.0	100.0	100.0
Copper . . .	66.7	91.5	73.3	73.6
Gold	59.0	64.9	58.5	53.2
Brass	18.4	...	21.5	23.6
Tin	10.0	14.0	22.6	14.5
Iron	12.0	12.35	13.0	11.9
Lead	7.0	8.27	10.7	8.5
Platinum . . .	10.5	7.93	10.3	6.4
German Silver .	5.9	...	...	6.3
Bismuth . . .	...	...	1.9	1.8

This similarity between bodies as regards their thermal and electric conductivities extends also to the decrement which their conductivity suffers when their temperature is increased.

In Art. 168 the decrement of the electric conductivity of iron between 0° and 100°C as determined by Matthiessen and Von Bose was found to be 38.26 per cent., while for the same metal and between the same limits of temperature Forbes, as we have just seen, has found a decrement of 24.5 and 15.9 per cent. in the thermal conductivity of his iron bars. The numerical value of the decrement for heat is thus considerably smaller than that obtained by Matthiessen for electricity.

279. Difference between transmission of heat and transmission of temperature. If the definition of thermal conductivity be considered, it will be found that it takes account of the quantity of heat referred to some unit which passes across a substance in unit of time.

Suppose now that we have two bars of different substances, but precisely of the same conductivity, and also of the same shape, and that we heat the ends of both to the same extent. If we allow a sufficiently long time to elapse, we shall no doubt find the distribution of temperature in both bars to be the same. But if we examine them both at the end of a short time, such as a minute, it does not follow that at the distance, say, of one inch from the heated end, they will both have the same temperature. The two cases are very different. In the former, the bar has attained a permanent temperature condition, and the flow of heat outwards is entirely spent in radiation and convection. If therefore two such bars of equal conductivity be coated with the same substance, so that their external surface is the same, then both bars will be similarly affected by radiation and convection. Referring therefore to previous articles, there is evidently no reason why any of the elements should be different in the two bars. Both will therefore have the same curve of temperature.

But in the second case, when we only allow a minute to elapse, the state of things is very different. Here the particles of the bar are in the act of rising in temperature; a great portion of the flow of heat is therefore spent in increasing the temperature of the bar. Now it may take much more heat to raise a given slice of the one bar one degree in temperature than it will take to raise a similar portion of the other.

The following experiment in illustration of this has been made by Professor Tyndall. Take two precisely similar prisms, one of bismuth and one of iron, and coat the ends of each with white wax, and place them with their coated ends upwards on the lid of a hot vessel. The wax will first melt on the bismuth, although by the table of Art. 278 it will be seen that iron is the best conductor. The reason of this is, that it requires more heat to raise the iron one degree in temperature than it does to raise the bismuth.

280. Safety-lamp. The present is perhaps the best opportunity of alluding to the safety-lamp, the action of which depends to a great extent on the withdrawal of heat by wire gauze. If a surface of wire gauze be lowered into the flame of a jet of gas, it will seem to crush the flame down before it so that none will appear above.

If now the flame be extinguished while the gauze is held in this position it may be ignited above the gauze, in which case there will be no flame below. It would thus appear that the flame cannot pass through the gauze, and the reason is that the heat of the flame is transferred in a great measure to the mass of metal which is placed upon it, by which means the temperature is so much lowered that combustion is stopped.

An ingenious and useful application of this principle was

devised by Sir Humphry Davy. He found by experiment that a lamp surrounded by wire gauze might burn in an explosive atmosphere without communicating sufficient heat through the meshes of the gauze to produce explosion, so that a miner furnished with a lamp of this kind, and using it with proper care, will be secure from the action of fire-damp.

CONDUCTIVITY OF NON-HOMOGENEOUS SOLIDS
AND OF CRYSTALS.

281. Owing to their want of continuity, powders and tissues, such as wool, fur, feathers, &c., are very bad conductors of heat. The heat has in its course to pass so often from the substance into the air, and from the air back again into the substance, that its progress is extremely slow.

In substances which possess a fibre, the conducting power for heat in a direction across the fire is generally different from what it is in the direction of the fibre.

MM. De La Rive and De Candolle were the first to remark this in the case of wood, for which they found that the conductivity was greater along the fibre than across it, a result which has been confirmed by Professor Tyndall. It has also been found by MM. Svanberg and Matteucci that bismuth conducts both heat and electricity better along the planes of cleavage than across them.

We are chiefly indebted to De Senarmont for our knowledge of the conduction of heat in crystals. He cut thin slices in different directions out of crystals, and piercing their thickness by small holes in the centre, he passed a wire through them along which a constant electric current was made to pass: the wire thus became very hot, and the heat was conducted on all sides of the hole. The slice of crystal was coated with wax, and the result of the heating of the crystal by means of the wire was a general melting of the wax all round the wire. If the substance was of equal conductivity in all directions then the wax melted in a circle, but if the conductivity was unequal it melted in an ellipse. The border of the melted portion represented by this method an isothermal line or curve possessing the same temperature throughout, this temperature being that of melting wax. De Senarmont thus determined that in quartz and calc-spar the axis of symmetry is the direction of greatest conductivity, while for a plate cut in a plane perpendicular to the axis of symmetry the conductivity is equal in all directions.

A crystal of idocrase, however, conducts best at right angles to its axis. De Senarmont has obtained the following laws :—

1. If we could imagine a crystal of the first system, such as rock-salt or fluor-spar, to be heated in a point in its centre, the isothermal surface would be a sphere, or the conductivity will be equal in all directions.

2. If the crystal be of the second or third system, (symmetrical around one axis,) then the isothermal surfaces of such a crystal, heated internally at a point, would be ellipsoids of revolution, the axis being in the direction of the axis of symmetry.

3. But if the crystal be of the system characterised by three unequal axes, then the isothermal surfaces are ellipsoids with three unequal axes.

CONDUCTIVITY OF FLUIDS.

282. The conductivity of liquids may be determined in the following manner. In Fig. 60 let there be a vessel of water in which we place a differential thermometer, one bulb being near the surface and one near the bottom. Now place a vessel containing boiling water or boiling oil on the surface, and it will be found that the heat from this vessel will penetrate downwards very slowly, so that for a long time the differential thermometer will scarcely be affected. Water is

thus proved to be a very bad conductor of heat. If we wish to try mercury, let the vessel of Fig. 12 be filled with mercury, and let a little alcohol on the surface be set on fire. It will be found that the thermometer will soon begin to rise, thereby shewing that mercury is a much better conductor than water. In the next chapter it will be shewn that heat is communicated in liquids more by convection than by conduction. It is believed that the conductivity of gases is, like that of liquids, extremely small; but this is a subject of which little is known, the experimental difficulties being very great.

Fig. 60.

CHAPTER VIII.

Convection of Heat.

CONVECTION IN LIQUIDS.

283. It was stated in the last chapter that liquids, such as water, are very bad conductors of heat, and an experiment was described in which a vessel of water was heated on the upper surface—the effect travelling downwards very slowly.

The heating of the water would however have been greatly hastened if the vessel had been heated from below instead of at the top, and the difference between the result in the two cases is due to a process termed Convection, which we shall now describe. As the lower strata of water in such a vessel become heated the particles expand; thus becoming specifically lighter than those above them. Their tendency is therefore to rise to the top, and to be replaced by colder particles descending from above, just for the same reason that a cork rises to the surface of water, or a balloon rises in the air. By introducing a little colouring matter, such as fragments of cochineal, the course of these currents may be observed, and it will be found that there is a central current ascending from below and side currents descending from above, after the manner of Fig. 61. In the Geysers of

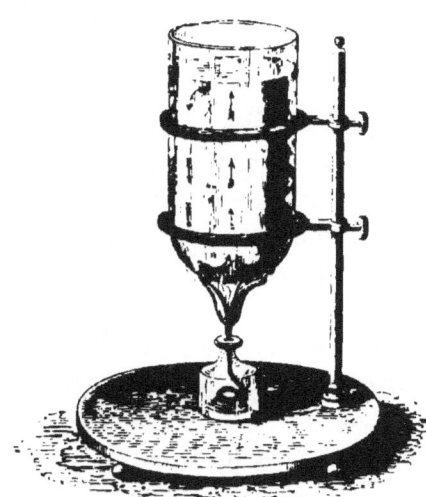

Fig. 61.

Iceland, which are large tubes of water heated from below, we have a natural instance of convection on a very large scale; and travellers relate that a small piece of paper thrown into the centre of the pipe is drawn to the side, and thence carried downwards by the descending current.

Another very good instance of the operation of convection is that described in Article 99, from which we see that the surface particles of a lake cooled at the top become specifically heavier, and descend until the whole body of water has attained the temperature 39°.2 Fahrenheit, this being the point of maximum density of water. When the whole lake has attained this temperature the process of convection is at an end; and if the surface particles be cooled still farther, they become lighter, not heavier; and instead of descending, remain at the top.

284. It will thus be observed that convection depends upon two things. In the first place, it depends upon the extent to which the liquid expands under heat; thus, for instance, if a body hardly expanded at all its convection would be very feeble. In the second place, convection depends upon the force of gravity. Were there no gravity there would be no convection; indeed the very term *specifically heavier* has a reference to gravity : so that if this force did not exist it would be a matter of no consequence what part of a vessel of water we heated,—the effect of the heating would always be the same.

CONVECTION IN GASES.

285. Convection takes place in air and gases even more energetically than in fluids, the coefficient of expansion of a gas on account of heat being comparatively great. Many familiar instances might be mentioned in illustration of the convection of air : thus, the air from a fire, being lighter than that around it, rises upwards, sometimes carrying with it small particles of solid matter, which become visible in the form of smoke. Even where there is no opaque matter mixed with the air, the currents which form convection are rendered visible in another way. As air expands its index of refraction becomes less, and the result of this is an apparent unsteadiness and indistinctness in objects viewed through heated air, which may be noticed above a lime-kiln, or in the air near the ground on a very hot day.

286. Trade winds, &c. In nature we have convection

of air on a very large scale. The air of the equatorial zone expands under the powerful influence of a vertical sun, and, becoming lighter, ascends, while its place is supplied by cold air from the regions north and south of the equator. Let us confine our attention to the northern hemisphere, and consider the air which rushes south to supply the place of the air carried upwards in the equatorial regions.

The earth, it is well known, revolves from west to east: the body of air therefore which approaches the equator from the north comes from a place of smaller to a place of greater velocity of rotation, it therefore lags behind, or in other words, appears to go towards the west; this current of air will therefore not blow directly from the north, but will rather be a current from the north-east. In like manner the cold air from the southern hemisphere blowing towards the equator will form a current from the south-east. These two currents blowing towards the equator in the two hemispheres are called the two *Trade winds*.

Having thus considered the cold winds which come to replace the air carried upwards at the equator, let us now endeavour to trace the course of this equatorial air. When it has mounted to the upper regions of the atmosphere it proceeds northwards and southwards towards the poles; and, going from a region of greater to a region of less velocity of rotation, it gains upon the earth, or in other words, goes eastward. Could we ascend into the upper regions of the atmosphere at the equator, we should there find currents blowing from the south-west in the northern hemisphere, and from the north-west in the southern. These winds are called the *Return-Trades*, their direction being opposite to that of the trade winds.

At the equator this return current is very high, so that even the summits of the Andes are probably beneath it. Volcanic explosions have however sometimes occurred in these regions with sufficient force to drive ashes up into the return current, which, when they regained the earth, at a considerable distance off, told by the course they had taken the direction in which the upper strata of air were moving.

As the return current proceeds north it gradually descends. At Teneriffe it has already fallen below the summit of the mountain, and it reaches the earth at about our own latitude; so that the south-west wind is perhaps more prevalent than any other in the British Isles : on the other hand, we are also often exposed to the trade wind in the form of a cold wind blowing from the north-east.

The land and sea breezes are probably produced by similar causes. During the day the land is more heated than the sea, and a vertical current is produced, carrying upwards the land air, which is replaced by air from the sea—this is the *sea breeze.* But after sunset the land cools more rapidly than the sea, and the cooled, and therefore heavier, land air moves seawards, thus producing the *land breeze.*

287. Law of cooling due to a gas. It has been already shewn (Art. 229) that a body placed in vacuo and surrounded by an enclosure of lower temperature than itself will gradually lose heat. If the body be surrounded not by a vacuum but by gas, it will lose heat more rapidly than in vacuo, and the difference between its velocity of cooling in the two cases is due to the presence of the gas. Thus the whole velocity of cooling of a body in air or gas is due partly to radiation and partly to the gas, but it is only the latter cause with which we are at present concerned. The velocity of cooling due to gas, or, which is the same thing, the amount of heat carried off momentarily from a body by gas, was investigated by MM. Dulong and Petit at the time when they also ascertained the law of cooling in vacuo.

This research was a very troublesome one, for the temperature of the thermometer, and the density, temperature, and chemical nature of the gas, had all to be varied before the exact law could be ascertained. The following results were obtained by these experimentalists.

1. *The velocity of cooling due to the sole contact of a gas is entirely independent of the nature of the surface of the body.* Sir J. Leslie was probably the first to make this remark in a general way, and the truth of his remark has been well confirmed by the accurate experiments we are now describing. Thus, as far as gas or air is concerned, a silvered thermometer will cool just as rapidly as a blackened one; but as far as radiation is concerned, it will cool less rapidly than the blackened one.

2. *The velocity of cooling due solely to the contact of a gas is proportional to the excess of temperature raised to the power* **1.233.** From this law also we see the difference between cooling in vacuo and the cooling due to a gas. In vacuo the effect for the same excess of temperature of the thermometer above the enclosure varies also with the temperature of the enclosure (Art. 231), whereas in the case of a gas, the effect depends only on the excess of temperature.

3. *The cooling power of a given gas and for a given excess of temperature depends not on the* DENSITY *but on the* PRESSURE *of the gas.* The following expressions give the relation between the velocity of cooling and the pressure (p) for the different gases, the excess of temperature being supposed constant throughout :—

For atmospheric air the velocity of cooling varies as $p^{.45}$,
for hydrogen .. .. $p^{.38}$,
for carbonic acid .. .. $p^{.517}$,
for olefiant gas .. .. $p^{.501}$.

Combining this last law with the previous ones we see that

the expression for the velocity of cooling due to a gas will have the following form—

$$\text{Velocity of cooling} = m\,p^{a}\,t^{1.233};$$

where m is a constant, depending partly on the dimensions of the body and partly on the nature of the gas; p is the pressure expressed in millimètres; a is an index, which we have given above for four different gases; and t is the excess of temperature in Centigrade degrees.

In order to express the cooling power of a gas in absolute units we must refer once more to a research of Mr. Hopkins already quoted (Art. 235). Let C denote the quantity of heat which would be carried off by a gas in one minute from a square foot of *any kind of surface* $t°$C above the surrounding gas, of which the pressure, expressed in millimètres, is p, the unit of heat being that amount of heat which would raise the temperature of 1000 grains of distilled water 1°C, then

$$C = .0372 \left(\frac{p}{720}\right)^{.45} t^{1.233} \text{ for atmospheric air.}$$

Combining this determination with the researches of Dulong and Petit, we find

$$C = .1288 \left(\frac{p}{720}\right)^{.38} t^{1.233} \text{ for hydrogen,}$$

$$C = .0359 \left(\frac{p}{720}\right)^{.617} t^{1.233} \text{ for carbonic acid,}$$

$$C = .0497 \left(\frac{p}{720}\right)^{.501} t^{1.233} \text{ for olefiant gas.}$$

Example. Let it be required to find the *whole amount of heat due to convection and radiation united* which leaves a square foot of surface of dry chalk in one minute, the temperature being 50°C, while that of the surrounding enclosure is 14°C; the enclosure being filled with hydrogen of the pressure of 760 millimètres. By reference to Art. 235 we find the whole expression for loss of heat in this case to be

$$V = R + C = 8.613\, a^\theta\, (a^t - 1) + .1288 \left(\frac{760}{720}\right)^{.38} t^{1.233} ;$$

or, since $\left.\begin{array}{l} \theta = 14 \\ t + \theta = 50 \\ a = 1.0077 \end{array}\right\}$, we have

$$V = 8.613 \times 1.0077^{14}(1.0077^{36} - 1) + .1288 \left(\frac{760}{720}\right)^{.38} 36^{1.233} = 13.958.$$

It ought however to be borne in mind that all these are to a great extent empirical formulæ, which represent the experiments made, and which are useful in so far as they enable us to calculate approximately the loss of heat due to radiation and convection in any case in which all the particulars are given.

CHAPTER IX.

Specific Heat.

288. In order to arrive at a complete knowledge of the laws which regulate the distribution of heat through space, we must be able to measure the amount of heat which a body absorbs, or parts with, when its temperature is changed to a given extent, and also when it changes its state. To do this it is necessary to adopt some unit of heat, and we shall use in this work as our thermal unit the quantity of heat necessary to raise one pound of water from 0° to 1°C.

In the present chapter we shall treat of the amount of heat which a body absorbs, or gives out, when its temperature rises or falls to a given extent. This is called *specific heat*, and we define the specific heat of a given substance to be the quantity of heat necessary to raise one pound of the substance 1°C in terms of that necessary to raise one pound of ice-cold water 1°C reckoned as unity. Thus, if a pound of any substance required as much heat to raise it from

100° to 101°C as would raise $\frac{3}{10}$ths a pound of water from 0° to 1°C, then we should say that the specific heat of this substance at this temperature was 0.3.

METHODS OF MEASURING SPECIFIC HEAT.

289. I. Method by mixture. Three different methods of measuring the specific heat of substances have been proposed. They are known as (1) the method by mixture, (2) the method by fusing ice, and (3) the method by cooling. In the first of these, or the method of mixtures, the experiment is made in the following manner. Take a known weight of the substance of which the specific heat is desired, and heat it to a known temperature, then mix it rapidly with a known weight of water at an inferior temperature (say at 0°C), and notice the temperature of the mixture. If we are at liberty to suppose that none of the heat has been otherwise disposed of, we have at once all the means of determining the specific heat of the substance in question. Thus, let x denote the unknown specific heat of the substance, and let m be its mass, and t its temperature; also let M be the mass of water at 0°C with which it is mixed, and let θ be the temperature of the mixture. Then the quantity of heat lost by the substance will be $mx(t-\theta)$, while that gained by the water will be $M\theta$. Since the whole quantity of heat remains the same, the one of these expressions must equal the other. Hence $mx(t-\theta) = M\theta$, from which x may be easily found. As an example of this method, supposing that 3 lbs. of mercury at 100°C have been mixed with 1 lb. of ice-cold water, and that the temperature of the mixture is 9°C, what is the specific heat of mercury? Here we have $m = 3$, $\theta = 9$, $t-\theta = 100-9 = 91$; hence

$$3x \times 91 = 9 ; \qquad \therefore \quad x = \frac{9}{273} = .033 \text{ nearly} :$$

so that the specific heat of mercury is only $\frac{1}{30}$th of that of water.

In this process it is assumed that the specific heat of mercury is constant between 100° and 9°C, or rather it is the mean specific heat between this range that is determined by the experiment.

A serious objection to this method consists in the unavoidable loss of heat which is likewise incapable of accurate measurement. For in the example given above the heat of the mercury is not all confined to the mixture, but part of it is spent :

1. In warming the vessel which contains the mixture,
2. In warming the agitator and the thermometer,
3. In dissipation from the sides of the vessel;

and unless we have the means of estimating exactly the loss of heat from all these sources we shall not be able to obtain a good result.

290. II. Method by fusion of ice. The second method of measuring specific heat is by the fusion of ice.

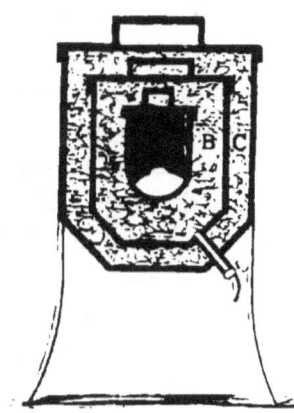

Fig. 62.

In this method we have an inner vessel A (Fig. 62) which contains the substance on which the experiment is made. This vessel is placed in the interior of a larger vessel B, the space between them being filled with melting ice. The vessel B, again, is in the interior of a still larger vessel C, the space between them being, again, filled as before with melting ice.

Since the exterior of the vessel B is at the temperature 32° Fahr., we may imagine that the ice in this vessel will only melt through means of the hot substance which is placed in A. If therefore we know not only the weight but the temperature of the substance in A, and also the quantity of ice which has been converted into water in consequence of this hot substance parting with its heat, we have the means of finding the specific heat of the substance in *A*. A stop-cock connected with *B* serves to carry off the water formed through melting of the ice, and hence, by weighing this water, we know approximately the quantity of ice melted in *B*, and if we know the quantity of heat necessary to convert ice into water we can find the heat given out by the substance in *A*. The chief objection to this instrument is that we cannot measure accurately the amount of water produced since a certain amount remains adhering to the ice.

291. III. Method by cooling. The third means of estimating specific heat is by the method of cooling. If two similar substances be exposed to the same cooling influence it is manifest that the one which has the smallest specific heat will cool fastest. Thus, suppose that we have two thermometers with blackened bulbs of precisely the same size, the one being filled with mercury and the other with water; further, let these instruments both cool from a common temperature under precisely the same circumstances. It will be found that the mercurial thermometer will cool more than twice as fast as the water one. For although the weight of the mercury is more than 13 times that of the water, yet the specific heat of mercury is only one-thirtieth of that of water, and hence while the same amount of heat leaves both instruments in one minute, yet this heat will produce on the water thermometer only $\frac{13}{30}$ths of that diminution of temperature which it produces on the mercurial one. The idea of measuring the specific heat of bodies first originated with Black, who was also the discoverer of latent heat; and many numerous and important experiments have since been made on this subject by a number of observers.

SPECIFIC HEAT OF SOLIDS.

292. Some of the latest experiments in this branch of the subject have been made by Regnault, who used the method of cooling. In these experiments the substance was reduced to a fine powder and enclosed along with a delicate thermometer in a vessel which was exposed to the cooling influence. Although every precaution was used the result of this process was not satisfactory; one objection was that the heat was not conducted sufficiently fast from the powder to the sides of the vessel which contained it. Another is that the specific heat of the same substance in the solid state depends to some extent on the mechanical treatment which it has received. Regnault has also investigated the specific heat of various solid substances by the method of mixtures.

293. Rise of specific heat of solids with temperature. It was first shewn by the experiments of Dulong and Petit that *the specific heat of a solid is greater at a high temperature than at a low one.* The following table embodies the results of these experiments.

Substance.	Mean Specific Heat	
	Between 0° and 100°C.	Between 0° and 300°C.
Iron	0.1098	0.1218
Mercury	0.0330	0.0350
Zinc	0.0927	0.1015
Antimony	·0.0507	0.0549
Silver	0.0557	0.0611
Copper	0.0949	0.1013
Platinum	0.0355	0.0355
Glass.	0.1770	0.1990

It will be noticed that for all the substances in the above table the specific heat is greater at high temperatures, with the exception of platinum, for which the specific heat remains the same between the limits of the experiment. Probably the reason of this is that the highest temperature of experiment was very much below the melting-point of this metal, and it has been found by Regnault that the variation of specific heat with temperature is much more rapid when the substance approaches its melting-point. M. Pouillet, by means of the method of mixtures, has obtained the specific heat of platinum at still higher temperatures. His results are as follows—

Mean Specific Heat of Platinum

Between 0° and	100°C		0.0335
,, 0 ,,	300		0.0343
,, 0 ,,	500		0.0352
,, 0 ,,	700		0.0360
,, 0 ,,	1000		0.0373
,, 0 ,,	1200		0.0382

The constancy of the specific heat of platinum renders this metal serviceable as a pyrometer, and a piece of platinum may be used for estimating the temperature of a furnace. When it has attained the temperature of the furnace it is taken out and plunged into a known quantity of ice-cold water. By means of the rise of temperature produced it is easy to calculate approximately the temperature of the platinum, and hence of the furnace.

294. Circumstances which influence the specific heat of solids. The specific heat of a solid has been found to depend on the mode of aggregation of its molecules and on the nature of the mechanical action to which it has been subjected. *In general whatever augments the density diminishes the specific heat, and whatever diminishes the density augments the specific heat; and it is perhaps owing to expansion that the specific heat of a body increases with its temperature.* The more carbon is divided the greater is its specific heat. The following table exhibits the specific heat, in their different states of aggregation, of carbonate of lime, sulphur, and carbon.

Carbonate of Lime.		Sulphur.	
Aragonite	0.2085	Recently melted.........	0.1844
Iceland spar	0.2085	Melted less than 2 months..	0.1803
Chalk.................	0.2148	Melted less than 2 years ..	0.1764
White marble...........	0.2158	Natural crystals	0.1776

Carbon.

Animal charcoal....................	0.2608
Wood charcoal	0.2415
Coke	0.2008
Graphite........................	0.2018
Diamond	0.1468

SPECIFIC HEAT OF LIQUIDS.

295. Regnault has determined the specific heat of a number of liquids by the following method. The liquid under experiment is contained in a reservoir *R* (Fig. 63) which is

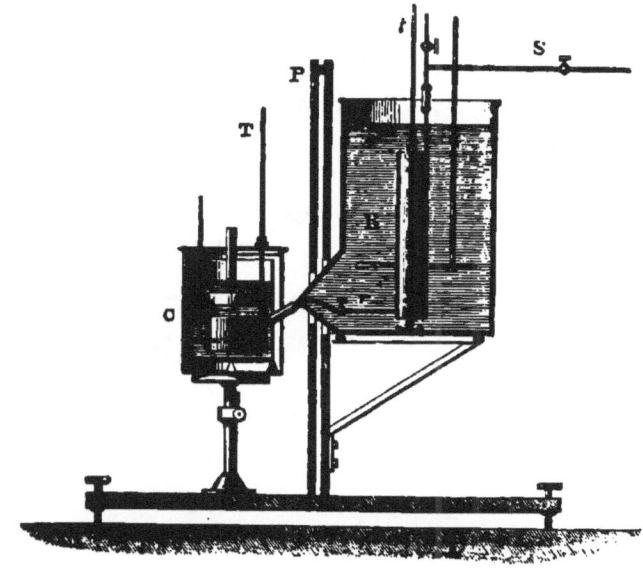

Fig. 63.

immersed in the middle of a bath, and by agitating the water of this bath a definite temperature is communicated to the liquid in R. By opening the stop-cock at r and bringing to bear at the same time an atmospheric pressure upon the liquid, it is driven through the tubes at r into a vessel contained in the calorimeter C. Having entered the calorimeter and having disposed of its surplus heat, the temperature of the water of the calorimeter is observed by means of the thermometer T, and this affords the means of estimating the specific heat of the liquid. The calorimeter is defended by means of a screen P from the heat of R.

Generally speaking a substance when liquid has a greater specific heat than when solid, a fact which was discovered by Irvine. Thus the specific heat of ice is only one-half that of water.

296. Variation with temperature of the specific heat of liquids. *The specific heat of liquids increases in general with the temperature and at a rate exceeding that of solids.* Thus bromine has between $-6°$ and $10°C$ the mean specific heat 0.10513, while between $13°$ and $58°$ it has the mean specific heat 0.11294.

The specific heat of water at various temperatures has been especially studied by Regnault, who has obtained the following result.

Mean Specific Heat of Water

From 0° to 40°C	1.0013
„ 0 „ 80	1.0035
„ 0 „ 120	1.0067
„ 0 „ 160	1.0109
„ 0 „ 200	1.0160
„ 0 „ 230	1.0204

SPECIFIC HEAT OF GASES.

297. In this branch of our subject there are two sets of determinations to be made. We must find, in the first place, the specific heat of gas under constant pressure; and in the second place, the specific heat of gas under constant volume.

In a future part of this work it will be shewn how these two are connected together.

Many experimentalists have been engaged in these determinations. Before the time of Regnault one of the most exact researches was that of Delaroche and Bérard, which was crowned by the Academy of Sciences. These experimentalists produced a current of gas of uniform velocity which was first heated to 100°C by being passed through tubes enveloped in boiling water, and was then cooled in its passage through a calorimeter, to which it abandoned its excess of heat. It ought likewise to be mentioned that Joule made an accurate determination of the specific heat of air.

After many years' trials Regnault finally adopted a modification of the method of Delaroche and Bérard.

His apparatus was constructed so as to fulfil the following requirements—

1. To obtain a gaseous current of constant velocity, which velocity might also be regulated at will.

2. By means of a bath to give a determinate temperature to the gaseous current.

3. To construct a calorimeter in which the gas would entirely dispose of its excess of heat.

In order to obtain a gaseous current of constant velocity the following arrangement was adopted. The gas, after being dried and purified, was forced into a large reservoir R (Fig. 64) of 35 litres capacity. A manometer attached to the reservoir at m indicated the pressure of the gas. The reservoir was surrounded by a large mass of water agitated by means of an annular plate a. The gas would thus take the temperature of this water—this temperature being denoted by the thermometer T. Suppose, in the first place, that the reservoir is filled with gas and that the stop-cock l is shut. Opening now the stop-cock at l this gas will escape through

the tube shewn in the figure, passing spirally through an
arrangement at *S*, by which a certain high temperature is,

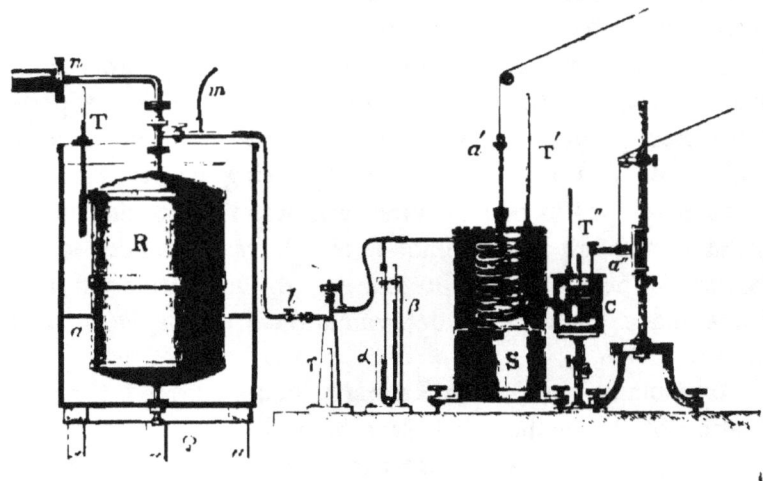

Fig. 64.

given to it, then parting with this excess of heat to a calorimeter at *C*, and ultimately escaping (say) into the air. At
the end of the experiment suppose that the stop-cock at *l* is
once more shut. Knowing the pressure and temperature of
the gas in *R* at the beginning and end of the experiment, if
the chemical constitution of the gas be known, and if it obeys
Boyle's law, the weight of gas passed through the calorimeter
will be known. If Boyle's law do not hold, it is yet possible,
though with more difficulty, to ascertain the weight of gas
used, but into the details of the method of doing so we will
not enter. The weight of gas consumed during the experiment is thus known, but in order to obtain a definite result
something more is necessary; the velocity of the current of
gas through the apparatus ought to be constant throughout
the experiment. It is clear that without some special arrangement this current will not be constant, because the

excess of pressure in the reservoir R will be greater at the commencement of the experiment than at the end of it when a quantity of this gas has been used. There is, however, an arrangement r by means of which the opening through which the gas escapes from the reservoir into the apparatus may be enlarged or contracted at pleasure. A manometer to the right of r, having one of its limbs open to the atmosphere, indicates the excess of pressure of the gas in the tube, and if the screw at r is turned in such a manner that throughout the whole experiment the excess of pressure denoted by this manometer is constant, then will the velocity of the current be constant also. Agitators a', a'' are attached to the source of heat and the calorimeter, and it was ascertained by Regnault that the gas in passing through S really attained the temperature (indicated by T'') of the fluid (oil) in S. It was further ascertained that the gas lost none, or extremely little, of its heat in passing between S and the calorimeter, and that in passing through the vessel of the calorimeter, which was arranged in a spiral form so as to present as much surface as possible to the surrounding water, the gas issued with a temperature the same as that of the water of the calorimeter indicated by the thermometer T'''. Finally it was ascertained that the pressure of the gas was as nearly as possible the same before its entrance into the calorimeter and after its exit therefrom.

To simplify matters we may suppose the pressure of the outward air constant throughout the experiment.

In this experiment therefore a known weight of gas having a known temperature (that of the bath) was made to pass with a constant velocity and at a constant pressure through the calorimeter, where it was reduced in temperature to that of the water of the calorimeter. The specific heat of a gas under constant pressure was thus found.

298. Results of Regnault's experiments. The following facts were determined by these experiments:—

1. *The specific heat of a given weight of a gas which is approximately perfect, and which therefore follows the gaseous laws previously indicated* (Art. 148), *does not vary with the temperature of the gas.*

2. *The specific heat of a* GIVEN WEIGHT *of such a gas does not vary with the pressure or density of the gas, and hence the specific heat of a* GIVEN VOLUME *of such a gas varies as its density.*

3. *The specific heats of equal volumes of the simple and incondensible gas are equal, but this equality does not hold for gases easily condensed, such as chlorine and bromine. It holds, however, for compound gases which are formed without condensation, such as hydrochloric acid and nitric oxide.*

4. *These laws do not hold for condensible gases—the specific heat of carbonic acid gas, for instance, increases with the temperature.*

299. The following table is derived from Regnault's determinations.

Specific Heat of Gases and Vapours under Constant Pressure.

Gas or Vapour.	Equal.	
	Vols.	Weights.
Air	0.2375	....
Oxygen	0.2405	0.2175
Nitrogen	0.2368	0.2438
Hydrogen...............	0.2359	3.4090
Chlorine	0.2964	0.1210
Bromine	0.3040	0.0555
Nitrous oxide	0.3447	0.2262
Nitric oxide	0.2406	0.2317
Carbonic oxide..........	0.2370	0.2450
Carbonic acid	0.3307	0.2169
Bisulphide of carbon	0.4122	0.1569
Ammonia..............	0.2996	0.5084
Marsh gas	0.3277	0.5929
Olefiant gas	0.4160	0.4040
Chloride of arsenic	0.7034	0.1142
Chloride of silicon	0.7778	0.1322
Perchloride of titanium	0.8564	0.1290

Gas or Vapour.	Equal.	
	Vols.	Weights.
Perchloride of tin..........	0.8416	0.0939
Sulphurous anhydride	0.3414	0.1554
Hydrochloric acid	0.2333	0.1852
Sulphuretted hydrogen......	0.2857	0.2432
Water	0.2989	0.4805
Alcohol...................	0.7171	0.4534
Wood spirit	0.5063	0.4580
Ether	1.2266	0.4797
Chloride of ethyl	0.6096	0.2738
Bromide of ethyl	0.7026	0.1196
Sulphide of ethyl	1.2466	0.4008
Cyanide of ethyl	0.8290	0.4261
Chloroform	0.6461	0.1567
Dutch liquid..............	0.7836	0.2293
Acetic ether	1.2184	0.4008
Benzole	1.0114	0.3754
Acetone	0.8264	0.4125
Oil of turpentine	2.3776	0.5061
Terchloride of phosphorus ..	0.6395	0.1347

In the first column of this table the common volume is that occupied by one pound of air, while in the second column the common weight is one pound. Also the specific heat of one pound of liquid water is taken as the unit, so that the heat required to raise a pound of atmospheric air one degree under constant pressure is only 0.2375 of that required to raise a pound of water one degree.

300. Influence of the state of a substance on its specific heat. *The same body has a higher specific heat in the liquid than in the solid state, while in the gaseous condition, again, its specific heat is less than when it is liquid.* Thus, for instance, the specific heat of water is twice as great as that of ice, and more than twice as great as that of steam.

The following table exhibits the dependence of the specific heat on the physical state of the substance.

Substance.	Specific heat.		
	Solid.	Liquid.	Gaseous.
Water	0.5040	1.0000	0.4805
Bromine	0.0833	0.1060	0.0555
Tin	0.0562	0.0637	....
Iodine	0.0541	0.1082	....
Lead	0.0314	0.0402	....
Alcohol	....	0.5475	0.4534
Bisulphide of carbon ..	....	0.2352	0.1569
Ether	....	0.5290	0.4797

ATOMIC HEAT.

301. Atomic heat of simple bodies. In 1819 Dulong and Petit made experiments on the specific heat of thirty elementary bodies, and discovered that for equal masses of each substance the specific heat is in the inverse proportion of the atomic weight. Regnault has made a number of experiments with the view of testing the accuracy of this law, and the following results have been chiefly obtained by him. (The atomic weights are those given in Williamson's Chemistry for Students, p. 100.)

Elements.	Specific heat of equal weights.	Atomic weight.	Product of specific heat into atomic weight.
Sulphur............	0.1776	32	5.6832
Tellurium..........	0.0474	129	6.1146
Magnesium	0.2499	24	5.9976
Zinc	0.0955	65	6.2075
Cadmium	0.0567	112	6.3504
Aluminium	0.2143	27.5	5.8932
Iron	0.1138	56	6.3728
Nickel	0.1091	58.5	6.3823
Cobalt	0.1070	58.5	6.2595
Manganese	0.114	55	6.2700
Tin	0.0562	118	6.6316
Tungsten	0.0334	184	6.1456
Copper	0.0951	63.5	6.0389
Lead.............	0.0314	207	6.4998
Mercury (solid) . ..	0.0319	200	6.3800
Platinum	0.0324	197	6.3828

Elements.	Specific heat of equal weights.	Atomic weight.	Product of specific heat into atomic weight.
Palladium	0.0593	106.5	6.3154
Rhodium	0.0580	104	6.0320
Osmium	0.0306	199	6.0894
Iridium............	0.0325	197	6.4025
Iodine	0.0541	127	6.8707
Bromine (solid)	0.0843	80	6.7440
Potassium	0.1696	39	6.6144
Sodium	0.2934	23	6.7482
Lithium	0.9408	7	6.5856
Arsenic..	0.0814	75	6.1050
Antimony..	0.0508	122	6.1976
Bismuth	0.0308	210	6.4680
Thallium	0.0336	203	6.8208
Silver	0.0570	108	6.1560
Gold	0.0324	196	6.3504

It appears from this table that *the product of the specific heat by the atomic weight is very nearly the same for all the elementary bodies.* The differences in this product may be accounted for by supposing that the different elements experimented on were not all in the same physical state, some of these being near their melting-points and others at a great distance from them.

302. Atomic heat of compound bodies. Neumann and Regnault have determined that *in all compound bodies of similar atomic composition the specific heats are inversely as the atomic weights.* The product of the specific heat into the atomic weight for one class of compounds may however be different from that for another class of compounds. Thus Regnault gives the following table for the specific heat of bichlorides.

	Specific heat.	Atomic weight.	Product of specific heat into atomic weight.
Chloride of Barium (Ba Cl²)......	0.0896	208	18.64
„ Strontium (Sr Cl²)....	0.1199	158.5	19.00
„ Calcium (Ca Cl²)	0.1643	111	18.23
„ Magnesium (Mg Cl²)..	0.1946	95	18.49
„ Lead (Pb Cl²)	0.0664	278	18.46
Perchloride of Mercury (Hg Cl²) ..	0.0689	271	18.67
Chloride of Zinc (Zn Cl²)........	0.1362	136	18.52
Perchloride of Tin (Sn Cl²)	0.1016	189	19.20

While for carbonates we have the following table.

	Specific heat.	Atomic weight.	Product of specific heat into atomic weight.
Carbonate of Lime (Ca C O³)	0.2086	100	20.86
„ Barytes (Ba C O³) ..	0.1104	197	21.75
„ Strontium (Sr C O³)..	0.1448	147.5	21.36
„ Iron (Fe C O³)......	0.1934	116	22.43

It thus appears that the numbers of each table agree very well together, but the numbers of the one table do not agree well with those of the other.

CHAPTER X.

Latent Heat.

303. It has been already remarked (Art. 91) that a large quantity of heat is required by bodies in order to enable them to pass from the solid into the liquid, or from the liquid into the gaseous state. This heat which is absorbed by bodies during their passage from one state to another, does not as a rule manifest itself by producing an increase of temperature, and it has on this account been called latent heat; so that we may with much' propriety affirm regarding water—

Water at o°C = ice at o°C + latent heat of liquefaction ;

or regarding steam—

Steam at 100°C = water at 100°C + latent heat of vaporisation.

Latent heat was discovered by Black, and the principles of this branch of science were first taught by him in 1762.

LATENT HEAT OF LIQUEFACTION.

304. Latent heat of water. Black first attempted to measure the latent heat of water in the following manner. He suspended in a room of the temperature of 64° Fahr. two similar glass vessels, one containing melting ice and the other ice-cold water; and he noticed that at the end of half an hour the water had attained the temperature of 40° Fahr., while the ice did not reach this temperature until ten hours and a-half had elapsed. He argued that the quantity of heat absorbed by the vessels was very nearly proportional to the time of exposure, and by this means he attempted to estimate the amount of heat absorbed by ice while passing into the state of water. Afterwards Black adopted the method of mixtures. The following example will illustrate this method of experiment.

It is found that a pound of water at 212° mixed with a pound of water at 32°, gives two pounds of water at a temperature equal, as nearly as possible, to 122°, this temperature being the mean of those of the two components; if however a pound of ice at 32° Fahr. be mixed with a pound of water at 212°, we have two pounds of water at 51° Fahr. only. A correct experiment of this kind gives us the means of measuring the latent heat of water. For we see that when equal weights (one pound each) of boiling and ice-cold water are mixed together, we have water at 122°, while when the same weights of boiling water and melting ice are mixed together we have water at 51° only. There is thus a difference in the total heat of the two mixtures equal to that required to raise two pounds of water from 51° to 122°, or through a range of 71° Fahr. Now since the heat of the boiling water was the same in each experiment, this difference must necessarily represent the heat required to liquefy one pound of ice. We thus see that it requires as much heat to liquefy one pound of ice at 32° as it does to raise two pounds of water through a range of 71° Fahr., or one pound of water through a range of 142° Fahr., or 142 lbs. of water through a range of 1° Fahr.

If we take as our unit of heat the quantity of heat necessary to raise one pound of water through 1° Fahr., we have therefore the latent heat of water represented by 142; but since we have taken as our unit (Art. 288) the amount of heat necessary to raise one pound of water from 0° to 1°C, we find, in accordance with this standard and as the result of this experiment, the latent heat of water to be

represented by $142 \times \dfrac{5}{9} = 78.9$ units of heat nearly.

305. Many distinguished philosophers have attempted since the days of Black to estimate the latent heat of water, and amongst these we may name Provostaye and Desains, Regnault, and finally Person. The experimental arrangements necessary for the estimation of latent heat are however so similar in principle to those required for estimating specific heat, that it will be unnecessary to give the details of the various experiments—let us rather state the results obtained. Provostaye and Desains used melting ice in their experiments, while Regnault employed both snow and melting ice. The united result of these experiments was to give 79.25 units of heat as the most probable value of the amount required to liquefy one pound of ice.

306. The experiments of M. Person are well worthy of an attentive study as affording at the same time evidence that the change which takes place when ice becomes water is to some extent gradual and not quite abrupt.

M. Person in his experiments employed ice at a temperature inferior to its melting-point.

In one of these the ice was at − 2°C, and it may be desirable to describe here in a few words how the latent heat of liquefaction of ice is to be derived from an experiment, where the ice used is below its melting-point. When such ice is melted we may imagine, for convenience sake, that the heat applied has two separate offices to perform. First of all, it has to raise the ice from its present temperature to the melting-point; and secondly, it has to liquefy this melting ice. It is the quantity of heat requisite to perform this latter office that is generally regarded as a measure of the latent heat; while that necessary to perform the former office may be estimated by knowing the temperature of the ice used and the specific heat of this substance. Thus we have seen (Art. 295) that the specific heat of ice is one-half that of water, or 0.5. In the above experiment, therefore, where the ice was at − 2°C, we might imagine one unit of heat necessary to raise the ice from this temperature to 0°C; while the remainder of the whole heat required to melt the ice might be taken to denote the latent heat of liquefaction. Now on this supposition Person found that the latent heat of liquefaction, as determined by this and similar experiments, was 80 units instead of 79.25, as found by Regnault and others.

M. Person, in continuing his investigations, was able satisfactorily to account for this difference. He found that a pound of ice at − 2°C requires two units of heat instead of one to raise it to 0°C; in fact it would appear as if the ice between − 2°C and 0°C had already begun to absorb part of the heat of liquefaction, and thus that the absorption of latent heat in order to be complete required a certain range of temperature.

Presuming this to be the case with ice it will at once be seen that, as far as such observations are concerned, latent heat simply resolves itself into an enormous increase of specific heat between certain narrow limits of temperature, and that in truth latent heat begins to be absorbed when the specific heat begins to increase; or, in other words, these two terms are only two different ways of expressing one and the same action.

We thus derive from these experiments of Person a basis for the theory of the gradual liquefaction of ice—a theory which we have already seen (Art. 101) has been applied with much success by Principal Forbes in order to account for the phenomenon of regelation.

307. Latent heat of other liquids. M. Person has made numerous experiments on the latent heat of other liquids besides water, and has obtained the following results :—

Substance.	Latent heat of one pound	
	In thermal units.	Water = 1.
Water	79.25	1.000
Phosphorus	5.034	0.063
Sulphur	9.368	0.118
Nitrate of soda	62.975	0.794
Nitrate of potassa	47.371	0.598
Tin	14.252	0.179
Bismuth	12.640	0.159
Lead	5.369	0.067
Zinc	28.13	0.355
Cadmium	13.66	0.172
Silver	21.07	0.266
Mercury	2.83	0.035

LATENT HEAT OF VAPORISATION.

308. Latent heat of steam. Black, the discoverer of latent heat, was the first who attempted to estimate the latent heat of steam. The subject has since engaged the attention of many eminent men, and amongst others of Watt, Rumford, Despretz, Southern, and Clément & Désormes. Finally, Regnault has discussed the subject with great exactness.

The object of Regnault's experiments was to determine the quantity of heat which must be furnished to one pound of water at 0°C, in order to convert it wholly into saturated vapour at a given pressure; that is to say, how much heat must be supplied to this pound of water in order, first, to raise its temperature from 0°C to a certain temperature without evaporation; and, secondly, to evaporate it entirely at that temperature and under the pressure which corresponds to it.

The following was the experimental method pursued by Regnault. In order to obtain the formation of aqueous vapour at a constant high temperature, the same arrangement was adopted as that used in making experiments on the pressure of aqueous vapour; that is to say, the water was made to boil under the pressure of an artificial atmosphere, while the vapour so formed was condensed in a condenser almost as fast as it was furnished. The formation of aqueous vapour at a high and constant temperature might thus be obtained (see Fig. 28).

To this arrangement in the present experiment a system of two calorimeters was added. In this experiment we may therefore suppose the calorimeters to be supplied at one end with saturated steam of a given constant pressure and temperature, which, having passed through the calorimeter, is condensed into water of a known temperature, having in the meantime given out a measurable quantity of heat. Suppose, for example, that a pound of steam at 100°C in passing through a calorimeter filled with water at -1°C heated up 637 lbs. of water from this temperature to 0°C, the condensed water of the steam having also the temperature 0°C, then from this experiment Regnault conceived himself entitled to suppose that the total heat (as he terms it) of steam at 100°C is 637. He conceived that he was entitled to infer that if a pound of water at 0°C was first of all heated without evaporation to 100°C, and at that temperature totally converted into steam, the total quantity of heat necessary to do all this would be 637 units. We shall see in a subsequent part of this work that this inference is quite correct; in the meantime we content ourselves with defining what Regnault meant by the total heat of steam, and in stating by what experimental means he imagined he had obtained it.

Regnault also made experiments at low pressures by another method.

The following table embodies the results of all his experiments :—

Total Heat of Steam.

Temperature of the saturated vapour.	Total heat.
0°	606.5
10	609.5
20	612.6
30	615.7
40	618.7
50	621.7
60	624.8
70	627.8
80	630.9
90	633.9
100	637.0
110	640.0
120	643.1
130	646.1
140	649.2

Temperature of the saturated vapour.	Total heat.
150	652.2
160	655.3
170	658.3
180	661.4
190	664.4
200	667.5
210	670.5
220	673.6
230	676.6

The latent heat of steam at any temperature is very easily derived from the total heat given in this table. Thus it takes 637 units first to heat a pound of water at 0° to 100° and then to evaporate it at that temperature, but it takes as nearly as possible 100 units to heat it from 0° to 100°; so that 637 — 100 = 537 units denote the latent heat of steam at 100°C.

309. Latent heat of other vapours. Andrews and Favre & Silbermann have made numerous experiments on this subject. The following table embodies the results derived by Andrews—the liquid is supposed always to be evaporated at the temperature of its boiling-point:—

Latent Heat of Vapours.

Substance.	Latent heat of one pound	
	In thermal units.	Steam = 1.
Water	535.9	1.000
Wood-spirit	263.7	0.492
Alcohol	202.4	0.378
Formiate of methyl	117.1	0.219
Acetate of methyl	110.2	0.206
Formic ether	105.3	0.196
Acetic ether	92.68	0.173
Ether	90.45	0.169
Bisulphide of carbon	86.67	0.162
Oxalic ether	72.72	0.136
Terchloride of phosphorus	51.42	0.096
Iodide of ethyl	46.87	0.087
Iodide of methyl	46.07	0.086
Bromine	45.60	0.085
Perchloride of tin	30.53	0.057

If we compare this table with that of the latent heat of liquids, we shall find that in both water stands at the head of the list; that is to say, the latent heat of liquefaction of ice is greater than that of any other solid, also the latent heat of vaporisation of water is greater than that of any other liquid.

BOOK III.

ON THE NATURE OF HEAT, ITS SOURCES, AND CONNECTION WITH OTHER PROPERTIES OF MATTER.

CHAPTER I.

Remarks on Energy—(Historical and Preliminary).

310. OUR ideas regarding the nature of Heat have recently undergone a great change. Formerly this agent was regarded as a species of matter, but of the class of the imponderables, since no evidence of the weight of Heat could be obtained, inasmuch as a hot body does not weigh more than the same body when cold; but very lately scientific opinion has unanimously decided that Heat is not a species of matter, but rather a species of motion. Contemporaneously with this change in our conception of Heat, a great general law, which binds together the various kinds of energy, molecular and visible, has become known under the title of the principle of the conservation of energy. As this law is intimately connected with that conception which regards Heat as a species of motion, we shall begin this branch of our subject by a short sketch of this great and important principle.

311. Perpetual motion. Almost from time immemorial certain curious and perplexing questions in various branches of knowledge have thrust themselves prominently forward, so as almost to haunt the human mind.

In chemistry the famous speculation was the possibility of transmuting other metals into gold; while in physics it was the possibility of perpetual motion.

These questions may appear visionary, but they have not been without an indirect influence upon the progress of knowledge, and without doubt an intelligent denial of the possibility of perpetual motion leads at once to the fundamental principles of the science of energy.

We shall afterwards see that there are two forms of the idea of perpetual motion : one of these may be very easily stated. The use of any machine, it is well known, is to do work. We need not here define 'work,' for its meaning will at once be understood. Now to do some kind of work is the object of every machine. But in order to keep a machine going it has always been found necessary to perform, either continuously or periodically, some operation upon this machine. Thus you must yourself keep constantly working at a turning-lathe, or a coffee-mill, in order that either of these machines may do work; and though a clock may go for a long time by itself, yet it has to be wound up periodically. When we come to a steam-engine, or even to a living being, such as a man or a horse, the case is somewhat different; yet the difference is not very great. Both of these have to be fed regularly, the one with fuel and the other with food, in order that they may continue to work.

Now one form of the idea of perpetual motion thinks it is possible to construct a machine which can go on doing external work without the application of any external agency, either constant or intermittent. May there not, it is said, be some hidden, unknown material agent, that gives us this great desideratum? It is the most difficult thing in the world to prove a negative, especially in such a case as this,

for our knowledge of the various forces of matter is extremely limited. It is only in the case of a clock or similar
machine that we can prove the impossibility of perpetual
motion of this kind; in other cases we are driven simply
to deny this possibility. But this denial, intelligently made,
leads us at once to the principle of the conservation of
energy, which asserts that the amount of energy in a material
system left to itself is a constant quantity, and that the only
change is from one form of energy to another; so that,
do what you may, you can only get a definite and limited
amount of work out of any machine that is not periodically
supplied with energy in some other form.

312. Definition of energy. I. Kinetic energy. Before proceeding any further·let us attach a more definite
idea to the word 'work;' and to enable us to do so we may
call to our aid the all-pervading force of gravity, against
the action of which our efforts are so frequently directed.
Let us agree to consider a one-pound weight raised up
vertically one foot in vacuo against gravity as representing
the performance of unit of work. It is necessary to say in
vacuo; for if, for example, the weight be made of wood and
the medium be water, it is evident that we perform no work
by lifting the wood one foot higher in the water; on the
other hand, we should perform work by causing it to
sink. A pound weight raised one foot in vacuo against
gravity is therefore to be taken as unit of work performed.

Now according to this standard it is easy to perceive
that the pound weight raised two feet will represent the
performance of two units of work, if raised three feet the
performance of three units, and so on. Further, a two-
pound weight raised one foot will denote two units of work
done, and a three-pound weight raised one foot three units,
and so on. In fine, if the mass of matter be m pounds, and
if it be raised f feet against the force of gravity, which we

may suppose to be nearly the same for all points at the earth's surface, then the work done = *mf.*

313. Let us now study the action of this force of gravity in producing velocity; and in order to do so let us suppose that the foot and the second are our units of space and time, while our unit of velocity is represented by a body moving at the rate of one foot in a second, and our unit of acceleration is the production of unit velocity by a force which has acted for one second. Under this convention the force of gravity, or *g*, will be denoted by 32.2, since when a body is allowed to fall under the action of gravity for one second, it is found to have acquired the velocity of 32.2 feet in one second. If we consider how far this body has fallen in one second in order to acquire this velocity, we shall find the distance to be 16.1 feet; and if, on the other hand, we project a body upwards with the velocity of 32.2 feet per second, it will rise against gravity 16.1 feet in height. A pound weight projected vertically upwards with the velocity of 32.2 feet per second is therefore capable of doing 16.1 units of work before it comes to rest.

Again, it is found that a body, if allowed to fall for two seconds under the influence of gravity, will have acquired the velocity of 64.4 feet in one second, and that during this time it will have fallen 64.4 feet. A pound weight projected vertically upwards with the initial velocity of 64.4 feet per second, will therefore rise 64.4 feet in height, and will do 64.4 units of work before it comes to rest.

We thus see that a double velocity enables the body to do four times as much work—in fine, in order to find out how much work a body one pound in weight projected upwards with the velocity *v* is capable of doing, we have only to ask how high it will rise. This will be given by the following formula :—

$$\text{Height of Ascent or Work Done} = \frac{v^2}{64.4}. \qquad (A)$$

Thus, if the velocity be 32.2, we have by this formula—

$$\text{Work} = \frac{(32.2)^2}{64.4} = 16.1 \, ;$$

but if the velocity be 64.4, we have—

$$\text{Work} = \frac{(64.4)^2}{64.4} = 64.4, \text{ as already stated.}$$

314. A little consideration will shew us that it is not necessary for the body to be moving with this velocity *vertically upwards* in order to be capable of doing this work; indeed, we have only selected the force of gravity as one of the most prominent forces *against* which work is done; but the moving body may likewise be made to do work *against* a spring, or even by means of a single fixed pulley or otherwise it may be made to raise another body against gravity. In fact, taking the words 'work done' in their most general sense, as representing space moved over against the action of any force, we see that the above formula (*A*) will hold good without reference to the direction in which the one-pound weight is moving; and if we consider the pound as denoting the unit of mass, we have the following general expression for the work capable of being done against any force by a body of mass m and velocity v—

$$\text{Work} = \frac{m \, v^2}{64.4}; \qquad (B)$$

the unit of work being always the amount represented by raising one pound one foot against terrestrial gravity, or the foot-pound as this is termed. It ought to be borne in mind that if the force against which the work is done is much more powerful than gravity, then a comparatively small space passed over against the action of this force will denote a large amount of work. Thus, for instance, if the force were constant and twelve times as powerful as gravity, then an inch passed over against this force would be equivalent to a foot against gravity. A body, such as a pound weight, moving with a certain velocity may therefore be said to have a certain amount of energy* stored up in it in virtue of this velocity. This energy is termed *energy of motion, or kinetic energy;* (κίνησις, *motion*).

315. II. Potential energy. Suppose now that this pound weight moves vertically upwards with the initial velocity of 32.2 feet per second, it will rise, we have seen, to the height of 16.1 feet. When this height has been attained the velocity is all spent, and the body may be supposed to be for an instant at rest. Its *kinetic* energy is therefore all spent, since it has no velocity; but this has not been spent without some equivalent benefit being attained: the *kinetic energy* has in fact been spent in acquiring for the body a *position of advantage with regard to the force of gravity*, in virtue of which, when it falls to the point of projection, it will have reacquired the same amount of velocity, and therefore of kinetic energy, with which it originally started upwards. When the pound weight has attained its extreme height of 16.1 feet it has therefore *converted its energy of motion, or kinetic energy, into energy of position, or potential energy* (*a conception due to Professor W. Thomson*), and when it has again fallen it has *reconverted its potential energy into kinetic energy.*

There is thus as much energy in the pound weight at the summit of its flight as at the moment of its discharge, only it is of a different kind in the two cases, being in the first potential and in the second kinetic energy; and, further, at any intermediate point of its course the energy of the pound weight is partly potential and partly kinetic;

---

* The term 'energy' is due to Young : it means the power of doing work against gravity or any other force.

but the sum of these two kinds of energy is constant throughout its range, so that in the varying motion of the pound weight there is neither creation nor destruction of energy, but simply a transmutation from one form to another.

316. The case of a pendulum is almost precisely similar to that just mentioned, for when the bob of a pendulum is passing its lowest point its energy is all kinetic; while at its highest point the energy is all potential. We may pass on at once from the case we have considered to any machine, and assert that the energy of such a machine left to itself, and neither doing work upon other bodies nor having work done upon it, is strictly constant and limited, although it may vary from kinetic to potential, and from potential back again to kinetic energy, according to the geometric laws of the machine. As far as regards the combinations of ordinary mechanics this principle was clearly enunciated by Newton, and was even to some extent recognised by Galileo.

By both these philosophers a machine was regarded not as a means of creating energy, but rather of transforming it from a less convenient to a more convenient kind; and if we study the mechanical powers, as they are called, we shall find their office is strictly limited to this. The truth of this will be seen at once from a very simple illustration. If we take a lever, one of whose arms is ten times as long as the other, a ten-pound weight at the end of the short arm will balance a one-pound weight at the end of the long one; but the one-pound must fall ten feet in order that the ten-pounds may rise one foot. Now according to the definition of 'work' already given, the work spent upon the long arm by the one-pound weight falling will be 10 units, while that gained by the short arm rising will also be 10 units.

The product of the weight into the space moved over against gravity is the same for both arms; but while the space-factor of this product is the larger one for the long arm, the weight-factor is the larger one for the short arm.

317. Functions of a machine. It thus appears that all we can do by the lever or the other mechanical powers is to increase the one factor at the expense of the other; that is to say, either to gain force by losing space, or to gain space by losing force. We may generalise this statement so as to make it applicable to all possible machines, and we may view these as instruments which when supplied with energy in one form convert it into other forms according to the law of the machine.

318. Conversion of mechanical energy into heat. It is not in ordinary mechanics that the difficulty of recognising the principle of the conservation of energy consists, but rather when visible motion has been transformed into molecular motion, or when the opposite transformation has taken place. Thus, for instance, when an anvil is struck by a hammer, what becomes of the energy of the blow? or when a railway train is stopped by the break, what becomes of the energy of the train?

319. The true explanation of this difficulty has done more than anything else to forward the theory of the conservation of energy, and it is only of late years that the problem has been completely solved.

In considering the subject of percussion and friction, two simultaneous phenomena claim our attention. In the first place, the energy of the hammer and of the railway train disappear from the immediate cognisance of our senses —from that category which embraces visible potential and visible kinetic energy.

In the next place, by repeated strokes of the hammer upon the anvil we have the production of heat, nay even of a red heat if the process be conducted sufficiently long and be sufficiently rapid; and in like manner the stoppage of a railway train produces heat; indeed we may see sparks flying out from the break-wheel on a dark night.

For a long time this production of heat was regarded as inexplicable, because, heat being looked upon as a species of matter, it could not be imagined where all this heat came from. The only sort of explanation was, that in the processes of friction and percussion heat might be drawn from neighbouring bodies, or there might be a diminution in the thermal capacity of the two bodies acting on each other, so that caloric was supposed to be squeezed, or rubbed, out of them, although it is not easy to see why the same effect should take place with two such different actions as friction and percussion. Davy, about the end of last century, was one of the first to refute this explanation by a very simple experiment. This consisted in rubbing two pieces of ice violently together until it was found that both were nearly melted by friction. The explanation of a diminution in thermal capacity was evidently inapplicable in this experiment, since water contains more heat than ice; and other experiments performed by Davy combined to shew that the heat produced in such cases is not abstracted from neighbouring bodies. The result derived by Davy from these experiments was that heat is a species of motion of the corpuscules of bodies.

About the same time Count Rumford was engaged in boring cannon at the arsenal in Munich, and was struck with the very great amount of heat developed by this operation; the source of this heat appeared to him to be inexhaustible, and he was therefore led to attribute it to motion.

Rumford, moreover, estimated approximately the quantity of heat produced by a definite amount of mechanical energy, and pointed out that the agitation of liquids, such as churning, might form a very good means of determining the mechanical equivalent of heat. A complete determination of this equivalent was however reserved for Joule, but his experiments will form the subject of another chapter.

320. Conversion of heat into mechanical energy.
The converse problem, or the rationale of the conversion of heat into mechanical energy, was first undertaken by Carnot, a French philosopher. He shewed that mechanical effect is only produced by heat when there is a transference of heat from a body of higher to a body of lower temperature. He likened, very ingeniously, the mechanical power of heat to that of water, shewing that just as a body of water at the same level can produce no mechanical effect, so neither can bodies at the same temperature produce any mechanical effect; and just as you must have a fall of water from a higher to a lower level in order to obtain mechanical effect, so likewise you must have a fall of heat from a body of a higher to one of a lower temperature. Carnot, in his researches, adopted the old or material theory of heat, and his principle therefore required to be modified so as to suit the dynamical theory. This was done nearly simultaneously by Rankine, Clausius, and W. Thomson. Further remarks on this subject we must defer to a future chapter.

321. Various principles of the science of energy.
It may be desirable at this stage to distinguish between three principles or laws connected with energy. The first of these is the principle of the conservation of energy, which asserts that energy is as indestructible as matter itself, and as a whole is neither created nor destroyed, but merely changes its form.

The second problem embraces the laws which regulate the change of form, consistently of course with the great law of conservation, and consistently also with the third law, or that of the dissipation of energy. Mr. W. R. Grove has done good service in pointing out how the various forms of energy are correlated, and many of those philosophers who have been engaged with the conservation of energy, such as Joule, Helmholz, Thomson, Rankine, &c., have necessarily advanced the subject; nevertheless, the complete laws which regulate the transmutation of the various kinds of energy into one another are as yet very imperfectly known. Rankine especially has given the laws of transmutation of energy in the most general form possible.

The third law, or that of the dissipation of energy, will be considered in a future part of this work.

322. Various forms of energy. Before concluding this chapter we will give a list of the various forms of energy, and state very briefly some of the more prominent transmutations from the one into the other. In the first place, all these forms may be divided into two classes :—

I. VISIBLE ENERGY, or energy of visible motions and arrangements.

II. MOLECULAR ENERGY.

In the first of these classes, under the head of visible energy, we have—

A. *Visible kinetic energy ;* that is to say, the energy of a body in visible motion.

B. *Potential energy of visible arrangement ;* that is to say, a body in a position of advantage with regard to the force of gravity, the force of a spring, or any other force acting through visible spaces. A head of water is a very good instance of this kind of energy, and every one is familiar with the work a head of water is capable of accomplishing.

In the class of visible energy we may embrace those vibrations of bodies which give rise to sound. A body in vibration is very similar to an oscillating pendulum, in which case we have already seen (Art. 316) that the energy is alternately kinetic and potential.

In the class of molecular energy we have—

C. *The energy of electricity in motion.* When a current of electricity passes along a wire the wire will be heated to some extent, but if it be a very good conductor the heating effect will be comparatively small. In such a case we know that much more energy has passed through a given length of the wire than can be accounted for by the heating effect produced. This is the energy of electricity in motion.

D. *The energy of radiant heat and light.* This is a species of energy which is capable of passing through inter-planetary space without sensible loss; it is also capable of passing through certain bodies with very little absorption.

We imagine radiant light and heat to consist of a vibratory motion of the molecules of matter. The energy of a molecule passing radiant light is therefore perhaps similar to that of a vibrating body or pendulum; that is to say, it is alternately potential and kinetic.

E. *The kinetic energy of absorbed heat.* When radiant heat and light are absorbed, or when a body becomes heated by any means, we have reason to believe that a great portion of the energy of this absorbed heat is transformed into a peculiar motion of the molecules of the body.

F. *Molecular potential energy.* Part of the absorbed heat is also spent in producing energy of expansion or separation of the molecules of matter against the force by which they are attracted to each other. It is thus spent in producing a species of potential energy, molecular attraction being the force in this case, just like gravity, or the force of a spring, in the case of the potential energy of visible motion. There are besides other forms of molecular potential energy.

G. There is also *the potential energy caused by electrical separation*. Thus two separated spheres, one charged with positive and the other with negative electricity, attract each other. A position of advantage is thus obtained with respect to the force of electricity analogous to that which is obtained with respect to the force of gravity when a stone is separated from the earth.

H. There is also *the potential energy caused by chemical separation*. In the expansion produced by heat we have chiefly one molecule separated from another of the same body; but in chemical separation we have one element of a compound body separated from the other, and in this separation we have obtained a position of advantage with respect to that very powerful force known as chemical affinity.

It is not of course pretended that there may not prove to be some kind of energy which is not embraced in this list, or that no two of these varieties here given are reducible into one. The list is simply one of convenience.

323. Now with regard to these various forms of energy, the principle of the conservation of energy asserts that for a body left to itself, or for the entire material universe, we must have—

$$A + B + C + D + \&c. = \text{a constant quantity};$$

on the other hand, the various terms of the left hand member of this equation must be considered as variable quantities, subject however to the above limitation, but capable of being transmuted into one another according to certain laws.

324. Laws of transmutations of energy. The following are amongst the most important cases of transmutation of these energies into one another :—

A, or visible kinetic energy, is transmuted into **B**, or the potential energy of visible motion, when a weight is projected upwards above the earth; into **C**, or electricity in motion (ultimately into heat), when a revolving conductor is brought between the poles of a powerful magnet.

As far as we know at present, **A** is not directly transmuted into **D**, or radiant light and heat; it is transmuted into **E** and **F**, which embrace the energy, both kinetic and potential, of absorbed heat, when friction stops a body in motion and the body becomes heated in consequence; into **G**, or the potential energy of electrical separation in the machine which produces frictional electricity. The electrical separation produced makes it harder to drive the machine. **A** is possibly not converted directly into **H**, or chemical separation.

B, or the potential energy of visible motion, is generally converted first into **A**, or visible kinetic energy, and through it into other forms of energy. It is converted into **A** when a stone is rolled down a mountain, or when a head of water is made to drive a mill-wheel.

C, or the energy of electricity in motion, is converted into **A**, or visible kinetic energy, when two wires conveying electrical currents in the same direction attract each other; a certain amount of the strength of the two currents is thus spent in producing the kinetic energy of the visible motion as they approach each other; into **E** and **F**, or absorbed heat, when an electric current passes through a body which presents any resistance to its passage; into **H**, or chemical separation, when a current of electricity is made to decompose a body.

D, or the energy of radiant light and heat, is converted into **E** and **F**, or absorbed heat, when radiant heat is absorbed by a body; into **H**, or chemical separation, when a ray of sunlight decomposes chloride of silver.

E and **F**, or the energy (kinetic and potential) of absorbed heat, is converted into **A** and **B**, or the energy (kinetic and potential) of visible motion, in the case of any heat-engine;

into **C**, or the energy of electricity in motion, in thermo-electric currents (Art. 163); into **D**, or radiant light and heat, when a hot body radiates, which it always does; into **G**, or electrical separation, when tourmalines and other gems are heated (Art. 167); into **H**, or chemical separation, when a body is decomposed by heat.

G, or electrical separation, is transformed into **A**, or the kinetic energy of visible motion, when two bodies oppositely electrified approach each other; into **C**, or the energy of electricity in motion, when they are connected together by a wire or when a spark passes.

H, or the potential energy of chemical separation, is transmuted into **C**, or the energy of electricity in motion, when a voltaic battery of zinc and copper-plates is in action; into **E** and **F**, or heat, when a body burns in air, or generally when chemical combination takes place; into **G**, or electrical separation, when two dissimilar metals are brought into contact.

325. These are some of the chief instances of trans-mutation of energy. In the remainder of this work we shall confine our attention to those transmutations in which the energy of heat embraced under the heads D, E and F is converted into other forms of energy, or in which other forms of energy are converted into heat.

CHAPTER II.

Relation between Heat and Mechanical Effect.

FIRST LAW OF THERMO-DYNAMICS.

326. Allusion has already been made to the experiments of Davy, in which ice was melted by the friction against each other of two pieces of this substance; and also to those of Rumford, in which the friction of boring cannon was found to produce great heat, sufficient even to cause a considerable quantity of water to boil. The opinions of these philosophers were also quoted, in both of which it was distinctly stated that in friction motion is converted into heat. Motion is, in fact, *annihilated* as visible motion, while at the same instant heat is *created*. Visible motion is likewise converted into heat in certain cases of deformation, in compression, in percussion, and also in a vibrating body, in which the energy of vibration is ultimately converted into heat; but this transmutation can best be studied in the case of friction.

If, therefore, by means of friction, percussion, &c., there is a transmutation of mechanical energy into heat, it becomes an experimental question of great importance to ascertain how much mechanical energy is required to produce one unit of heat; or in other words, what is the relation between the unit of mechanical energy and the unit of heat; the latter unit being chosen as the amount of heat necessary to raise one pound of water from 0°C to 1°C. We have, in fact, to inquire how far a pound of water must fall under the influence of gravity in order to acquire mechanical energy by the fall which, when entirely converted into heat, will raise its temperature 1°C.

327. Joule's experiments. I. Fluid friction. This experimental question has lately been answered by Joule. His experiments began in 1843 and were continued until 1849. During this time he had learned to perfect his apparatus and to eliminate the various sources of error in such a manner that the results of different processes coincided in giving almost identical values for the mechanical equivalent of heat.

His experiments on the friction of fluids were conducted

in the following manner. A known weight is attached to a pulley as in Fig. 65, the axle of this pulley resting upon

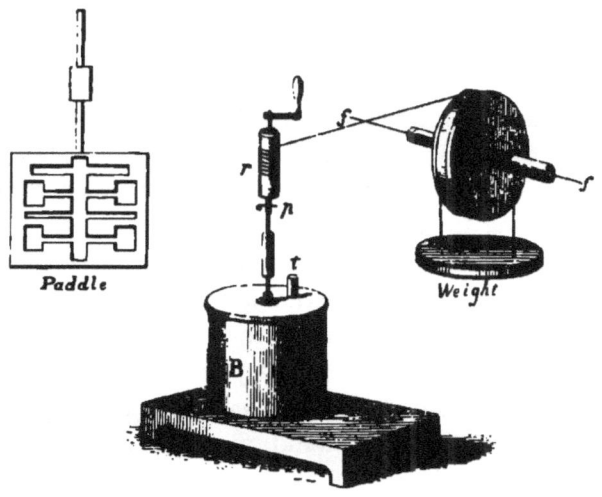

Fig. 65.

friction rollers at f and f'; a string passing over the pulley is also wrapped round the roller r, so that by descent of the weight a rapid motion round a vertical axis is communicated to this roller.

This roller communicates its motion to a system of paddles placed in a fluid which fills the box B. A vertical section of one of these paddles is given in the figure. There are eight sets of these revolving between four stationary vanes, which thus prevent the liquid from being whirled in the direction of rotation. The mechanical energy employed in producing the rotation was measured by the descent of a known weight through a known distance, and by undoing a small peg p the weight could be wound up again without moving the paddles in B. Great care was taken to correct for the amount of energy expended in friction of the axles of the pulleys employed. In this experiment it is evident that the mechanical energy of the weight is expended in fluid friction in the box *B*, and by this means is ultimately converted into heat. A delicate thermometer at *t* gives the temperature with great exactness, and, the usual precautions being taken to eliminate the effects of radiation and conduction, it is evident that the amount of heating effect may be accurately measured, and by knowing the thermal capacity of the box and its contents this may ultimately be expressed in terms of the unit of heat. Joule also made experiments on the friction of iron. In these a disk of cast iron was made to rotate against another disk of cast iron pressed against it; the whole being immersed in a cast-iron vessel filled with mercury. By all these experiments it was found that the quantity of heat produced by the friction of bodies, whether solid or liquid, is always proportional to the quantity of work expended, and that the number of units of work in foot-pounds necessary to raise by 1° Fahr. the temperature of one pound of water taken at about 50° was as follows :—

772.692 from friction of water mean of 40 experiments.
774.083   „   mercury   „   50   „
774.987   „   cast iron „   20   „

328. II. Magneto-electricity. Other methods were used by Joule; one of these took advantage of magneto-electricity, and was essentially the same experiment which was afterwards put in the following form by Foucault.

If a metallic disk or top in rapid rotation be brought between the poles of a powerful electro-magnet, it will almost immediately be brought to rest. The effect is exceedingly curious, and if it be asked what becomes of the energy of the rotation, the answer is that it is converted into heat, and that in consequence the temperature of the disk will be found to have increased. If the disk be turned by hand the effect is very strange; it is found almost impossible to move it while the electro-magnet is in its neighbourhood, but when the current is broken it is of course exceedingly easy to do so. At the expense of much labour the disk, so revolving between the poles of the magnet, may be heated until it is too hot to be touched.

Joule's final results coincided in giving 772 foot-pounds as the mechanical equivalent of the heat necessary to raise one pound of water (weighed in vacuo and taken between 55° and 60°) through 1°Fahr.; whence, if we adopt one pound of water raised 1°C as our unit of heat, we find that this will be represented by $772 \times \dfrac{9}{5} = 1390$ foot-pounds nearly. Strictly speaking, this determination is for the value of gravity at Manchester, and for the specific heat which water has between 55° and 60° Fahr.

329. III. Condensation of gases. Before leaving this subject it will be desirable to consider the method of deriving the mechanical equivalent of heat from the condensation of gases. Many familiar experiments shew that when a gas is suddenly compressed there is a production of heat, and that when suddenly expanded there is an absorption of heat.

Séguin and Mayer had already suggested the use of gases and vapours for the purpose of determining the mechanical equivalent of heat; and air, the substance chosen by Mayer, was no doubt very good for such a purpose; nevertheless, the suggestions of these philosophers do not seem to have been accompanied with a clear appreciation of all the data necessary to a complete proof.

330. Joule, however, in his experiments supplied what was wanting in order to derive a good determination of the mechanical equivalent of heat from the known gaseous laws. By compressing air forcibly into a receiver surrounded by water he found that the water was considerably heated. It is not, however, correct to infer without further experiment that the amount of heat produced in this case is the exact equivalent of the energy expended in compressing the air. A familiar instance will make this clear. By a blow of a hammer upon a small quantity of fulminating mercury it is exploded and produces a considerable amount of heated gas, but we are not at liberty to suppose that all the heat thus developed is merely the mechanical equivalent of the energy of the blow, as will be evident by supposing such an extreme case as a ton of the fulminating powder. .

Evidently the substance is in different molecular conditions at the end of the experiment and at the beginning, and it may be supposed with much truth that the heat produced is nearly all due to the conversion into a kinetic form of a certain potential energy present in the compound. Now in the experiment above described, in which air is compressed, the air is evidently in a different molecular condition after compression, for the particles are much nearer together. The first thing therefore is to determine how much, if any, of the heat produced may be due to this change of molecular condition of the air, and how much to the work expended in compressing the air.

331. The following very ingenious experiment performed by Joule is conclusive in shewing that the mere change of distance of the molecules of a permanent gas neither produces nor absorbs heat to an appreciable extent. In Fig. 66 we have two strong vessels, of which *A* contains compressed air, say under the pressure of 20 atmospheres; *B*, on the other hand, is a vacuum. The two vessels are connected with each other by a tube having a stop-cock which we may suppose to be shut. The whole apparatus is plunged into a vessel of water. After the temperature of the water has been very accurately ascertained, open the stop-cock, and thus allow both vessels to have the same pressure.

When the experiment is finished it will be found that there is no change in the temperature of the water. The

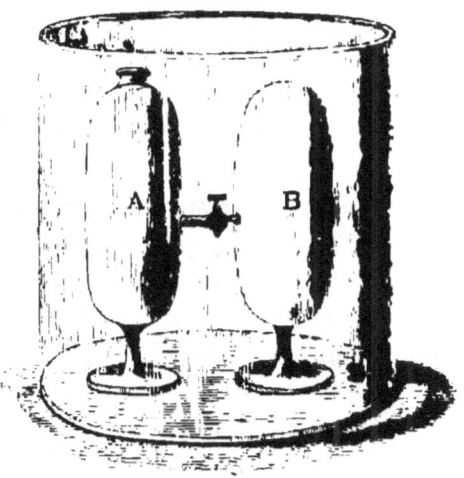

Fig. 66.

prevalent idea is that when air expands it becomes colder, and that when condensed it becomes hotter; but Joule by this experiment has shewn that no appreciable change of temperature occurs when air is allowed to expand in such a manner as not to develope mechanical power. It follows as an inference that when air is compressed the rise of temperature is scarcely at all due to the mere diminution of the distance between the particles, but almost entirely to the mechanical effect which must be spent on the air before this condensation can be produced.

332. Specific heat of gas of constant volume. In a previous part of this work a distinction was made between the specific heat of a gas of constant volume and that of the same gas of constant pressure, and the determinations therein exhibited were those of Regnault.

His determinations give the specific heat of various gases under constant pressure; that is to say, when the gas remains at the same pressure during the various temperatures to which it is exposed.

Experimentally it would be very difficult to find the specific heat of a gas of constant volume; nevertheless, the one specific heat can be obtained from the other without trouble by means of the knowledge derived from the experiments of Joule.

Thus let us consider a rectangular prismatic vessel one foot in section (Fig. 67), and suppose that we have a cubic foot of air under the ordinary pressure of 15 lbs. to the square inch contained in it, the temperature being 0°C; the whole pressure on the surface *aa*, which shuts in this air, will therefore be 15 × 144 = 2160 lbs. We may suppose, for the sake of simplicity, that there is no atmosphere above this air, and that it is kept down by a veritable weight of 2160 lbs. above it. The weight of this cubic foot of air will at 0°C be 1.29 oz.

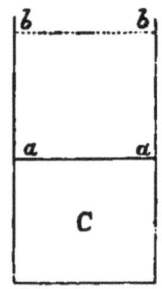

Fig. 67.

avoirdupois, and if it be raised in temperature through an interval of 272°C its volume under the same pressure will be exactly doubled; that is to say, it will have raised the weight 2160 lbs. one foot high and done work represented by 2160.

Now according to Regnault's determination the specific heat of air is 0.237; that is to say, it will only require 0.237 of the amount of heat necessary to raise a pound of water one degree in temperature, in order to raise a pound of air under constant pressure one degree in temperature.

Hence the amount of heat necessary to raise this air from 0°C to 272°C under constant pressure will be—

$$\frac{1.29}{16} \times 0.237 \times 272 = 5.19 \text{ heat units.}$$

In this expression the first factor refers to the weight of the air, the second to its specific heat, and the third to its increase of temperature. But in the course of this increase of temperature work equal to 2160 mechanical units, or

(Art. 328) $\frac{2160}{1390} = 1.554$ heat units, has been done.

Hence, of all the heat expended upon this air, or 5.19 units, 1.554 units have been spent in work. Hence also 5.19 — 1.554 or 3.636 units denote the amount of heat consumed in the mere heating of the particles.

But, according to Joule's experiment, if the air had throughout been confined to one cubic foot, and afterwards made to occupy two cubic feet without doing any work, the whole heat of the particles would be the same in the second case as in the first. But we have seen that the mere heat consumed in heating the particles occupying the two cubic feet is 3.636 units; hence this also will represent the heat required to raise the air remaining at the constant volume of one cubic foot through 272°C. It thus appears that if 5.19 be used to represent the specific heat of this air under constant pressure, 3.636 will represent its specific heat of constant volume.

According, therefore, to our usual method of measuring specific heat, $0.237 \times \frac{3.636}{5.19} = .166$ will denote the specific heat of air, the volume of which remains constant during experiment.

SECOND LAW OF THERMO-DYNAMICS.

333. Reversible engines. Having now described at some length the first law of thermo-dynamics, or that which relates to the conversion of work into heat, let us proceed to consider the second law, which relates to the conversion of heat into work.

The following proof of this law is deduced from that given by Professor W. Thomson.

In establishing this very important principle recourse is had to a conception of Carnot, to whom this branch of science is so much indebted, notwithstanding that his idea of the nature of heat was erroneous.

This conception is that of an engine completely reversible in all its physical and mechanical agencies. Such an engine must be supposed to have a source of heat and also a refrigerator, the temperature of the first being of course higher than that of the second, and it produces work while it transfers heat from the source to the refrigerator. If worked forwards, such an engine will produce a certain amount of work from a certain amount of heat which leaves the source; but if worked backwards, owing to its complete reversibility, it will, at the expense of a similar amount of work, bring back the same amount of heat into the source.

334. Now it may easily be shewn that a completely reversible engine will produce as much mechanical effect as can be produced by any heat engine, with the same temperatures of source and refrigerator, from a given quantity of heat. For let there be two heat engines A and B, of which B is a reversible engine, both working between the same temperatures, and if possible let A derive more work from a given quantity of heat than B. Now if A be worked forwards, a quantity of work W is produced by it, during the conveyance of a quantity of heat Q from the source of heat.

If B were worked forwards, a quantity of work w (less than W by hypothesis) would be derived from the same quantity of heat Q; but since B is completely reversible if worked backwards it would restore to the source of heat a quantity of heat Q by the expenditure of a certain amount of work w (less than W).

Thus we have—

A working forwards and producing an amount of work W by carrying heat $= Q$ from the source.

B working backwards and spending an amount of work w (less than W) in order to carry heat $= Q$ to the source of heat.

But, since the work produced by A is greater than that spent by B, A may be made to work B, and hence the whole arrangement becomes self-acting; while, on the whole, the source neither gains nor loses heat, and work equal to $W - w$ is produced during each double cycle of operations. Now, as far as this problem is concerned, we may suppose all the bodies surrounding the source (with the exception of the refrigerator) to be of the same temperature as the source, and therefore, if the hypothesis with which we started is correct, we may go on continually producing work by the mere presence of a refrigerator, or body of lower temperature; while, at the same time, no heat is conveyed from the bodies of higher temperature which are supposed to surround this refrigerator.

Since however, consistently with the conservation of energy, heat must disappear *as heat* in order to produce this work, we see that this heat must in this supposed case really come from the body of low temperature; that is to say, work is produced by abstracting heat from a body of already low temperature. A little reflection will shew that such a process might be carried on for ever, and would therefore result in a kind of perpetual motion; but since we cannot admit the possibility of such a case, we must suppose our hypothesis to be erroneous.

But our hypothesis was that of two engines A and B, of which the latter is reversible, working between the same source and refrigerator, A could produce more work than B out of the same quantity of heat. We are thus driven to the conclusion that under similar circumstances B produces as much work as A; and therefore that the test of maximum work under given circumstances is *reversibility*.

335. Reversible engines of infinitely small range. In the next place let us take a mass of any substance (for the sake of simplicity we may suppose it to be fluid), and let each unit of its surface be subjected to the uniform pressure p, also let its volume be v while its temperature is t.

Next imagine this substance to form our heat engine; that is to say, let us imagine certain operations at different temperatures to be performed on this substance whose result is that heat is transmuted into work.

And here it is well to observe that we need not trouble ourselves about the practicability of making such an engine; all that we need care about is that our conception is mechanically conceivable.

Now, in the first place, let us reckon pressures and volumes along two axes at right angles to one another as in Fig. 68, and let us suppose our substance to have a volume v denoted by og, its pressure p being represented by ag. Now, *in the first place*, let it expand from volume v to $v + dv$, its temperature being kept constantly t; at the end of this expansion its volume may be supposed to be oi and its pressure ib, necessarily less than ga; let it now, *secondly*, be allowed to expand further, without either emitting or absorbing heat, till its temperature goes down through an exceedingly small range to $t - \tau$ (τ being very small); c may now be taken to denote the place of the substance in our

scale of pressures and volumes; *thirdly*, let it be compressed at the constant temperature $t - \tau$ (differing infinitely little from t), so much
that when, *fourthly*, the volume is further diminished to
the original volume v without
the substance being allowed
either to emit or absorb heat,
its temperature may be t.

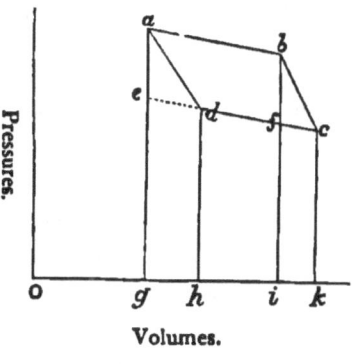

Fig. 68.

336. Here, then, we have
first of all two expansions,
and next two similar compres-
sions bringing back the body
to its original state, and the
first compression is the reverse of the first expansion, while
the second compression is the reverse of the second expansion, and all are supposed to be extremely small.

Evidently, therefore, the line which denotes the first compression will be parallel, but opposite in direction to that
which denotes the first expansion, and the same will hold for
the other two lines; so that, provided all the movements be
sufficiently small, the four positions of the body will be the
four corners of a parallelogram $abcd$. Now the work done
by the body during the expansion between a and b (equal to
the mean pressure on unit of surface multiplied by the
volume passed over) will be denoted by the area $abig$, also
that done by the body between b and c will be denoted by
the area $bcki$. Hence the whole work *done* BY *the body* between a and c will be denoted by the area $abckg$.

In like manner the work *performed* AGAINST *the body* during
the compression between c and d will be the area $cdhk$, and
that done against the body by the further compression between
d and a will be the area $dhga$. Hence the whole area $ckgad$
will denote the whole work *done* AGAINST *the body*.

Now the difference between the area *abckg*, or the work done by the body, and the area *ckgad*, or the work done against the body, is the parallelogram *abcd*.

Hence this parallelogram denotes the whole surplus work *done* BY *the body* in its cycle of operations.

337. In the next place, the whole heat abstracted from the source of higher temperature *t* is that required to heat the body as it increases in volume from v to $v + dv$, this operation being performed at the temperature *t*, while, on the other hand, when the body is finally restored to this temperature *t* it has only the volume v.

Heat corresponding to the volume $v + dv$ is therefore taken from source *t*, while heat corresponding to the volume v is restored to this source.

Hence the whole heat abstracted from source *t* is that required to increase the volume of the body at the constant temperature *t* from v to $v + dv$.

This may be called $M dv$.

338. Let us now suppose the cycle of operations to take place, or the engine to be worked backwards starting from *c* and from the lower temperature $t - \tau$.

First, let the body contract in volume without giving or receiving heat until it becomes of the temperature *t*.

Next, let it be further contracted at the constant temperature *t* through the volume dv.

Thirdly, let it expand without giving or receiving heat till it falls to the temperature $t - \tau$. And

Fourthly, let it expand at the constant temperature $t - \tau$ through the volume dv.

It will be seen that in this cycle the body goes from *c* to *b* and from *b* to *a* having *work done* UPON *it;* while it goes from *c* to *d* and from *d* to *c* having *work done* BY *it*.

The *work done* UPON *it* is represented therefore by the larger area *abckg*, and *that done* BY *it* by the smaller area *adckg*; and on the whole there is a surplus of *work done* UPON *the body* denoted by the parallelogram *abcd*. At the same time it will be noticed that in the second operation, where the body is contracted from $v + dv$ to v (going from b to a) at the temperature t, there is a surplus supply of heat brought to the source equal to $M dv$.

339. Thus when this engine was worked in a direct manner we had *work produced* equal to the area *abcd*, while heat was *drawn from the source* equal to $M dv$. Now when the engine is reversed we have *work spent* equal to the same area *abcd*; while heat is *brought to the source* equal as before to $M dv$. A body acted upon in this manner forms therefore a reversible engine, and we are entitled to apply to it the reasoning of Art. 334, and to conclude that whatever be the substance employed between the limits of temperature t and $t - \tau$ if the heat drawn from the source or $M dv$ remain constant, the work done, or the area *abcd*, will also remain constant; in other words, for the same temperature-limits the ratio between $M dv$ and the area *abcd*, or $\dfrac{M dv}{\text{area } abcd}$, is constant, whatever be the substance used.

340. The area *abcd* is easily found thus :—

Produce *cd* to cut *ag* in *e*. Now area *abcd* = area *abfe*, since they are on the same base and between the same parallels, but area *abfe* = *ae* × perpendicular distance between *ae* and *bf* = *ae* × *gi*. Hence area *abcd* = *ae* × *gi*.

Now if the operation denoted by the body going from *c* to *d*, namely the contraction of volume at the fixed temperature $t - \tau$, be continued until the original volume v is reached, that is, up to the line *ag* which limits this volume, we should be brought to the point *e*; *eg* would thus denote the pressure of the body at temperature $t - \tau$ and at volume v; while *ag* is the pressure at the same volume, but at temperature t.

Hence *ae* denotes the change of pressure of the body at constant volume *v* while the temperature falls from *t* to *t*−*τ*. If we consider the pressure to be a function of the temperature *t*, *ae* will thus be represented by $\frac{dp}{dt}\tau$; that is to say, by the differential coefficient of this function multiplied by the small temperature-change *τ*.

Again, *gi* is evidently the change of volume or *dv*. Hence—

$$\text{Area } abcd = ae \times gi = \frac{dp}{dt}\tau\,dv.$$

341. Carnot's function. Hence also—

$$\frac{M\,dv}{\text{area } abcd}, \quad \text{or} \quad \frac{M\,dv}{\frac{dp}{dt}\tau\,dv}, \quad \text{or} \quad \frac{M}{\frac{dp}{dt}\tau}$$

is constant for the same temperature *t* and range *τ* whatever be the substance used, but if in going from one substance to another we always adhere to the same value of *τ*, or keep the small fall of temperature the same, it will thus become a constant multiplier, and we may therefore dispense with it and assert that $\frac{M}{\frac{dp}{dt}}$ is constant for the same temperature whatever be the substance used. In other words, $\frac{M}{\frac{dp}{dt}} = \phi(t)$;

that is to say, it is a function of the temperature only, and does not vary with the nature of the substance.

This very important common property of all bodies was first discovered by Carnot.

342. Probable form of this function. Since therefore this function is the same for all substances, in order to determine its form let us take some one body whose laws are best known. Let us, for instance, take a perfect gas, and consider in the first place the relations which subsist between the temperature and pressure of such a gas whose volume is v. This is very easily found, for if P denote the pressure of this gas at o°C, its pressure at $t°$ will be $P(1 + at)$. (Art. 63.)

Now we have reason to conclude from the experiment of Joule (Art. 331) that the molecular heat of the particles of a perfect gas whose temperature is constant is independent of the volume of this gas, being the same for a great volume as for a small one. The heat absorbed when such a gas expands at a constant temperature is therefore the exact equivalent of the work done in expansion.

Hence the mechanical equivalent of $M dv$, that is to say of the heat absorbed while the gas increases in volume at the constant temperature t from v to $v + dv$, will be denoted by the work done, that is, by p v or $P(1 + at)dv$.

Hence if we use J to denote the multiplier by which our heat-unit must be multiplied in order to produce its mechanical equivalent (that is to say, $J = 1390$ (Art. 328)), we shall have—

$$JM dv = P(1 + at)dv ; \qquad \therefore \quad M = \frac{P(1 + at)}{J}.$$

But again, since $p = P(1 + at)$, we have $\frac{dp}{dt} = Pa$; and hence

$$\frac{M}{\frac{dp}{dt}} = \frac{P(1 + at)}{JPa} = \frac{1 + at}{Ja}. \qquad (1)$$

343. This therefore is most probably the true value of the function $\phi(t)$, and the expression may be rendered yet simpler by the following assumption.

Instead of considering o°C as our zero of temperature, let us, while adhering to Centigrade *degrees*, take however a different *zero* to start from. Let this zero be such that our new temperature shall be proportional to $(1 + at°\text{Cent.})$, so that if the ratio of this proportion be some number m we shall have

New temperature $= m(1 + at°\text{Cent.})$.

Hence at o°C we shall have new temperature or $T_o = m$;

and at 1°C   ,,   ,, $T_o + 1 = m(1 + a)$.

Subtracting the upper expression from the lower, and since $a = .0037$ (Art. 64), we find—

$$1 = am; \qquad \therefore \quad m = \frac{1}{a} = \frac{1}{.0037} = 270 \text{ nearly.}$$

Hence at o°C $T_o = 270°$, according to our new notation, and generally—

$$\text{New temp.} = \frac{1}{a}(1 + at°C) = \frac{1}{a} + t°C \text{ or } t°C = \text{new temp.} - \frac{1}{a}.$$

Making this substitution in (1), we have—

$$\frac{M}{\dfrac{dp}{dt}} = \frac{1 + a\left(\text{new temp.} - \dfrac{1}{a}\right)}{Ja} = \frac{\text{new temp.}}{J}. \qquad (2)$$

344. Perfect engines of great range. We have hitherto confined our observations to a perfect engine working through an infinitely small temperature-range; let us now attempt to find how much work will be produced from a given quantity of heat by an engine working between a source of temperature T_S and a refrigerator of temperature T_R, according to the new scale of temperature just mentioned. In discussing this problem let us (adopting the words of Professor W. Thomson) suppose the great engine to consist of or to be broken up into an infinite number of perfect engines, each working within an infinitely small range of temperature and arranged in a series of which the source of the first is the given source, the refrigerator of the last the given refrigerator; while the refrigerator of each intermediate engine is the source of that which follows it in the series. In order to make this reasoning perfectly clear we may follow out the analogy suggested by Carnot, in which he compares the mechanical energy derived by carrying heat from a body of a higher to one of a lower temperature to the mechanical energy of water falling from a higher to a lower level. The imaginary breaking up of the great engine into an infinite number of small engines is thus analogous to the breaking up of a great waterfall into a vast number of very small stages. But we must not pursue the analogy too far.

Now each of these small engines will in any time emit less heat to its refrigerator than is supplied to it from its source by the amount which represents the mechanical work which it produces. Now let q denote the quantity of heat which such an intermediate engine discharges into its refrigerator in any time; while $q + dq$ denotes the quantity which it draws from its source in the same time; also let t and $t + dt$ denote the temperatures (on the new scale) of the refrigerator and source of this intermediate engine.

345. Denoting as before by J the mechanical equivalent of unit of heat, then the work done by this small intermediate engine in the given time will be equal to

$$J dq. \tag{3}$$

But since dt replaces τ of Art. 335—that is to say, since it denotes the difference of temperature between the source and refrigerator of our small engine—we shall have the following proportion :—

Work done : heat drawn from source or $q :: \dfrac{dp}{dt} dt\, dv : M dv.$

Hence—

$$\text{Work done} = \frac{q}{M} \times \frac{dp}{dt} dt = q \times \frac{J dt}{t} \quad \text{(Art. 343)}. \tag{4}$$

Now since (3) and (4) are both different expressions for the work done, we may equate them together. Hence we have—
$$J dq = J q \frac{dt}{t}; \text{ and hence } \frac{dq}{q} = \frac{dt}{t}. \tag{5}$$

Let us now, in Fig. 69, represent the temperatures (t) (new scale) of the various intermediate engines by lines of abscissæ starting from the origin O; while we raise ordinates to denote the whole quantity of heat (q) that has passed during the time under consideration through an intermediate engine of temperature t denoted by the corresponding abscissa; and let us join the extremities of these ordinates so as to form a line. It is very easy to shew that this line will be a straight line. For $ea = q$ and $ec = dq$, also $Oa = t$, $ab = dt$. Now if Oed be a straight line, we have—

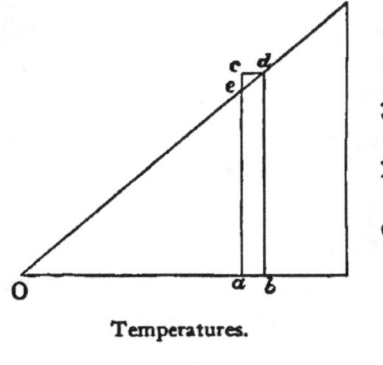

Quantities of heat.

Temperatures.

Fig. 69.

$$ec : ea :: ed : eO :: ab : aO;$$

that is to say—

$$dq : q :: dt : t; \text{ or } \frac{dq}{q} = \frac{dt}{t}.$$

The condition (5) is therefore fulfilled by a straight line of this description; and indeed we may arrive at the same result by a direct integration of (5).

346. Work done by perfect engines. Having thus determined that the line Oed is a straight line, the work done by the great engine can be very easily found; for let T_S and T_R be the temperatures (new scale) of the source and refrigerator of this great engine, while Q_S is the quantity of heat which passes from its source, and Q_R is the quantity of heat which passes through its refrigerator in a given time. Q_S and Q_R are thus ordinates of Fig. 69, while T_S and T_R are the corresponding abscissæ; and we have, since Oed is a straight line—

$$Q_R : Q_S :: T_R : T_S; \qquad \therefore \quad Q_R = Q_S \frac{T_R}{T_S}.$$

Also—

$$Q_S - Q_R = \frac{Q_S (T_S - T_R)}{T_S}.$$

But since during a given time while the given quantity of heat Q_S leaves the source it is only the smaller quantity Q_R which reaches the refrigerator, it is evident from the principle of the conservation of energy that the difference, or $Q_S - Q_R$, must have been transmuted into mechanical effect. Hence—

$$J(Q_S - Q_R) = \frac{JQ_S(T_S - T_R)}{T_S}$$

is the quantity of work produced by the engine in this time; that is to say, this expression represents the amount of work produced by a prefect engine working between temperatures T_S and T_R (new scale) during the time that a quantity of heat $= Q_S$ is conveyed from the source. It is unnecessary to notice the importance of this result in the theory of steam engines and of heat engines in general.

347. Absolute zero of temperature. One peculiarity of this expression remains to be remarked. If $T_R = 0$, then the work produced is JQ_S; that is to say, all the heat Q_S which leaves the source is converted into work. Since we cannot possibly have more work than this from this quantity of heat, we are therefore precluded from supposing that T_R may be a negative quantity; that is to say, it would seem that on this scale there can be no negative temperature or it would seem that the zero of this scale is the absolute zero of temperature. We shall again return to the subject of the absolute zero of temperature.

CHAPTER III.

History of Heat Engines.

348. In the last chapter heat engines were discussed, but rather from a theoretical than a practical point of view.

Y

A mechanically conceivable but nevertheless unattainable machine called a perfect engine was there imagined, and it was shewn that such an engine, having a given temperature of source and refrigerator, is only able to convert into mechanical effect, or utilize, a certain definite proportion of the heat which leaves its source. In fine, the principles of the process by which heat is converted into work in such engines were given; so that by knowing the temperatures of source and refrigerator of a perfect engine it could at once be told what proportion of heat is utilized.

But in practice engines are not perfect, and by no means produce the greatest possible amount of work which perfect engines of the same temperature of source and refrigerator are capable of producing, although of late years the efficiency of heat engines has been very greatly increased.

Such machines also have hitherto been worked almost exclusively by steam, so that the history of heat engines is in fact that of the steam engine.

This history is one of great interest, and it is extremely instructive to trace the attempts to make use of steam from their infancy to our own day, in which the steam engine plays so very prominent a part.

349. Hero's engine. In giving a short sketch of the history of the steam engine we may with much propriety limit ourselves to those attempts to produce by means of steam some motion of a useful kind which have been either made or at least suggested; and in this sketch the first engine which we shall have to describe is the Eolipyle of Hero of Alexandria, who flourished about 120 B.C.

This machine is represented in Fig. 70.

The principle is very obvious, and is founded upon that law of motion which asserts that all action has an equal and contrary reaction as far as momentum is concerned. Thus when a musket is discharged the equivalent to the forward momentum of the ball and ignited gas is the recoil of the gun barrel, but the mass of the latter being much greater the velocity is of course much smaller.

In like manner when a rocket is ignited the reaction to the down rush of gas is the upward flight of the rocket.

The same principle applies to Hero's Eolipyle, which consists of a globe having two nozzles with narrow apertures, as in Fig. 70. This globe contains a quantity of water, which is made to boil by the application of a lamp (not shewn in the figure). As the heat is applied the vapour is forcibly discharged through the nozzles, these nozzles may therefore be compared to musket barrels; so that at each nozzle there is a recoil which is the exact equivalent of the momentum of the issuing steam. This recoil will not however be momentary but continuous, since the issue of the steam is continuous. Now the nozzles are so arranged that these forces of recoil form a couple, tending to produce a rapid motion of rotation of the globe about its axis.

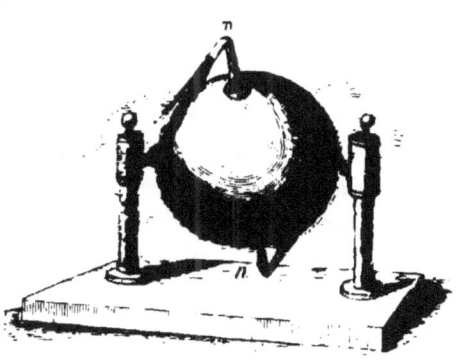

Fig. 70.

350. Blasco de Garay. Passing over the Middle Ages, we have information that in the year 1543 Blasco de Garay, who was in the service of Charles V of Spain, succeeded in applying the motive power of steam so as to propel a ship of 200 tons burthen in the harbour of Barcelona at the rate of three miles an hour. This, if well authenticated, is a very extraordinary fact.

351. Porta, De Caus, and Worcester. J. B. Porta

(1580), Solomon de Caus (1615), and the Marquis of Worcester (1663) appear to have independently conceived an application of steam of a kind somewhat like the following.

Our readers are no doubt familiar with an accident that sometimes happens with a common kettle if the lid be too tight and the level of the water be above the orifice of the spout; the pressure of the steam formed acts upon the surface of the water so as to drive it out at the mouth of the spout.

Now it seems to have been contemplated by these three inventors independently that the pressure of steam might thus be employed to raise a column of water, and by this means to do work; but it seems very doubtful if these conceptions ever led to the construction of a machine of any magnitude.

352. Papin. In 1690 Dr. Papin, a Frenchman, whose name we have already mentioned (Art. 123), conceived the idea of applying the motive force of steam to raise a piston, while its descent might be effected by the condensation of the steam creating a vacuum.

For a long time it was thought that Papin did not carry his project into execution on a scale of any magnitude, but a correspondence has recently come to light which appears to shew that Papin not only conceived the idea of such a machine, but had this idea carried into effect. If we presume this to be the case, a very high rank must be given to Papin in the history of the steam engine.

353. Savery. In the year 1698 Captain Savery took out a patent for an engine for the purpose of raising water from mines.

The machine of Captain Savery was in reality a lift and force pump worked by means of steam. In the lift and force pump two operations are performed. In the first place, by the ascent of a piston a vacuum is formed in a chamber from which a pipe proceeds down to the reservoir of water, beneath the surface of which the extremity of this pipe is plunged. On account of this vacuum the external pressure of the atmosphere on the reservoir forces the water up this pipe, and ultimately into the chamber of the pump; while a valve opening upwards prevents it from returning.

The piston has, however, another office to perform: it drives the water out of the body of the pump into a side pipe, which it is thus forced to ascend, its descent being prevented as before by a valve.

Now in Savery's engine a receiver communicating by means of a pipe with the reservoir of water was filled with steam. The supply of steam was then shut off, and the steam condensed by means of a jet of cold water;—a vacuum was thus formed and the external pressure of the air on the surface of the reservoir forced the water up the pipe into the receiver, its return being prevented by means of a valve. When the receiver was thus nearly filled with water a communication with the boiler was again opened, and the pressure of the steam upon the water in the reservoir forced it up a pipe to a height determined by this pressure, its return being prevented by a valve.

The defects of this engine of Savery's are very manifest, and it was never extensively used: one great disadvantage was that the height to which water could be raised by this engine was dependent on the pressure of steam in the boiler; so that to carry water any considerable height an enormous pressure would be required.

354. Newcomen. Newcomen & Cawley conceived in 1705 the same idea that had previously occurred to Papin, namely to make use of steam to move a piston. It is evident that if by an arrangement of this kind a considerable pressure is exerted on every square inch of a piston of considerable area, and that if this piston is made to move through a considerable space, a great amount of useful work may be done.

In Newcomen's engine as finally constructed we may imagine the piston to be at the top of the cylinder, while the cylinder itself is filled with steam; the communication with the boiler is now cut off, while at the same time a jet of cold water made to play in the cylinder condenses the steam.

A vacuum is thus formed, and the pressure of the air upon the upper surface of the piston pushes it down with great force:—in descending the piston is made to perform useful work. When the piston has reached the bottom of the cylinder the communication with the boiler is again opened, the atmospheric pressure is thus balanced, and the machine itself by a simple arrangement is made to pull the piston up to the top of the cylinder.

When the piston has arrived at the top the communication with the boiler is once more cut off, the steam condensed, a vacuum formed, and the external pressure of the air made to force the piston down, performing as before useful work in its descent, and so on again. It will be seen that this is in reality an atmospheric engine, and though in many respects objectionable, it was a form of engine that continued in use until the time of Watt.

355. Watt. Separate condensation. In the year 1763 James Watt, philosophical instrument maker to the University of Glasgow, was appointed to repair a model of a Newcomen engine that was used by the Professor of Natural Philosophy. He soon perceived the disadvantages attending the construction of this engine, and was led, after laborious study and much opposition, to realize certain improvements of the steam engine which have immortalized his name.

Watt perceived that in order for the piston of such an

engine to descend with force it is necessary that there should be little pressure of steam opposed to that of the atmosphere, and hence that the cylinder, previously filled with steam, must be cooled, so as to condense the steam. But before another down stroke takes place it is necessary that this very same cylinder should be filled with steam of the ordinary atmospheric pressure, and hence that the cylinder should be hot.

It is, therefore, essential to this arrangement that the same cylinder should be heated and cooled alternately; but this produces a great waste of heat, and it soon occurred to Watt that the condensation might be performed in a separate vessel. In fact, the observations of Watt had led him to the result that we have stated in a previous part of this work (Art. 116), namely, that if vapour of water be introduced into two communicating vessels of different temperatures the pressure of the vapour will soon fall so as to correspond as nearly as possible with that due to the inferior temperature.

Watt's idea was therefore to keep the cylinder always as hot as possible, and when it was wished to condense the steam, to open up a communication between the cylinder and a separate chamber kept cold by the constant injection of water. By this means a vacuum might readily be made without the necessity of cooling down the cylinder.

356. Air-pump. Another improvement was the air-pump. Watt saw that this water of injection would soon get heated, and that by its means also atmospheric air might be carried into the condenser. The usefulness of this separate chamber would thus be greatly impaired unless some arrangement were made for pumping out the heated water and the air.

This was done by an air-pump driven by the engine itself; and in order to economise heat as much as possible the boiler was fed by means of this heated water.

This arrangement of separate condensation must be regarded as one of the greatest of Watt's discoveries, for by means of it instead of alternately heating and cooling the same cylinder, the cylinder was always kept as hot as possible and the condenser always as cold as possible.

357. Double action. Another improvement of Watt was to transform the atmospheric engine into a steam engine, and to make this steam engine double acting. In the engine of Newcomen it was essential that the cold atmosphere should have access to the interior of the cylinder; but Watt devised the plan of using the pressure of steam instead of that of air. In this plan when the piston is at the top of the cylinder, the steam below the piston is now condensed, the communication with the boiler being shut off, while steam from the boiler is admitted above the piston, which thus descends with force; but when at the bottom of the cylinder the steam above the piston is shut off from the boiler and condensed, while steam from the boiler is allowed to pass beneath the piston—which is thereby driven upwards with force.

By this arrangement neither cold water nor cold air is admitted into the cylinder, the object being to keep the cylinder always as hot as possible which is accomplished by means of a non-conducting envelope or jacket.

358. Expansive working. One other great improvement of Watt requires to be mentioned.

If the communication of the cylinder with the boiler be uninterrupted during the whole time of the stroke of the piston, and if the resistance to the ascent of the piston be uniform, and of course less than the pressure of the steam, the velocity of the piston will gradually increase to the end of the stroke, when its momentum will be suddenly destroyed. Available work will by this means be converted into heat of percussion (an unavailable form), while the engine itself will also suffer in consequence of these blows. Watt checked this by shutting off the communication with the boiler before the piston had yet finished its stroke. The remainder of the stroke would thus be performed under the continually diminishing pressure of the expanding steam, and things might be so regulated that the piston would reach the top of the cylinder with little or no velocity. Other improvements were introduced into the steam engine by Watt, and also since his day, but these have been chiefly of a mechanical nature and are therefore foreign to the subject of this work.

359. It will be observed that the leading idea in the engine we have described is to produce work as economically as possible, and that this was effected mainly by the improvements of Watt.

The following table will render this evident. It represents the performance in foot-pounds of different engines for one bushel (somewhat less than 100 lbs.) of coal consumed both before and after the era of Watt.

1769	Atmospheric engine (Smeaton)	5,590,000
1772	„ „	9,450,000
1776	Watt	21,600,000
1778	„ (expansive working)	26,600,000
1830	Cornish engines	86,585,000

360. Definition of horse-power. In an engine we have however another point to consider besides the economy with which it works;—this point is the rate at which it works, or how much work it produces in a given time. The unit of this measure is usually the horse-power. An engine is said to be of one horse power when it will raise 33,000 lbs. one foot high in a minute, this being the average rate of work of the strongest London horses: it is said to be of 10 horse power when it will do ten times this work in one minute, and so on.

361. It will appear as a consequence of the principles deduced in the last chapter that the economy of an engine will be increased by increasing the range of temperature between its source and refrigerator; but this could scarcely be done to any great extent in the steam engine, for if the temperature of the water in the boiler is very high the pressure is enormous. Whether on this account any other vapour or gas might not be employed with greater economy is a practical question which has not yet been decided.

362. Locomotive engine. Stephenson. Our object in this sketch has been to furnish the reader with a short account of those improvements in engines which have reference to heat, and before concluding it we cannot do better than describe certain appliances in the locomotive engine. This form of engine is adapted for carrying itself and a load swiftly on iron rails, and was improved very much by George Stephenson: of late years it has played a very prominent part in the world's history. In this engine the principle of condensation cannot be adopted, as that would lead to a large increase in the weight of the engine in order to hold the necessary water. We have not therefore, as in the ordinary engine, the pressure of steam on one side of the piston and a vacuum on the other, but we have the pressure of steam on one side and that of the air on the other; in fine, in the locomotive the steam is generated at high pressure, and instead of being condensed is blown off into the air.

The locomotive boiler is eminently adapted to vaporise water as quickly as possible; in order to produce this result metallic tubes conveying the heated air of the furnace are made to go through the boiler, thus exposing as great an area of the boiler as possible to the action of the heat. Another feature of the locomotive is the blast-pipe, or pipe by means of which the waste steam is made to escape through the chimney, and in so doing to supply a powerful draught to the fire. By this arrangement the fire is urged most when the engine is going most quickly, and when there is therefore most need of rapid combustion.

CHAPTER IV.

Connection between Heat and other forms of Energy.

CONNECTION BETWEEN HEAT AND ELECTRICITY IN MOTION.

363. Conversion of electricity in motion into heat. Heat is the ultimate form of energy generally assumed by a current of electricity. Thus when a Leyden jar is discharged a momentary flash of light is seen, and if we consider voltaic currents we know that there is often a great display of heat in those portions of a circuit which most resist the passage of the electrical current.

Until recently it was supposed by some that the electric flash was the direct production of light through the union of the two electricities, and that this flash did not imply the existence of ordinary matter in a heated state; but of late years it has been shewn that the electric flash is probably due to a small portion of some kind of matter intensely heated. Thus when a jar is discharged, or the spark is taken between the terminals of a Ruhmkorff's machine, this spark consists of a small quantity of the matter of the terminal, in a gaseous state and at a very high temperature, combined with a small portion of the air or gas existing between the terminals also intensely heated. Indeed, we can analyse by the prism the light of such a spark, and we find that this light gives the spectrum of the substance composing the terminal in a state of vapour superimposed upon the spectrum of the air or other gas existing between the terminals. Great light has recently been thrown upon the nature and peculiarities of the electric discharge by the recent introduction of spectrum analysis, and also by the researches of Mr. J. P. Gassiot.

When we come to consider the ordinary voltaic current its heating effect is immediately apparent. Large quantities of wire may be heated to fusion by this current, and the light from charcoal-points a little separated is the most brilliant which can be produced by artificial processes. Indeed, the heating effects, and consequently the energy of voltaic electricity, far exceeds that of statical electricity, although the intensity of electrical separation is greater in the latter.

364. Viewing voltaic electricity as an agent capable of measurement continually passing along the wire of a circuit, the following are the laws which regulate its calorific effect.

Let I denote the *quantity* of electricity which passes in *unit of time* across the section of a wire, or, in other words, let I denote the *intensity* of the current which proceeds along the wire, then the heat produced is proportional to I^2, and also to the electric resistance R of the wire, that is to say, the heat varies as $R I^2$.

Again, R, or the electric resistance, is proportional to the length of the wire, and hence a double length of wire will offer a double resistance; while it is inversely proportional to the area of the cross section of the wire, so that a wire of double sectional area only interposes half the resistance.

We thus see that in such a current if the wires used be of the same material the heat developed is directly proportional to the square of the intensity of the current and also to the length of the wire, while it is inversely proportional to the area of the cross section of the wire. For wires of different material but of equal lengths and sectional areas the heating effect is inversely proportional to the electric conductivity.

365. The reason is very easily seen why a current passing along a wire should develope twice as much heat in one which is twice as long, and also why in a wire of half the section it should develope twice as much heat, but it is not quite so apparent why the heating effect should vary as the square of the intensity. This may, however, be very easily explained. Suppose we have two wires of single thickness coiled together, while currents of single intensity are sent simultaneously through each wire—we may if we choose imagine the one current to go through the one wire, and the other current through the other wire. Here then we have a double current going through a double wire, while of course twice as much heat is developed as when a single current goes through a single wire; but when this double current is made to go through a single wire twice as much heat will be developed as when it goes through a double wire; that is to say, four times as much heat as when a single current goes through a single wire.

366. It is not within the province of this work to give the theory of the voltaic battery: we will therefore suppose that our readers are already conversant with the arrangement of a simple battery consisting of a number of pairs of copper and zinc. Now it is well known that in such a battery, when the circuit is complete, the intensity of current, or quantity of electricity, which passes in an unit of time through every cross section of this circuit is the same. The intensity being the same for every cross section of the circuit, if we imagine that all the energy of the current is expended in heating the circuit, and if we know the electric conductivity of the various materials of which the circuit is composed, the laws already stated furnish us with the means of finding the distribution of the heat in the different parts of the circuit.

Thus there will be a great heating effect where the resistance is great, and a small heating effect where this is small.

To give a numerical example. Suppose one part of the circuit is composed of a foot of silver wire .05 inch in thickness, while another part is composed of 5 inches of gold wire .01 inch in thickness; it is required to find the relative heating effect of the current in those two parts of the circuit. Calling that produced in the first wire unity, we shall have that in the second wire represented by—

$$1 \times \frac{100}{78} \times \frac{5}{12} \times \frac{(.05)^2}{(.01)^2} = 13.35;$$

where the first multiplier is on account of the difference of substance (see Art. 168), the second on account of the difference of length, and the third on account of the difference of section.

Knowing thus the relative distribution along the different parts of the circuit of the heating effect, the whole amount of heat produced may be found by bearing in mind the nature of the process which supplies the heat in such a battery. There is, in fact, a chemical action that goes on between the zinc and the acid in virtue of which electricity is produced: the zinc is in truth burned, and the electrical energy given out is simply proportional to the quantity of zinc consumed. This electricity is finally converted into heat by the resistance of the circuit.

Joule has shewn that if the same quantity of zinc be combined with the acid in an ordinary vessel it will give out the same amount of heat as it would if the combination took place by means of the voltaic arrangement, and he has expressed an opinion that heat of combination is in *all* cases first produced as electricity.

The difference between the two processes is not therefore a difference in the amount of heat produced from the same combination—indeed, according to the laws of the conservation of energy there could be no such difference—but it consists in the peculiar distribution of this heat. In the voltaic arrangement, by interposing a resistance in the circuit, heat might be produced many miles from the cells; whereas in ordinary chemical combination of the zinc with the acid, the heat is of course entirely confined to the vessel in which the combination takes place.

367. Conversion of heat into electricity in motion. Allusion has already been made to the thermo-electric currents produced when a circuit composed of two different metals has the two junctions unequally heated (Art. 163), and it has been stated that in a circuit of bismuth and antimony the current will go from the bismuth to the antimony across the heated junction, while it goes from the antimony to the bismuth across the cold junction. Suppose now that we have a circuit with both junctions of the same temperature, and that heat is abstracted, let us say, by radiation from the junction C (Fig. 71); this junction will therefore lose heat, while, at the same time, an electrical current will be established in the circuit in the direction of the arrowheads.

Now an electrical current denotes energy; and since there is no access of energy to the system that might become transformed into such a current—but the reverse, since the system is losing heat by radiation—it is clear that some other form of energy must disappear from this system in order to produce this current.

We should naturally look for a disappearance of some of the heat of the system, and it was on this principle that Joule and W. Thomson explained the fact (first discovered by Peltier) that a current of electricity passing across a junction in the direction from bismuth to antimony causes cold. For it would naturally appear that if a current of electricity has such a cooling effect, it ought to be (as it is) when passing from the bismuth to the antimony, and not when passing from the antimony to the bismuth. For let us refer once more to Fig. 71. Since the junction at C is colder than that at H, and since in consequence a current is passing across C in the direction of the arrow-head, if this current has a cooling effect at one of the junctions it ought to be at H, for evidently if it cooled C (already colder than H) and heated H (already hotter than C) it would result that an electric current, and hence energy capable of performing work, might be associated with the conveyance of heat from a cold junction towards a hot one; that is to say, from a cold substance to a hot one: but would not this be in violation of the principle propounded in Art. 334?

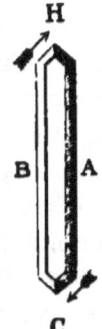

Fig. 71.

CONNECTION BETWEEN HEAT AND MOLECULAR POTENTIAL ENERGY.

368. Latent heat. In most bodies when heated and allowed to expand freely the heat has a double office to perform. A great part of it is no doubt spent in communicating a peculiar motion to the molecules of the body, but some of it is also spent in doing work against the molecular forces of the body. More especially is this the case when a body changes its condition, that is to say, passes from the solid to the liquid or from the liquid to the gaseous state; and we may in such cases suppose a very large portion of the heat required to produce this change of state to be spent in doing work against molecular forces.

It will be necessary here to make a remark with regard to the latent heat of vapours, and especially that of steam. Experimentalists have sometimes defined the total heat of saturated steam of any temperature to be the quantity of heat required to convert a unit of weight of water at o°C into steam of this state.

Now it has been well remarked by Professor W. Thomson that the amount of heat necessary to do this depends on the mode in which the change of state is effected. No doubt the real quantity of heat (kinetic and potential) of a pound of the vapour of water at a certain temperature and pressure is constant, while the heat of a pound of liquid water at o°C is also constant; but in passing from the one state to the other work is generally done, and the operation may be so varied that in some ways more work will be done than in others. Thus Thomson remarks that the final quantity of heat required to evaporate a quantity of water at o°C, and then, keeping it always in the state of saturated vapour, to bring it to the temperature 100°C, cannot be so much as three-fourths of the quantity required first to raise the temperature of the liquid to 100°C and then to evaporate it at that temperature.

Now in a determination of the total heat of aqueous vapour made by Regnault let us see how the experiment was performed. It was conducted virtually in the following manner. To one extremity of the calorimeter a vessel was attached containing water, which was made to boil at a certain constant temperature; and this vapour of water in passing through the calorimeter was given out at the other end as liquid water, let us say, of the same temperature, having been in the meantime robbed of a certain amount of heat, which remained in the calorimeter and was there measured.

Now it is evident, Thomson remarks, that since no external work is done by this arrangement, and therefore since no heat is converted into work, the whole amount of heat absorbed at the one end in converting the water into vapour at a constant temperature of ebullition is given out at the other in reconverting this vapour into water. Regnault's total heat of steam (Art. 308) is therefore the quantity of heat that would be required first of all to raise the water without evaporation to the proper temperature, and then to convert it wholly at that temperature into saturated vapour.

369. Gradual change of molecular state. We have spoken of the molecular change that generally accompanies change of temperature of a body; if, however, a body when at a high temperature be suddenly cooled, its particles have not had time to acquire their proper position for the reduced temperature, and they are therefore thrown into a state of constraint. Prince Rupert's drops, formed by dropping melted glass into water, form examples of this class. Now all such bodies tend as far as possible to assume a more natural condition; and on this account a Prince Rupert's drop, if the surface be only slightly scratched, breaks into small pieces. We have seen also that the recently blown bulb of a thermometer gradually contracts. Probably these changes, whether abrupt or gradual, are attended with an evolution of heat, and depote the conversion of potential into kinetic molecular energy.

In other bodies a process of a more complete kind goes on; and there is, in fact, a new arrangement of particles, in virtue of which many of the properties of the body are changed. We see this take place in sulphur, phosphorus, iodide of mercury, &c. In all such cases molecular energy leaves the potential to assume the kinetic form, or it leaves the kinetic form to assume the potential.

CONNECTION BETWEEN HEAT AND THE POTENTIAL ENERGY OF CHEMICAL SEPARATION.

370. Transmutation of the potential energy of chemical separation into heat. In accordance with what has been stated, it is natural to expect that if a definite quantity of carbon or of hydrogen be united to oxygen or burned under given conditions a definite quantity of heat will be produced. Thus a ton of coal or of coke will give out, as it burns, a definite quantity of heat, neither more nor less. Although this almost seems to be self-evident, yet the difficulties attending a correct estimation of the heat-equivalent of the chemical action which takes place in this and similar combinations are very great. In order to exemplify these difficulties let us suppose that 12 pounds of carbon (a solid) are united to 32 pounds of oxygen (a gas) at a given pressure, the temperature of the constituents being 0°C : the result is the production of 44 pounds of carbonic acid gas. If we wish to find how much heat is due to chemical action we must first of all preserve the heat of combustion so as to measure it by a calorimeter. By this means it may be possible to estimate the whole amount of heat rendered sensible ; but something more is still desired if we wish to know the exact heat-equivalent of the chemical combination which has taken place. In order to ascertain this it will be necessary to know—

(1) The total amount of molecular energy (both kinetic and potential) in the carbon C

(2) The total amount of molecular energy in the oxygen O.

(3) The total amount of molecular energy in the compound $C O^2$.

Now it will be found that (3) is greater than the sum of (1) and (2), the difference denoting the amount of chemical potential energy which has been transmuted into heat. That is to say, the molecular energy of the compound *less* the molecular energy of both constituents united is *equal to* the heat produced by chemical action.

But we have no certain means of estimating directly the whole molecular energy either of the components or of the compound produced, for we cannot deprive any of these bodies of the total amount of its molecular energy and thus measure its amount. We may no doubt by means of measurements of specific and latent heat arrive at conclusions more or less probable regarding the molecular energy of bodies, but these conclusions cannot be regarded as certainties; and besides, they are founded on experiments of a very difficult nature. It being thus impossible with our present knowledge to estimate with certainty (1), (2), and (3), it is also impossible to estimate with certainty

$$(3) - \{(1) + (2)\} \;;$$

—an expression which represents the heat-equivalent of chemical action.

371. But though we perhaps cannot in this sense estimate the quantity of energy produced by chemical action, we can cause a certain definite quantity of carbon in a definite molecular state and at a definite temperature to combine with oxygen at a definite temperature and pressure; and when the carbonic acid gas which is the product of combustion has been brought to this same definite temperature and pressure we can find how much heat has been evolved in the process of combustion. Determinations of this nature have been made by many chemists, among whom may be named Crawford, Lavoisier, Dalton, Davy, Dulong, Despretz, and more recently Andrews, Hess, and Favre & Silbermann. As the experiments of Andrews were performed with unusual accuracy we shall now shortly describe his method of observation.

372. Andrews' experiments. When the experiments of Andrews were made on gases these were introduced into

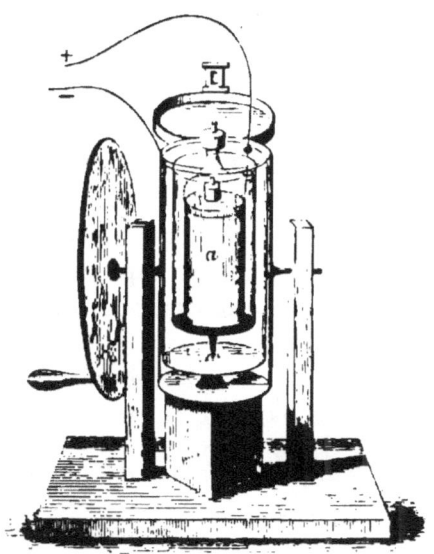

Fig. 72.

a vessel of sheet copper thin, but strong enough to resist the force of the explosion. The copper vessel *a* (Fig. 72), containing the mixed gases, was introduced into another of larger capacity, which was filled with water; the latter vessel was suspended in a cylinder which had a moveable cover at each end, and the whole was finally enclosed in an outer vessel also cylindrical. This outer vessel was capable of being made to rotate round a horizontal axis by means of the arrangement shewn in the figure. Before commencing the operation the apparatus was made to rotate for some time, in order to bring all its parts into a uniform temperature: this temperature was then measured by a very delicate thermometer. The apparatus was then brought into connection with a voltaic battery, so arranged that a fine platinum wire passing through the gas was by means of the current brought to a red or white heat, and the gas in consequence made to explode. The orifice of the calorimeter was then quickly closed with a cork, the lid shut down, and the whole made to rotate for 35 seconds, in order to distribute the temperature uniformly throughout the apparatus. The thermometer was then again introduced and the increase of temperature observed; by this means, and by knowing the calorific capacity of the apparatus, the amount of heat produced by the explosion might be determined.

A somewhat different form of apparatus was used when solid bodies were burned in oxygen, but the principle of the experiment was the same.

373. The following tables give some of the results obtained by Andrews and Favre & Silbermann :—

Units of heat developed during combustion in Oxygen.

Substance burned.	Pounds of water raised 1°C by the combustion of one pound of each substance.	Compound formed.	Observer.
Hydrogen	34462	H^2O	Favre & Silbermann
„	33808	„	Andrews
Carbon	8080	CO^2	Favre & Silbermann
„	7900	„	Andrews
Sulphur	2220	SO^2	Favre & Silbermann
„	2307	„	Andrews
Phosphorus	5747	P^2O^5	„
Zinc	1301	ZnO	„
Iron..	1576	Fe^3O^4	„
Tin	1233	SnO^2	„
Copper	602	CuO	„
Carbonic oxide ..	2431	CO^2	„
„ ..	2403	....	Favre & Silbermann
Marsh gas	13063	.. ..	„
„	13108	....	Andrews
Olefiant gas..	11942	....	„
„	11858	....	Favre & Silbermann
Alcohol	6850	....	Andrews
„	7183	....	Favre & Silbermann

Units of heat developed during combustion in Chlorine.

Substance burned.	Pounds of water raised 1°C by the combustion of one pound of each substance.	Compound formed.	Observer.
Hydrogen	23783	H Cl	Favre & Silbermann
Potassium	2655	K Cl	Andrews
Zinc	1529	Zn Cl^2	,,
Iron...........	1745	Fe^2 Cl^6	,,
Tin	1079	Sn Cl^4	,,
Antimony	707	Sb Cl^5	,,
Arsenic	994	As Cl^3	,,
Copper	961	Cu Cl^2	,,

Units of heat developed by the action of Bromine.

Zinc	1269	Zn Br^2	Andrews
Iron...........	1277	Fe^2 Br^6	,,

Units of heat developed by the action of Iodine.

Zinc	819	Zn I^2	Andrews
Iron...........	463	Fe^2 I^6	,,

374. Metallic precipitates. Andrews has likewise made a number of experiments on metallic precipitates, and he finds as a result that the quantity of heat developed during the mutual action of two metals, A and B, when an equivalent of A displaces an equivalent of B from any of its salts, is the same, whatever be the nature of this salt, provided that in all the salts B is in the same state of oxidation.

We are thus provided with a means of arranging the metals, beginning with that metal which evolves most heat when used to displace the metal at the other extremity of the series. This furnishes the following list :—

1. Zinc.	5. Mercury.
2. Iron.	6. Silver.
3. Lead.	7. Platinum.
4. Copper.	

It is interesting to observe that this is exactly the electro-chemical order of these metals, zinc being the most electro-positive and platinum the most electro-negative.

This prepares us for the following conclusion, also deduced by Andrews.

If there be three metals *A*, *B*, *C*, such that *A* will displace *B* and *C* from their combinations, while *B* will displace *C*, then the heat developed by substituting *A* for *C* will be equal to that developed by substituting *A* for *B* *plus* that developed by substituting *B* for *C*.

Compare this with the fact that the electro-motive force between *A* and *C* is equal to that between *A* and *B* *plus* that between *B* and *C*, and we are thus led to imagine that the electro-motive forces which are really due to contact of dissimilar bodies are also the very forces which cause heat when chemical combination ensues, potential energy being then converted into kinetic energy by the rushing together of the particles under the attracting forces.

Andrews has also made experiments from which it may be inferred that the quantity of heat given out when different acids combine with an equivalent of the same base is nearly the same, while however the same acid combined with different bases produces different amounts of heat.

375. Nature of flame. This may be the fittest place to say a few words on the nature of flame, for the knowledge of which we are much indebted to Davy.

Let us take a flame of ordinary gas.

This substance consists of carbon united to hydrogen, and is perfectly transparent.

Now when a gas flame is lit we find the lowest part next

the burner to have a very feeble luminosity; this part consists of gas more or less heated which has just escaped from
the pipe but has not yet united with the oxygen of the air:
its temperature is not perhaps very high, but even if it were
high, so long as this gas does not change its nature it will
give out but little light, the reason being that it absorbs but
little (Art. 221). As this gas proceeds upwards it comes
into the presence of the oxygen of the air and unites with it;
but as the hydrogen of the gas unites more rapidly at first,
the consequence is that a number of particles of carbon
are set free. Now these small particles are intensely heated
by the combustion that is going on when they are set free,
and, being at the same time exceedingly opaque, they give
out when heated a great deal of light; indeed, we have
already seen (Art. 227) how great is the radiation from
lamp-black.

The illuminating power of the flame is therefore due to
these carbon particles which are afterwards burned nearer the
border of the flame, forming carbonic acid gas. The products
of combustion are therefore water and carbonic acid gas.

**376. Heat absorbed when salts dissolve, and the
converse of this.** During the solution of salts in water
heat is generally absorbed, and the temperature of the liquid
falls; nevertheless in a few cases there is an evolution of heat
when certain anhydrous salts are dissolved.

This is probably due to the preliminary formation of a
solid hydrate, a process which is generally accompanied by
heat, as, for instance, when hydrate of baryta is formed.

On the other hand, heat is evolved during the deposition
of a solid from a supersaturated solution.

377. Heat evolved during the solution of gases.
We have already noticed (Art. 134) that when a gas is ab-
sorbed by water a considerable evolution of heat takes place.
We may suppose that this consists not only of the heat due

to chemical combination but also of that due to the latent heat of gaseity which is evolved when the gas passes from the gaseous to the liquid state.

Thus—

1. When water unites with a gas and the product is liquid we have great heat developed.

2. When water unites with a liquid (such as sulphuric acid) and the product is liquid, we have generally still heat; but

3. When water unites with a solid and the product is liquid, we have often an absorption of heat; while

4. If the product is solid we again have heat.

In the cases now described it would seem to be change of condition as much as chemical action which determines the result as far as heat is concerned.

Heat is also produced when a gas condenses on the surface of a solid.

Pouillet has also shewn that heat is produced in capillary action.

378. Transmutation of heat into the potential energy of chemical separation. When certain bodies are heated they are decomposed; thus, for instance, when carbonate of lime is heated it gives out its carbonic acid, also when slaked lime is heated it gives out its water and is changed into quick lime. Heat is thus transmuted into the potential energy of chemical separation.

Radiant heat (at least those rays which are called chemical rays) may be directly transformed into the potential energy of chemical separation.

Thus when such rays fall upon chloride of silver we have a chemical change produced which is made use of in photography.

It is believed that this change consists in the decomposition of the salt into its constituents, and that silver is deposited.

CONNECTION BETWEEN HEAT AND THE POTENTIAL
ENERGY OF ELECTRICAL SEPARATION.

379. We have already noticed (Art. 167) that when certain crystals are heated there is a development of statical electricity.

The most prominent laws of the relation between heat and other forms of energy are those which have now been given.

CHAPTER V.

*Dissipation of Energy.   Sources of Energy.   Concluding
Problems.*

DISSIPATION OF ENERGY.

380. It will have become apparent from the preceding chapters that we can no more create energy than we can create matter, and that all we can do is to make the best possible use of the store of energy at present existing in the universe around us.

Now some forms of energy are of more service to us than others, and we ought therefore to inquire which of the various forms of energy are the most serviceable and which are the least so.   Having come to definite ideas on this subject it becomes one of the most interesting, as well as one of the most important, problems to look around us and review the various stores of available energy which have been put at our disposal by the Author of the Universe.

381. We have already seen (Art. 317) that a machine only transmutes energy from one form to another, and that in consequence it is impossible for any machine unless supplied with energy of some kind, either continuously or periodically, to go on doing work; and that in this sense perpetual motion is impossible.

It will also be seen by Art. 334 that we may modify the usual conception of perpetual motion in a way that will render it not inconsistent with the law of the conservation of energy, although it is nevertheless equally impossible. Indeed, it will appear that the reasoning of Chapter II of this book is founded on the assumption that it is impossible to convert heat into mechanical energy by abstracting it from a substance of lower temperature than the substances around it, because if this were possible a perpetual motion would be possible also; nevertheless, such a perpetual motion is not inconsistent with the principle of the conservation of energy. Now when we come to examine more closely into the results of this chapter we see that the impossibility of this form of perpetual motion is intimately connected with the fact that heat tends to diffuse itself.

382. The following example will make this plain. Suppose a machine to work in a room that neither conducts nor radiates heat to other bodies; that is, in fact, isolated as far as regards the reception or communication of energy with the rest of the universe.

Suppose, further, that the source of this machine is supplied with heat, and that in consequence of this the machine does work. Next suppose that this work, by means of friction or otherwise, is immediately reconverted into heat, and then carried again to the source of the engine.

Will not such an engine, it may be asked, go on working for ever? There is nothing in the law of the conservation of energy that forbids this result, for the energy of the chamber is supposed to be constant, while a constant proportion of this energy is supposed to exist always in the shape of mechanical work. The possibility of this arrangement is connected therefore with the possibility of *wholly* reconverting the heat produced by the mechanical motion into motion, which is again to be converted into heat, and from heat into motion, and so on for ever.

To assume the most favourable circumstances, let us suppose that there is absolute zero of temperature in the chamber, except at the source of the engine; then, assuming the truth of the results of Chapter II, we may conclude that if a quantity Q of heat be taken from the source it will be wholly converted into work. Suppose, again, that the work is reconverted into heat in a box similar to the chamber itself—that is to say, neither conducting nor radiating heat—and that this heated box is taken back to the source, reconverted there entirely into work, and so on.

No doubt this arrangement would be, in its literal sense, a perpetual motion—but not in the technical sense, as no external work is produced. When, however, we come to analyse the conditions we have imposed upon the materials employed, we find that they are such as never occur in nature; there is, in fact, no body that neither conducts nor radiates heat, and it is this tendency to diffusion in heat that prevents the arrangement from being possible. Owing to this tendency it is impossible either to procure a chamber which neither conducts nor radiates, or to produce a perfect zero of temperature. Now this latter is quite essential to the perpetuity of our supposed arrangement; for, without such a zero, while all the work is converted into heat only a portion of the heat is reconverted into work.

The work will thus at every cycle bear a continually diminishing proportion to the heat, and the final result will be a uniform distribution of this latter form of energy.

383. This example, in which the results of Chapter II are taken for granted, forms of course no new proof of the impossibility of this kind of perpetual motion, because the assumption of this impossibility is the foundation of the argument of this chapter. But the example serves to shew that this impossibility is intimately connected with the diffusive nature of heat.

384. All this has been clearly shewn by Professor W. Thomson, to whom the principle of the dissipation of energy is due.

He has shewn that when mechanical energy is transmuted into heat by friction or otherwise there is always a degradation in the form of the energy; and inasmuch as this heat cannot be entirely converted back again into work from its diffusive nature, the final result of continually converting mechanical motion into heat will be that the amount of mechanical motion obtainable from the system will be always growing less, until ultimately all the energy has taken the unavailable form of equally diffused heat.

That this form of energy is unavailable will be acknowledged at once by recalling to mind the statement that to get work from heat you must have bodies of different temperatures.

385. Suppose now that we have a ton of water at 212°, while all the other substances around us are at 32°, we have in this ton of water an instrument capable of affording us a certain amount of mechanical work by using it as the source of a perfect engine. There is a certain amount of *available work* in this ton of water, and do what we may we cannot get it to give more, although it may very probably, if improperly used, give less work. It would appear that by no artifice can we increase this amount any more than we can increase the available work of a head of water of given contents and height of fall.

It might perhaps be thought that this would be possible if we could convert the heat of this water into the potential energy of chemical decomposition; could we not use it to decompose a certain amount of some compound substance whose components have a great attraction for one another, so that by the reunion of these components a very high temperature might be produced; the heat of 212° would thus be converted into heat of a higher temperature which would be more *available?* or might not the radiant heat from the water be used to produce some kind of chemical decomposition, and thus the same result be obtained?

It is believed that any such result is, to say the least, unlikely; in fact, it has been remarked by Professor W. Thomson that an intimation to this effect seems to be given by nature, for we have no reason to think that either absorbed or radiant heat of low temperature is capable of producing powerful chemical changes of this nature.

There is no reason to think that this stratagem of bringing in chemical decomposition will increase the amount of available work to be obtained from one ton of hot water, and in our ignorance of the ultimate constitution of matter it would appear that the principle of the degradation and dissipation of energy, just as that of the conservation of energy, should be recognized as a principle having very strong claims to recognition, and as increasing these claims every day by the new facts which its employment as an instrument of research is constantly bringing to light.

At the same time it is but just to state that the principle of the conservation of energy is at present more fully · established than that of the dissipation of energy.

386. Regarding, therefore, uniformly diffused heat as a form of energy utterly unavailable, and regarding mechanical energy as ultimately tending to assume this degraded form when it is reduced by friction, percussion, or otherwise, the question arises, Are there any influences at work tending thus to degrade the motions of the universe? Now we know very well that all motions on the surface of our earth ultimately tend to be dissipated and converted into equally diffused heat; we know also that the heat of the sun and stars tends to assume this degraded form; but does the same reasoning apply to celestial motions? This leads us to ask if there is a material medium pervading space; for if there is such a medium, however attenuated, something analogous to friction must necessarily take place, and the result would appear to be the conversion, at a rate more or less rapid, of the mechanical energy of the universe into the degraded form of diffused heat.

387. Medium pervading space. We have several reasons for assuming the existence of such a medium.

1. The various phenomena of light are best explained on the supposition that this agent consists of undulations in a medium pervading space.

Our proofs in favour of the undulatory theory of light are strengthened if we acknowledge the principle of the conservation of energy.

For the experiments of Mr. Bennet shewed all absence of momentum when the concentrated light of the sun was made to strike a piece of paper attached to the end of a straw delicately suspended, and acting as a lever which would change its position with the smallest momentum. Now let H denote the quantity of heat that struck the paper in unit of time. Then assuming for a moment that light consists of particles ˙projected with great velocity from a heated body, that is to say, assuming the emission theory of light, and assuming also that in accordance with the principle of the conservation of energy the energy of the blow given to the paper by these particles has been converted into heat, JH will denote this energy during an unit of time, but if m denote the mass and v the velocity in feet per second of the light-particles, then (Art. 314) the energy is denoted by $\dfrac{mv^2}{64}$.

Hence—
$$JH = \frac{mv^2}{64}.$$

Now H, or the heating effect, can be determined by observation, also v, or the velocity of light (in feet), is known; and hence the momentum, or mv, may be easily deduced; and it is thus found that this ought to have been quite perceptible in this experiment.

But as it was not perceptible we must conclude that light particles do not give a blow, and hence that the emission theory of light is not true; and if this theory be not true, we must have recourse to the undulatory or some similar theory which assumes the existence of a medium pervading space.

2. The continual shortening of the path of Encke's comet leads us to the same conclusion; that is to say, to a belief in the existence of a material medium pervading space.

If, therefore, there be a resisting medium pervading space, the visible motions of the universe must gradually be lessened in consequence; unless indeed we assume the existence of some unknown completely restorative process; but such a process is inconsistent both with the principle of the degradation of energy, and also with the shortening of the path of Encke's comet, whatever weight this may have.

There can, in fine, be little doubt that if we suppose the principle of the degradation of energy to hold throughout the universe it implies an element of decay in the present order of things, and the final transmutation of all available energy into uniformly diffused heat, unless we suppose the constitution of the universe to be such that this process of degradation will last an infinite time.

For a clear statement of this subject we may refer our readers to an article on ' Energy' that appeared lately in the *North British Review*, from which many of these remarks are taken.

SOURCES OF ENERGY.

388. Let us now consider shortly the various supplies of energy of different kinds with which we are furnished, and also the *ultimate sources* of these supplies.

Of potential forms of energy we have—

1. The potential energy of fuel.
2. The potential energy of food.
3. The potential energy of a head of water.
4. The potential energy derived from the tides.
5. The potential energy of the chemical separation implied in native sulphur, native iron, &c.

Then with regard to kinetic forms of energy, we have—

6. The kinetic energy of air in motion.
7. The kinetic energy of water in motion.
8. We may add to this catalogue the direct rays of the sun which are available for certain purposes; and also
9. The energy that may be derived from the unequal temperature of different parts of the earth.

389. Fuel and food. The potential energies of fuel and food are of essential importance to our existence.

By fuel we mean certain substances which are capable of combining with oxygen, and of supplying us as they so combine with a large amount of heat of high temperature.

Coal is the most important of such substances; and we can employ it either to warm ourselves and our habitations by means of the heat which it produces, or as an agent for generating mechanical effect in our various heat engines.

When we come to consider from what original source of energy the chemical separation of fuel is derived, we see that it is due to the sun's rays. These rays acting upon the leaves of plants produce those decompositions which form fuel. The energy of the sun's rays have in fact been transmuted into the potential energy of chemical separation.

This fact seems to have been recognized at a comparatively early period by Herschel and the elder Stephenson, and a curious tale is current about the latter, who, though well aware that it was the sun that drove his engines, could not give a very clear explanation of the subject; nevertheless the statement is undoubtedly true.

It is indeed true that the rays of the sun acting upon the leaves of plants in those remote ages when coal beds were being formed have laid up for man a stock of energy of inestimable value.

Food has the same origin as fuel, with the exception that vegetable food is being produced by the sun year by year, while the greater portion of our fuel, as we have just seen, has been produced ages ago. And here we may remark a very prominent distinction between vegetables and animals as regards energy. Vegetables serve to transmute the energy of the sun's rays into fuel and food. Animals, again, consume this food and transmute it partly into useful work but partly into the degraded form of diffused heat.

Joule, Carpenter, and Mayer seem to have been aware of the restrictions under which living beings are placed by the laws of energy, and to have seen that the power of an animal, as far as energy is concerned, is not *creative* but only *directive*.

A clear view of this subject was probably also held by Rumford, who remarked that if a certain amount of fodder were consumed by a horse he will do more work for it than would be done by an engine in which this fodder was burned as a source of heat. Finally, Helmholz has treated this question, as well as the whole subject of energy, in a very able manner. An animal is in fact an engine, and just as an engine must be fed with fuel, so an animal must be fed with food.

390. Head of water. We thus see that the sun's rays are the ultimate source of fuel and food, and we have no difficulty in recognizing the same cause as the origin of the energy derived from a head of water. It is the sun that produces rain by promoting evaporation; his energy is consumed in lifting the water of the earth to a higher level, and we are thus enabled to make use of the potential energy of this elevated water.

391. Tidal energy. The energy capable of being derived from the ebb and flow of the tides has however a different source.

This was recognized by Kant; Mayer also and J. Thomson (the former of whom was the first to give his conclusions a general publicity) shewed that the ebb and flow of the tides being due to the earth's revolving on her axis under the moon's force, the energy of the tides is really taken from the energy of the earth's revolution; part of which is thus ultimately dissipated in the heat of friction caused by the tides: and the astronomical phenomenon known as the secular acceleration of the moon's mean motion is now supposed to be partly caused by a very slow lengthening out of the sidereal day caused by loss of the earth's motion of rotation from this effect of the tides.

It is clear that this action would be arrested when the rotation of the earth was so much diminished that she always turned the same face to the moon, for then there would be no tidal ebb and flow and consequently no friction; and Professor Frankland in a lecture at the Royal Institution, as well as Thomson and Tait in their treatise on Natural Philosophy, have independently remarked that the much more powerful influence of the earth upon the fluid matter of the moon during the course of ages has probably stopped the rotation of our satellite so far as to cause her always to present the same face to the earth. We thus see that any work we derive from tidal action is abstracted from the motion of rotation of the earth.

392. Native sulphur, &c. The potential energy of the chemical separation implied in native sulphur, iron, &c., is, it may be, the primeval form of energy, but the amount of this energy so far as we know is very small, though the interior of the earth may be wholly made up of matter in an uncombined form. As a source of energy it is at present of no importance.

393. Air and water in motion. The kinetic energy of air in motion, and the kinetic energy of water in motion, are both chiefly due to the sun.

394. Unequal temperature of the globe. Little energy is likely to be derived from the unequal temperature of different parts of the earth, for such differences of temperature are comparatively small, and consequently only a very small proportion of the whole amount of heat transferred from the higher to the lower temperature can be turned to practical account.

395. Now if we group together the really serviceable members of the list of sources of energy we find that they consist of the potential energies of fuel, of food, of a head of water, and of tidal ebb and flow, together with the kinetic energies of air in motion and of water in motion. All these either are or may be of immense service to man.

396. Coal. Of the different forms of fuel coal is one of the most important, and the exhaustion at no very distant date of this source of energy has been of late very much and very properly discussed.

There appears to be little doubt that the progress of civilisation forces us to draw each year more and more largely upon our stores of coal, and there is no doubt that when once the deposits near the surface have been exhausted those at a greater depth will have a much smaller real value.

For the time, the capital, and the labour spent in bringing a ton of coal from a great depth to the surface ultimately resolve themselves into so much available energy spent in accomplishing this : now if a considerable portion of the available energy of a ton of coal is spent in bringing it to the surface, the ultimate value to us of this ton of coal is greatly impaired.

If the question be asked, What shall we do when coal fails? The only reply is, Make as much use as possible of water and tidal power, and of the energy of air in motion, and plant trees.

It is difficult to think of anything else, or to deny the fact that, as far as we are able to judge, the exhaustion of our coal beds will be a very serious loss of power.

397. The sun. It thus appears that if we except tidal power, the sun's rays are the ultimate source of the available forms of energy with which we are surrounded.

We cannot, therefore, do better than direct attention to this most wonderful source of energy.

We remark, in the first place, that the sun's radiant light and heat are not perhaps the only kind of energy which we derive from our luminary.

It has been discovered by General Sabine that the various disturbances of terrestrial magnetism are due to the sun, but probably not to his radiant heat and light. Now these magnetic disturbances are invariably accompanied by the aurora borealis, and also by currents of electricity in the surface of the earth, or earth-currents as they are called.

It would appear, from an investigation by the author of this work, that auroræ and earth-currents are to be regarded as secondary currents due to small but rapid changes in the earth's magnetism, and that the body of the earth may be likened to the magnetic core of a Ruhmkorff's machine, the lower strata of the atmosphere forming an insulator, while the upper and rarer, and therefore electrically conducting strata, may be likened to the secondary coil.

In this analogy the sun may perhaps be likened to the primary current which performs the part of producing changes in the magnetic state of the core.

But in the Ruhmkorff's machine the energy of the secondary current is derived from that of the primary current. If this analogy holds good the energy of the aurora borealis may in like manner come from the sun; but in our ignorance of the method in which the sun affects terrestrial magnetism this may be considered to be somewhat doubtful. Be this as it may, the radiant heat of the sun constitutes by far the greatest part of the energy which we receive from him, and it has for a long time been an object of speculation from what source the sun derives his light and heat *.

398. Actinometric observations. In the first place, let us briefly allude to the attempts that have been made to estimate the amount of the sun's radiant energy, and then let us attempt to speculate on its most probable source.

Instruments for measuring the intensity of the sun's radiant heat have been devised by Herschel and Pouillet. The instrument of the latter he calls a pyrheliometer, and it is constructed on the following principle :—

A shallow cylindrical box (Fig. 73) made of iron or steel is filled with mercury. Into this box, and therefore into this mercury, a thermometer is introduced, the stem of which is suitably protected.

At the other extremity of the instrument we have a disk of the same diameter as the box.

Now if the instrument be pointed in such a manner that

---

* The radiation from the sun is not entirely confined to his visible disk. There are orange-coloured protuberances or flames which are seen to surround his disk during a total eclipse, and which have been proved by Mr. Warren de la Rue to belong to our luminary.

the shadow of the box, thrown by the sun, coincides with the disk, then we may be sure that the sun's rays impinge perpendicularly on the surface of the box.

Fig. 73.

The experiment consists of three parts—

First, let the instrument, sheltered from the sun, be permitted to radiate its heat into the clear sky for five minutes. Let the heat lost be r.

Next, let it be turned to the sun for five minutes. Let the heat gained be R.

Finally, let it (at its increased temperature) be allowed to radiate into the clear sky as before for five minutes, and let the heat lost be r'.

Now, since r denotes the radiation into clear sky before heating, and r' the same after heating, the radiation into the clear sky during the heating will be very nearly a mean between the two, or $\dfrac{r + r'}{2}$; but it is evident that this radiation takes place even when the instrument is receiving the sun's rays, and tends therefore to diminish the heating effect produced by these rays.

Hence, therefore, the whole heating effect will be—

$$R + \frac{r + r'}{2}.$$

Observations have been made by Herschel and Forbes with Herschel's actinometer, and by Pouillet with his own instrument.

From all these observations it is probable that, taking the earth's hemisphere which is illuminated, one-half of the radiant heat of the sun may perhaps reach the ground, the other half being absorbed by the atmosphere. Taking this into account, and imagining for a moment that the earth has no atmosphere, it is calculated that the amount of solar heat received by the earth in one year would liquefy a layer of ice, 100 feet thick, covering the whole surface of the earth.

If we bear in mind that the solar heat which reaches the earth in any time is only $\frac{1}{2,300,000,000}$ of the heat which leaves the sun, we may obtain some idea of the enormous heating power of the radiation from our luminary.

399. Origin of the sun's heat. The most plausible theory of the origin of the sun's heat is that which supposes that the primeval potential energy of gravitation has been converted into heat for the sun's particles.

The rudiments of such an idea seem to have occurred to Mayer and to Waterston; but Professor W. Thomson has worked it out in such a manner as almost to prove that there is no other known power capable of producing such a stupendous result.

According to this theory we may imagine the particles of matter when originally created to have been at a distance from each other, but endued with the power of gravitation, forming in fact a chaotic mass.

As these particles rushed together heat would be produced, just as when a stone is hurled from the top of a precipice heat is the ultimate form into which the potential energy of the stone is converted.

It is probable that this cause, by storing up an amount of heat in the sun, is sufficient to account for his wonderful outpouring of light and heat during a long series of ages.

CONCLUDING PROBLEMS.

400. Before concluding this treatise let us bring before our readers two problems, both connected with the dynamical theory of heat.

401. Effect of pressure in lowering the freezing-point of water. In a previous part of this work (Art. 92) it was mentioned that the application of pressure lowers the freezing-point of water, and that Professor J. Thomson was the first to suggest and prove that this would be the case, while the experiment was first made by Professor W. Thomson.

The following explanation of this effect of pressure upon ice is that given by Professor J. Thomson.

Suppose we have a quantity of mercury constantly kept at 0°C as our source of heat, and also a quantity constantly kept at $-\tau$°C (τ being small) as our refrigerator. Suppose also that we have a cylinder, of which the sectional area is one square inch, and that this cylinder contains one cubic inch of water at 0°C; the water will thus be one inch high in the cylinder. Suppose now that a pressure equal, let us say, to one atmosphere of 15 lbs. weight is placed above the surface of the water in this cylinder, and imagine, for the sake of simplicity, that the specific heat of the materials of the weight and of the cylinder is exceedingly small, so that if heated or cooled it is merely the specific heat of the water that we have to consider.

Let this arrangement be now used as a heat engine, and let us first suppose that the cylinder is placed in the mercury at o°C. Let it next be taken out of this mercury (the contained water being unfrozen) and plunged into the mercury of the refrigerator at $-\tau°$; the water will in course of time be frozen, and while freezing it will expand and finally occupy 1.089 cubic inches; hence the weight of 15 lbs. will have been raised nearly .09 inch, or .0075 of a foot. Suppose now that the cylinder is again transferred to the mercury at o°C, the ice in the cylinder will in course of time become water and occupy once more its old level one inch high in the cylinder. There will thus be a void space equal to .0075 of a foot, through which the weight may be made to fall, thus doing useful work when the process of melting is finished. We have thus obtained work = $15 \times .0075 = .113$ foot-pounds for every cycle of operations. Now during each cycle it will be seen that an amount of heat equal to the latent heat of fusion of a cubic inch of water is conveyed from the higher to the lower temperature. We thus know the quantity of heat conveyed from the source to the refrigerator, as well as the quantity of work done. But we also know that this arrangement (Art. 334) cannot possibly give us more work under the circumstances than a perfect engine : in fact we shall see at last that the arrangement is a perfect engine; that is to say, there must be a certain difference in temperature between the source and the refrigerator. This difference of temperature is easily found.

The latent heat of fusion of a pound of ice (Art. 306) is 80 heat units, and hence that of a cubic inch of water, or 253 grains, will be $80 \times \dfrac{253}{7000} = 2.89$ heat units. Multiplying these by their mechanical equivalent, or 1390 (Art. 328), we find. the total amount of energy transferred from the higher to the lower source during a complete cycle to be 4017. But we have seen that during this process mechanical energy = .113 is obtained. Now we know by Art. 346 that in a perfect engine the energy utilized bears to the whole energy of the heat carried from the source to the refrigerator the same proportion as the absolute temperature of the source does to the temperature difference between the source and refrigerator.

Hence, since 270° (Art. 343) is the absolute temperature corresponding to 0°C, we have the following proportion—

$$4017 : .113 :: 270 : \tau; \qquad \therefore \ \tau = .0076°\text{C} = .0137° \text{ Fahr.}$$

Now if the pressure under which the water expands into ice be doubled or become two atmospheres, or 30 lbs. per square inch, twice as much work will be done by this arrangement and twice the above temperature difference between the source and the refrigerator will be absolutely necessary; in fact, for each atmosphere of pressure it is necessary to have a difference of .0137° Fahr. This is only another way of stating that for each atmosphere of pressure the freezing-point of ice will be reduced .0137° Fahr. For a pressure of 16.8 atmospheres this would give 0°.230 Fahr., a result which agrees very closely with 0°.232 Fahr.—the temperature reduction in the freezing-point of water found experimentally by Professor W. Thomson for this same pressure.

A little consideration will shew that the arrangement we have here sketched for producing work by means of the freezing of water is in reality a perfect engine.

402. Temperature. If we refer to Art. 67 of this work it will be found that the whole subject of temperature has been left in a somewhat unsatisfactory condition.

When we analyse our conception of temperature we find it to be this—

If two bodies, such as water and mercury, be brought together, and if neither parts with any of its heat to the other, then each of these two bodies is of the same temperature. If the water parts with some of its heat to the mercury, the water is said to be of a higher temperature than the mercury. On the other hand, if the water receives heat from the mercury, then the water is said to be of a lower temperature than the mercury.

It will be seen that this definition of temperature is very similar to our definition of hardness. If when two bodies are brought together A scratches B, then A is said to be harder than B; but if B scratches A, then B is said to be harder than A.

Now by means of this definition of temperature or of hardness we are quite able to construct a scale of temperature or of hardness in which we are certain that a body having a definite place in the scale shall be less hot or less hard than that above it, but more hot or more hard than that below it. We may be able to do all this without at the same time being able to estimate either temperature or hardness quantitively, and without being able to say that the temperature or hardness of a certain body is precisely half-way between the temperature or hardness of two other bodies.

It may, however, be asked, Do we not then measure temperature by means of thermometers? To this it may be replied, We do not measure temperature: by liquid thermometers we measure expansion; by the air thermometer either expansion or pressure.

We insert a liquid into a glass envelope, and finding that it increases in bulk a certain amount between 0° and 100°C, we *assume* that half the increase of bulk will denote a temperature half-way between these two points.

We then try different liquids and make them into standard

thermometers, but finding they disagree slightly among themselves, we pronounce them unsatisfactory.

We then try permanent gases of sufficient tenuity, and finding that while they all slightly disagree with liquid thermometers they quite agree amongst themselves, we consider them satisfactory.

403. Before proceeding further it is well to observe that some very eminent scientific men have supposed that our subdivision of a certain temperature difference is in the nature of things arbitrary, and that all we can do is to subdivide this difference between two temperatures by means of a certain instrument which may be easily reproduced and always remains comparable with itself. Thus, for instance, if we can blow bulbs of invariably the same kind of glass, these when filled with pure mercury will form thermometers always comparable with themselves, and will thus afford us a thermometric scale. But if we fill these bulbs with water instead of with mercury, we produce another set of thermometers also comparable among themselves, but not quite comparable with the mercurial thermometers.

It may be asked, Which of the two are we to adopt?

It may also be asked, Even if our mode of subdividing a temperature difference be essentially arbitrary, may not some one conventional mode be better than others?

Now if we take permanent gases of sufficient tenuity we know that by their means we can produce thermometers comparable with one another, even although we vary the nature of the gas. In such thermometers we measure either the *volume* or the *pressure* of the gas. But if instead of measuring the pressure or the volume we measure the *quantity of heat that enters into our gas* on the convention that equal increments of heat denote equal increments of temperature, we here obtain a scale precisely the same as that obtained by measuring the volume or the pressure of the gas, since the specific heat of the permanent gases remains constant.

Yet, again, Professor William Thomson has shewn that if we measure a temperature difference by the proportion of a certain quantity of heat Q, passing from the higher to the lower temperature, capable of being converted into mechanical effect (Art. 346), we obtain a temperature scale holding for all bodies, whether liquid, solid, or gaseous, and also precisely the same as that of the air thermometer.

Finally, in the case of gases of which the molecular constitution is comparatively simple we have some grounds for supposing that we have at last succeeded to some extent in ascertaining what kind of motion constitutes heat. According to this theory, which has been lately greatly developed by Clausius and Maxwell, the particles of gases are supposed to be in continual motion backwards and forwards on account of the heat they contain; in fact, they knock against the sides of the containing vessel, and it is this knocking that constitutes the pressure: also on this account they tend to intermingle with one another even against the influence of specific gravity, and it is this which constitutes gaseous diffusion. We thus see why the pressure of a gas increases when it is heated.

But the test of a theory consists even more in the new facts which it brings to light than in the facts already known which it serves to explain, and Professor Maxwell by means of this theory has brought to light a new fact in fluid friction.

It may be stated thus—

Suppose a moveable horizontal disk to oscillate by means of a suitable arrangement very slowly in a receiver between two fixed disks near the moveable disk.

If the receiver be full of air it is found that the friction of the air rubbing against the oscillating disk will ultimately

bring it to rest. If now we approximately exhaust the receiver and leave in say only $\frac{1}{100}$th of the full air, we shall
find that this frictional effect of the air tending to stop the
disk is as strong as when the receiver was full of air. Professor Maxwell, starting with the above theory of gaseous
motion, anticipated this fact: it has since been verified by
him experimentally.

There are besides this other facts which tend to confirm
the truth of this theory of gaseous molecular motion.

We have therefore good grounds for supposing the nature of the molecular motion of gases to be known to some
extent.

Now it may be shewn on this theory that if there are
specimens of two gases, either of the same or of a different
chemical constitution, and if the various molecules of the
one have each a greater *energy of motion* than the molecules of the other, there will be a conveyance of heat from
the first to the second, or from the gas with greater molecular energy to that of less.

The absolute temperature of a gas according to this
theory may therefore with propriety be denoted by the
molecular energy of the molecules of that gas.

Again, it may also be shewn in accordance with this
theory that the pressure of a gas is proportional to the
molecular energy of its particles, and hence the pressure
of a gas according to this theory is proportional to its
absolute temperature; and it follows that the air thermometer agrees with this mode of measuring temperature.
On all accounts therefore the air thermometer would seem
to be the preferable means of measuring temperature.

TABLE I.

Shewing the elastic force of aqueous vapour in inches of mercury at the latitude 53° 21' for each degree Fahr. from −30° to 432°.

Temperature.	Force in inches of mercury at 32° at sea level. (Lat. 53° 21'.)	Temperature.	Force in inches of mercury at 32° at sea level. (Lat. 53° 21'.)	Temperature.	Force in inches of mercury at 32° at sea level. (Lat. 53° 21'.)
°	in.	°	in.	°	in.
−30	0.0099	+ 1	0.0459	+ 32	0.1810
29	0.0105	2	0.0481		
28	0.0111	3	0.0503	32	0.1810
27	0.0117	4	0.0526	33	0.1883
26	0.0123	5	0.0551	34	0.1959
25	0.0130	6	0.0576	35	0.2038
24	0.0137	7	0.0603	36	0.2119
23	0.0144	8	0.0630	37	0.2204
22	0.0152	9	0.0659	38	0.2291
21	0.0160	10	0.0689	39	0.2381
20	0.0168	11	0.0721	40	0.2475
19	0.0177	12	0.0753	41	0.2571
18	0.0186	13	0.0788	42	0.2672
17	0.0196	14	0.0823	43	0.2775
16	0.0206	15	0.0861	44	0.2882
15	0.0216	16	0.0899	45	0.2993
14	0.0227	17	0.0940	46	0.3108
13	0.0238	18	0.0982	47	0.3226
12	0.0250	19	0.1027	48	0.3349
11	0.0262	20	0.1073	49	0.3476
10	0.0275	21	0.1121	50	0.3607
9	0.0289	22	0.1171	51	0.3742
8	0.0303	23	0.1223	52	0.3882
7	0.0317	24	0.1278	53	0.4026
6	0.0332	25	0.1335	54	0.4175
5	0.0348	26	0.1395	55	0.4329
4	0.0365	27	0.1457	56	0.4488
3	0.0382	28	0.1522	57	0.4653
2	0.0400	29	0.1589	58	0.4822
1	0.0419	30	0.1660	59	0.4997
0	0.0439	31	0.1733	60	0.5178

B b

Temperature.	Force in inches of mercury at 32° at sea level. (Lat. 53° 21'.)	Temperature.	Force in inches of mercury at 32° at sea level. (Lat. 53° 21'.)	Temperature.	Force in inches of mercury at 32° at sea level. (Lat. 53° 21'.)
°	in.	°	in.	°	in.
61	0.5364	106	2.292	151	7.729
62	0.5556	107	2.360	152	7.922
63	0.5755	108	2.430	153	8.120
64	0.5959	109	2.502	154	8.321
65	0.6170	110	2.576	155	8.527
66	0.6388	111	2.652	156	8.737
67	0.6612	112	2.729	157	8.951
68	0.6843	113	2.809	158	9.170
69	0.7081	114	2.890	159	9.393
70	0.7327	115	2.974	160	9.621
71	0.7580	116	3.059	161	9.853
72	0.7841	117	3.147	162	10.090
73	0.8109	118	3.237	163	10.332
74	0.8386	119	3.329	164	10.579
75	0.8671	120	3.423	165	10.831
76	0.8964	121	3.520	166	11.088
77	0.9266	122	3.619	167	11.350
78	0.9577	123	3.720	168	11.617
79	0.9898	124	3.824	169	11.889
80	1.0227	125	3.930	170	12.167
81	1.0566	126	4.039	171	12.450
82	1.0915	127	4.150	172	12.739
83	1.1274	128	4.264	173	13.033
84	1.1643	129	4.381	174	13.333
85	1.2023	130	4.500	175	13.639
86	1.2413	131	4.622	176	13.951
87	1.2815	132	4.747	177	14.268
88	1.3228	133	4.874	178	14.592
89	1.3652	134	5.005	179	14.922
90	1.4088	135	5.139	180	15.258
91	1.4537	136	5.275	181	15.600
92	1.4998	137	5.415	182	15.949
93	1.5471	138	5.558	183	16.304
94	1.5958	139	5.704	184	16.666
95	1.6457	140	5.854	185	17.034
96	1.6971	141	6.006	186	17.410
97	1.7498	142	6.162	187	17.792
98	1.8039	143	6.322	188	18.181
99	1.8595	144	6.485	189	18.577
100	1.917	145	6.651	190	18.981
101	1.975	146	6.822	191	19.392
102	2.035	147	6.996	192	19.810
103	2.097	148	7.173	193	20.236
104	2.160	149	7.354	194	20.669
105	2.225	150	7.540	195	21.110

Tempe-rature.	Force in inches of mercury at 32° at sea level. (Lat. 53° 21'.)	Tempe-rature.	Force in inches of mercury at 32° at sea level. (Lat. 53° 21'.)	Tempe-rature.	Force in inches of mercury at 32° at sea level. (Lat. 53° 21'.)
°	in.	°	in.	°	in.
196	21.559	241	51.78	286	110.32
197	22.016	242	52.72	287	112.05
198	22.480	243	53.67	288	113.81
199	22.953	244	54.64	289	115.60
200	23.435	245	55.63	290	117.40
201	23.924	246	56.62	291	119.23
202	24.422	247	57.64	292	121.08
203	24.929	248	58.66	293	122.95
204	25.445	249	59.71	294	124.85
205	25.969	250	60.76	295	126.77
206	26.502	251	61.84	296	128.71
207	27.045	252	62.92	297	130.68
208	27.597	253	64.03	298	132.67
209	28.158	254	65.15	299	134.68
210	28.728	255	66.28	300	136.72
211	29.308	256	67.43	301	138.79
212	29.898	257	68.60	302	140.88
213	30.50	258	69.79	303	142.99
214	31.11	259	70.99	304	145.13
215	31.73	260	72.20	305	147.30
216	32.35	261	73.44	306	149.49
217	32.99	262	74.69	307	151.70
218	33.64	263	75.96	308	153.95
219	34.30	264	77.24	309	156.22
220	34.98	265	78.55	310	158.51
221	35.66	266	79.87	311	160.83
222	36.35	267	81.21	312	163.18
223	37.05	268	82.56	313	165.56
224	37.77	269	83.94	314	167.97
225	38.50	270	85.33	315	170.40
226	39.23	271	86.75	316	172.86
227	39.98	272	88.18	317	175.35
228	40.74	273	89.63	318	177.86
229	41.52	274	91.10	319	180.41
230	42.30	275	92.59	320	182.98
231	43.10	276	94.10	321	185.59
232	43.91	277	95.63	322	188.22
233	44.73	278	97.18	323	190.88
234	45.57	279	98.75	324	193.57
235	46.42	280	100.34	325	196.29
236	47.28	281	101.95	326	199.05
237	48.15	282	103.58	327	201.83
238	49.04	283	105.23	328	204.64
239	49.94	284	106.91	329	207.49
240	50.85	285	108.60	330	210.36

Tempe-rature.	Force in inches of mercury at 32° at sea level. (Lat. 53° 21'.)	Tempe-rature.	Force in inches of mercury at 32° at sea level. (Lat. 53° 21'.)	Tempe-rature.	Force in inches of mercury at 32° at sea level. (Lat. 53° 21'.)
°	in.	°	in.	°	in.
331	213.27	365	332.52	399	498.22
332	216.21	366	336.68	400	503.90
333	219.18	367	340.88	401	509.63
334	222.18	368	345.13	402	515.41
335	225.21	369	349.41	403	521.24
336	228.28	370	353.73	404	527.12
337	231.38	371	358.10	405	533.06
338	235.51	372	362.50	406	539.04
339	237.68	373	366.95	407	545.07
340	240.88	374	371.44	408	551.16
341	244.12	375	375.98	409	557.30
342	247.38	376	380.55	410	563.48
343	250.69	377	385.17	411	569.73
344	254.02	378	389.84	412	576.02
345	257.39	379	394.54	413	582.36
346	260.80	380	399.29	414	588.76
347	264.24	381	404.09	415	595.22
348	267.72	382	408.92	416	601.72
349	271.23	383	413.81	417	608.28
350	274.78	384	418.73	418	614.90
351	278.37	385	423.71	419	621.56
352	281.99	386	428.73	420	628.29
353	285.65	387	433.79	421	635.07
354	289.35	388	438.90	422	641.90
355	293.08	389	444.06	423	648.79
356	296.85	390	449.26	424	655.73
357	300.66	391	454.51	425	662.73
358	304.51	392	459.80	426	669.79
359	308.39	393	465.15	427	676.90
360	312.32	394	470.54	428	684.07
361	316.28	395	475.98	429	691.30
362	320.28	396	481.46	430	698.58
363	324.32	397	487.00	431	705.92
364	328.40	398	492.58	432	713.32

TABLE II.

Shewing the elastic force of aqueous vapour in inches of mercury at the latitude 53° 21' from 0° to 100° Fahr. for every two-tenths of a degree.

Temperature.	Force in inches of mercury at 32° at sea level. (Lat. 53° 21'.)	Temperature.	Force in inches of mercury at 32° at sea level. (Lat. 53° 21'.)	Temperature.	Force in inches of mercury at 32° at sea level. (Lat. 53° 21'.)
°	in.	°	in.	°	in.
0.0	0.0439	6.4	0.0587	12.8	0.0781
.2	0.0443	.6	0.0592	13.0	0.0788
.4	0.0447	.8	0.0597	.2	0.0795
.6	0.0451	7.0	0.0603	.4	0.0802
.8	0.0455	.2	0.0608	.6	0.0809
1.0	0.0459	.4	0.0614	.8	0.0816
.2	0.0464	.6	0.0619	14.0	0.0823
.4	0.0468	.8	0.0625	.2	0.0831
.6	0.0472	8.0	0.0630	.4	0.0838
.8	0.0476	.2	0.0636	.6	0.0846
2.0	0.0481	.4	0.0642	.8	0.0853
.2	0.0485	.6	0.0647	15.0	0.0861
.4	0.0490	.8	0.0653	.2	0.0868
.6	0.0494	9.0	0.0659	.4	0.0876
.8	0.0499	.2	0.0665	.6	0.0884
3.0	0.0503	.4	0.0671	.8	0.0892
.2	0.0508	.6	0.0677	16.0	0.0899
.4	0.0512	.8	0.0683	.2	0.0907
.6	0.0517	10.0	0.0689	.4	0.0916
.8	0.0522	.2	0.0695	.6	0.0924
4.0	0.0526	.4	0.0702	.8	0.0932
.2	0.0531	.6	0.0708	17.0	0.0940
.4	0.0536	.8	0.0714	.2	0.0948
.6	0.0541	11.0	0.0721	.4	0.0957
.8	0.0546	.2	0.0727	.6	0.0965
5.0	0.0551	.4	0.0734	.8	0.0974
.2	0.0556	.6	0.0740	18.0	0.0982
.4	0.0561	.8	0.0747	.2	0.0991
.6	0.0566	12.0	0.0753	.4	0.1000
.8	0.0571	.2	0.0760	.6	0.1009
6.0	0.0576	.4	0.0767	.8	0.1018
.2	0.0581	.6	0.0774	19.0	0.1027

Tempe-rature.	Force in inches of mercury at 32° at 32° at sea level. (Lat. 53° 21'.)	Tempe-rature.	Force in inches of mercury at 32° at sea level. (Lat. 53° 21'.)	Tempe-rature.	Force in inches of mercury at 32° at sea level. (Lat. 53° 21'.)
°	in.	°	in.	°	in.
19.2	0.1036	28.2	0.1535	37.2	0.2221
.4	0.1045	.4	0.1548	.4	0.2238
.6	0.1054	.6	0.1562	.6	0.2255
.8	0.1063	.8	0.1575	.8	0.2273
20.0	0.1073	29.0	0.1589	38.0	0.2291
.2	0.1082	.2	0.1603	.2	0.2309
.4	0.1092	.4	0.1617	.4	0.2327
.6	0.1101	.6	0.1631	.6	0.2345
.8	0.1111	.8	0.1645	.8	0.2363
21.0	0.1121	30.0	0.1660	39.0	0.2381
.2	0.1131	.2	0.1674	.2	0.2400
.4	0.1141	.4	0.1689	.4	0.2418
.6	0.1151	.6	0.1704	.6	0.2437
.8	0.1161	.8	0.1718	.8	0.2456
22.0	0.1171	31.0	0.1733	40.0	0.2475
.2	0.1181	.2	0.1749	.2	0.2494
.4	0.1192	.4	0.1764	.4	0.2513
.6	0.1202	.6	0.1779	.6	0.2532
.8	0.1213	.8	0.1795	.8	0.2552
23.0	0.1223	32.0	0.1810	41.0	0.2571
.2	0.1234	.2	0.1825	.2	0.2591
.4	0.1245	.4	0.1839	.4	0.2611
.6	0.1256	.6	0.1854	.6	0.2631
.8	0.1267	.8	0.1869	.8	0.2651
24.0	0.1278	33.0	0.1883	42.0	0.2672
.2	0.1289	.2	0.1898	.2	0.2692
.4	0.1300	.4	0.1913	.4	0.2713
.6	0.1312	.6	0.1929	.6	0.2733
.8	0.1323	.8	0.1944	.8	0.2754
25.0	0.1335	34.0	0.1959	43.0	0.2775
.2	0.1347	.2	0.1975	.2	0.2796
.4	0.1359	.4	0.1990	.4	0.2818
.6	0.1370	.6	0.2006	.6	0.2839
.8	0.1382	.8	0.2022	.8	0.2861
26.0	0.1395	35.0	0.2038	44.0	0.2882
.2	0.1407	.2	0.2054	.2	0.2904
.4	0.1419	.4	0.2070	.4	0.2926
.6	0.1431	.6	0.2086	.6	0.2948
.8	0.1444	.8	0.2103	.8	0.2971
27.0	0.1457	36.0	0.2119	45.0	0.2993
.2	0.1469	.2	0.2136	.2	0.3016
.4	0.1482	.4	0.2153	.4	0.3039
.6	0.1495	.6	0.2169	.6	0.3061
.8	0.1508	.8	0.2186	.8	0.3085
	0.1522	37.0	0.2204	46.0	0.3108

Tempe-rature.	Force in inches of mercury at 32° at sea level. (Lat. 53° 21'.)	Tempe-rature.	Force in inches of mercury at 32° at sea level. (Lat. 53° 21'.)	Tempe-rature.	Force in inches of mercury at 32° at sea level. (Lat. 53° 21'.)
°	in.	°	in.	°	in.
46.2	0.3131	55.2	0.4361	64.2	0.6001
.4	0.3155	.4	0.4392	.4	0.6043
.6	0.3178	.6	0.4424	.6	0.6085
.8	0.3202	.8	0.4456	.8	0.6127
47.0	0.3226	56.0	0.4488	65.0	0.6170
.2	0.3251	.2	0.4521	.2	0.6213
.4	0.3275	.4	0.4553	.4	0.6256
.6	0.3299	.6	0.4586	.6	0.6300
.8	0.3324	.8	0.4619	.8	0.6344
48.0	0.3349	57.0	0.4653	66.0	0.6388
.2	0.3374	.2	0.4686	.2	0.6432
.4	0.3399	.4	0.4720	.4	0.6477
.6	0.3424	.6	0.4754	.6	0.6521
.8	0.3450	.8	0.4788	.8	0.6567
49.0	0.3476	58.0	0.4822	67.0	0.6612
.2	0.3501	.2	0.4857	.2	0.6658
.4	0.3527	.4	0.4891	.4	0.6704
.6	0.3554	.6	0.4926	.6	0.6750
.8	0.3580	.8	0.4962	.8	0.6796
50.0	0.3607	59.0	0.4997	68.0	0.6843
.2	0.3633	.2	0.5033	.2	0.6890
.4	0.3660	.4	0.5069	.4	0.6938
.6	0.3687	.6	0.5105	.6	0.6985
.8	0.3714	.8	0.5141	.8	0.7033
51.0	0.3742	60.0	0.5178	69.0	0.7081
.2	0.3769	.2	0.5215	.2	0.7130
.4	0.3797	.4	0.5251	.4	0.7179
.6	0.3825	.6	0.5289	.6	0.7228
.8	0.3853	.8	0.5326	.8	0.7277
52.0	0.3882	61.0	0.5364	70.0	0.7327
.2	0.3910	.2	0.5402	.2	0.7377
.4	0.3939	.4	0.5440	.4	0.7427
.6	0.3968	.6	0.5479	.6	0.7478
.8	0.3997	.8	0.5517	.8	0.7529
53.0	0.4026	62.0	0.5556	71.0	0.7580
.2	0.4055	.2	0.5595	.2	0.7632
.4	0.4085	.4	0.5635	.4	0.7683
.6	0.4115	.6	0.5675	.6	0.7736
.8	0.4145	.8	0.5714	.8	0.7788
54.0	0.4175	63.0	0.5755	72.0	0.7841
.2	0.4206	.2	0.5795	.2	0.7894
.4	0.4236	.4	0.5836	.4	0.7947
.6	0.4267	.6	0.5877	.6	0.8001
.8	0.4298	.8	0.5918	.8	0.8055
55.0	0.4329	64.0	0.5959	73.0	0.8109

Temperature.	Force in inches of mercury at 32° at sea level. (Lat. 53° 21'.)	Temperature.	Force in inches of mercury at 32° at sea level. (Lat. 53° 21'.)	Temperature.	Force in inches of mercury at 32° at sea level. (Lat. 53° 21'.)
°	in.	°	in.	°	in.
73.2	0.8164	82.2	1.0986	91.2	1.4628
.4	0.8219	.4	1.1057	.4	1.4720
.6	0.8274	.6	1.1129	.6	1.4812
.8	0.8330	.8	1.1201	.8	1.4904
74.0	0.8386	83.0	1.1274	92.0	1.4998
.2	0.8442	.2	1.1347	.2	1.5091
.4	0.8499	.4	1.1420	.4	1.5185
.6	0.8556	.6	1.1494	.6	1.5280
.8	0.8613	.8	1.1568	.8	1.5375
75.0	0.8671	84.0	1.1643	93.0	1.5471
.2	0.8729	.2	1.1718	.2	1.5567
.4	0.8787	.4	1.1794	.4	1.5664
.6	0.8846	.6	1.1870	.6	1.5761
.8	0.8905	.8	1.1946	.8	1.5859
76.0	0.8964	85.0	1.2023	94.0	1.5958
.2	0.9024	.2	1.2100	.2	1.6056
.4	0.9084	.4	1.2178	.4	1.6156
.6	0.9145	.6	1.2256	.6	1.6256
.8	0.9205	.8	1.2334	.8	1.6356
77.0	0.9266	86.0	1.2413	95.0	1.6457
.2	0.9328	.2	1.2493	.2	1.6559
.4	0.9390	.4	1.2573	.4	1.6661
.6	0.9452	.6	1.2653	.6	1.6764
.8	0.9515	.8	1.2734	.8	1.6867
78.0	0.9577	87.0	1.2815	96.0	1.6971
.2	0.9641	.2	1.2896	.2	1.7075
.4	0.9704	.4	1.2979	.4	1.7180
.6	0.9768	.6	1.3061	.6	1.7285
.8	0.9833	.8	1.3144	.8	1.7391
79.0	0.9898	88.0	1.3228	97.0	1.7498
.2	0.9963	.2	1.3312	.2	1.7605
.4	1.0028	.4	1.3396	.4	1.7712
.6	1.0094	.6	1.3481	.6	1.7821
.8	1.0160	.8	1.3566	.8	1.7930
80.0	1.0227	89.0	1.3652	98.0	1.8039
.2	1.0294	.2	1.3738	.2	1.8149
.4	1.0361	.4	1.3825	.4	1.8260
.6	1.0429	.6	1.3912	.6	1.8371
.8	1.0497	.8	1.4000	.8	1.8482
81.0	1.0566	90.0	1.4088	99.0	1.8595
.2	1.0635	.2	1.4177	.2	1.8708
.4	1.0704	.4	1.4266	.4	1.8821
.6	1.0774	.6	1.4356	.6	1.8935
.8	1.0844	.8	1.4446	.8	1.9050
82.0	1.0915	91.0	1.4537		

TABLE III.

Shewing the elastic force of aqueous vapour in millimètres of mercury at the latitude of Paris (48° 50′) for each degree centigrade from −32°C *to* +230°C.

Temperature.	Elastic force.	Temperature.	Elastic force.	Temperature.	Elastic force.
°	mm.	°	mm.	°	mm.
− 32	0.320	− 1	4.263	30	31.548
31	0.352	0	4.600	31	33.4c6
30	0.386	+ 1	4.940	32	35.359
29	0.424	2	5.302	33	37.411
28	0.464	3	5.687	34	39.565
27	0.508	4	6.097	35	41.827
26	0.555	5	6.534	36	44.201
25	0.605	6	6.998	37	46.691
24	0.660	7	7.492	38	49.302
23	0.719	8	8.017	39	52.039
22	0.783	9	8.574	40	54.906
21	0.853	10	9.165	41	57.910
20	0.927	11	9.792	42	61.055
19	1.008	12	10.457	43	64.346
18	1.095	13	11.162	44	67.790
17	1.189	14	11.908	45	71.391
16	1.290	15	12.699	46	75.158
15	1.400	16	13.536	47	79.093
14	1.518	17	14.421	48	83.204
13	1.646	18	15.357	49	87.499
12	1.783	19	16.346	50	91.982
11	1.933	20	17.391	51	96.661
10	2.093	21	18.495	52	101.543
9	2.267	22	19.659	53	106.636
8	2.455	23	20.888	54	111.945
7	2.658	24	22.184	55	117.478
6	2.876	25	23.550	56	123.244
5	3.113	26	24.988	57	129.251
4	3.368	27	25.505	58	135.505
3	3.644	28	28.101	59	142.015
2	3.941	29	29.782	60	148.791

Temperature.	Elastic force.	Temperature.	Elastic force.	Temperature.	Elastic force.
°	mm.	°	mm.	°	mm.
61	155.839	108	1004.910	155	4088.56
62	163.170	109	1039.650	156	4196.59
63	170.791	110	1075.370	157	4306.88
64	178.714	111	1112.090	158	4419.45
65	186.945	112	1149.830	159	4534.36
66	195.496	113	1188.610	160	4651.62
67	204.376	114	1228.470	161	4771.28
68	213.596	115	1269.410	162	4893.36
69	223.165	116	1311.470	163	5017.91
70	233.093	117	1354.660	164	5144.97
71	243.393	118	1399.020	165	5274.54
72	254.073	119	1444.550	166	5406.69
73	265.147	120	1491.280	167	5541.43
74	276.624	121	1539.250	168	5678.82
75	288.517	122	1588.470	169	5818.90
76	300.838	123	1638.960	170	5961.66
77	313.600	124	1690.76	171	6107.19
78	326.811	125	1743.88	172	6255.48
79	340.488	126	1798.35	173	6406.60
80	354.643	127	1854.20	174	6560.55
81	369.287	128	1911.47	175	6717.43
82	384.435	129	1970.15	176	6877.22
83	400.101	130	2030.28	177	7039.97
84	416.298	131	2091.94	178	7205.72
85	433.041	132	2155.03	179	7374.52
86	450.344	133	2219.69	180	7546.39
87	468.221	134	2285.92	181	7721.37
88	486.687	135	2353.73	182	7899.52
89	505.759	136	2423.16	183	8080.84
90	525.450	137	2494.23	184	8265.40
91	545.778	138	2567.00	185	8453.23
92	566.757	139	2641.44	186	8644.35
93	588.406	140	2717.63	187	8838.82
94	610.740	141	2795.57	188	9036.68
95	633.778	142	2875.30	189	9237.95
96	657.535	143	2956.86	190	9442.70
97	682.029	144	3040.26	191	9650.93
98	707.280	145	3125.55	192	9862.71
99	733.305	146	3212.74	193	10078.04
100	760.000	147	3301.87	194	10297.01
101	787.590	148	3392.98	195	10519.63
102	816.010	149	3486.09	196	10745.95
103	845.280	150	3581.23	197	10975.00
104	875.410	151	3678.43	198	11209.82
105	906.410	152	3777.74	199	11447.46
106	938.310	153	3879.18	200	11688.96
107	971.140	154	3982.77	201	11934.37

Tempe-rature.	Elastic force.	Tempe-rature.	Elastic force.	Tempe-rature.	Elastic force.
°	mm.	°	mm.	°	mm.
202	12183.69	212	14902.22	222	18058.64
203	12437.00	213	15197.48	223	18399.94
204	12694.30	214	15497.17	224	18746.07
205	12955.66	215	15801.33	225	19097.04
206	13221.12	216	16109.94	226	19452.92
207	13490.75	217	16423.15	227	19813.76
208	13764.53	218	16740.90	228	20179.61
209	14042.52	219	17063.29	229	20550.48
210	14324.80	220	17390.36	230	20926.40
211	14611.32	221	17722.13		

INDEX.

Latent heat, first taught by Dr. Black, 84; what it is, 278, 336; of steam, 283, 337.

Lavoisier's measurement of dilatation, 26.

Laws, of dilatation of solids, 24; of dilatation of crystals (Mitscherlich), 37; of dilatation of liquids, 52; Boyle's law, 53; of expansion of gases (Gay Lussac's law), 55; of dilatation of gases (Regnault), 61; of fusion, 82; of solidification, 87; of maximum pressure in vacuo (Dalton), 96; of mixtures of gas and vapours, 96; of evaporation, 107; of Leidenfrost's phenomenon, 114; of relation between volume and temperature of gases, 121; of density of gases, 133; of relation between temperature and refraction (Gladstone and Dale), 148; of electric currents (Seebeck), 148; of radiation of heat, 159; of reflection of dark heat, 173; of refraction, 175; of polarization, &c., 179; of radiation (exchanges), 190; of internal radiation, 198; of absorption and radiation, 204; of velocity of cooling, 209; of radiation from black bodies, 214; from gases, 217; of dew, 231; of fluorescence, 235; of flow of heat across a wall, 243; of conduction of crystals, 255; of cooling due to a gas, 260; of specific heat of solids, 267, 268; of liquids, 270; of gases (Regnault), 274; of atomic heat, 277; of energy, 298; of thermodynamics, 301.

Leidenfrost's phenomenon, 113.

Length, standard of, 65–67.

Leslie's differential thermometer, 22; first to freeze water by evaporation, 101; experiments on reflection of dark heat, 170; table of results, 171; on radiation and reflection, 185; on oblique radiation, 188; on law of cooling in gases, 261.

Light, its heat reflected, 172; and

heat, probably identical, 179; heat, and sound, analogy of, 204; absorption of, 226; energy of, 298.

Light rays, equilibrium of, 198.

Linear dilatation of uncrystallized solids, 26–36.

Liquefaction and solidification, 80–93; latent heat of, 279.

Liquids, dilatation of, 39–52; electric conductivity of, 155; convection in, 256; specific heat of, 269.

Locomotives, 330.

Machines, functions of, 294.

Magnetism, effect of temperature on, 155; disturbances of, due to the sun, 358.

Magneto-electricity, experiments by Foucault, 304.

Magnus on dilatation of crystals, 38; of gases, 55; on mixed liquids in a confined space, 97; on boiling-points of saline solutions, 110; on the effect of air dissolved on boiling-point, 111.

Malus on polarization, 177.

Marcet's experiments on boiling-point, 110.

Marchand on Leidenfrost's phenomenon, 114.

Marianini on electric conductivity, 155.

Marriotte's law of dilatation of gases, 54.

Mason's wet and dry bulb hygrometer, 142.

Material medium pervading space, 352.

Matteucci on conduction of heat in bismuth, 254.

Matthiessen's absolute expansion of mercury, 46; table of electric conductivity, 154.

Maximum thermometer, 20.

Maxwell on motion of gases, 367.

Mayer on expansion of gases, 305; on animal energy, 355; on tidal energy, 356; on solar heat, 361.

UNIVERSITY OF OXFORD.

Clarendon Press Series.

THE DELEGATES of the Oxford Press understand from eminent Schoolmasters and others who are authorities upon education, that there is still great need of good School Books and Manuals.

They are told that Editions with good English notes of many of the Greek and Latin Classics read in the higher classes of the Public Schools are required; that text-books, both English and Foreign, are much needed for the use of Schools, especially with reference to the Local Examinations held by the Universities; that good English and other Grammars, and Exercise-books adapted to them and with a copious supply of Examples, are much needed and that there is a great and urgent want of Delectuses, Analecta, and generally of books of Selections from Authors, for use in Schools;—

That the Histories now read in Schools are greatly below present requirements, and in some cases there are absolute deficiencies; and that the want of good books on History is much felt in the Law and Modern History School in the University;—

That English Treatises on Physical Science, written with clearness and precision of language, and adapted for use in the higher classes of Schools, and in the Natural Science School of the University, do not exist.

They believe that the University may with propriety and efficiency do much towards remedying the defect. They have therefore determined to issue a series of Educational Works, hoping to supply some existing wants, and to help in improving methods of teaching.

B

The departments of Education which they propose to deal with at present are the following :—

I. CLASSICS.   The Delegates hope to issue

  1. Works suitable for the Universities and the highest forms of Schools; or

  2. Books for School-work generally, beginning from the very rudiments.

II. MATHEMATICAL WORKS; both for University Students, and also with especial regard to the needs of Middle Class Schools.

III. HISTORY.   Here again there will be two classes of books :—

  1. Short Histories, such as may be useful for the History School, or for general reading;

  2. School Histories, with all the necessary appliances for education.

IV. LAW.

V. PHYSICAL SCIENCE.   The experience of teachers in the University and elsewhere has already pointed out several desirable works, and has also gone some way towards providing the books required.

VI. ENGLISH LANGUAGE AND LITERATURE, which will comprise a carefully compiled series of Reading Books, Exercise Books, and Grammars.

VII. MODERN LANGUAGES.

VIII. A MISCELLANEOUS CLASS; including Handbooks on Art, Music, Literature, and the like.

IX. A SERIES OF ENGLISH CLASSICS.

The DELEGATES OF THE PRESS *invite suggestions and advice from all persons interested in sound education; and will be thankful for hints, &c., addressed to the Rev.* G. W. KITCHIN, *Walton Manor, Oxford.*

Just Published.

1. Chemistry for Students. By A. W. WILLIAMSON,

Phil. Doc., F.R.S., Professor of Chemistry, University College, London. (Crown 8vo., cloth, price 7s. 6d.)

Also: Solutions of the Problems in " Chemistry for Students." By the same Author. (Sewed, price 6d.)

"Within less than four hundred pages of a handy little volume, in type not fatiguing to the eye, Professor Williamson here gives to the student an outline of the leading facts and principles of inorganic and organic chemistry.

"Very few men are able to compress, within such limits, so large a topic, and of those who should attempt to do so almost all would fail to keep together soul and body of the science. Even in large treatises there is a tendency to part principles from facts. Having taken the life out of the body in a few preliminary chapters, the learned expositor confines all further attention to the corpse. While this is true of many a large book, in a small book we get usually facts alone or principles alone, if not the two in a state of repulsion. Professor Williamson is accurately technical and so concise that at a glance his pages might seem to contain only the *caput mortuum* of a great science. But let a chapter be read, and the truth appears that the student who reads such a book as this is in the hands of a singularly skilful teacher who knows how, without waste of a word, to fix intelligent attention. Out of experiments and observed facts arranged in a clear logical order he developes principles, and points to the part they play in the world's life. Step by step the student is led, not blindfold but with his attention constantly directed to the landmarks on his way. For example, the book begins by telling the learner how to make oxygen. There is a diagram of the arrangement necessary, and a clear explanation of the process of getting the gas from chlorate of potash or manganese. Then there is an equally clear account (with a diagram) of Lavoisier's experiment for getting oxygen out of the common air. * * * * *

"A volume constructed in this way is really a too rare example of what a good elementary text-book in any science ought to be: the language brief, simple, exact; the arrangement logical, developing in lucid order principles from facts, and keeping theory always dependent upon observation; a book that keeps the reason of the student active while he strives to master details difficult but never without interest, and that furnishes him with means for practising himself in the right management of each new tool of knowledge that is given to him for his use."—*Examiner.*

2. Greek Verbs, Irregular and Defective; their

forms, meaning, and quantity; embracing all the Tenses used by Greek writers, with references to the passages in which they are found. By W. VEITCH. New and revised edition. (Crown 8vo., cloth, 616 pp., price 8s. 6d.)

"The 'Clarendon Press Series' makes an excellent start, and if its succeeding volumes are to combine anything like the distinctive

merits of the first, it is destined to supersede every other series already
in use.   Mr. Veitch's work on the *Irregular and Defective Greek Verbs*
is as signal a proof as could be furnished that a book designed to assist
the learner or the advanced student may be convenient in size and yet
exhaustive in treatment, may be quite original in investigation and yet
fall readily into the educational channel, may confine itself to the
strictest exposition of phenomena, and yet be fresh with the force of
character and lively with the humour that belong more or less to all
inquiring and independent minds.

    *   *   *   *

"We shall not pretend to review the treatise of an author who
stands very nearly, if not altogether, alone in knowledge of his subject.
Mr. Veitch is indeed as independent of the praise or the censure of
critics as any author need care to be.   It is one of his claims to the
gratitude of scholars that, in spite of the premature and almost
universal desertion of the field of rigid, textual scholarship, for the
easier, showier, and pleasanter field of aesthetic or literary disquisition,
he has persevered in his forsaken and solitary path, and has produced a
work unique of its kind, full of fresh and lasting contributions to our
knowledge of the Greek language, and intellectually vivacious and
incisive on nearly every page.   Open the book anywhere, and instances
of erroneous doctrines corrected, of omissions (common to all our
lexicons) supplemented, of new theories propounded and vindicated,
occur at once. * * * * Let the critical reader compare Mr. Veitch's
treatment of such a compound as ἀνορθόω, for example, with its handling
by other critics, and he will at once see how incomparably more trust-
worthy Mr. Veitch is as a guide not only for the pupil and teacher,
not only for the writer of Greek prose and verse, but also for the con-
stituter of texts and for the advanced amateur scholar.   Indeed there
is scarcely an authority, whether editor, lexicographer, or grammarian,
British or Continental, whom Mr. Veitch has not occasion to correct,
modify, or supplement.   The German Dindorf, the Dutch Cobet, the
French Littré, the English Liddell and Scott, are a few among living
scholars who are repeatedly brought to the touchstone of comprehensive
induction and acute judgment, while the dicta of departed authorities
are canvassed with a freedom which would be almost cruel, were it not
uniformly so just.   We congratulate Mr. Veitch on the completion, and
the Clarendon Press on the publication, of a work which will reinstate
our scholarship in that esteem which the Germans have almost ceased
to entertain for it since the days of Porson and Elmsley, and which will
have the merit not only of purifying the fountain-heads of classical
education, but of affording the youthful scholar an example of that
moral singleness of purpose and undeviating search for truth which are
even rarer than the intellectual gifts that have been lavished on its
execution."—*Spectator.*

"The book before us by Mr. William Veitch is quite a wonderful
contribution to critical knowledge of Greek, and has been selected
by the Delegates of the Clarendon Press to lead off a new series of
educational works.   Its great distinction, in the first place, is that
it is all derived from original reading.   Mr. Veitch has not learned

the anatomy of the language from anybody's anatomical plates ; he has dissected the body for himself. He has gone with a careful finger through the Greek texts, and the Greek texts in their latest recensions, marking every noticeable form, and checking by his own personal examination the *dicta* of other critics. * * * * The book is useful, indeed we may say indispensable, to scholars, in the widest sense of the word. It takes a larger range than its mere title would imply ; and besides being a supplement to our best Lexicons, such as that of Liddell and Scott, contains touches of fine philology which would have delighted Porson and Elmsley. Indeed, the perusal of it recalls to our memory the description of Elmsley with which Hermann concluded his review of our countryman's edition of the *Medea:*—'Est enim P. Elmsleius, si quis alius, vir natus augendae accuratiori Graecae linguae cognitioni, ut cujus eximia ac plane singularis in pervestigandis rebus grammaticis diligentia regatur praeclaro ingenio, mente ab auctoritatibus libera, animo veri amantissimo, neque aut superbia, aut gloriae studio, aut obtrectandi cupiditate, praepedito.' It is a pleasant sign of the increased communication between the northern and southern parts of the United Kingdom that the Clarendon Press should have volunteered to bring this learned treatise before the world ; and Mr. Veitch gratefully acknowledges the service in his preface. His book will soon become a text-book in all the great English public schools, and will doubtless by-and-by come to be known and appreciated also in the country in which it was written."—*Pall Mall Gazette.*

3. **An Elementary Treatise on Heat, with** numerous Woodcuts and Diagrams. By BALFOUR STEWART, LL.D., F.R.S., Director of the Observatory at Kew. (Crown 8vo., cloth, price 7s. 6d.)

"In this work the Author endeavours to place before his readers in an elementary form the facts and principles of the Science of Heat, and also to give some of the most prominent practical applications of our knowledge of this subject. He begins with the study of well-ascertained facts, and proceeds onwards to general principles.

"The work is divided into three parts:—

"1. The study of the various Effects produced on Bodies by Heat. Many of the most recent investigations, and the apparatus used in conducting them, are described at length ; and numerical examples are given to help the student to attain to the accuracy needful in physical researches.

"2. The Laws which regulate the Distribution of Heat through Space. This part includes radiation, conduction, convection, and the measurements of specific and latent heat. Theoretic views are here first introduced.

"3. The Nature of Heat, its Sources, and Connexion with other Properties of Matter. In this part heat is viewed as a species of motion ; and the leading principles of the Science of Energy, by which heat becomes related to other forms of motion, are discussed.

"The work is chiefly intended for students of Physical Science; but it is hoped that it may also interest general readers by placing before them some of the most remarkable and most practical and valuable truths arrived at by modern researches into the nature and qualities of heat."—*From the Author's Preface.*

4. Specimens of Early English; being a Series of

Extracts from the most important English Authors, Chronologically arranged, illustrative of the progress of the English Language and its Dialectic varieties, from A.D. 1250 to A.D. 1400. With Grammatical Introduction, Notes, and Glossary. By R. MORRIS, Esq., Editor of "The Story of Genesis and Exodus," &c. (Crown 8vo.)

This work seeks to set before students of the English language a systematic view of its older forms and their development, as exhibited in writers of the latter part of the thirteenth and the whole of the fourteenth centuries : a most important period in the history of our language, though it has been but imperfectly investigated even by the best writers on the subject. Existing text-books on the history of English literature and language not only pass over much that is important in this period, but they also deal in a very unsatisfactory way with many chief authorities, whose style, language, and position are thought to be sufficiently illustrated if twenty or thirty lines are devoted to them. There is in fact no real knowledge of this period to be met with. This present work is intended, partially at least, to fill this blank. It presents a series of specimens selected so as to form a connected and continuous whole. Each passage chosen is of considerable length (the extracts varying from 200 to upwards of 1200 lines); so that the grammar, vocabulary, and manner of each author are completely represented to the student.

These specimens are arranged in chronological order, and illustrate the leading *dialects* of the early English period. They will be found to be (for the most part) new; having been chosen from works which have not usually been quoted and are not well known. In many cases the passages are re-edited from the best MSS. ; a few of them now appear for the first time.

The work has a grammatical Introduction, Notes, and a Glossary; and it is hoped that it may be within the reach and capacity of all who take an interest in the *origines* of our mother-tongue. It lays bare some of the strong foundations on which our language is built up; it throws some light on the ethnological and historical characteristics of its period; religion, manners, domestic habits, ranks and orders, of a very important time in the annals of this country are illustrated by it.

It is, however, specially intended for students in colleges in which the English language forms a part of the regular routine of instruction, and for candidates for the Civil and Indian Civil Service.

In course of Preparation.

I. CLASSICS.

1. Sophocles. By the Rev. LEWIS CAMPBELL, M.A.;
Professor of Greek at St. Andrews, late Fellow of Queen's
College, Oxford.

2. Homer, Iliad I–XII. By D. B. MONRO, M.A.,
Fellow of Oriel College, Oxford.

3. Homer, Odyssey I–XII.

4. —— Odyssey XIII–XXIV. By ROBINSON ELLIS,
M.A., Fellow of Trinity College, Oxford.

5. A Golden Treasury of Greek Poetry, being a col-
lection of the finest passages in the principal Greek Poets, with
Introductory Notices and Notes. By R. S. WRIGHT, M.A.,
Fellow of Oriel College, Oxford. [*In the Press.*
Also, to follow: A Golden Treasury of Greek Prose. By R. S.
WRIGHT, M.A., Fellow of Oriel College, and J. E. L. SHADWELL,
B.A., Student of Christ Church.

6. Horace. With English Notes and Introduction.
By the Rev. E. WICKHAM, M.A., Fellow of New College,
Oxford. Also a small Edition for Schools.

7. Livy I–X. By J. R. SEELEY, M.A., Fellow of
Christ's College, Cambridge; Professor of Latin, University
College, London. Also a small edition for Schools.

8. Cicero. Select Letters. By the Rev. A. WATSON,
M.A., Fellow of Brasenose College, Oxford.

9. Cicero. The Philippic Orations. By the Rev. J. R.
KING, M.A., Fellow of Merton College, Oxford.

10. Selections from the less known Latin Poets. By the
Rev. NORTH PINDER, M.A., late Fellow of Trinity College,
Oxford.

11. Xenophon's Anabasis (for Schools). With English Notes and Maps, by J. S. PHILLPOTTS, B.C.L., Fellow of New College, Oxford; Assistant Master in Rugby School.

12. The Commentaries of C. Jul. Caesar. Part I. The Gallic War, with English Notes, &c., by CHARLES E. MOBERLY, M.A., Assistant Master in Rugby School; late Scholar of Balliol. Also, to follow: Part II. The Civil War: by the same Editor.

13. Select Epistles of Cicero and Pliny (for Schools). With English Notes, by the Rev. C. E. PRICHARD, M.A., late Fellow of Balliol.

14. Selections from Plato (for Schools). With English Notes, by the Rev. B. JOWETT, M.A., Regius Professor of Greek, and J. PURVES, B.A., Balliol College.

15. The Elements of Greek Accentuation (for Schools): abridged from his larger work by H. W. CHANDLER, M.A., Fellow of Pembroke College, Oxford.

16. Cornelius Nepos (for Schools). With English Notes, by OSCAR BROWNING, M.A., Fellow of King's College, Cambridge, and Assistant Master at Eton College.

II. MATHEMATICS.

1. An Elementary Treatise on Quaternions. By P. G. TAIT, M.A., Professor of Natural Philosophy in the University of Edinburgh; late Fellow of St. Peter's College, Cambridge.

2. A Course of Lectures on Pure Geometry. By H. J. STEPHEN SMITH, M.A., F.R.S., Fellow of Balliol College, and Savilian Professor of Geometry in the University of Oxford.

III. HISTORY.

1. A History of Germany and of the Empire, down to the close of the Middle Ages. By J. BRYCE, M.A., Fellow of Oriel College, Oxford.

2. A History of British India. By S. OWEN, M.A., Lee's Reader in Law and History, Christ Church; and Reader in Indian Law in the University of Oxford.

3. A History of Greece. By E. A. FREEMAN, M.A., late Fellow of Trinity College, Oxford.

4. A Constitutional History of England. By the Rev. W. STUBBS, M.A., late Fellow of Trinity College, Oxford, and Regius Professor of Modern History.

5. A Church History of the First Three Centuries. By the Rev. W. W. SHIRLEY, D.D., Canon of Christ Church, and Professor of Ecclesiastical History.

IV. LAW.

1. The Institutes of Justinian, with Notes and an English Translation. By J. BRYCE, M.A., Fellow of Oriel College, Oxford.

2. Commentaries on Roman Law; from the original and the best modern sources. In Two Volumes, demy 8vo. By H. J. ROBY, M.A., formerly Fellow of St. John's College, Cambridge; Professor of Law at University College, London.

V. PHYSICAL SCIENCE.

1. A Treatise on Natural Philosophy. In four Volumes. By W. THOMSON, LL.D., F.R.S., Professor of Natural Philosophy in the University of Glasgow, and P. G. TAIT, M.A., Professor of Natural Philosophy in the University of Edinburgh; late Fellow of St. Peter's College, Cambridge. *Vol. I. nearly ready.*

2. Also, by the same Authors, a smaller work on the same subject, forming a complete Introduction to the subject, so far as it can be explained by the help of Elementary Geometry and Algebra. *[In the Press.*

3. Forms of Animal Life. Illustrated by Descriptions and Drawings of Dissections. By G. ROLLESTON, M.D., F.R.S., Linacre Professor of Physiology, Oxford. *[In the Press.*

4. On Laboratory Practice. By A. VERNON HARCOURT, M.A., Lee's Reader in Chemistry at Christ Church, and H. G. MADAN, M.A., Fellow of Queen's College, Oxford.

5. Geology. By J. PHILLIPS, M.A., F.R.S., Professor of Geology, Oxford.

6. **Handbook of Astronomy, Descriptive and Practical.** With very numerous illustrations and tables. By G. F. CHAMBERS, F.R.A.S.   *[In the Press.*

VI. ENGLISH LANGUAGE AND LITERATURE.

1. **On the Principles of Grammar.** By the Rev. E. THRING, M.A., Head Master of Uppingham School.

   Also, by the same Author, a Gradual, designed to serve as an Exercise and Composition Book in the English Language.

2. **The Philology of the English Tongue.** By the Rev. J. EARLE, M.A., late Fellow of Oriel College, Oxford, and late Professor of Anglo-Saxon.

3. **Reading Books.** i. For junior classes in Schools, in Prose and Verse, Two Volumes. ii. Advanced, in Two Volumes. By the Author of "Mademoiselle Mori."

4. **Typical Selections from the best English Authors** from the Sixteenth to the Nineteenth Century, (to serve as an higher Reading book,) with Introductory Notices and Notes, being a Contribution towards a History of English Literature.

VII. FRENCH.

By Mons. JULES BUÉ,

Honorary M. A. of Oxford ; Taylorian Teacher of French, Oxford ; Examiner in the Oxford Local Examinations from 1858.

1. **A French Grammar.** A complete theory of the French language, with the rules in French and English, and numerous Examples to serve as first Exercises in the language.

2. **A French Grammar Test.** A book of Exercises on French Grammar; each Exercise being preceded by Grammatical Questions.

3. **Exercises in Translation No. 1, from French into** English, with general rules on Translation; and containing Notes, Hints, and Cautions, founded on a comparison of the Grammar and Genius of the two languages.

4. Exercises in Translation No. 2, from English into
French, on the same plan as the preceding book.

5. Exercises on French Idiomatic Locutions.

6. A new method of French Analysis.

7. Theory of French Pronunciation.

VIII. MISCELLANEOUS.

1. The Principles of Music. By the Rev. Sir F. A.
GORE OUSELEY, Bart., M.A., Mus. Doc., Professor of Music,
Oxford.

2. A Handbook of Pictorial Art, with numerous Illustrations, and Practical Advice. By the Rev. R. ST. JOHN
TYRWHITT, M.A., late Student and Tutor of Christ Church.

IX. ENGLISH CLASSICS.

*Designed to meet the wants of Students in English Literature:
under the superintendence of the Rev. J. S. Brewer, M.A., of
Queen's College, Oxford, and Professor of English Literature
at King's College, London.*

THERE are two dangers to which the student of English
literature is exposed at the outset of his task;—his reading
is apt to be too narrow or too diffuse.

Out of the vast number of authors set before him in books
professing to deal with this subject he knows not which to
select: he thinks he must read a little of all; he soon
abandons so hopeless an attempt; he ends by contenting

himself with second-hand information; and professing to study English literature, he fails to master a single English author.

On the other hand, by confining his attention to one or two writers, or to one special period of English literature, the student narrows his view of it; he fails to grasp the subject as a whole; and in so doing misses one of the chief objects of his study.

How may these errors be avoided? How may minute reading be combined with comprehensiveness of view?

In the hope of furnishing an answer to these questions the Delegates of the Press, acting upon the advice and experience of Professor Brewer, have determined to issue a series of small volumes, which shall embrace, in a convenient form and at a low price, the general extent of English Literature, as represented in its masterpieces at successive epochs. It is thought that the student, by confining himself, in the first instance, to those authors who are most worthy of his attention, will be saved from the dangers of hasty and indiscriminate reading. By adopting the course thus marked out for him he will become familiar with the productions of the greatest minds in English Literature; and should he never be able to pursue the subject beyond the limits here prescribed, he will have laid the foundation of accurate habits of thought and judgment, which cannot fail of being serviceable to him hereafter.

The authors and works selected are such as will best serve to illustrate English literature in its *historical* aspect.

As "the eye of history," without which history cannot be understood, the literature of a nation is the clearest and most intelligible record of its life. Its thoughts and its emotions, its graver and its less serious modes, its progress, or its degeneracy, are told by its best authors in their best words. This view of the subject will suggest the safest rules for the study of it.

With one exception all writers before the Reformation are excluded from the Series. However great may be the value of literature before that epoch, it is not completely national. For it had no common organ of language; it addressed itself to special classes; it dealt mainly with special subjects. Again; of writers who flourished after the Reformation, who were popular in their day, and reflected the manners and sentiments of their age, the larger part by far must be excluded from our list. Common sense tells us that if young persons, who have but a limited time at their disposal, read Marlowe or Greene, Burton, Hakewill or Du Bartas, Shakspeare, Bacon, and Milton will be comparatively neglected.

Keeping, then, to the best authors in each epoch—and here popular estimation is a safe guide—the student will find the following list of writers amply sufficient for his purpose: Chaucer, Spenser, Hooker, Shakspeare, Bacon, Milton, Dryden, Bunyan, Pope, Johnson, Burke, and Cowper. In other words, Chaucer is the exponent of the Middle Ages in England; Spenser of the Reformation and the Tudors; Hooker of the latter years of Elizabeth; Shakspeare and

Bacon of the transition from Tudor to Stuart; Milton of Charles I and the Commonwealth; Dryden and Bunyan of the Restoration; Pope of Anne and the House of Hanover; Johnson, Burke, and Cowper of the reign of George III to the close of the last century.

The list could be easily enlarged; the names of Jeremy Taylor, Clarendon, Hobbes, Locke, Swift, Addison, Goldsmith, and others are omitted. But in so wide a field, the difficulty is to keep the series from becoming unwieldly, without diminishing its comprehensiveness. Hereafter, should the plan prove to be useful, some of the masterpieces of the authors just mentioned may be added to the list.

The task of selection is not yet finished. For purposes of education, it would neither be possible, nor, if possible, desirable, to place in the hands of students the whole of the works of the authors we have chosen. We must set before them only the masterpieces of literature, and their studies must be directed, not only to the greatest minds, but to their choicest productions. These are to be read again and again, separately and in combination. Their purport, form, language, bearing on the times, must be minutely studied, till the student begins to recognise the full value of each work both in itself and in its relations to those that go before and those that follow it.

It is especially hoped that this Series may prove useful to Ladies' Schools and Middle Class Schools; in which English Literature must always be a leading subject of instruction.

A General Introduction to the Series. By the Rev. PROFESSOR BREWER, M.A.

1. Chaucer. The Prologue to the Canterbury Tales; the Knight's Tale; the Nun's Priest's Tale. Edited by R. MORRIS, Esq., Editor for the Early English Text Society, &c. &c.

2. Spenser. Faerie Queene, Book I., with the Poet's letter to Sir Walter Raleigh. Edited by the Rev. G. W. KITCHIN, M.A., formerly Censor of Christ Church.

3. Hooker. Ecclesiastical Polity, Book I. Edited by the Rev. R. W. CHURCH, M.A., Rector of Whatley; formerly Fellow of Oriel College.

4. Shakspeare. The English Historical Plays; the five Great Tragedies; Julius Caesar; and The Tempest. Edited by the Rev. W. G. CLARK, M.A., Fellow of Trinity College, Cambridge, and Public Orator; and J. ALDIS WRIGHT, M.A., Fellow of Trinity College, Cambridge.

5. Bacon. Essays; Advancement of Learning. Edited by J. ALDIS WRIGHT, M.A.

6. Milton. Allegro and Penseroso; Comus; Lycidas; Paradise Lost; Samson Agonistes.

7. Dryden. Stanzas on the Death of Oliver Cromwell; Astraea Redux; Annus Mirabilis; Absalom and Achitophel; Religio Laici; the Hind and Panther. Edited by the Rev. PROFESSOR BREWER, M.A.

8. Bunyan. Grace Abounding; The Pilgrim's Progress.

9. Pope. Essay on Man, with the Epistles and Satires. Edited by the Rev. M. PATTISON, M.A., Rector of Lincoln College, Oxford.

10. Johnson.   Rasselas; Lives of Pope and Dryden.
Edited by the Rev. J. FRASER, M.A., Rector of Ufton-Nervet;
formerly Fellow of Oriel College.

11. Burke.   Thoughts on the Present Discontents; the
two Speeches on America; Reflections on the French Revolution,
Edited by GOLDWIN SMITH, M.A., Fellow of University College,
Oxford; late Regius Professor of Modern History.

12. Cowper.   The Task, and some of his minor Poems.
Edited by the Rev. T. L. CLAUGHTON, M.A., Vicar of Kidder-
minster; formerly Fellow of Trinity College, Oxford, and
Professor of Poetry.

The volumes will be (as nearly as possible) uniform in shape and
size; and at the same price. There will be a brief preface, biographical
and literary, to each; and each will have such short notes only as are
absolutely needed for the elucidation of the text.

Published for the University of Oxford, by MACMILLAN and CO.,
London and Cambridge.

www.ingramcontent.com/pod-product-compliance
Lightning Source LLC
Chambersburg PA
CBHW021326110726
47900CB00005B/1370